GLORY BOYS

Harry Bingham was born in England in 1967. After graduating from Oxford University, he worked as an investment banker for ten years. In 1997, he left banking to care for his disabled wife and to write his first book, *The Money Makers*. He lives near Oxford with his wife and dogs, and writes full time. To find out more about publications by Harry Bingham, go to www.harpercollins.co.uk and register for AuthorTracker.

By the same author

The Money Makers
Sweet Talking Money
The Sons of Adam

HARRY BINGHAM

Glory Boys

HarperCollins*Publishers*

HarperCollins*Publishers*
77–85 Fulham Palace Road
London W6 8JB

www.harpercollins.co.uk

A Paperback Original 2005
1 3 5 7 9 10 8 6 4 2

ISBN 0 00 715795 9

Set in Sabon by Palimpsest Book Production Limited,
Polmont, Stirlingshire

Printed and bound in Great Britain by
Clays Ltd, St Ives plc

To my beloved N, my writing partner

*'But it is beautiful to unfold our souls
And our short lives'*

Prohibition is an awful flop.
   We like it.
It can't stop what it's meant to stop.
   We like it.
It's left a trail of graft and slime,
It's filled our land with vice and crime,
It don't prohibit worth a dime,
    Nevertheless we're for it.

From F. P. A., *New York World*

'The aeroplane was very easy to fly and very forgiving to pupils' mistakes, even to the extent of (usually) not killing them when they spun it to the ground . . . To start off with, and for some reason I could never understand, [it] seldom seemed to catch fire after a crash.'

Allen Wheeler, *Flying Between the Wars*

PROLOGUE

To begin with, it looked like nothing. A nick on the horizon. A moving dot. A speck of red and white against the smoky Georgian blue.

Herb Johnson, standing bolt upright on his wagon, followed it with his eyes. The little plane was flying low, carving an unsteady course between the twisting hills. Every now and then it rose sharply upwards, before beginning a slow glide earthwards again.

The town could boast four war heroes, but Herb Johnson was the only one to have seen the front line in France. Consequently, he was also the only guy in town to have seen an airplane. He wanted to hang on to the sight alone; be the only man in town to see it. He looked for a while, then sat back down on the wagon board and settled his hat back on his head.

'Good God in the morning!' he hollered. 'Airplane! Airplane! Airplane!'

Something was wrong.

That much was obvious. The plane, now directly overhead, was gasping for breath. The engine would fire properly for a couple of beats, then choke, then fire again, then cut completely, then spurt back into temporary life.

1

'That feller didn't oughta stay up there,' remarked Jeb Holling, with a considered tobacco-speckled spit on the ground. 'That engine ain't holding him up too good.'

The machine was a biplane, with red wings, a red nose and a clean white fuselage that seemed too bright in the sun. When the plane banked a little, they could see the pilot, no more than a leather-helmeted head and a pair of shoulders. Some of the kids waved, but the pilot must have been a surly type, because he wouldn't wave back, not even to say hi to a bunch of kids who'd never seen an airplane before, let alone right up close, floating over their town like a giant dragonfly.

'Ain't so easy,' said Johnson, who had quickly and delightedly established himself as the town's aviation expert. 'Them planes need an air-eo-drome. In France . . .'

The plane came back again, lower this time. They could see the pilot's face better. They could see his lips moving, and he was waving this time, one leather-gauntleted hand gesticulating out of the cockpit, though in an angry kind of way, hardly the way to wave at kids. The engine was still bad and when it cut out, you could almost see the flashing propeller blades slow down.

'Like to see it come down on my place,' said one farmer from out of town. 'Terraced fields like mine, it'd be like landing on a flight of steps.'

'There's the woods round by Williams Point,' said another man. 'That'd be the place all right. Come down into the trees . . .' His words petered out, as he realised that his picture of airplanes roosting in the treetops probably contained more than an ounce or two of inaccuracy.

It was a kid who saw the truth first. Little Brad Lundmark, a red-headed kid, looking a couple of years younger than his fifteen years, yelled it out. 'He wants to land here. He wants to come down right here!'

The kid was right. The pilot was criss-crossing overhead and waving. The plane continued to bob crazily in the air, pulling upwards when the engine was sound, drifting down when it sputtered. And when you thought about it, Main Street in Independence was about the only hard flat place for miles around. If you excluded those places which were dotted with cows or drainage ditches or trees or houses, then you might have to cross right over into Anderson County before you could find a better place to land.

'Quick,' said Johnson, anxious to regain his ebbing leadership. 'Clear a space there, will you?'

Everyone pushed and shoved, until they had cleared a circle some forty or fifty feet wide. Herb Johnson winked and waved at the pilot, inviting him to come on down. Once again, the kid knew best.

'He needs the street,' shouted Lundmark. 'He needs the whole street.'

Instantly, the street was cleared. Horses were led down side alleys. A couple of buggies were hauled and pushed to the side of the road. There were only five cars in town, but the one belonging to Gibson Hennessey, owner of the General Store, didn't start too well in the heat of the day, so it was decided to leave them all. Men, women and kids, ran indoors to watch from windows, or stood in the shade of the verandas, until the whole town was lined up in two long rows that quivered with expectancy.

The red-winged plane banked for a final turn. Right overhead, the engine roared into life, then cut. There was an anxious-delicious moment when it seemed the plane must surely crash, but the engines fired again, strongly enough for the pilot to get his machine under control for landing. For a moment or two, the plane disappeared behind the two-storey warehouse belonging to the Agricultural-Mercantile on the edge of town. People craned forwards, desperate to see it again.

Then, when they did, they leaped back again in shock. The plane was headed right at them, diving towards the road from no distance at all. The propeller was a flashing

3

disc. The plane's nose was a fat red bullet aimed straight at the town.

Somebody screamed. The plane plunged. Wheels slammed hard into the earth.

Then everything happened at once. The plane tore down the street. For a few moments, it looked as though the impossible landing would take place without mishap. Then the tail-skid snagged on a pothole. The plane's motion altered suddenly and drastically. The fuselage slewed violently round. An axle or a wheel-strut broke. One of the wingtips hit the ground and splintered. The plane skidded sickeningly along the ground, crunching up the end of its lower wing as it moved. It came to rest with the nose four feet from the barber's shop window, as though about to pop in for a shave.

The pilot's cockpit was lost in the dust he'd kicked up. The engine was silent. The propeller blade began to slow. Somewhere a piece of wood cracked loudly. The airplane sank.

For a moment, just for a moment, everything fell silent.

PART ONE

Beginning

Afterwards, people like to sit and figure out when it all started.

Mostly people talk about the crash landing, the hot May day in 1926 when an airplane fell clean out of the sky. But there are others who look a little further back. They talk about when the troubles in town first started. They talk about the Volstead Act, the law which prohibited the sale of alcohol the length and breadth of America. They talk about politics and the good old days and the general decline in moral values.

But when you think about it properly, you can see that there is no beginning. Not really. If it hadn't been for the Great War, there wouldn't have been Prohibition. If it hadn't been for the Wright brothers, and Santos-Dumont in France, and all the other guys who spent their lives coaxing chunks of wood and metal to jump into the air and fly, then there wouldn't have been airplanes, and every-thing in this story is to do with airplanes.

But if you want to talk about beginnings, then you have to go back to the start. Right to the start. And that wasn't Santos-Dumont or the Wright brothers, or even Langley and his doomed experiments over the gloomy Mississippi.

The beginning was an English guy, name of Sir George Cayley.

Cayley was born in 1773, when George Washington was still a British subject and the good folks of Boston were filling their harbour with forty-five tons of best Bohea tea. Cayley was another one of these guys who ought to have been born with feathers. He wanted to fly. He spent his whole life working on the problem. But unlike all those who had gone before, Cayley got a whole lot of things pretty right.

Up until Sir George, anyone designing a flying machine thought about birds. Birds flap their wings and that's the whole deal. They get their lift from wings. They get their forward motion from wings. Most of what stops birds rolling around in the sky like corks in a waterfall is built into the wings as well. Lift, thrust and control. All in the same neat instrument.

But that's birds. Sir George's particular spark of genius was to see that what worked for birds would never work for humans. So he split the three problems and tackled them separately. He conducted careful scientific experiments on lift, drag and streamlining. He tackled the issues of stability, pitch-control and general aircraft design. He did some tough mathematics and some solid science.

And he got there. He designed the airplane. For lift, he chose a pair of fixed wings, shaped like an aerofoil. For thrust, he chose an airscrew – what we'd call a propeller. And to give his flying machine control, he designed a tail fin and rudder, not a whole lot different from what you see sticking to the ends of airplanes today.

If you want to see the first ever drawing of a working airplane, you'll find it in the notebooks of good old Sir George. Of course, the gallant knight only had steam engines to play with. There was no way a steam engine of his day would develop enough horsepower to lift itself, an airplane and a human being all together. But he built gliders though, good ones. You want to know when the first true airplane flight in history took place? Answer: in 1853, when Sir George ordered his coachman out of his coach and into a glider. The glider soared happily into the air, flew five hundred yards across a Yorkshire valley, then came to a bumpy rest. The coachman, already the world's first airplane pilot, wasn't too keen on becoming the world's first airplane casualty and he handed in his notice. Cayley, an old man now, quit building gliders and died almost fifty years before the Wright brothers left earth at Kitty Hawk.

So, if you want a beginning, there it was.

Lift, thrust, control. Three problems. Three solutions. The start of everything.

1

The pilot lifted his goggles and removed his helmet, all in the same motion. He let helmet and goggles drop to the floor. The air was still cloudy with dust and his eyes pricked.

With an automatic hand, he checked his switches (all off) and the cockpit fuel pipes (all sound). He sniffed to detect any escaping gasoline. The air stank of petrol, but the pilot had never been in a crash where the air smelled any other way. The pilot flexed his left leg, then his right leg, then both arms, then ran his hands over his back, neck and head. His left foot was sore where the rudder bar had snagged it, but apart from that, he seemed to have escaped uninjured. His left arm struck the instrument panel a couple of times softly.

'Sorry, sweetheart,' he muttered.

He lifted himself to the lip of the cockpit and stepped down to the ground. The movement made him grimace. Not because of the pain in his foot, but because the undercarriage should have been lifting the fuselage well clear of the ground. But the plane no longer had an undercarriage to speak of, and the fuselage was lying prostrate on the ground like a beached sea animal.

The pilot undid his flying jacket, wiped his forehead on his arm and stepped, blinking, away from the dust and the plane wreck into the brilliant glare of the sun.

And that was how they saw him first. Long afterwards, that was how most of them would remember him as well. A man a little less than medium height. Not big built, but light on his feet. Poised. A sense of athleticism held a long way in reserve. Fair hair very closely cropped. Skin deeply tanned. Eyes of astonishing blueness. His face lined but still somehow young. Or perhaps not young exactly, but alert, watchful. And smiling. That was how they first saw him.

Smiling.

The pilot was used to being stared at, but even for him this was something new. Independence, Georgia boasted a population of 1,386 and right now the pilot was being given the chance to inspect almost every last one of their number.

He wiped his forehead again. Leather flying clothes make a whole lot of sense six thousand feet up in an eighty-mile-an-hour wind. They make a lot less sense the second you touch earth. He shrugged off his jacket and advanced a few more paces. The town had grouped itself into a semicircle around him and was staring at him, like he was something out of the Bible.

'Hi, folks,' he said. 'Seen better landings, huh?'

He laughed. Nobody else moved. They were still staring, still in awe.

'Thanks for clearing a way for me. Things were getting kinda tough up there.'

There was a bit of shuffling amongst the townsfolk and one of them was pushed to the front.

'Good afternoon, sir,' he said. 'My name's Herbert Isiah Johnson, and on behalf of Independence and Okinochee County and on behalf of . . . of . . . everyone, we'd like to welcome you to Georgia.'

Johnson's mumblings broke the spell. People surged forward.

'Gee whizz, Ma, did you see the wing go pop . . .?'

'Spark plugs, was it? I once saw that on a Model-T. Lousy sparks . . .'

'You OK, pal? You shouldn't be walking any, not after . . .'

'He didn't take a left. You go past the Ag-Merc, you have to jink a little to the left . . .'

'I said them things weren't safe to use. If the good Lord . . .'

But amidst the crush of people, there was no one more determined than Brad Lundmark, the red-headed kid who'd first understood the pilot's need to land. Within seconds of seeing the pilot emerge safely from the wreckage, Lundmark was running. First he ran hard, round a corner, into a simple two-storey house on Second Street. He was inside for about twenty seconds, then came racing out again. He tore back the way he'd come and hurtled into the thick of the crowd. Doggedly, he fought his way to the front.

'Excuse me, sir. Sir, excuse me, please. Please, sir . . .'

There was something in Lundmark's single-mindedness which made other people quit talking, until he found himself talking into a vacuum.

'Sorry. Sorry. Just . . .' He held out the things he'd fetched from the house. They were a well-chewed pencil and a photo. The photograph had been neatly clipped from the pages of a boy's magazine. It was unmistakably a picture of the pilot, a few years younger and stiffly dressed in military uniform. 'Captain Rockwell, sir, I wonder if I could have your autograph.'

2

'Oh for God's sake!'

Willard Thornton, a dazzlingly good-looking actor of twenty-something, felt sick.

It wasn't the plane, a neat little Gallaudet, that upset him, but the take-off site. The Gallaudet had been precariously winched up on to the roof of the Corin Tower, twenty-five storeys above ground. The tar roof was flat, a hundred feet square. A low parapet had run round the outside, but had been removed for filming. The place where the blocks had been wrenched away showed up white against the tar. A camera crew stood sullenly, underdressed for the wind that flicked across from the mountains. The cameraman jabbed a finger at the sky.

'We oughta go. We're losing light. But what do I care? It's your picture, buddy.'

Willard scowled again. The cameraman was right. This was his movie. He was actor, writer, director, producer, financier – and right now there was a decision to be made. He thought of the stunt he was about to pull and felt another bout of nausea rise towards his throat.

'OK, OK,' he commented, 'only Jesus Christ!'

'Jesus Christ is about right, darling,' said Daphne O'Hara, taking a cigarette from the cameraman's mouth and smoking it down to the butt. O'Hara (or Brunhilde Schulz, to give her the name she was born with) was dressed in a silver evening gown, with enough paste diamonds to

12

bury a duchess. The wind was wrapping her dress hard against her legs and her carefully set hair was beginning to unravel.

'The light,' said the cameraman.

'Forget the light. It's my hair, sweetheart.'

'Oh for God's sake! Let's do it.'

Willard felt angry and out of control. The cast and crew were on their thirteenth week of filming their feature, *Heaven's Beloved*. They already had enough film in the can to make a six-hour movie. But Willard was a realist. He'd seen the rushes. And they were bad. Badly done, badly shot, and dull. Deadly dull. The script had been hastily revised. Stunts had been shoved in in a desperate effort to lift the story. Willard had grown to loathe any mention of the budget.

And now this. The Gallaudet stood in one corner of the roof, with the wind on its nose. They'd selected the plane for its low take-off speed, but even so, Willard guessed, they wouldn't be fully airborne by the time they reached the edge. Would he have enough lift and forward speed to keep his tail clear as he left the roof? He didn't know. If the tail caught, would it hook him downwards, or just give him a fright? He didn't know, but felt sick thinking about it. In the past, he'd preferred to hand the tough stunts over to professional stuntmen, but his last two stuntmen had quit on him after rows over money. In any case, it was only flying wasn't it?

'OK. Ready?'

The camera crew positioned themselves. The production guys fussed over the Gallaudet. Then Willard and O'Hara burst from the steel doorway onto the roof. Willard pointed dramatically at the Gallaudet, then the two actors raced across to it.

O'Hara struck a pose by the rear cockpit, which meant, 'No! Surely not!' Willard stuck out his chin and looked darkly resolute. 'But we have to!' Willard stepped behind

O'Hara to help her in. 'Keep your hand away from my fucking ass,' she said.

The two actors clambered inside. It was the sort of move which Willard found difficult. He hated the idea of looking bad on camera but could never quite get the hang of making an ungainly move, such as swinging his leg over the cockpit rim, in a way that made him look good. He tutted with annoyance and said, 'Again!'

They got out and in again. Willard's second attempt was worse than his first, and what's more he grazed his hand in the process. Willard wanted to do it over, but was aware of O'Hara behind him, smoking like a steam train and swearing darkly in her native German.

'That'll do,' he said, annoyed.

The camera crew took a few shots of them in the cockpit. The wind rose. Willard knew he ought to cancel the shot and wait until conditions were better. But O'Hara was being wooed by United Artists – Douglas Fairbanks himself had lunched with her – and Willard knew it was only a matter of time before she quit. There was another, stronger flutter of wind. Ten knots gusting to twelve or thirteen. Wind was good because what mattered in take-off was wind speed, not ground speed. But too much wind was bad, because of the risk of the airplane being blown straight back into the side of the building. Willard's sickness came back, stronger.

The lead production guy said mildly, 'Thornton, I think . . .'

'Yes. Get her started. Jesus Christ!'

The production crew swung the propeller. The engine roared into life. The propeller flashed into a blur. The cameramen positioned themselves. O'Hara stopped smoking and swearing, and flashed a dazzling smile at the cameras. Beneath the wheels, Willard could feel the wooden chocks being pulled away. The graze on his hand was red and angry. He hoped it wouldn't show on film.

14

He jammed the throttle forward. The pitch of the engine rose into a full roar. The little plane began to roll forwards. The edge of the building rushed towards them. The Gallaudet's wheels reached the edge. Her tail was lifted, but the main gear was nowhere close to being airborne. She plunged sickeningly over the edge and was lost from sight.

3

The wall at the end of the barn wasn't solid, but built of vertical wooden slats to allow the entrance of light and air. The golden evening sunshine poured in and lay in bars across the floor. In the middle, amidst a debris of straw and spilled grain, the airplane sat. It looked oddly at home, like an obsolete piece of agricultural equipment or perhaps an exotic animal lying down to rest. It was a peaceful scene, but somehow sad. The plane looked like it had been shut away to die.

For the first time since his unconventional arrival, Captain Abraham 'Abe' Rockwell had a moment alone with his plane. He walked slowly round the battered craft. The hull was badly scraped and there were patches where the plywood had been smashed away completely. Aside from that, there was damage to one of the propeller blades, damage to the lower left wingtip, and the utter destruction of the plane's undercarriage.

But Abe's manner wasn't simply the manner of an equipment-owner attempting to quantify the damage. He didn't just feel the plane, he stroked it. He ran his hand down the leather edging of the cockpit and brushed away some cobwebs that were already being built. When he got to the nose of the aircraft, he pulled his sleeve over his hand and cleaned up the lettering that read, '*Sweet Kentucky Poll*'. Dissatisfied, he went to the engine, fiddled with a fuel-pipe, pulled it free and dribbled a little fuel onto a rag.

Then he set the pipe back in place and scrubbed at the name with the gasoline-soaked cloth. This time, he got the name as bright as he wanted and he straightened.

Straightened and stopped. He turned and spoke directly into the heap of straw that filled the opposite end of the barn.

'It's rude to stare.'

Seeing that the straw made no answer, Abe picked up an axe handle from the floor and tossed it onto the top of the heap.

'Ow!'

The straw wriggled and a red head emerged.

'I said it's rude.'

'Sorry, sir. I . . .'

'Yes?'

'Nothing.'

Abe waited a short moment, then shrugged. 'If it's nothing, then you won't mind leaving.'

'No, sir.'

The red head attached itself to a skinny kid, who slid down the straw pile and landed with a soft thwack. 'Sorry, sir.' The kid, whom Abe recognised as the autograph-hunter from earlier, glanced across into a corner of the barn, then brushed himself off, ready to leave. Abe followed his glance. There was a bucket of warm water there, soapy and still steaming, a bath sponge floating on the surface.

'Wait.'

The kid stopped.

'You came to clean her?'

The kid nodded. 'Doesn't matter, sir. I can do it later. Sorry.'

Abe shook his head. The gesture meant: Don't leave yet.

'D'you have a name?'

'Lundmark, sir.'

'Your ma and pa think of giving you a first name to go along with that?'

'Yes, sir. Bradley. Brad.'

'Mind if I use it?'

'No, sir.'

'OK, Brad, now I'm not over-fond of this "sir" business. I'm not in the army now and I don't want to be. If you want to call me something, I'm happy with just plain Abe. If that's too much for you, you can call me Captain. Understand?'

'Yes. Yes, Captain.'

'Good.'

There was a pause. The slatted evening light was moving round, bringing new parts of the airplane into view and hiding others. Abe found a cobweb he'd missed before and brushed it away absent-mindedly.

'We'll start at the nose.'

Abe brought the bucket over to the plane and the two of them began to wash her, nose to tail, removing the dust and the flaking paint and the burned-on oil and the scatter of straw-dust and insects. For about fifty minutes they worked mostly in silence, changing the cleaning water from a pump in the yard outside. Then, as the light began to fade, Abe threw down his sponge.

'Hell,' he said. 'That's not too bad. For a moment back there, I thought the landing was gonna turn out rough.'

Still clutching his sponge, the kid turned to Abe. 'You've smashed up worse 'n that?'

'Yeah, plenty worse.'

The kid's eyes, which had been large before, grew moon-shaped and moon-sized. Abe, irritated with himself, added sharply: 'Anyone who flies enough will have a few bad smashes. Most machines fold up pretty easy. The accidents mostly look worse than they are.'

'Yes, sir.'

'Captain.'

'Yes, Captain.'

'You ever been up in a plane?'

18

Brad Lundmark shook his head, the way he might have shaken it if the Archangel Gabriel had asked if he was acquainted with Paradise.

'If you got some time to help me out here over the next week or two, I'll give you a ride. What d'you say?'

'Oh, yes! Sure thing, Captain! Gee! I promise I'll –'

'Hey, hey, it's OK. It's only a plane ride. If I've got any cash left after we've fixed her up, I'll give you a couple of bucks a day as well, but no promises.'

Abe rummaged in the rear cockpit and brought out a fur-lined sleeping roll which he threw out under the wing. Lundmark looked shocked.

'Captain, there's a boarding house just down the block. You can't –'

Abe pulled his shirt off, took the sponge and the bucket of water, and scrubbed himself hard all over. He sluiced water through his close-cropped grey-blond hair, until it stuck up in spikes, and rubbed hard at the back of his neck, where there had been a line of sweat and grime.

'That's better.'

Abe fiddled in his luggage for a spare shirt, which he pulled on. Lundmark noticed that the cuffs and collar were old and worn.

'Brad?'

'Yes, Captain?'

'I gotta have food. Poll here's gotta have fuel. She's got some pretty bad hospital bills coming up. One thing I can't afford to spend money on is a bed.'

Lundmark shook his head. 'That ain't right. If you explained who y'are to Mr Houghton at the hotel, why I'm sure he'd –'

'He'd tell me to pay for my bed just like anyone else. Brad, I'm gonna lie under the wing of my airplane. Can you think of a better place for a guy to sleep?'

Lundmark shook his head.

'No, Captain. Say –'

But what he was about to say, Abe would never know. There was a minor commotion in the yard outside. Somewhere a small dog barked angrily. Then four men appeared in the barn door against the violet air. They were dressed in dark suits and ties, which they wore with Sunday stiffness. One of the men – six feet plus, mid-fifties, lean, intelligence in his face, moustache – spoke.

'Good evening to you, Captain Rockwell. My name's Gibson Hennessey, owner of the General Store down there. On behalf of the town, I'd like to apologise for being so neglectful earlier. I want to assure you that we didn't mean no disrespect. It wasn't 'til the kid here informed us who you were, that we realised we had a hero of the United States in our midst.'

Abe's blue eyes gave nothing away, but his mouth possibly hardened a little before he answered. 'I didn't feel no disrespect, Mr Hennessey. I didn't exactly let you know I was coming.'

'No, indeed.'

'And I'm plenty happy with the barn here.'

The second of the men laid his hand across his chest. He was a plump man, fat and buttery. ''Low me to introduce myself. Ted Houghton's my name, proprietor of the Independence Hotel and Bar, only these days I ain't got a bar. I'd be only too honoured, if you'd accept my hospitality for the duration of your stay.'

'Right, and any assistance we can give in getting your airplane all fixed up, you just ask.'

The two sides fought gently for a minute or two. Abe wanted no fuss. He just wanted to fix up his plane and move on. But there was no escape. Surrounded by the four dignitaries, Abe was escorted back to the centre of town, feeling like a prisoner on his way to the jailhouse.

'The folks here wanted to show their appreciation . . .' murmured Hennessey, as a crowd of two hundred people stood and cheered Abe's arrival. A collection of schoolkids performed a rendition of the 'Star-Spangled Banner'. A man, whose name Abe didn't catch, made a truly dismal speech of welcome. Abe was expected to reply at length, but he just stood on the hotel steps and said, 'I'm mighty grateful to you all. Thank you.'

There was another round of applause. Half the schoolkids thought an encore of the 'Star-Spangled Banner' was in order, but luckily the effort sputtered quickly out. Abe was bundled into the hotel where he was the guest of honour at a five-course dinner, ending with a vast sponge cake in the very approximate shape of an airplane.

By eleven o'clock, Abe had finally escaped to his room.

He rooted around in his bags for a tattered pack of Pall Mall cigarettes, then stretched out on his bed and lit up. With the oil lamp set low, he lay on his back and breathed smoke at the ceiling. His face was tired and he looked ready to sleep.

For ten minutes, he lay and smoked. Then a couple of circular marks on the wall high up behind the wardrobe caught his eye. Swinging his feet lightly to the floor, he took a chair over to the wardrobe and examined them.

The marks were gouged right through the plaster through to the room next door. The top of the wardrobe still had a little white dust beneath the marks, indicating either that the hotel didn't dust very often or that the marks were relatively recent.

Captain Abe Rockwell had earned his rank as a pursuit pilot in the United States Army. Before the war, he'd been an auto mechanic, then a racing driver. When war had broken out, he'd decided to switch trades. He'd thrown in his job racing cars. He'd wangled his way out to France as a mechanic attached to one of America's newly formed flying squadrons. He'd fixed planes by day, and by evening more or less taught himself to fly. Despite being over-age and lacking either a commission or a college education, he nevertheless persuaded the authorities to give him a chance in the cockpit. He'd repaid their faith. His first victory over a German machine had come within two weeks. Another three months had seen his fifth victory – and his official recognition as one of America's few fighter-aces. By the end of the war, he'd been promoted to captain, had command of a squadron, and had had nineteen victories officially confirmed. Of the American pilots to have survived the war, only Ed Rickenbacker had shot down more enemy planes.

Abe was a military man who'd seen plenty of combat, plenty of action. He knew what bullet holes looked like, and these were bullet holes.

4

Willard didn't get headaches. He didn't get them from heat. He didn't get them from noise. He didn't even get them after a jugful of martinis, when everybody else was looking as white and fragile as a porcelain teacup. But he had one now.

He stepped inside. The shades were down and the interior was cool and dim. Reflections from the pool outside trembled on the ceiling. Willard closed the door, and the voices grew small and distant. He had been holding a letter in his hand, which he let drop on the carpeted floor. The letter was from his accountant. A stunt plane they'd used but hadn't insured had just smashed up. Another eighteen thousand bucks had slid uselessly down the pan.

He sank into a deep chair and sat slumped, hardly moving.

Willard felt lousy, when all the time he knew he should be happy. After all, he was a lucky man, born into a lucky family.

His great-grandfather had begun it all, manufacturing handguns and rifles for sale to the country's wild frontier. The business had prospered. The Civil War had turned Thornton Ordnance into one of the country's biggest profit-makers, one with international reach. The nineteenth century had been a good one for wars and the firm had benefited from every one. When the Great War had broken out in Europe in 1914, Thornton Ordnance entered its most profitable phase. Junius Thornton – Willard's father – made money hand over fist. On America's entry into the war, profits had doubled, then doubled again.

But it wasn't just Willard's family which had been touched with magic. He had been too. Willard had been a student at Princeton when Germany, in a fit of lunacy, began unrestricted submarine warfare against American shipping, thus propelling America into the war. Willard's studies hadn't exactly been going badly, but they certainly hadn't been going well. Willard happened to meet a British pilot and saw the way the man had used his war stories to pull any girl he wanted.

And so, one sunny autumn's day and with almost no prior consideration, Willard had taken the plunge. He'd joined up. He sought a pilot's commission and got it. Within three months of that sunny October day, he was in France, a lieutenant in the US Army Flying Corps.

He hadn't been there a week before he regretted it.

On his first flight over enemy lines, he was almost killed. On his second flight, he returned with bullet holes plugging his upper starboard wing and the tail mounting. Within three weeks, Willard could count four lucky escapes – and not one time when he'd even got a shot away at the enemy.

That had to change and it did.

By a fluke, Willard was transferred to the Ninety-First Squadron, under the command of Captain Abraham 'Abe' Rockwell.

Before letting his newest recruit out on patrol, Rockwell ordered Thornton to take to the air, twenty-five miles behind the lines, to take part in a dummy patrol and dogfight. Willard thought he'd done OK, but Rockwell had torn Willard's combat-flying to pieces. Over the next two weeks, he'd reassembled it, from the ground up.

When Willard was allowed back into the air, he scored his first kill on his very first patrol. He wasn't the best pilot in the sky, but he was no longer a dangerous novice. By October 1918, he'd brought down three German machines – just two short of the magical number, which would turn him from a fine pilot into an officially recognised flying ace.

Rockwell had seen the younger man's desire and, in the first week of November, assigned him to fly against the enemy *Drachen* – gas-filled observation balloons, that rose from fixed steel cables a mile back from the collapsing German front. The assignments were simple and dangerous. Simple, because there was nothing easier than shooting at a giant inflammable balloon. Dangerous, because the Germans curtained their precious balloons with intense and accurate anti-aircraft fire. Willard accepted his assignment gravely. Before each flight, he was so afraid, he vomited secretly in the hangar toilet. But he'd hit his targets and escaped being hit himself. On November 8, three days before Armistice was declared, Willard downed his second *Drache*. A *Drache* counted the same as an airplane. By the time peace broke out, Willard Thornton was a flying ace. He returned to America, a hero.

He hadn't been the bravest pilot, or the best. He hadn't scored anywhere near as many kills as Rockwell or Rickenbacker. But none of that mattered. He was an ace – and he was stunningly good-looking. Up-close, far away, carefully staged or thrillingly informal: there just wasn't an angle that made him look bad. Sandy-haired, blue-eyed, wide-chinned, strongly built. His smile was terrific, his eyes enticing, his mouth full and kissable. He was dazzling to look at and he knew it.

Hollywood saw the potential and was quick to move. The studios fought to get his signature on a movie deal. One of the studios had a guy literally follow him round with a blank contract. Willard rose to the bait and signed.

His first picture had billed him as 'Willard T. Thornton, America's *favourite* ace'. A movie-going public, still enchanted with its war-time heroes, flocked to see it. For a few brief weeks, Willard's had been one of the most recognisable faces in America. The second picture had sold well. The next two movies had done OK. The last two had sagged, flopped, sunk from sight.

But Willard had grown up a little. He knew enough to make a picture of his own – '*Heaven's Beloved*, a picture of class'. He'd asked his father for finance. His father had put him in touch with Ted Powell, a Wall Street banker. Willard had made his pitch – and Powell had bought it. And although the picture was over-schedule, although Daphne O'Hara had just quit right in the middle of filming, although costs were out of control and his precious stunt plane had just crashed, Willard's luck was staying the course.

Ted Powell continued to believe, continued to come up with cash. The original sixty-thousand dollar loan had mushroomed. First to eighty, then to a hundred, then to one-twenty, then to an 'open-ended loan facility' – banker-speak for don't-even-ask.

Willard was a lucky man, born into a lucky family.

5

The Lundmark kid showed up at seven o'clock sharp, with a pot of coffee and a couple of rolls.

'Feeding me, huh?'

Abe had been up at dawn, and found nobody yet awake at the hotel. Sooner than wake anyone, he'd come directly to the barn. He'd shaved in a can of hot water brewed over a primus stove, then stripped to the waist and washed under the yard pump. Right now, he was stretched out on a bale of straw, rubbing soft wax into his flying boots and mending a small tear on his jacket.

'I just thought . . . if you don't want it, I can . . .'

'No, Brad, I want it. There are a couple of mugs in there,' said Abe nodding at the rear cockpit of the broken plane. 'Green canvas bag.'

Lundmark approached the plane like it was holy, and came away with a single mug.

'Don't drink coffee? You're missing out.'

Abe sipped his coffee and took a bite of the bread roll.

'We'll get to work shall we? We'll need to send away for a new blade,' Abe indicated the busted propeller. 'Aside from that, if we can find some timber and a forge, I haven't seen anything we can't fix.'

'Really? Wow! You can get it going again, Captain?'

'Careful, Brad. She's a lady.'

'Huh? Oh. I mean, *her*. Sorry.'

'Reckon we can. First thing is to send a wire to my

friends at Curtiss. Get a new blade out here. There a post office in town?'

'Sure, Captain . . .' Lundmark's reply wasn't exactly confident.

Abe was silent for a minute. He'd flown over the town, searching the ground for landing sites. He brought the view to mind. There are an infinity of obstacles that can smash up an aircraft. A cow. A ditch. A rickety fence with a single strand of wire. A boulder. A pothole. A tree stump.

Or telegraph wire. During the war, a friend of Abe's had been shot up in a dogfight over enemy lines. With fabric streaming from one wing and controls mushy from German bullets, the plane had limped home. Struggling in to land, barely skimming the tree-tops, the plane had struck a line of telegraph wire. The wheels had snagged. The nose had been yanked down. Pilot and plane had dived into the ground at seventy miles an hour.

Abe thought back to his view of the town from above. No wires. 'There's no telegraph, is there? Where we gotta go? Brunswick?'

A tiny hesitation. Then: 'Yeah, Brunswick. Joe Borden takes his cart in on a Tuesday. I guess we could ask him.'

'Good.'

Abe paused. He'd seen something else from the sky; something that had puzzled him then and was puzzling him even more now. 'A mile south of here,' he said, 'there's another town.'

'Uh-huh.' The kid was non-committal, but evasive. He began cleaning invisible muck from a side of the aircraft which enabled him to keep his expression concealed.

'There's no other town marked on my map. It's Rand McNally, 1921. I've never known 'em to be wrong before. Not that wrong anyways.'

'It's called Marion. It's kind of new. Grew up a lot the last couple of years.'

'That's a lot of growing.'

'I guess.'

The kid clearly didn't want to talk, and, though Abe's intense blue-eyed stare held the boy a few moments longer, he allowed the matter to drop. But it was a puzzle. It wasn't just that Rand McNally hadn't marked the town. It was where the town was and what it was.

What it was, first of all. From the air, Abe had seen large white houses, big yards, motor cars, even a couple of swimming pools. The contrast with the sun-bleached timbers and dusty streets of Independence was even stronger when darkness fell. Whereas Independence couldn't boast a single electric bulb, the town below had been a blaze of light. The thump of oil-fired generators had thudded softly through the night.

Then there was the matter of where it was. Independence stood in a low range of hills on the edge of the Okefenokee swamps. Between Independence and Jacksonville there were salty marshes, mangrove swamps, a maze of creeks running out to the ocean. Independence was connected to the rest of the world only by a single-track unpaved road, plus the railway which ran just inland from the coast.

Why on earth had a slice of the brash new America wound up in these back-of-beyond swamp lands? Where was the money coming from to finance those new houses, the big cars? And why was the kid Lundmark lying to him about having to hike in to Brunswick to find a telegraph?

Abe could remember the view from the sky perfectly well. Marion, Independence's mysterious new neighbour, had a line of telegraph wire running directly into it from the south. If Abe wanted to send a telegram, he only had to stroll a mile downhill.

6

The cigar smoke hung blue-grey in the projector beam. The first reel snickered to an end and the screen filled with light. Willard jumped up to change the reel.

'That dame,' said Ted Powell, prodding the air with his cigar, looking every inch like the Wall Streeter that he was. 'Is she meant to be the same as the first one?'

'Brunhilde Schulz? O'Hara?'

'Blondie back there. The one who just got kidnapped by the bank robbers.'

'O'Hara quit on us. Right in the middle of filming. Breach of contract. We found a girl who looked OK from a distance, but all the close-ups are of O'Hara.'

'Is that why the backgrounds are funny?'

'They're not that funny.' Willard fiddled the second reel into place, poking the fragile celluloid through the little rollers. The lamp inside the projector was burning hot and the whole apparatus was scorching to the touch. 'Ow! Here. You'll like this next bit.'

The next bit was the skyscraper scene.

'That's me in the plane. I did this stunt myself.'

'Funny place to park an airplane.'

Willard and the girl who really was O'Hara bounded out onto the roof. They looked dramatic – tragic – resolute. Then they bounded into the plane. The next shot had the propeller whirling and Willard clenching the muscles in his jaw.

'Plane that starts itself,' commented Powell. 'Nice.'

'She's only a Gallaudet and she didn't start herself. We're doing things cheap here, Powell. Cheap as we can without . . . without . . .'

'I was kidding, Will. And call me Ted.'

The plane rolled to the edge of the building, then plunged out of view. The next shot, taken from a neighbouring rooftop, showed the little Gallaudet dive nose-first for the ground. After falling ten or twelve storeys, the nose had come up and levelled out. There was another close-up of the hero: resolute – victorious – defiant. Then a shot of the Gallaudet flying out of sight, while a group of hoodlums poured out onto the roof and began shaking their fists at the sky.

'Jesus Christ!' said Powell.

'Pretty good stunt, isn't it?'

'Looks like you just fell clean off the edge.'

'We *did* just fall.'

'Something wrong with the airplane?'

'No. It's a question of air speed. You have to build speed before you can climb. And it was a dive, not a fall. Saying "fall" makes it sound bad.'

'I saw a picture recently where they pulled a stunt like that.'

'*Breaking Free*. They had it in *Breaking Free*.'

'Yeah, maybe. Only there, the airplane flew, it didn't just fall. You sure your plane was OK?'

'They had a catapult. We thought about using a catapult, only it wouldn't have been very realistic.'

'Realistic . . .?'

The two men watched in silence to the end of the reel. They watched the girl be captured twice more by the hoodlums and be rescued back both times. The best stunt showed the girl being snatched by an airplane from a speeding car. The girl didn't look too much like O'Hara and the pilot didn't look too much like Willard, but it was a good stunt all the same.

The second reel snickered to its close. Willard got up again, tweaking the cuffs of his shirt from his jacket sleeve so they showed up better. He'd just spent four hundred bucks on a set of silver cuff-links and it annoyed him when they didn't show. Powell stood up to flex his back. The cigar smoke filled the room like a migraine.

'How's distribution coming along? If I was going to be picky about it, I'd have to remind you that your first repayments were due last week.'

'Distribution?' said Willard. 'Don't you even want the third reel?'

'Oh, there's more? Sure . . .'

The reel ran on in ugly silence. Willard watched it with new eyes and found himself hating every frame of it. A picture of class, indeed! The picture was pitiful, truly pitiful.

He owed Ted Powell one hundred and ninety-four thousand bucks.

7

There was plenty to do.

The first thing was to cut away the ruined fabric and assess damage to the wooden structure beneath. Using knives sharpened in a little engine oil on the step of the barn, Abe and Brad cut away the torn cotton and piled it up in the yard to burn later.

As the ship's frame began to come into view, Abe was relieved to see that the main wing-struts were scuffed and cracked, but basically intact. The plane looked more like a skeleton now; but there was something fast and hungry in her look as well. He whittled splints for the cracked spars and screwed them carefully into place, wrapping twine round the joins for extra strength.

Then Abe stripped the engine, so he could clean, oil and reassemble it. As he'd known from the outset, it had been a faulty valve in the fuel-line which had created a blockage in the feed. It had been the work of five minutes to locate the problem and fix the valve. Most engine problems were like that. Little tiny niggles, which sometimes killed you, sometimes didn't.

As the first week merged into the second, the new undercarriage began to take shape. Abe had some ideas on putting a cowling around the wheel base to reduce drag. By stretching cotton tightly over an arrangement of hoops and battens, he succeeded in putting his ideas into practice. Poor old Poll looked like she was wearing her winter stockings, but he promised her that she'd like them once she was airborne.

When the structural work was all done, he and Brad wound swathes of cotton around the exposed frame, pulling it tight so the fabric was hard and taut. Then they painted her: red and white, the colours Abe had used ever since his days as a barnstormer. Then, to protect the paint and fabric, they painted her again with cellulose dope, a kind of aviator's varnish.

The battered airplane began to look herself again; perhaps better.

Abe usually worked alone – he usually did pretty much everything alone – but he liked working with the kid. The kid's enthusiasm was uncanny. His aptitude too. Again and again Brad reminded Abe of himself at the same age. It was almost like working with a version of himself plucked from twenty years into the past.

As the days passed, Abe had counted another twenty-three bullet holes in the buildings around Independence. The glossy boomtown down the hill still seemed to be invisible. There was still no explanation of why Independence was the only town in America which still treated ex-army pilots as descended demi-gods. Abe kept his eyes open and his mouth shut.

On the evening of the tenth day, Abe was sitting alone in the hotel dining room, eating cold pie and potatoes. Then, just as he was finishing, Gibson Hennessey, the tall store-keeper, wandered in. The two men nodded a greeting.

'Ed Houghton looking after you OK?'

Abe thought of the mountainous puddings he'd been subjected to – each one of them 'in his honour'.

'Yeah. Sometimes even better than that,' he commented.

'Ted's right hospitable when he wants to be, especially in the pudding-making department.' Humour flickered round the storekeeper's mouth, before his voice changed again. 'You won't take this bad, I hope, but there's a little whiskey to be had, if you were a whiskey-drinking man.'

'From time to time.'

The storekeeper wandered over to the shelves where the glasses were kept. He helped himself to a couple and led the way upstairs, clearly knowing which room Abe had been given. At the door, he stood back politely and let Abe open up.

The room was the best in the hotel, but simple enough for all that. There was a deep and comfortable bed, a dressing table and chair, a wardrobe, and a small green armchair which emitted puffs of dust if anyone sat on it. There were a couple of oil lamps, grown smoky from needing their wicks trimming. A thin curtain moved sluggishly in front of the open window.

'This OK for you?' said Hennessey, looking around. 'I got a better room over at my place if you want it, only I figured you'd be happier without a troop of little Hennesseys yelling and screaming the whole time.'

'You figured right.'

'*I'd* probably be happier, matter of fact.'

Abe pulled off his boots and stretched out on the bed. Not satisfied with his first attempt at getting comfortable, he pounded and pummelled his pillows into shape, before lying back with a sigh. Hennessey put the two glasses on the table and produced a pint-bottle wrapped in brown paper from his coat pocket. He poured the whiskey and handed Abe a glass.

'Local moonshine. Been going long before Volstead, keep

35

going a long time after. It's always had quite a following in Independence.'

Abe sipped. The whiskey was good and he drank again. They'd been varnishing again today, and, though Abe liked the smell, it always made him dizzy. The whiskey helped.

'Mind if I smoke?' Hennessey produced a packet from his pocket and offered them to Abe. The pilot shook his head, but told Hennessey to go ahead. For a while, the two men were silent together, Hennessey smoking by the open window, Abe lying, eyes half-closed, on the bed. Eventually the storekeeper broke the silence.

'Being a famous man and all, I guess you get a lot of attention? Even when you don't announce your presence by putting your machine right down on Main Street.'

Nothing in Abe's manner changed, except that beneath his lids, his eyes grew more alert.

'Truthfully, Hennessey? I haven't been received like this for five years.'

The storekeeper smiled. 'No shortage of patriotism in Independence. That's the trouble with this country, see. Short memories. People ought to remember more.' He finished his cigarette and tossed the glowing butt in a wide arc out onto the dirt street outside. He watched it go.

'That's the trouble with America, huh?' said Abe softly. 'And what's the matter with Independence?'

The tall storekeeper turned from the window. 'What makes you think there's anything wrong?'

Abe closed his eyes and rested the glass of whiskey on his chest. 'Only everything I've seen since coming. That's all.'

Hennessey nodded. Some of his pleasure in their little drama left his face. It was replaced by something sadder and older.

'What's wrong with Independence?' he repeated. 'Everything's wrong. Everything bar the whiskey.'

8

'Two hundred thousand dollars? Two hundred exactly?'

Junius Thornton, Willard's father, named the figure. You need to be a rich man to name a sum like that and show no feeling aside from a businesslike care for arithmetical exactitude.

'One ninety-four. I rounded up.'

'One ninety-four, I see.' The older man nodded. He had his son's strong face and broad bones, but whereas Willard looked handsome, Junius just looked heavy. He looked the way a boxer might look, if he'd been hauled out of the ring and given five thousand dollars to spend at Brooks Brothers. 'I had no idea pictures were so expensive.'

'It's not just the actors. You need the cameramen and the stunt guys. We used a lot of airplanes and . . . it adds up.'

'Yes, I see. I'd never thought about it.'

There was a pause. Willard flicked at his trouser leg with irritation. Whoever had last pressed them had put the crease in the wrong place, so that the old one was still showing up like a shadow of the new. Willard wished he'd noticed before dressing that morning. The silence ran on.

'Well, anyway,' said Willard eventually, 'Ted's on at me about his money. I can't help admitting I feel a little peeved. He's not being quite gentlemanlike. I mean he can't possibly think there's a problem, can he?'

'I don't know,' said his father. 'I don't know the nature of your arrangement.'

'It was a loan, of course. But I mean to say, the understanding was always . . .'

'Yes?'

'Well, he never said anything about chivvying me, like some Lenox Avenue rent collector.'

'But perhaps you never said anything about failing to repay him.'

'Oh for heaven's sake! Don't take his side. It's not like that.'

There was another pause, an even longer one this time. Sometimes, silences are shared. They belong equally to both people in the conversation. But not always. This one wasn't. This one was strictly the property of the older man. Willard's scalp tightened. Noises from the street outside seemed like an invasion. Eventually, the older man lifted his gaze.

'You haven't made it very plain why you wanted to see me. But, if I have it right, you are asking me to settle your debt with Ted.'

'Yes. Yes, I am.' Willard had been intending to ask for some money in addition. It had been a long time since he'd seen any income, and after selling his Hollywood villa and settling his other debts, he'd only have around twenty-five thousand dollars in the world. To ninety-five per cent of Americans, twenty-five thousand dollars would have felt like an impossibly large fortune. To Willard, it felt like the breadline.

'You seem equally confident that I shall agree.'

'And I should hope so! Lord, it's not as though I've ever asked for money before.'

'No. No, indeed.'

His father slid open a drawer and drew out a slim case in unmarked black leather. Inside, Willard knew, there was a chequebook issued by the Morgan Bank; America's most

38

prestigious bankers – and ones who offered their services only to the very, very wealthy. Junius picked up the fountain pen from his desk, uncapped it, examined the nib, dried it carefully on the pink blotter, then wrote out two cheques. He examined the nib again and frowned before screwing the cap back on the pen. He placed the chequebook back in the drawer and closed it.

All this time, Willard was silent and sulky. But if he'd been honest with himself, it hadn't been too bad. His father had been difficult, but not nearly as bad as he might have been. He'd known some fellows back in college who'd had the most furious fights over money. All in all, he'd got off lightly. His headache drummed away, but wasn't any worse.

His father took a dry sheet of blotting paper and held it down over the cheques, rubbing from side to side with a thick forefinger. He didn't say why he'd written two. He didn't say anything about how much he'd written the cheques for. They stayed invisible beneath the blotter.

'Willard, in a way I'm pleased that we should be having this conversation.'

'Yes, Father,' his son responded, not quite clear what conversation it was they were having.

'I am fifty-seven, as you know. I expect I shall have another thirteen years or so at the Firm. Perhaps less. I shan't attempt to push myself if my health turns poor.'

'No. Quite right. Worst thing to do. Did you ever meet poor old Noggy Edwards' pa? He . . .'

Junius waved a finger. 'Your concern for my health is creditable, but is not what I wish to discuss.'

'No. Quite. Sorry.'

'It has always been my expectation that you should succeed me. My hope, I should say. My hope.'

'Well, of course! I mean, after all –'

The older man didn't so much interrupt as simply continue, trampling whatever Willard had been about to say. 'But the Firm is a very demanding organism. It turns a profit because I compel it to turn a profit. Making money is never just a question of holding your hat out.'

Willard shook his head. His headache was squarely back now, like an angry bruise. He sat with his hand pressed to his temple.

'It isn't clear to me yet if you have the . . .' the businessman groped for the correct word. He couldn't find it and shook his head. 'If you have what it takes. Brains. Guts. Desire. Ambition. Everything it takes to be a man.'

Willard opened and closed his mouth. 'Lord, Father, I've just turned twenty-five. I'd say I've accomplished rather a lot. Not just during the war, but in Hollywood . . .'

'Your time in California has been an unmitigated disaster.' Junius held one of the two cheques up and shook it. 'I have the proof of that here. You did well enough as a pilot although, as I remember, you decided to serve your country at much the same time as Princeton was wondering if it had done wrong in allowing you a place.'

'Oh heavens! Mr Rooney and his conic sections! I . . .' Willard's hand dropped away from his head. He jutted his chin. His manner was defiant, but also cowed. He didn't argue.

'I don't wish to belittle your accomplishments. You are my son and I continue to have faith in you. I suggest we let the past dwell in the past and instead look to the future.'

Willard nodded agreement. 'Oh, yes. Give me half a chance and I –'

His father interrupted. 'I have always assumed, perhaps wrongly, that in due course you wish to lead the Firm. I have thought you would wish to do this, because I have been unable to believe that a son of mine should wish for anything else. But it is a decision you must make for yourself. Do you wish to lead the Firm? Yes or no?'

Willard stuttered for a second or two. He stuttered because he hadn't expected the question and because he was never entirely comfortable in his father's presence. His father hated people who mumbled or repeated themselves or didn't complete their sentences. Willard had a tendency to do all these things and his bad habits grew worse under his father's gaze.

But the answer itself was as clear as day. Of course he expected to lead the Firm. Willard was a Thornton, the only son, the natural and rightful heir to the family throne. Of course he would one day lead the Firm.

'Gosh, yes, Pa. As a matter of fact, I was about to say, isn't it time I began? I mean, the movie business is one thing, but it's hardly . . . I'd like to start, Pa. I think I'm ready.'

Willard hadn't come into the room with any intention of getting started at the Firm. But now that his father had raised the issue, the answer seemed obvious. The movie business had turned sour. It was time he started at the Firm. He was the heir anointed. He was ready to lift his crown.

His father nodded massively.

'Good. I should not have wished your answer to be any different.'

Willard began to feel a surge of relief. His father would never want him to start work with a two hundred thousand dollar debt around his throat. His father could cancel the debt, give him a position, get him started. Willard supposed there would be hard work to put up with, but, for all his playboy past, he wasn't afraid of hard work.

'That's wonderful, Papa, I –'

The businessman raised a finger, stopping his son in mid-flow. He placed the two cheques face up on the blotter and pushed the blotter across the desk so Willard could see them both clearly.

The first one was written out for twenty-five thousand dollars and Willard moved his glance aside with a flicker of irritation. The second cheque was better. Much better. 'One million dollars precisely.' The figures were so many that the older man had had difficulty fitting them into the

41

space designated. Willard felt an almost overpowering urge to reach out and take the money.

But first there was a question. He lifted his eyes.

'Father?'

'You may take whichever cheque you choose. You may take the million dollars. You can pay off Ted. You can make pictures. You can do whatever it is you wish to do. But you will have nothing to do with the Firm. There are professional managers available these days, who will conduct business in a first-rate way. As for the future, I shall treat you as I propose to treat the girls. I shall give each of them a large gift upon marriage. That's this, in your case.' He tapped the million-dollar cheque in front of him. 'Thereafter there will be nothing further during my lifetime. When your mother and I pass on, you and the girls will inherit everything in equal fifths.'

'Or?' asked Willard in a whisper.

'Or you may take the smaller cheque. You got yourself into debt. You must get yourself out of debt. If you succeed in doing so, I believe you will have the wherewithal to make a creditable leader of the Firm.'

'But two hundred thousand dollars, Pa. I . . .'

The businessman didn't soften his expression at all.

'You may come to whatever accommodation with Ted Powell you can. I would not expect him to make any special allowance for you because you are my son. But he is a good finance man. He'll be reasonable.'

Willard stared back at the cheques. The large one and the small one. Both, in their different ways, represented a life sentence of a sort. Willard's headache thundered in his temples. He felt like a small boy asked to do a man's job.

'As I say,' said the older man, 'the choice is yours.'

9

Hennessey finished speaking.

It was gone midnight. Outside, a few dogs howled, a few birds called, the breeze set up a low murmur that ran from tree-top to tree-top. Abe's blue eyes, the brightest thing in a dingy room, had been fixed on his companion for the past hour and a half. Hennessey had smoked twelve cigarettes, Abe just one. Though the pint bottle of whiskey stood within easy reach of both men, it was still nearly full. Abe hadn't even finished his first glass.

There was a long silence which extended beyond the two men out into the whispering night beyond.

'That's a hell of a story, Hennessey.'

'You can call me Hen. Everyone does.'

The story was this.

Four or five years back, Independence was like every town the length and breadth of America. It wasn't too good, it wasn't too bad. It wasn't too rich, it wasn't too poor. The sheriff was busy now and again, but so was the preacher. Folks made money, they made love, they made merry, they made out.

Then, in the early days of 1921, things began to change. At first, it was nothing so extraordinary. A big block of land down in the river bottom was sold to out-of-towners. Up the hill in Independence, people laughed. The land down by the river was marshy and prone to flooding, pretty

43

near useless for farming. There were jokes made about cows learning to swim, about harvesting corn from a rowboat.

But the laughter died. Construction crews were brought in. The land was drained. The river was contained behind concrete walls. Houses and villas were thrown up: big, lavish affairs with oil-fired generators, electric lights, air conditioning, indoor bathrooms, one for every bedroom. That part of it was exciting – unsettling maybe, but exciting.

Then people began to arrive. The houses became occupied, the villas filled up.

'There's gambling down there,' said Hennessey. 'Blackjack, poker, craps, roulette, the lot. And booze too, of course.'

'Gambling? It's hardly Palm Beach down there, Hen.'

'Different type of customer. Palm Beach is for rich guys on vacation. They take a swim, they take the air, they take in a casino. Marion ain't like that. It's for serious gamblers. Folk who like the fact that there are no cops in shouting distance. The town is run by hoods, for sure, but I'd say that their clients were mostly just as rough.'

Abe thought again about the view of Marion from the air. There was a single-track rail spur linking the town to the coastal express line and a single-track dirt road heading out towards Brunswick. Neither route looked like it carried a lot of traffic.

'Marion's tough to get to, isn't it?'

The storekeeper nodded. 'They run a kind of buggy service out to the railroad and back. But hard-to-get-to is part of their pitch. They attract the kind of folks who don't get on with cops.'

'And they haven't been the best of neighbours, right?'

The question had made Hennessey reach for another cigarette, which he lit before answering. 'I guess we didn't make a great first impression. Certain parties up here in

Independence feel mighty strongly about old John Barleycorn and the whole Prohibition thing. Those parties called the cops, the county government, the *County Gazette*, generally made a bit of a noise.'

'And?'

'The cops came, took a look, said far as they were concerned Marion was full of law-abiding citizens going about their law-abiding business. They told us to shut up.'

'And?'

'And that night a couple of cars came up from Marion full of goons and Tommy guns. They shot us up. They weren't really trying to kill anyone, just trying to let us know how they felt about things. We had four people hurt, plenty of damage to property. So then a bunch of people made a complaint not just to the county but to the state Capitol in Atlanta.' The storekeeper dragged on his cigarette until a quarter-inch glowed red on the tip. He stared at it as if it held an answer to all the problems of the world. 'The cops never came. The letters never got answered. But the folk who'd signed those letters had their houses torched, shots fired at them, livestock shot dead in the field, crops burned. Two men were beaten so badly they could hardly see.'

Abe looked intently at the storekeeper. 'The house behind the store has a new front, Hen.'

'Yes, I was lucky. I got to the fire before it had done too much damage. I don't give a damn for Prohibition. I don't see why federal government should meddle in county business. But then again, I don't like the idea that some goons could go buy themselves the laws they wanted. I don't like the way they take out their guns at the first sign of trouble.'

'And now?'

'They want us gone. That sound crazy? But it's true. They just plain don't want us as neighbours. Course they

45

got jobs down there. Poor folks' jobs. Would be coloured jobs, 'cept we never had too many coloureds round here. Cleaning floors, mending roads, that type of thing. But aside from that, they want us gone. It's little things, but it's all the time. Farmers wake up, find somebody's fired their hayrick. Houghton here gets his place smashed up 'bout once a year. Me, I've had my own problems. If anybody even whispers about resisting, it isn't long before they're jumped on and beaten to a pulp. We've had one person blinded, six hurt so bad they can't walk without help, and one very brave man killed. And people are leaving. There are easier places to live, easier places to make a buck. They want us gone, Captain. They're killing the town.'

Silence filled the room. The breeze outside had fallen almost silent and the thumping beat of the electricity generators down in Marion could be heard.

'That's one heck of a story, Hen.'

The older man nodded, reached for his pack of cigarettes and found it empty. 'The hell with it,' he said, flinging the pack away from him.

'Sounds like you don't plan on quitting.'

Hennessey made a gesture with his hands, which could have meant just about anything. 'I have a steel plate on my door and bars over my windows. I have a gun in the shop and another one by my bed. I've stayed because I don't like quitting, but not everyone feels that way. No reason why they should.'

Abe blew out. 'Sheez, Hen . . . Listen, tell me more about the booze.'

'What's to say? You want a drink, I'd say the bars in Marion were pretty nicely stocked.'

'I didn't mean that. The way you tell the story, the gambling came first and the booze came second. I don't figure it like that.'

'I don't follow.'

46

'Think about it. If you wanted to make money out of gambling there are plenty of places you could pick. Marion doesn't look like the most obvious choice. On the other hand, if you were thinking of making money from booze, then Marion looks like a million-dollar bet. It's connected to the sea by a few miles of river. The coast is quiet and open. It's as close as you want to Bimini and the other islands. The local coastguard has its hands full trying to keep booze out of Miami and Jacksonville. How much time will they spare trying to keep it out of Marion?'

Hennessey nodded. 'Yeah, they bring it in all right. They've got a big shed on the river. But still, how much can one bunch of hoods and gamblers drink?'

'There's a rail line. A spur running right down to the coastal express.'

'Yeah. Twenty, thirty years ago some folks from the north found kaolin upriver from here. They built a rail line, then the kaolin ran out and the business folded. But the line's still there.'

'I don't think Marion drinks all the booze it brings in.'

'They load it onto the railroad, you think? Could be. I wouldn't say no. Hell, who knows what goes on in a goon's mind?'

Abe didn't answer that. Still lying on the bed, he stretched like a cat, right down to his toes. Then he rolled over, reached for his glass of whiskey and swallowed what remained.

'What I'm wondering,' he said, 'is what goes on in a storekeeper's mind. And specifically, why a storekeeper should go to a lot of trouble to tell a beat-up pilot a lot of things that aren't any of his business.'

Hennessey picked up the whiskey bottle, thought about pouring himself another glass, but thought better of it and set it back on the table. He looked suddenly old, tired and unshaven. When he spoke his voice had none of its earlier guile or subtlety.

'We need your help,' he said. 'We need you to save us. You're all there is.'

10

Ted Powell was six foot, an athletic mid-fifties, and had a face that smiled almost constantly. The smile was deceptive. That was a thing Willard would learn to remember. Ignore the smile. Look at the eyes. The smiles were like a gentleman's agreement. They looked nice and meant nothing.

'Welcome to Powell Lambert,' said Powell, as they strode along to his corner office. 'Your first time on the Street, I imagine. You get here OK? No trouble parking?'

'Parking? I came by cab.'

'Oh! Cab?'

'Sure. I –'

'And I assumed you'd come by airplane! What? Our roof isn't good enough for you?'

'I – uh –'

Willard smirked in embarrassment, but Powell had begun to laugh away at his own joke. 'It's a good roof. Nice and flat. Or have you decided to quit falling off skyscrapers? Ha, ha, ha! Hell of a stunt that.' He zoomed his hand vertically down like a stone. 'America's favourite ace! Ha, ha, ha!'

'I guess we should have paid for the catapult.'

'That was a stinker of a movie, eh, Will? A stinker.' Powell's face didn't change as he said this. It was still smothered by smiles and tobacco smoke.

'Well you know, I wouldn't quite –'

'You want to know my favourite bit? It was the bit where Blondie has to jump off the clock-tower and there you are right underneath in an airplane. You know –' Powell leaned forward. His face grew serious and he wagged his finger for extra emphasis. 'You know, I think you were right about the catapult. I just don't think that would have been realistic.'

Willard leaned back. He prided himself on a sense of humour, but Powell was pushing things too far. 'I'm sorry you didn't like the movie,' he said stiffly.

'Ha, ha, ha! I didn't say I didn't like it. I said it was a stinker. I *liked* it. Boy! I *liked* it.' He roared with laughter, a series of guffaws that subsided into chuckles and then into silence. 'So . . . you're six weeks late on your first repayment. Second instalment due in two and a half weeks.'

'Yes. That's what I wanted to come and talk about.'

Powell's cigar had run into some kind of problem, and he was puffing away over a lighted match to get things started again. 'Hmm? Eh? Oh, needn't have done, Will. No need.'

'Well, obviously, our income fell rather short of what we'd hoped.'

Powell was shaking his head. It wasn't clear if he was taking issue with Willard's words or the disobedience of his cigar. 'No, no . . . Not *our* income. *Your* income.'

'Very well, if you prefer, but in any case –'

Powell was done with his cigar. He waved it at Willard. 'I made you a loan. If I'd been dumb enough to come in for some equity, then you could say *our* income. That's the beauty of lending. I don't care if the movie was a beaut or a stinker, you pay me back just the same.'

'And I fully intend to.'

'Right. Otherwise you end up bankrupt.' Powell was still smiling.

'I hardly think you need to speak to me in those terms.'

'I'm calling in the loan. The whole of it. Due in two and

a half weeks. Margaret, my secretary, will give you written notice before you leave.'

'But I have eight months. We agreed. There were to be at least eight months.'

Powell wagged a finger. 'You're in default. The rules change. Read the contract.'

Once again the suggestion of migraine came to press on Willard's temples. Somewhere in the last few weeks and months, his world had changed. Not for the better. Very much for the worse.

'Powell, may I be candid?'

'Call me Ted.'

'Ted, I'd like to be candid.'

'Nothing to stop you.'

'I haven't any money. Nowhere near enough.'

'Bad thing to tell your banker, my boy.'

'I guess I figured you already knew.'

Powell smiled. He was very calm for a man owed almost two hundred thousand dollars by someone with no money. Willard noticed this and felt even more unsettled.

'I guess you could run along to Pappy. From what I hear, it's been another great year for guns and bombs.'

'Yes.'

Willard knew that Powell was right. After a sharp collapse in profits after the end of the war, the Firm had begun to rebuild. 'Strengthen the Old; Build the New' was Thornton's watchword. By 1922, Willard's father had proudly announced that the Firm's profits would equal those of 1916. Since then, each year had continued better than the one before.

'Look, I have spoken to Father and he's offered to bail me out if necessary. Most handsomely, as a matter of fact.'

'Excellent. Money in two and a half weeks, then.'

Willard shook his head. Up until a few weeks ago, life had seemed simple. He had looks, he had luck, he had charm, he had money. But things had grown complex;

51

horribly so. Life had come to seem like a puzzle with a million moving parts and only one correct solution.

He hadn't simply accepted his father's ultimatum. The choice of cheques and the conditions that rode with them felt humiliating and unfair. But all his arguing had been useless – and, as a matter of fact, it hadn't really been an argument. An argument takes two and the businessman hadn't even bothered to raise his voice. Willard might as well have been throwing sand against granite for all the difference he'd made.

So the scene ended as it had begun, with a choice. Willard could bail himself out and give up his future throne. Or he could take the smaller cheque, extricate himself from his mess with Powell, and take his proper place beside his father, the heir anointed.

'Listen, Ted, my father has offered to clear my debt, but I'd sooner, if I can, clear the debt myself.'

Powell stopped puffing, stopped smiling. His face was suddenly very cool, very still.

'You wish to clear the debt yourself?'

'Yes. Yes, Ted, I do.'

'I see. And how do you propose to do that, may I ask?'

11

Abe said no.

What else could he have said? A foxy old storekeeper wanted Abe to save the town from a bunch of gangsters down the hill. From all Hennessey had said, it was clear that the gangsters were well-established, well-organised and well-financed. Even supposing that Abe felt like playing the hero – and he didn't; he truly didn't – what could one man do in such a situation? The cops, the county, the state had all proved useless or worse. How could one man, working alone, do anything to help?

So he said no. Positively, certainly and finally no.

Hennessey had accepted his answer, or pretended to. But the next day, Hennessey returned to Abe's slatted barn-cum-workshop, warm and cordial as ever. The storekeeper's ostensible mission was a concern about getting Main Street ready for Abe's impending take-off.

'The street'll be fine. I just need everyone well clear,' said Abe.

'There are some potholes. I'm getting 'em filled. Should be done by the end of today.'

'Thanks.'

'And them trees at the end of the road. They ain't gonna be in the way?'

'I'll wait for the right wind. If I get the conditions right, I'll either clear the trees or have room enough to slip left of them.'

Hennessey shook his head. 'That ain't right. We owe you a proper send-off. I'll have 'em felled. The worst ones, anyhow.'

Abe felt caught between two feelings. On the one hand, he was pleased to get Main Street properly cleared for a take-off. On the other hand, friendly as Hennessey was, Abe suspected him of ulterior motives.

'Didn't you hear me last night, Hen? I said no.'

'Sure I heard.'

'Listen, I know how to fly a plane. I can fix an engine if it breaks. And if my plane happens to have a gun on it, I'm a pretty good guy for shooting at other airplanes. That's it. That's me. That's all.'

'Sure, I understand. Probably I was dumb for asking.'

'You knew that before. But you still went ahead and asked.'

'It wasn't because you can fly a plane, Captain. It's because you've got it here.' The storekeeper struck his heart. 'And here.' He tapped his forehead.

'I reckon you've got plenty in both those places yourself.'

'Hah!' Hennessey made a hacking noise in his throat. 'My wife's got a sister over in Atlanta. If things get bad enough here, we got another place to go. Things being how they are, I don't see I'd get a lot for the store, but –' he shrugged '– there are others who lost a whole lot more.'

'I'm sorry, Hen. I'd have helped if I could.'

'I expect you're right. Probably nothing you could do for us anyway.'

'I don't think there is.'

'OK, then. You can't blame me for asking.'

'No blame.'

The storekeeper shook his head, dismissing the subject. 'Say, though, before you leave, why not take supper with Sal Lundmark tomorrow? She'd love to have you round. Brad wanted to ask you, but was kind of shy. You've got yourself one heck of an admirer there.'

Abe looked sharply at the storekeeper, whose face was a picture of innocent friendliness. Abe suspected him of being up to something, but didn't know what. In any case, Brad had been a terrific helper and Abe wanted to find a way of saying thank you.

'Sure. He's a good kid. I'd like that.'

Hennessey got up to go. The plane still sat in the barn, as she had done since the first day, but there was nothing sad about her appearance now. The plane was trim and clean. Her engine smelled of fresh oil and gasoline. The fabric over her wings was hard and taut, a series of gleaming curves, that seemed only waiting for the command to leap into the air and ride it.

'There much more to do here, Captain?'

Abe nodded out towards the yard. He'd nailed a long roofing batten to an old horse-hitching post. On the top of the pole, a ribbon of white silk hung limply in the breeze.

'The take-off site's kinda short. Lowering the trees will help, but I'll still want a bit of breeze in my face before starting out. And I'll probably want to go not long after sun-up, before the air's heated too much.'

'Hot air's a problem?'

'A plane needs lift to get airborne. Cold air's got more lift than hot.'

'So that's all you're waiting for? A wind from the south and a bit of cold air?'

'Uh-huh. Aside from that, we're ready to go.'

The storekeeper was taken aback. He'd seen the way the plane had smashed up on landing. He hadn't realised Abe could be ready to move on again so fast. But he controlled his expression and nodded.

'You'd best go over to Sal Lundmark's tonight, then. Wouldn't want to keep you here unnecessarily.'

'No.'

'I'll tell her to expect you.'

'Thanks.'

Hennessey walked to the barn door and the white dust and beating sun outside. He looked back at the barn, the plane and the pilot. 'Don't mention it,' he muttered. Then he headed out, back to Main Street and his store. He had a cigarette between his lips and was searching his pockets for matches when he heard a movement behind him. It was the airman, a strangely troubled expression on his face.

'Hen, last night you asked me to do something for you. You asked me to help you and the town here out of a fix, a real bad one. I said no.'

The storekeeper nodded, his face shadowed by the brim of his hat from the fierce overhead sun.

'I said no for two reasons and I only told you one of them. The reason I told you about had to do with the jam you're in. It's not clear to me – as a matter of fact I don't think it's clear to you – what one man could hope to do. Even if I wanted to, I don't see as I could do anything to help.'

'Uh-huh. And the other reason?' Hennessey spoke slowly as though the sun was stealing energy from his words. The storekeeper's cigarette was still between his lips, still unlit.

'The other reason is me. Before the war, I was a race-track driver. When the war came, I did everything I could to get out to France, because I thought I'd be able to fly planes and fight them. And I was right. I was right about that part. But I hadn't understood something then, which I understand now.'

He stopped speaking. His jaw actually locked and he looked as though he wasn't going to speak another word. It took Hennessey a moment or two to realise that Abe hadn't simply paused, so it was only after a few seconds that the storekeeper stepped closer and prompted, 'Yes?' When Abe spoke, his answer was so quiet that only the baking stillness of the air allowed Hennessey to catch it.

'A man's got to want to play the hero. And at first I did, I guess. I was crazy for it. But then they promoted me, gave me a squadron. And I changed, or maybe the war changed me. I wanted nothing to do with any of it. But I had no choice. I was a serving officer with orders to carry out. What I did, I did because I had to. To the best of my abilities. But I'm not the man you thought I was, Hen. I'm sorry.'

The storekeeper nodded, his mouth slightly open and a dark crease running between his eyebrows. He looked surprised or disbelieving. But the look was only temporary. He held up his cigarette, still unlit. He smiled like a man who looks around for his glasses and finds them on his nose. He lit the cigarette and inhaled.

'I'll tell Sal Lundmark to expect you. You'll be getting a pot roast, I expect.'

'Pot roast sounds good.'

'And you should ask to see the kid's collection of flying stuff. He's nuts about it.'

'Yeah.'

The storekeeper looked up at Abe's makeshift windsock. The strip of white silk still hung down, as if in surrender. The two men nodded. Words still unspoken drifted just beyond them, out of reach. Then the storekeeper turned and walked away, shoes scrunching in the dazzling dust.

12

Powell accepted Willard's offer.

It was an offer that gave everything to Powell, nothing to Willard. Under the terms of the contract – drawn up by Powell's chief lawyer, then and there, under Willard's nose – Willard would begin work at Powell Lambert. He'd be a junior employee in the trade finance division, earning a handsome fifteen thousand dollars a year.

Only not.

Of the fifteen thousand dollar salary, Powell would withhold ten thousand in interest payments on the loan. As for the principal, almost nothing was said. Willard wouldn't even remotely be able to repay the loan from his earnings. When he tried to ask Powell about salary hikes and promotions, Powell dismissed the subject with a brusque jab of his cigar. The only thing Powell did say was, 'This is Wall Street. There's money to be made. If you have the gift, you'll make it. If you don't . . .' He shrugged.

And the meaning of the shrug was obvious. With the contract as it was written now, Willard was a virtual slave. If he couldn't find two hundred thousand bucks, then he'd be forced to work for Ted Powell for the rest of his life. During the war, Willard had been almost as frightened of capture as he had been of injury. But the barbed wire of a German prison camp could hardly have been more permanent than the contract he had just signed.

And why? Why was he doing what he was doing? Why

not take the million, clear the debt, go back out West, get on with life?

Two reasons.

The first was money. A million bucks sounded like a lot. But Willard was a realist. He owed Powell two hundred grand: so a million became eight hundred thousand. And what would Willard live on? In Hollywood he had spent more than a hundred thousand bucks a year. Eight hundred grand would run through his hands in six or seven years, maybe less. And after that, what? To most people, a million dollars would have seemed like the vastest fortune in the world. To Willard, it felt a hair's breadth from poverty.

But the second reason was the bigger one. He didn't know how to put it into words. It had to do with pride, with Willard's sense of himself.

From earliest childhood, he had understood this much: he was the son, the only son, the natural inheritor of the family kingdom. It had always been hard to convey to outsiders the intensity of that feeling. The name for one thing. No one in the family ever called the family business by its name, Thornton Ordnance. It was just the Firm, one word, implicitly capitalised. Willard's great-grandpa had made it. His grandpa had nourished it. His father had expanded it. It was Willard's destiny to do the same, to follow in their footsteps, to prove himself worthy of the family name.

And that pointed to a deeper reason still. Willard's father. Junius Thornton might speak as though it were entirely up to Willard whether or not he joined the Firm, but both men knew that was a lie. It mattered entirely, completely, utterly. If Willard had chosen not to fight for his place at the Firm, Junius wouldn't have excommunicated his son, but any respect would have vanished completely. Willard already knew too well how bruising his father's savage, iron-bound silences could be. A lifetime of such silence would have been too much to bear.

And so, as Willard picked up the pen that would sign away his freedom, somewhere in his deepest consciousness he understood this: that everything he was about to do, he was doing for his father.

13

The Lundmarks' home had a double door. A screen door closed shut against evening insects and a green-painted wooden door that was folded back inside the room. Inside, the room was lit by a single oil lamp. What with the wire mesh and the dim light, Abe hadn't been able to see very much of the interior. He knocked at the door, but out of politeness only, to let the folks inside know he was there. Without waiting, he went on in.

And he saw this: the kid, Brad, staring at him with those big wide-open eyes.

And this: the mother, Sal, her face and neck violently disfigured by red burn marks, her reddish hair growing thin and patchy through the burns on her scalp. And her eyes: pale blue, pretty, and completely blind.

And finally this: a photo on the mantelpiece, framed and spotlessly clean. It showed a man's face, nice looking and strong, Brad's father. Beneath the photo, an inscription: Stanford G. Lundmark, A Hero of Independence, 1881–1923.

Right away, Abe knew the nature of the storekeeper's game – a game perfectly calculated to change Abe's mind, if anything could. Muttering darkly, Abe assumed a smile and advanced. Sal Lundmark had dinner ready. She asked Abe to say grace, which he did, stiffly and out of practice. 'Let us thank the Lord for these His gifts of goodness. Amen.' Abe used the grace his father used to say, but finished wondering whether Sal had been expecting something longer and more ornate.

'Thank you, Captain.'

The conversation began awkwardly. Sal Lundmark had some kind of idea that Abe had to be treated a little better than royalty, maybe not quite as well as a procession of angels. She asked him if it were true that he'd met President Wilson – which he had. She asked him if the Prince of Wales had been as handsome in real life as he looked in his pictures – Abe said he had. She asked what the food had been like the time he'd been a guest of the French Prime Minister.

At that point, Abe had put his knife and fork down.

'Ma'am, I did a little flying in the war. Right afterwards, I met a few people, got given some medals, had a big fuss made of me. And you want to know something? I hated it. I like my airplane, I like any place that has airplanes in, and I like places that feel like home.'

There was a pause.

When Sal wasn't using her hands to eat, she rested them on the edge of the table so she could keep her orientation in the room. 'And your home,' she said uncertainly. 'Your home, I guess . . .'

'The place I grew up was a little farmhouse in Kentucky.' He looked around the cluttered room, which was about thirty feet long by fifteen wide. 'I'd say it was a little bit smaller than this, and we didn't have that fancy lean-to affair at the back. But don't worry,' he added, 'although this place feels kind of grand, you've made it homey. It's a pleasure to be here.'

She laughed. Abe laughed. Brad laughed with pleasure at seeing the ice broken. The conversation ran easily after that. Stanford Lundmark had worked as a carpenter and, when work was hard to come by, a farm labourer. Abe knew plenty about farming from his childhood, and they talked about good harvests and lousy employers.

Little by little, Sal opened up to speak about her

husband's death. He'd been one of the men who had first reported the Marion mobsters to the police. Their house had been burned to the ground, blinding Sal and almost killing her. Stanford had rebuilt the house, plank by plank. For a time things had been quiet, but then there had been more unprovoked assaults on Independence. Lundmark had had enough. He'd ridden down into Marion, aiming to sort things out, 'once and for all'. He'd got his wish, in a manner of speaking. He was gone for two days, before he was found with his head smashed in down among the cornfields on the north side of town.

'He must have been a hell of a man,' Abe murmured softly.

Sal nodded. Her eyes couldn't see, but they could still cry. There was a short silence.

'You must have been very proud,' he said.

She nodded. 'Very.'

Abe let the silence run a little longer, then changed subject. He asked Brad if he had collected any flying stuff other than the photo of Abe. He might as well have asked the Pope if he had an interest in prayer books. In an instant, the kid ran upstairs and came down with a whole boxful of photos, news stories, scrapbooks, pages torn from boys' magazines, movie posters.

Abe laughed. 'Sal, you know your son is a bit of an obsessionist?'

She smiled and wiped her eyes, but Brad was impervious to irony. He had a small mountain of material relating to Abe; vastly more than Abe had ever wanted to keep himself.

'And that's your Croix de Guerre,' said Brad, slapping down one photo. 'And that's your Légion d'honneur –' another photo '– And that's your Congressional, no, wait, *that's* your Distinguished Service Cross, the first one, three oak leaves, then I should have – yes – the Glory Boys piece. Boy! I used to know that article by heart.'

Brad dropped a newspaper article on the table. The

article was a syndicated reprint of a piece that had first appeared in the *New York Times*. Abe had been asked to do an interview with a war correspondent. Abe hadn't wanted to do it – he didn't like or approve of the way the press treated the war – and he had given a grudging thirty-minute interview to the journalist in question. That had been all. He'd forgotten the whole thing within five minutes. But then the article had appeared, splashed beneath a huge photo of Abe, 'Captain Rockwell of the Glory Boys'. The piece had caused a sensation. Nothing in it was untrue. Abe couldn't even claim that his words had been twisted or distorted. But if Abe had sought to avoid any possible glamourising of his unit and the war in the sky, he couldn't have failed more completely. The article made Abe out to be America's hero of heroes; his men to be the bravest of the brave. And it was good. Much though Abe hated it, the article was a superb piece of writing, syndicated, so it seemed, to every newspaper in America. And the name for the squadron had stuck. Abe was never just Captain Rockwell any more, he was always Captain Rockwell of the Glory Boys. The men in the squadron had been intensely proud and had painted the title on the nose and tail of every plane. Abe dated his true and abiding hatred of the war from the moment that article first appeared.

Brad went on digging out items from his collection. Abe rubbed his face, in deep discomfort. He did his best to change the subject.

'I hope it's not all me.'

'No, I've got everyone here. Everyone. I mean,' he added hurriedly, 'you were always my favourite. You and . . .'

'Me and Rickenbacker. Good choice. Rickenbacker was the best.'

Abe felt better now that the kid's interest was deflected onto other subjects, but one photo of himself as a young man was still visible on the top of the pile. He was wearing a lieutenant's uniform. He'd only just been commissioned, hadn't yet shot down a single plane, hadn't yet experienced a minute in combat. The photo was monochrome, of course, but somehow you could see the startling blue of the young man's eyes, just as startling as if a piece of sky had fallen down and got lodged there. The young man looked out with confidence and eagerness, as though knowing the place that history had written for him. Abe looked sharply away, as though allergic to the sight. When Brad happened to unfold a newspaper cutting that fell over the photo and covered it, Abe pulled his glance away with an almost visceral feeling of relief.

Sal stood up to make coffee. Abe wanted to help, but she said, 'You stay where you are. I don't need eyes to find the blamed coffee pot.' Meantime, Brad had dug out something that amused Abe. A folded movie poster advertised 'America's favourite flying ace', Willard Thornton.

'So *he's* the favourite,' laughed Abe. 'Hear that, Brad? America's favourite! What's all this about Rockwell and Rickenbacker?'

'Oh, him! I don't really . . . But say, Captain, he was ninety-first squadron as well. You must have –'

'Sure, I knew Willie Thornton, all right.'

'Wow! . . . I saw one of his movies once. In Jacksonville. I used to quite like him, but the picture was dumb. He shot down about eight machines in one fight.'

'I wouldn't know. I've never watched 'em.' He smiled. Will Thornton had arrived in the squadron much cockier than his flying skills warranted. But Abe had seen through the bluster. He'd put time into Thornton's training and the effort had paid off. Abe had come to trust his ability in a fight. If the young man had been able to get his instinctive selfishness under control, he'd have a fine future ahead of him.

'You keep in touch with him?'

'Not now, no, these movie actors, I doubt if they'd have time for an old beat-up flier like me . . . Say, though, if you wanted me to ask him to sign that movie poster for you, I expect he'd be happy to oblige.'

'Really, Captain? Gee whizz, I . . .' he trailed off, caught between his excitement at the idea and his desire to make sure that Abe knew he didn't have a rival for his admiration.

Abe took the poster. 'I'll mail it to him with a note. No promises, mind, but I expect he'll help out.'

Sal came to the table with the coffee. Abe forced the subject away from the war, back to farming and the price of corn. After twenty minutes, he pushed his chair back. 'Say, Sal, thanks for dinner. It was real good. Nice to eat home-cooked food once in a while.'

'You couldn't be more welcome, Captain.'

'Brad, I'm gonna be leaving town tomorrow. The take-off could be a mite tricky and I wouldn't want to carry a passenger, but I've heard there's a stretch of beach just south of Brunswick with room to land.'

'Oh, sure, Captain. A real good beach. Flat and wide. Not too soft neither.'

'Well, what d'you say you meet me there tomorrow? Say around noon, if you can get there. We'll do a little flying together before I head off south.'

'Oh boy! Mom, can I . . .?'

'Oh no, Captain, you don't want to do that. Brad doesn't need to –'

'D'you know what, ma'am? I think as a matter of fact he does.'

And that was that. Abe fixed the date. Poll was ready. Meantime, Hennessey had had the trees felled, the road levelled, any obstacles removed. Main Street, Independence looked almost like a real runway. Abe walked slowly back to the hotel. On the four wooden steps leading up to the hotel's verandah, there was a man visible only as a bunch of shadows and a red-tipped cigarette.

'Evening, Hen,' said Abe.

'Well, good evening to you. You're leaving tomorrow I guess?'

'Yep.'

'Enjoy your dinner?'

'You mean, did Sal Lundmark's blindness make me change my mind?'

'Either way.'

'I enjoyed my dinner, Hen. But as for changing my mind, I told you already.'

The storekeeper pulled the cigarette from his mouth and stared at the tip. Then he flicked it, still glowing, out into the street.

'A man's gotta try, though.'

'Sure.' Abe hesitated. He liked the storekeeper. The man had guts and honesty: characteristics which Abe prized above anything. 'If things work out, Hen, I'm going to be doing a little flying in these parts. I'm hoping to make a little money flying between Florida and the islands.'

'There money in that?'

'Don't know. Not much. Any case, I aim to find out.'

'Yeah, well, good luck.'

'Maybe I'll get in touch again sometime. If things work out. Any case, if you ever get a postcard from your Auntie Poll, you don't forget who sent it.'

'I won't.'

'Goodnight, Hen.'

'Goodnight, Captain.'

'And thanks. I'm only sorry I couldn't help.'

PART TWO

Lift

Heavier-than-air flight sounds impossible – and it is. People get confused because they think that planes must weigh a lot. But that's not true. Not true at all.

On the ground, of course, aircraft weigh something. But on the ground, they aren't really airplanes, they're just big chunks of metal with wings. The magic happens when the plane begins to roll forwards and air starts to move over those wings. At first, nothing much happens – nothing visible anyway. But, as the airspeed increases, the wings begin to experience lift. They're pulling upwards, cancelling gravity, making the plane lighter.

The airspeed gets faster. Once again, the lift on the wings increases. Invisible strings are pulling the plane upwards. As the airspeed goes on increasing, the lift begins to equal gravity. Push the plane through the air just a notch or two faster and the plane rises from the ground, not by some miracle of nature but because it's helpless to do otherwise.

And that's it.

That's why heavier-than-air flight never has been possible and never will be possible. Imagine the biggest, heaviest plane you've ever seen in your life. Imagine it one thousandth of a millionth of a millisecond before take-off. The plane may look like it's sitting on the ground, a clumsy metal skyscraper that's fallen over. But that's all illusion. That entire plane – pilot, passengers and all – has become absolutely weightless.

It's so light you could pick it up and throw it over the moon.

14

Abe quit, he turned his back.

One bright and breezy dawn, with a cool wind a steady ten knots from the south, Abe took Poll to the end of Main Street, opened her throttle, and roared upwards into the eggshell-perfect sky. He dipped his wings, once, twice, then flew away.

As the red-and-white plane danced away towards the ocean, the knots of onlookers broke up, back to their daily business or their morning grits. The last person left squinting into the morning sun was Hennessey Gibson. 'A nice guy that,' he muttered. 'Just a shame he wouldn't stay.'

Abe kept his date with Brad Lundmark. The Curtiss Jenny had been built as a trainer. It had two cockpits, front and rear, with full controls in each one. Abe took the kid up to fifteen hundred feet, then let the kid take over. Rudder bar left and right. Control stick up, down, port, starboard. Throttle full open, half-off, then full power again. Abe gave the kid two hours in the air. They did a couple of landings, a couple of take-offs. It was the best two hours of Brad Lundmark's life.

Abe dropped the kid back on the sand and filled the tank with gasoline from a red tin fuel can.

'So long, Brad.'

'So long, Captain.'

'You mind you look after your mom, OK?'

'Sure, Captain. I will.' On the last two words, Brad's voice twisted a little and rose half an octave. It was the sort of verbal stumble which probably means nothing. The boy immediately got his control back and added something else in a voice which was completely level and smooth. Only he'd looked away too. He'd darted his eyes quickly out to sea and kept them there 'til his voice had recovered.

The conversation ran on a littl... Abe still needed to stow the empty fuel can and clear a few stones away from his prospective take-off site. But the flier had become suddenly gruff, almost angry. They said goodbye again and shook hands. Then Abe took off, climbing aggressively. He headed south, long enough to be sure that Brad had already set off for home, but inside himself the flier was at war.

On the one hand there stood Hennessey and the blind Sal Lundmark, her dead husband and the stricken town. There stood the redhead Brad, the engine-obsessed image of the boy that Abe had once been. And on the other hand, there stood Abe himself; everything he was now, everything he'd ever learned about himself. The two sides struggled for mastery. Neither side won.

Angrily, treating his controls with uncharacteristic roughness, Abe brought Poll round in a long curve that would bring her back up the coast, five miles out to sea and a mile and a quarter above it. Then holding himself directly in between the Marion coast and the eye of the sun, he circled. The mouth of Okefenokee River, a few miles east of Independence, was marked by a cluster of ragged green islands and the branching tongues of a little delta.

Still angry, still grim, but always careful, Abe began to study the sea below. At first glance, the ocean seemed littered with vessels of all sizes, ploughing the violet-blue with trails of random foam. Abe watched until the shapes gradually resolved themselves into a pattern. The smaller ones were mostly fishing boats, tracking shoals of fish. Further out to sea, bigger ships were cruising, paralleling the coast. Abe looked at the whole pattern of shipping, but kept the Okefenokee River always in view.

He didn't see what he was looking for on that flight, nor any time that day. He felt relieved. The war that had been raging inside him had resolved itself in this way: he had given Hennessey and Brad and all the other figures in his head twenty-four hours exactly. If he found what he was looking for in that time, he'd continue to investigate. But if he didn't ... Waves of relief, of freedom, washed through him at the thought. Abe thought of flying Poll out over the ocean to the islands. The blue ocean with its alternate tints of purple and green, its crests of white, the far horizons, and only the sky above ... Abe hoped against hope, that the sea would stay empty.

When darkness fell, he unrolled his sheepskin sleeping roll on a beach a little way north of Brunswick. An hour before light the next morning, he woke up, walked waist-deep into the sea, where he dunked his head and scrubbed himself clean. Then he returned to shore, dressed and took off. By the time the sun nudged over the horizon, he was in position, lodged invisibly in the glare of dawn.

He watched the coast, watched the boats, searching for what he knew had to be there.

Searched, then, with a sinking heart, he saw it.

Two boats, the size of launches, broke from the green-fringed islands. They could have been fishing boats, only these launches were faster, sharper, lighter, keener. The two boats chugged out to sea, then headed south. Abe, holding

73

his position in the eye of the sun, his stomach churning with a feeling that he couldn't put into words, turned to follow.

15

It was 31 May 1926.

Willard stood, face washed and shoes shined, in Ted Powell's eighteenth-storey office. The banker was on the telephone and held up a finger, indicating that Willard should neither move nor speak. The call ran on for six minutes before Powell hung up. He stared at Willard.

'It's eight-thirty,' he said.

'You said I should come by first thing.'

'We start at eight.'

'Oh.'

'Never mind. Tomorrow. I'll show you around.'

Brusque and unfriendly, Powell shot his newest recruit around the premises. Powell never knocked on any door. He just threw them open and snapped out the name of each department or office as he did so. 'Typing Pool', 'Mail Room', 'Mr Barker and Mr Grainger, in charge of our trade finance operation', 'Legal', 'Letters of Credit', 'Settlements', and so on. Powell Lambert occupied four floors of its building. Although Willard saw everything at too great a speed to take it in, he was given the impression of a purposeful, dynamic, dedicated business enterprise. The more routine areas of the bank – the Typing Pool, the bay where the settlement clerks went about their business – were neat but functional. The parts of the bank open to clients or reserved for senior officers were kept immaculate and expensive: thick carpets, colonial period clocks, large mahogany desks, crystal light fittings.

The only time when Powell slowed down was in the Investment Bureau. The Bureau was lavishly furnished. It would have given off the air of a gentlemen's club, except that the undercurrent of a steely dedication to making money was stronger there than anywhere. Desks sat at long distances from each other across a wide green carpet. Young men, a couple of them no older than Willard, murmured into phones or sat at one another's desks calmly chatting. Unlike the less favoured areas, Willard witnessed no stiffening into silence when Powell walked in. He greeted his employees by their first names. They greeted him back, not bothering to rise, not ending their phone calls, sometimes greeting him with nothing more than a look and a nod.

Willard felt the difference in atmosphere instantly. If he'd ever imagined working behind a desk, then this was the sort of desk he'd like to occupy. Thus far on his tour, he had felt the cold chains of his contractual imprisonment rattling louder and louder with each new depressing stride. Here, it was different, brighter, hopeful. He looked up expectantly and Powell seemed to confirm his rising hope.

'Every part of Powell Lambert is important,' said Powell, 'but the Investment Bureau is worth everything else in the bank put together – good morning, Freddie. D'you get your revenge on the golf course, then? Ha! Thought as much. This is where the substantial profit-making activities of the firm are concentrated.' As he spoke those words, *'substantial profit-making activities'*, Powell's face screwed up as though he were speaking of something sacred. He paused, before adding in a different tone, 'That loan of ours.'

'Yes?'

'If you are ever to pay it off, it will be through your ability to earn exceptional returns on assets entrusted to you by the firm.'

'Gosh, you'd give me a chance in Investments one day?'

'I didn't say that. Your record in the moving picture business does not inspire confidence.'

Willard winced. He felt the crushing weight of his debt, his failure in the movies, of his father's doubts. Then, noticing that there was a part of the top, twentieth, floor that they had not visited, tried to win back some credit for himself by pointing it out.

'What's through there, Ted? Anything important?'

'That depends on what you consider important.'

'Oh?'

'It's lifting machinery. It drives the elevators. It means you are not obliged to climb seventeen flights of stairs on your way in to work. Does that strike you as important?'

'No.'

Powell made no answer, except to say, 'You will start out in Trade Finance. Downstairs.'

He strode downstairs, and marched Willard along a corridor to a door, marked 'Trade Finance'. He flung it open. Inside was a good-sized room, thirty foot by twenty, mahogany panelled to waist-height, painted dirty cream above. A big map of the United States was the only decoration, aside from a large black-and-white clock set in a frame of dark wood. The room was less bleak than the factory-conditions of the Typing Pool, but a long way from the studied luxury of the Investment Bureau. Looking at his new workplace, Willard felt his throat tighten with nerves.

There were five desks, plus a circular well-shaped one in the middle. A secretary sat in the middle of the circular one. Four young men sat at theirs, on the phone, bent over paperwork, or yawning and reaching for coffee. But as soon as Powell's frame was visible in the doorway, everything changed. The yawning man reached for his pen instead of his coffee. The secretary rolled her chair closer to Powell. The man on the phone finished his call. The room went still.

'Trade Finance,' said Powell, 'our main activity. This is the engine room of Powell Lambert, an important place.

And these are your colleagues.' Powell grinned meaning-lessly, letting his grin linger as his eyes patrolled. 'Hughes, McVeigh, Claverty, Ronson.' Powell named the four men in turn, jabbing at them with his finger as though they were bullocks at market. He didn't look at the secretary, let alone give her a name. 'You'll get on with them all. They'll tell you what to do. If you have any questions . . .' Powell tailed off, as though already bored.

'If I have any questions, I'll come to you. Sure. Thanks for the introduction, Ted.'

Powell's gaze flicked sharply around to Willard.

'If you have any questions, you will not so much as think of disturbing me with them. These men here will sort you out.'

'Certainly. Sorry. Of course.'

'And you will not call me Ted.'

'I'm sorry, Mr Powell, I thought you said I should call you . . .'

'When I said that, Thornton, you were not my employee.'

'Yes, Mr Powell.'

The silence lasted a second or two longer than it should have done.

'Well?'

'Nothing, sir. Thank you.'

Willard went to the empty desk and sat down.

16

Down in the swampy heat and dirt roads of southern Georgia, a little red-headed kid, aviation crazy as he was, got an envelope through the post. The letter contained a movie poster signed by Willard T. Thornton. It wasn't Lundmark's battered old poster, but a brand new one, large and glossy, with an extravagant signature in thick blue pencil that came pretty near to deleting the smaller figure of Willard's leading lady and co-star. Along with the poster there was a short note in a separate envelope addressed to Captain Rockwell. Brad didn't know where to find Abe, but he put the envelope aside in case.

And the poster?

There Brad had a problem. His main hero (by a long way) was Abe Rockwell. Next on the list was Ed Rickenbacker. A long, long way after that came some of the other names from the American war in the air and, definitely on the list but a fair way down it, came Willard Thornton. If Brad had just put his poster up, slap-bang on the wall of the sitting room, it would have looked as though he ranked Thornton right up with the best of them. The idea outraged Brad's sense of decency. So in the end, he compromised. The poster was too good not to be displayed, but Thornton didn't merit a place in either the sitting room or Brad's attic bedroom. And so Thornton's handsome face found itself in the lean-to. But the walls of the little room were covered with shelves, so Brad tacked it to the ceiling instead, where it hung upside down, looming down as though the movie star were about to come diving to earth. In the meantime, Brad had got out his father's old carpentry tools and built a frame for the photo which Abe had signed minutes after his abrupt arrival in Independence. The photo of Abe went on the mantelpiece, only a few inches sideways from the photo of Brad's father.

Abe in the living room, Thornton in the lean-to. Brad figured he'd got it just about right.

17

'Heck, Rockwell, nice to see you again. Darn nice. Very dang darn nice.'

General Superintendent Carl Egge of the Air Mail Service of the United States Post Office puffed up and down, pumping Abe's hand. The two men had known each other from two or three years before, when Egge had been in charge of the St Louis–Minneapolis sector of the transcontinental route and Abe had been his senior pilot.

'Nice to see you too, Egge.'

'Carl, please! Lord's sakes! Can you think of anything sounds dumber than Egge? Lord! I once worked right alongside a fellow with quite a name too. Can you guess what he was called? Huh? Give you a hint there. We made quite a famous pair.'

Abe knew perfectly well the name of Egge's former coworker, because Egge had told him on a dozen occasions in the past.

'No idea, Carl.'

'Jimmy Bacon. *Bacon*. Egge and Bacon. How about that?'

'Very good.'

'I'll say! Boy! Egge and Bacon! Quite a pair!'

Egge puffed and hooted his way into something like quietness. They talked a little about Egge's plans for the Air Mail Service, before Abe brought up the subject he'd come to discuss.

'Say, Carl, you ever thought of opening up an international route?'

'Hoo! Boy! Do you ever come up with some queer ideas! International? I should say not.'

'It's the next step.'

'Yeah, but you ever been to Canada?' Egge leaned forward and whispered confidentially. 'It's kinda snowy.' He leaned back. 'That's difficult flying, Captain. Heck, they're only letters.'

'Cuba.'

'Cuba? Coo-ba?'

'It's only ninety miles off the coast. In time, you could push the service on into the islands.'

'Cooo-ba? Habana, Coooooo-ba? Could be. Neat idea. Don't know how much mail there is.'

'I'd fly the route. Carry passengers. Take a little cargo. I just need the mail to get me started.'

'Heck, Rockwell, there's other routes I might be able to find for you. Not Cuba though.'

Abe shook his head. He couldn't say so, but it was Cuba that interested him, nowhere else. When he'd followed those two green-painted launches south from Marion, they'd headed down the Florida coast, skipping Bahama, Bimini and Andros, and made straight for the Puerto del Ingles, a little harbour a mile or two west of Havana. He'd continued to watch. In one single week he'd counted fifteen launches running south from Marion to Havana – and that meant the same number returning under cover of night. Fifteen launches, a hundred cases of booze on each, and a raw profit of thirty or forty bucks the case-load. Carry that on for fifty weeks a year, and there was a million-dollar racket running right under Gibson Hennessey's nose.

'Cuba would be a good start. You'd have your first international route right there.'

'No. No authority. Looks likely Congress will put airmail routes up for tender some time soon. But domestic ones. Boston–New York. Chicago–St Louis. That kind of thing. International? Who knows?'

'You don't get things if you don't push for them, Carl.'

'No, siree, you don't. And don't get me wrong. I think it's a good idea. You know me. I'd like all letters to go by plane. Stony Brook, North Dakota – whoosh!' His hand soared off the desk, like an airplane in take-off. 'Muddy Creek, South Dakota – whoosh!' His hand landed again, nose first, very fast. 'Your letter, ma'am. US Post Office at your service.' He saluted. 'Congress. It's Congress is the problem. Those guys can't think beyond costs. Look.' He held up his hands, wrist to wrist, in the shape of a cross and waggled them. 'My hands are tied. Sorry, pal. We got smart people in this country, only you know our problem? We got the government we got.'

'Cost? That's the problem?'

'Just a wee little bitty of an itty-bitty problem.'

Abe struggled with himself again. The temptation to quit was always there, never fading. If Egge denied him a route, then Abe could maybe give up on his plans with an easy conscience . . . But with Abe, the black dog Conscience never lay quiet for long.

'I'll do it for free,' he said, in a low voice.

'Beg pardon? For free?'

'It's the validation I want, not the revenue. I figure I'll get business more easily if people see Uncle Sam is happy to ride with me.'

Egge nodded solemnly. For all his fooling, he was a smart man, with an inflexible determination to build the US Air Mail Service. His nods grew slower and deeper.

'For free? A daily service?'

'Yes.'

Egge thought for a moment, then grinned. '*Correos del Estados Unidos*. Sounds good, huh?'

18

Willard sat down. Powell left the room. The door closed. Nothing moved.

Then one of the young men broke the stillness by standing up. He was below medium height, with dark curly hair, quick eyes and a look of amusement.

'"When I said that, Thornton, you were not my employee",' he quoted. 'Don't mind Powell too much, old fellow. He likes to be a bit fierce.' He held out his hand. 'I'm Larry Ronson, by the way. Most of us do have first names around here, though it's easy to forget it at times.'

The other men came over too.

Leonard McVeigh was a bull-necked red-head, with a strong grip and a look of military directness. He mangled Willard's hand, grunting 'Good to have you with us.' He held Willard's eyes for a second, as though checking to see how much competitive threat the newcomer might pose, before dropping back and letting the last two men come close.

'Iggy Claverty,' said one, as tall as Willard though not as broad, olive-skinned. 'And before you dare to ask, Iggy is short for Ignacio. And before you dare to speculate, yes my mother is Spanish but no, I am not secretly a Catholic; no, I do not stink of garlic; and no, I do not have three hundred poor relations living in Spain. Finally, before you decide what to call me, you should know that any use of the name Ignacio will buy you a kick in the seat of your pants.'

'OK, Iggy, I'll remember.'

The last man was Charlie Hughes. Right from that moment, Hughes struck Willard as a misfit. The other men – Ronson, Claverty, McVeigh – were the sort of fellows Willard had roomed with at Princeton. They were smart enough, good-looking enough, well dressed. Men like these had been the life-blood of Princeton, standard issue for the East Coast social scene. Willard's four sisters flirted with men like these. They petted with men like these. One day they'd marry men like these.

But not Hughes.

Hughes was no shorter than Ronson and not much lighter. But where you could imagine all the other men playing tennis or a game of ball or messing around in boats or on the beach, Hughes was different. He stood out. His hands were fidgety and nervous. His spectacles were thick and bookish. His clothes were decent enough, but the cut wasn't quite right, the fashions weren't quite of the moment, the poor fellow's tie wasn't even tied right.

'Hughes. Charlie Hughes. Hello. Nice to have you join us. Really.'

He nodded once too often, shook Willard's hand once more than he should have done.

Willard, whose instinct for these things was immaculate, instantly placed Hughes at the bottom of the pack. The pack-leader he guessed was probably Larry Ronson, for his intelligence and likeability, though Willard couldn't see Leo McVeigh being bossed around by any of them. That left Iggy Claverty, court jester to Ronson's prince. Willard's colossal debt and his bootblack-style income was a disaster whichever way he looked at it. But at least his new work colleagues were ones he was sure he'd get on with. His nerves began to recede.

'And allow me to introduce you to the sun of our little solar system, the flower of our garden, the lovely Miss Annabelle Hooper.'

Larry Ronson took Willard over to the secretary's circular desk. Miss Hooper, blushing, stood up to shake Willard's hand. She was mid-twenties, brunette, light blue eyes, freckled, petite. She was pretty, but unspectacular, the sort of girl you'd be happy to kiss, but not the sort you'd want on your arm anywhere important.

'Just Annie, for heaven's sake. Don't listen to Larry.'

'What, never?' said Willard. 'You're very stern.'

'Oh no!'

'Oh yes!' said Ronson. 'Powell barketh, but Miss Hooper biteth. And if she says she don't, then she speaketh not the truth. See this?' He held up a brown manila folder, perhaps half an inch thick. 'This may look like office stationery. It may feel, smell and – for all I know – taste like office stationery. But all that's a snare and a deception. These files will consume your life. They're the curse of Powell Lambert. Mr Claverty, if you please . . .'

Ronson handed the file to Iggy Claverty, who took it with an air of exaggerated ceremony. Bringing the file over to Willard, he held it out with both hands, as though the file were a precious gift being handed to a king. He bowed his head.

'May the torture commence.'

19

Abe sat at the back of a café on the waterfront. On the drink-slopped table in front of him, he had a glass of brown rum and a plate of rice and fish. A cheap mystery novel lay half-read by his elbow. Outside the café, ocean and sunlight combined to scrub the air so clean it sparkled.

Abe was a mail pilot now. For the Havana end of his business, he had rented a field a little way inland from the Puerto del Ingles. In Miami, he'd persuaded the city authorities to release land for their very own international airport. The Miami field was hardly less basic than the Havana one: comprising an oblong of sandy grass, three hundred yards at its longest, and a tin-roofed, steel-framed hangar. Each day for four weeks now, Abe took off from Miami not long after dawn with a bag of US mail for Havana. He washed off, walked down to the Puerto del Ingles, and took an early lunch, before returning to his airplane in the hope that the Cuban postal authorities wouldn't be more than a couple of hours late in bringing the US-bound mail. When it finally arrived, Abe flew it to Miami, job done.

Abe sipped his rum and went back to his novel. In the corner of the bar, a bunch of bootleggers from Marion were on their way to getting drunk. And they *were* bootleggers, of course. Here, in free and easy Cuba, there was no need to disguise the fact. True, the wooden crates they loaded into their boats were marked 'Maís de Aranjuez' or 'Jamón Serrano de Cuba'. But the markings meant nothing. Often enough the crates weren't even lidded properly. The bottles of Johnny Walker or Gordon's Gin shone out as plain as day.

Behind the bar, a home-made radio set tried its hardest to pick up a station from Miami. Mostly the set couldn't get a signal, just the whistle and crackle of empty space. Abe read. The bootleggers drank. The radio whistled.

After an hour or so, one of the bootleggers lurched up from his seat and came swaying past Abe's table. The bootlegger's bleary eyes focused on Abe's grey mailbag, and the leather helmet and goggles looped around the handles. The man stopped, stared – then inspiration struck.

'Hey Birdman!' he said, flapping his arms. 'Birdman, Birdman.'

He stopped and grinned again, as though expecting Abe to declare that was the first time he'd heard that joke in all his ten years of aviation. Abe did and said nothing. The bootlegger revved his brain to full throttle and came up with something else every bit as funny.

'Hey, Birdie. I wanna send a postcard, you gotta stamp?'

The man leered at his friends for applause, and got it. Abe said nothing, did nothing. The man cast around in the cavernous emptiness of his skull for anything else funny, but came away with nothing. He lingered a second or two, then headed off to get drinks.

That was that.

But then, just three days later, Abe was back in the same bar with the same bunch. The radio had, for once, found a jazz tune and was holding to it with a kind of feeble determination. This time another one of the bootleggers approached. Not drunk this time, and not offensive.

'Hey, pal, sorry about the other day. That birdman stuff. Guess that ain't funny, huh?'

'Not too funny, nope.'

'You ain't sore?'

'No.'

The bootlegger looked down at Abe's mailsack. It was a small bag. Mostly Abe carried just a few pounds of mail each way. At a commercial rate of a few nickels a pound, he'd have been a million miles from profit. Flying as he was for free, he was a million and one miles short.

'You carry mail? That's all?'

'Cargo, passengers, anything that pays.'

'You do OK at that?'

Abe shrugged.

'Guess you must.'

Abe shrugged again. A shrug wasn't a statement, so it couldn't be a lie. But the fact was that Abe hadn't had a single customer since starting business.

'You're sure you ain't sore? You didn't answer us today.'

'Answer you?'

'We signalled from the boat. We saw you coming in. Fired off a handgun. Da-da-da-da-da-dum. That didn't do nothing, so we shot off the rifle. Boom, boom.'

'I sit six feet from a ninety-horse engine in an eighty-mile-an-hour wind.'

'You didn't hear nothing?'

'Use a mirror. You want to signal, you need to flash.'

'Huh, OK.' The bootlegger shifted his weight from leg to leg. 'Sorry about the other day, OK?'

Abe shrugged.

'Listen, buddy, if you're a man for liquor, just let us know, OK? We can let you have some cheap. Wholesale, you know.'

'I'm OK. Thanks.'

'Right.' Chatting with Abe wasn't always easy, not if you wanted your conversational balls returned over the net. The bootlegger shifted his weight again. 'A mirror, huh?'

20

The torture commenced.

Powell Lambert's main business activity was trade finance. What this meant was that a manufacturer in one part of America – St Louis, say – might want to sell some goods to a buyer somewhere else completely – Seattle, for instance. The Seattle buyer would want the goods on credit, but the St Louis manufacturer would want his money right away. That was where Powell Lambert came in. As soon as the buyer and seller had agreed a purchase, Powell Lambert would promise to pay the St Louis men upfront, and collect payment in due course from Seattle. In exchange, Powell Lambert would charge a fee, half a per cent or thereabouts.

And that was it. The more trade Powell Lambert financed, the more the fees they earned. Every transaction had its own folder. Every morning, more folders arrived on Annie Hooper's desk for her to deal out to her five young men. She was nice about it. Sweet and understanding. But remorseless. Ruthless. The folders kept pouring in. She kept handing them out. There was no other way.

And the folders!

Each transaction sounded simple, but there were a myriad details to be attended to on each one. Insurance had to be arranged, transport arrangements checked, funds transferred, receipts obtained. Each time Willard thought he'd disposed of a file, another vicious little complication would rise up and drag him back. His working hours grew longer. His weekends vanished beneath the landslide. His prospects of repaying his debt seemed negligible. His hope of succeeding his father seemed laughable.

'*Yeee-aaargh*!'

It was five-thirty on a Friday afternoon. Larry Ronson's head disappeared beneath his desk with a long drawn-out liquid gurgle. After pausing a second for effect, he poked his head out around the corner and said, 'Miss Hooper, will you marry me?' Annie tutted and pulled her eyes away from him, a slight blush rising into her freckled cheeks. 'Silence will be taken to mean yes.'

'Larry, don't be silly.'

'Elope with me then. We'll live in sin in some crumbling Mexican palace with our sixteen children and spend our time writing rude postcards to Ted Powell.'

'It's five-thirty, anyway,' said Annie, looking around for her coat.

'That doesn't settle the question.'

'I'm off home, I mean.'

'Women today! So practical! Whatever became of romance? I'll dance with you down Broadway by the light of the silvery moon.'

'It's raining.'

'Streetlights. Silvery streetlights.'

Annie had her bag and her coat, and was settling a little cloche-style hat on her head. 'I'll see you Monday.'

'OK, how about a drink? I want to get so boiled I won't be able to find my feet.'

Willard had been expecting Annie to refuse one further time, but this time she paused. 'Well . . .'

'Excellent. Anyone else? Leo? No? Can't tear yourself

away, I presume?' Leo McVeigh's massive red head peered briefly up from his paperwork. He looked at Ronson, unblinking and expressionless, the way a butcher looks at a bull, the way a bull looks at anyone. He said nothing, just put his head back to his work and continued writing, his heavy black fountain pen moving evenly across the paper. Ronson opened his hands in a kind of what-can-you-expect-from-football-players gesture. 'Ignacio, old chap?'

Iggy Claverty glanced up briefly. 'You know an Ignacio, do you?'

'Iggy, you chump, I was asking if you wanted to come and toast the Eighteenth Amendment in a sea of alcohol.'

'Can't. I'm already drowning. Sorry.'

He waved his hand at the stack of brown files on his desk. He'd had a bad day that day. Willard had heard his swearing and sweating over some transport problem in one of the Dakotas. The stack of files in his 'out' pile was still much smaller than the stack of those on the 'in' side.

'Mr Thornton?'

Willard was about to echo Claverty's refusal and for the same reason, but the thought of an evening getting royally drunk was more temptation than he could handle.

'I'm in,' he said. 'Just let me get these damned things bundled up for the weekend.'

He swept the files that still needed to be dealt with into his briefcase – then glanced at Hughes, then at Ronson. So far Ronson had asked everyone to come except poor old Charlie Hughes, who was blinking away behind his spectacles, watching everything. Ronson clearly had no intention of asking Hughes. Hughes, equally clearly, had no intention of asking to come.

'Charlie,' said Willard, 'want a drink? Annie and Larry and I are going to get pickled.'

'Thanks, no, it's OK, I need to finish up, then get home. You folks go. Enjoy!'

Willard winced. Hughes always managed to get things a little bit wrong. People like Willard didn't use phrases like 'enjoy!'. He couldn't have explained why not, but the right sort of people never said that, the wrong sort of people did. But Willard was glad he'd asked. He was irritated by the way Ronson treated Annie Hooper as his own property. Annie would appreciate Willard's courtesy to the less fortunate. She had already made a handful of admiring comments about Willard's glamorous past, to which he'd responded with carefully offhand modesty.

'Let's go,' he said.

They went. First to a hotel that Willard knew about, where you could get anything you wanted as long as you didn't mind it served in a coffee cup. Then to a speakeasy off Broadway, where the drink was cheaper. To get in, you had to walk down a set of grimy, unlit steps to a shuttered steel door. Just inside, a watchman peered out to check the new arrivals weren't cops, before the door was unbolted and Willard and the others whisked inside. Once in, they drank cocktails because they wanted hard liquor, and because the cocktails were a way of disguising the taste of the grain alcohol, the industrial alcohol, and the under-brewed green moonshine which invaded every bottle of 'honest-to-God, straight off the boat' Scotch whisky in New York. Then finally, drunk as Irishmen on payday, they stumbled out into the street.

'I must say, Annie, you're a very good sport,' mumbled Willard. 'A very damned good sort. Ha! A damned good sort of sport! A sporting sort with a sort of –'

'There!' said Annie, pointing. 'A burger place. *Joe's Burgers*. Aren't you starving?'

Ronson followed her unsteady arm with an unsteady eye. 'Not necessarily a burger place,' he objected. 'Maybe that's the fellow's name. Mr Joe Burger. I should think the poor old gooseberry gets rather annoyed with people knocking him up and asking him for burgers. Poor old Mr B.'

The three of them swayed over to the burger stand. Annie hadn't drunk as much as either of the men, but she was every bit as sozzled. Willard and Ronson fought over which of them would be allowed to take her arm, and only declared a truce once Annie gave her left arm to Willard and her right one to Ronson.

Willard had enjoyed the evening, but he'd enjoyed it the way a prisoner on death row gets a kick out of a postcard from outside. Even now, drunk as he was, Willard felt his lack of freedom. Willard's salary, net of Powell's deduction for interest, left him hardly any better off than Annie. Unlike her, he had the use of a company apartment and the part of his father's twenty-five thousand he hadn't already spent. But he wasn't an Annie, a mouse content with crumbs. With a kind of reckless defiance, Willard had changed his spending habits almost not at all. In the past two weeks alone, he'd spent six hundred dollars on clothes, thirteen hundred dollars on new furniture, another few hundred dollars to have the seats in his Packard re-upholstered in pale calfskin. Before too long, his bank account would be as dry as a busted fuel tank. What he'd do then, he didn't know – he refused to think about it.

And that wasn't all. Six weeks since starting work, he was no further ahead. His loan was not a nickel smaller. His chance of repaying it not a hundredth of a per cent higher. All his life, Willard had known there were two sorts of people: the rich and the not-rich, the free and the unfree. He had always been of the first sort. Had been. He was the second sort now. He and his two colleagues stood in line, under a light July rain, belching and privately regretting their last cocktail.

'I must say,' said Ronson to Willard, 'you're a lot better than our last fellow.'

'Hmm?'

'You know. Martin. Our late-lamented colleague. Esteemed and lamented.'

Even in his drunken state, Willard pricked up his ears.

Arthur Martin had been the fifth member of the Powell Lambert 'engine room' before Willard's arrival. Willard had inherited his desk, his paperwork and even his company-owned apartment. All Willard really knew of the man was that he had been killed in an auto accident shortly before Willard's arrival at the firm.

'So, when was the auto smash? When did the poor fellow die?'

'Eh? You know,' said Ronson. 'You know.'

'Gentlemen, please,' said Annie, using her chin to point to a gap that had opened in the line ahead of them. The two men frog-marched Annie forwards until they had caught up.

'I don't know,' said Willard. 'If I knew, I wouldn't ask, would I?'

'Well . . .'

'It was only . . .'

Annie and Ronson both spoke at once, then stopped. Then Annie spoke alone.

'He died the Thursday before you arrived. We thought you knew.'

Willard felt a tiny prickle of something run through him. Afterwards, he thought maybe it was fear or the first premonition that something was wrong. But perhaps it was only the underbrewed moonshine talking. Perhaps the prickle was nothing more than a simple shudder in the rain. In any case, when Willard answered, he suddenly felt less drunk, less stupid.

'But that couldn't be. Powell had already told me which apartment I'd be staying in. He couldn't have done that, if the poor devil Martin was already there.' He didn't mention it, but the same was also true about the 'engine room'. There were five desks there, plus Annie's. The room couldn't have fitted another one. If arrangements had been made for Willard's arrival, wouldn't someone have thought to introduce an additional desk?

'It was, though,' said Annie. 'The Thursday before you came.'

'Powell must have been in a muddle. Good job in a way. You wouldn't have wanted to arrive with all your boxes and find . . . I mean, not a good job the fellow died, obviously. What I mean is, good job the place was empty.'

'Powell wasn't in a muddle,' said Willard, argumentatively. 'It wasn't just him, I mean I had to phone and confirm and collect keys and everything. It wasn't just a case of turn up, mister.'

'Then Martin must have been moving somewhere else, mustn't he? Couldn't have the two of you living on top of each other. Any case, Martin wasn't a decent sort, like you. Didn't appreciate the merits of a fine bottle of . . .'

The line moved forwards again but neither of the men had noticed. Annie wriggled free of their arms and stood ahead of them, asking them what sort of burger they wanted.

'Good old Joe Burger,' said Ronson. 'A veritable prince of gooseberries. Ruining his Friday evenings to help the starving.'

'Willard, what are you having?'

Annie turned to him, her fine brown hair damped down against her cheek. Willard stared at her blankly.

'Old chap, your mouth is hanging open. Mr B here will probably have to stuff it closed with one of his excellent pickled gherkins.'

Willard shook his head. *How had Ted Powell known that Arthur Martin's apartment and Arthur Martin's desk would be empty in time for Willard's arrival?* The question had no possible answer.

'I'm sorry,' he said. 'I'm not feeling hungry.'

He pulled away from them and walked fast uptown, hatless through the pattering rain.

21

Abe ran through the little belt of turbulence over the Florida coast, turned, applied a side-slip with the nose into the wind. Then, just before the ground came up, he levelled the wings and kicked Poll straight with the rudder. The wheels came straight and touched down. As Poll began to shake her speed off into the grass, he let the tail float down as the elevator lost authority. He was a little later than he'd expected, partly because of headwinds, partly because he'd overflown one of the Marion launches on its way south. These days, he'd got into a routine with the bootleggers. They'd flash to him, signalling their presence and he'd flip into an aerobatic routine: loops, spins, barrel-rolls, dives. Once he came so low over the water at the launch, that by the time his undercarriage flashed over their heads, one of the bootleggers had been scared enough to jump overboard. The stunts were much appreciated. In the café in the Puerto del Ingles, Abe was a mini-celebrity. His drinks were always bought for him. He was showered with gifts: cigars, booze, chocolate. His routines grew more elaborate, more complex.

For now, though, Abe just taxied over to the hangar and stopped. The blur of propeller blades slowed to a flicker, then to a halt. Abe climbed wearily from the cockpit, pulled helmet and goggles off, scrubbed his head, face and neck under a cold tap. The hangar wasn't just a place for Poll to come in out of the weather, it was Abe's home too. As well as room for Poll and room for all the maintenance equipment she needed, Abe had set up a camp bed and thin mattress. He also had a sheet, a blanket, a coat rolled into a pillow, a small table, two chairs, two enamel mugs and plates, a primus stove, and a bag which contained his entire wardrobe. Aside from what was in the hangar or on his back, Abe owned nothing in the entire world.

He dried off with an end of towel. The beat of an airplane engine still thrummed in his ears, but it sometimes did after a long flight. He rubbed the sides of his head with his palms and listened again. The thrumming was still there, and it was a sound different from Poll's. It was stronger, racier, deeper, cleaner. Abe jumped on an oilcan to get a better view, then saw it.

A plane was coming in from the south. She was flying low, steel-grey bodywork glinting in the sun. She was the most beautiful machine Abe had ever seen: a gloriously streamlined, squat-tailed biplane with stubby little wings and an engine asnarl with power. That she was a racing plane was obvious. That she was in trouble even more so.

The engine had a problem. It was running foul, firing wrong, missing beats. And there was another problem. Abe's airfield had been designed for Poll. Because Poll was slow, she didn't need much room to land or take off. And when the Miami authorities had approved the grant of land for an airfield, they had approved enough for Poll and not an inch more. The little racing plane didn't have room to land.

The little plane howled overhead, its engine note all wrong. Abe watched, helpless. The longest strip of clear space on the airfield was on the diagonal, but a line of telegraph poles ruled out that approach. The little plane came to the same conclusion. It buzzed off towards the south-west, but Abe knew that the south-west held few options. A beach was fine for Poll's slow and sturdy ways. But a racing plane could easily smash up on a beach. No. Abe corrected himself. Not could, would. *Would* smash up. Abe stared another moment, then ran to Poll. If he could get airborne fast, he could follow the pilot, and be on hand for the coming catastrophe.

But he was too late. The little plane came again. She was flying desperately low to the ground, tree-skimming and dune-hopping. Abe breathed slowly and evenly through his mouth. He silently urged the pilot not to do what he was about to do.

In vain.

The little plane sank lower. It was flying just twenty feet off the ground, dead level with the telegraph poles, dead level with the wire. It was an insane way to fly in any case, but here on the coast, with the turbulent ocean breezes making any manoeuvre vastly more difficult, it was beyond lunatic. The plane kept coming. Heading for the telegraph wire, heading for extinction.

The plane got closer – closer – closer – then at the last possible moment dipped its nose down. Like a terrier easing under a gate, the little plane scuffed its way beneath the wire. Its wingtips were so close to the telegraph posts on either side, Abe could virtually hear them twang. The pilot held his four feet of altitude another half second, then touched down on the airfield within mere yards of the boundary.

It was precision flying of the highest calibre, but the danger wasn't over.

The pilot had already cut his approach speed to the bare minimum, but the plane was still running too fast. The aircraft tore across the airfield, kicking up a storm of dust from its wheels, its tailskid digging into the sand. Slowly – too slowly? – the racer lost speed. The pilot was using full-back stick, to drive the tail down and maximise drag from the wings. All the same, the little plane bounded three-quarters of the way across the field – then four-fifths – then nine-tenths – then ended up, engine still running, just fifteen yards from a three-foot ditch.

After a short pause, the racer made a cautious turn and bumped slowly up to the hangar.

Up close, the machine was beautiful – stunning. Abe recognised the plane as one of the Curtiss R6 series of planes, purpose-built racers, winners of all the flying competitions in 1922 and 1923, and holders of the world speed record before the Europeans had snatched it back. The plane was power and force and beauty and speed. Abe was open-mouthed with envy and delight.

The plane came up and stopped. The air emptied of sound, huge and hollow after the noise.

Abe looked at the pilot, whose head poked out from a cockpit screened by a low windshield raked back hard from the nose. The pilot was only just visible in the cramped cockpit, dust- and oil-stained, still helmeted and goggled, but obviously young and boyish. The pilot caught Abe's glance and raised a gauntleted hand.

Abe nodded in answer.

The hand fell back and thumped the edge of the cockpit twice. The gesture meant 'Thanks, old girl', or maybe, 'Thanks and sorry'. It was a gesture Abe had used often enough. He knew the pilot's feelings: a mixture of relief, exhaustion, happiness, shock – a bubbling brew which took hours to settle.

The pilot took another few moments to gather himself, then pulled a face. The face might have meant something about luck and close shaves and being relieved, or it might just have been that his heart was still pounding in his chest and he was too tired to say anything sensible. Abe stood back, didn't try to rush things.

Then the newcomer pulled off his goggles and dropped them in the cockpit. He was young, terribly young, reminiscent of the boys who had served with Abe in France. Served and died, in so many cases. He stood back as the pilot got ready to jump out. For a second – or less, perhaps just half a second – the pilot paused, as though expecting Abe to step forwards and offer a hand. But maybe not. Shock could make even the most familiar things seem strange. In any case, the pause ended. The pilot put his hands to the side of the cockpit and rolled his body out and onto the ground. He was around Abe's height and, as far as you could tell anything about a person wrapped head to toe in sheepskin, thin.

'That was a heck of a landing. One of the best bits of flying I've ever seen.'

The pilot smiled and puffed out with relief. Then he put his hand to his head and removed his helmet.

Or rather, not.

Not *his* head, *his* helmet. But *her* head, *her* helmet. Abe goggled in astonishment as a pretty sandy bob emerged into the strong Miami light. The pilot's face *was* boyish, but it was boyish the way that the fashion plates in the women's magazines were boyish, fine-boned but unfussy, clear-skinned, fresh and direct. It was an attractive face, the sort of face a man could like straight away and never change his mind about.

The woman smiled.

'Hi.'

22

As problems went, it ought to have been a small one.

The Association of Orthodox Synagogues was expecting a consignment of 'Sacred Books and Sacramental Materials' from a Long Island based import-export outfit. The documents were in good order. The goods were in Long Island, ready for delivery. Insurance and transportation arrangements had been settled. But there was a problem.

The customer named on the delivery note was the Association of Orthodox Synagogues. But the beneficiary named in the insurance documentation was the Associated Synagogues of New York. Did it matter? Maybe not. But if there was a screw-up and Powell Lambert took a hit, then it would be Willard who suffered, no one else.

Larry Ronson wasn't around at the time Willard ran into the issue. Willard didn't like Leo McVeigh and didn't want to ask him. Iggy Claverty and Charlie Hughes were both there, but Willard guessed Claverty was bound to be flippant and Hughes fussy and nervous. Sunshine cut across the room, hurting Willard's eyes, reminding him of his time in the cockpit, when throwing the plane around in the sky made the sun bob and spin like a wild thing . . .

He strode across the room and pulled down a blind. Annie caught his eye and smiled at him. She smiled at him more than at Ronson now. Willard noticed and was pleased. He went back to his desk. The problem was still there. Sunshine still swam in through a flaw in the blind. The

Association of Orthodox Synagogues? The Associated Synagogues of New York? Which? Willard dialled a number, got no reply. To hell with it.

The documents both contained the same address, which was only a short walk away on the Lower East Side. Willard jumped up.

'I'm going out, Annie. Shan't be long.'

She smiled at him again and tucked a strand of light brown hair behind her ear. It was a menace that strand: always falling loose and needing to be put back, especially when she knew he was watching her. Willard didn't flatter himself that she was flirting, but he knew that she was very aware of his presence.

In a rare good mood, he strode north, but as he got closer, his mood evaporated. The neighbourhood was a poor one. There was something edgy in the air: smells of bad plumbing, decaying masonry, conversations that fell silent as he approached. He found the address: a shabby doorway at the bottom of a concrete staircase. A domestic argument droned angrily from a nearby room. There was no plate on the door. Split green linoleum rippled underfoot – Willard noticed it particularly, because he had just taken delivery of half a dozen pairs of handmade shoes. He was wearing a pair now, and his feet were sore and uncomfortable in the stiff new leather. He rang the bell.

No answer. He rang again. Then, just as he was about to give up and go, an Irishman, unshaved, wearing trousers and his undervest came to the door.

'Yeah?'

'Oh . . . Excuse me, I believe I must have the wrong address.'

'Who d'you want?'

'I understood that a Jewish religious organisation was based here. As I say, I must –'

'Huh? Kikes?'

There was a muffled shout from the dark interior beyond

the Irishman's shoulder. 'Uh . . . wait a moment, will you,' he said, and disappeared.

When he came back, he'd found a shirt from somewhere, but hadn't bothered to button it.

'Sure, you're right. At least, they're not here exactly, but . . . What d'you say your name was?'

'My name is Willard Thornton, representing the Trade Finance department of Powell Lambert.'

Willard handed the man a card, who blinked at it, and stuffed it into a greasy pocket. 'Jesus!' He pronounced the name the Irish way, Jay-sus.

'You can get a message to them?'

'I can, sure. There's a fellow, black coat and that, a rabbi. I guess he'll give you a call, maybe. Is that all you'll be wanting? OK.'

The door slammed shut. From inside, a burst of laughter crashed against the shabby plywood. Willard was suddenly angry. Whatever had just happened, he had the sense of being made a fool of. He folded his fist, wanting to smash it through the door, wanting a fight.

He didn't, of course, but when he got back to Powell Lambert, he sought out Ronson. Willard explained the problem in angry, affronted tones. Ronson looked serious.

'You think there might be a problem with this outfit?'

'It was no place to find a bunch of . . .' Willard swallowed the word 'kikes' and used the word 'rabbis' instead. 'The place was a shithole, Larry, honestly.'

'You worry somebody's playing us for suckers? That's your worry?'

'Well, good Lord, something didn't add up.'

'Maybe. On the other hand, there's no law against shitholes. And the thing with the insurance note, I've had that before. The insurance clerks just scribble down whatever the hell they want. No attention to detail. Now what I'd do if I were you . . .'

The conversation drifted into the comforting detail of

104

paperwork and insurance forms. Willard was grateful to Ronson for his help. Iggy Claverty came over and helped out too. The problem seemed resolved.

And that was all.

Or almost.

Going home that evening, Willard happened to ride in the same elevator as McVeigh. The two men exchanged a couple of words, then fell silent. The elevator moved slowly, people got in, got out. The compartment emptied. All the time, Willard felt McVeigh's heavy gaze pressing on him. When Willard turned, the big man, with his cropped red hair and football player's neck, was looking squarely at him, unblinking.

'Yes?' said Willard.

McVeigh shook his head.

'You've been staring at me all the way down,' Willard persisted.

McVeigh paused a second, then stepped half a pace closer. His head was too close. Though Willard weighed in at an athletic one hundred and eighty pounds, McVeigh must have had another forty pounds on him at least. There was something directly threatening in his attitude. Willard's anger flared. Whatever McVeigh's problem was, Willard had no intention of backing down.

'Careful,' said McVeigh. 'Asking questions, like you were today.'

'What d'you mean?'

McVeigh shrugged.

'What d'you mean? Why the hell shouldn't I ask questions?'

McVeigh came a little closer still. He had small blue eyes, lost beneath a broad expanse of forehead. 'Just be careful what you ask and who you ask. You wouldn't want to . . .'

The elevator hit the ground floor. Willard clanked open the inner door, then the outer one. The two men held their pose of near-aggression a second longer.

'I'll ask who I want, what I want, and I don't suppose I need to ask your permission, Leo.'

'That's up to you.' McVeigh looked like he was trying to take some of the heat out of the situation, but a muscle continued to clamp and unclamp in his jaw. 'You do what you like. Just remember . . . anyhow, goodnight.'

McVeigh turned and walked away. For a big man, he was light on his feet and fast. Willard found himself thinking *that man could be dangerous*. For the second time that day, he found his fist curled into a ball, wanting to thump something.

23

'I'm Hamilton, Pen Hamilton. Short for Penelope only no one ever calls me that.'

Abe shook her hand. 'Abe Rockwell. Welcome to Miami.'

'Abe Rockwell? Captain Rockwell? . . . Oh, gosh, what a way to meet you! Gee! . . .' The woman flier was briefly flustered by finding herself in front of one of the two or three most famous aviators in the United States, but Abe was used to this reaction and brushed it away. 'I can land the normal way too, you know,' she added.

'I bet you can.'

'I was lucky the sand was soft.'

'You were lucky you knew how to fly.'

'I don't know. I wasn't sure I needed to land. The engine was missing beats, but I still had power. Maybe I could have gone on.'

'It wasn't just the distributor blocks, maybe?'

Pen pulled an apologetic face: the first really girlish thing she'd done. The face said, 'I couldn't tell a distributor block from a humpback whale.'

'The distributor blocks on the magnetos,' Abe pursued. 'They get coated with carbon when the engine's running. But they were cleaned before you took off, right?'

'I'm sorry, Captain. I'm sure I ought to know, but I don't. They told me she was OK to go.'

Abe felt a jolt of irritation. During the war, he had no time for pilots who couldn't strip, clean and reassemble an engine.

107

The reason why Abe's squadron had the best serviced airplanes in the American Army was that Abe made his pilots responsible for the airworthiness of their equipment. It was an attitude he regarded as sacred. And by those standards, Pen Hamilton's ignorance was shocking, an insult to aviation.

And yet . . . Pen Hamilton was a woman. She had handled her machine with a rare combination of courage, force and delicacy. She had made a horrendous landing look almost easy – and was now handling herself not with bravado but with modesty. Abe let his irritation pass.

'The problem sounded to me like your magnetos. If so, you could have gone on to wherever you were going. I'll take a look, if you want. And please, Miss Hamilton, there's no need to –'

'Oh no, call me Pen, please.'

'Then I'm Abe. No Captains around here, if you don't mind.'

They grinned at each other, suddenly comfortable.

'You'll want to come in and get cleaned up. And something to eat or drink? I was about to have something myself.'

They went in.

Abe could see Pen noticing Abe's camp bed in the corner of the hangar, his makeshift kitchen, and his barren wardrobe, the logo on Poll's fuselage: a mailbag in the very approximate shape of a shield with the words 'US Mail' stencilled across it. She noticed something else too. Above Abe's crowded workbench ran a shelf at head height. The shelf was crowded with metal castings, polished, clean and free of dust. Pen looked at the collection with curiosity. The castings were models of aircraft, but not necessarily complete ones. Only four of the castings had nose cone, fuselage, tail, and a full set of wings, upper and lower on both sides. The rest were simply airplane pieces. A fuselage without wings. A wing without a body. A nose cone. A lot of nose cones. She picked up a few of the castings, ran her hands over them and put them down.

'You make these?'

'Uh-huh.'

'They're beautiful.'

'Yes.'

'And unusual. Beautiful and unusual.'

'Uh-huh.'

Since Abe didn't exactly seem full of chatter on the subject, Pen turned to a different topic. She indicated the mailbag stencilled on Poll's side.

'You're flying the mails?'

Abe nodded

'I didn't know there was a route . . . To Cuba, I guess?'

Abe nodded.

'Havana?'

Abe nodded.

'Every day? Over water?' She took in the information like a professional pilot, calculating the hazards, the safety margin, the rewards. 'You must hit quite some weather at times.'

Abe gestured at Poll. 'She's a strong girl. We get through.'

'Still . . .'

Pen washed her face and hands. Abe offered to walk out of the hangar so she could take a proper wash, but, since the washing facilities consisted of a cold tap and a tin water-scoop, Pen managed to resist. By the time she was done, Abe had laid out the only meal he could provide: bread, cold meat, some tomatoes, water. She came over to his little table. First she said she didn't want anything, then, when Abe pressed her, she ate hungrily.

A moment's awkward silence was covered by eating.

Abe wasn't shy of girls. True, he didn't see much of them. True, he'd never had a relationship that had lasted longer than a couple of months. But he wasn't shy, nor even inexperienced. He'd dated girls, petted girls, slept with girls. The reason why his relationships had quickly fallen apart was that he'd never really wanted them. Abe knew his priorities and they had never included women. So, aged thirty-six, he wasn't shy of girls, but he didn't spend much time with them either.

Pen bit into a tomato. It was overripe. The skin split and spurted juice across the table and down her chin.

'Sorry.'

'Don't worry.' Abe gestured at his linenless table, his bare accommodation. 'Sorry I haven't got anywhere better.'

'You . . .?' Pen began to ask the obvious question, then dropped it, embarrassed.

'Yeah, I'm living here for now. While I get the business started up. In time, I'd like to build a little. Extend the place at the back.'

Abe gestured at the cement block wall at the rear of the hangar. He knew enough about construction to be able to fix something up. It wasn't something he'd thought about before, but now that Pen had put him in mind of the idea, he liked it.

'You just carry mail?'

'Passengers too. If I can find any. Also cargo.'

'You get many passengers?'

'No.'

'Cargo?'

'I don't advertise much. I guess I ought to do a little more.'

He wasn't being candid. He had only ever placed one advertisement for business. Next door to the hangar, Abe had tacked on a tiny wooden lean-to which he had designated his office. The office held one chair, one table and – pinned to the door in sun and rain – a notice saying 'Passengers and cargo carried. All enquiries welcome'. Nobody had ever come to the office. Nobody had ever seen the advertisement.

'What d'you call yourself?'

'Huh?'

'The business. It's got a name, right?'

110

For a half-second, Abe struggled to remember what he'd written on the notice. Then he got it. 'Florida International Air Travel. Fancy, huh?'

'You've got an office in town or . . .?' Pen trailed off. She was getting the picture. 'People need to apply here, right? I've got friends down here. They're always running up the coast, or down to Key West and the islands. I'll have a word. Maybe I can send some clients your way.'

Her glance slid out of the empty hangar to the dusty grass. Aside from her own beautiful machine, there was only Poll: clumsy, old-fashioned, graceless. Abe could see Pen wondering how Abe thought he could recruit passengers without advertising and with only Poll to fly them.

Something in Abe hardened. He changed subject.

'That your plane?'

Pen's eyes were still focused out of the hangar door. At Abe's words she swept her gaze across to her own machine, her eyes softened, then she brought her gaze in, her pupils dilating as she took in Abe's face. She took a moment to answer and Abe ended up looking longer into her eyes than he'd expected. It was a curious sensation. The eyes were like his eyes: too blue, too clear, the face around too tanned to hold them. Only it wasn't that. There was something in the way Pen looked at him. It wasn't the way a woman looked at a man. Her look was direct, frank, open, unembarrassed. There was nothing flirtatious, but nothing modest either. She wasn't sexless, but she didn't have to bring her sex into the look that passed between them.

She dropped her eyes.

'Yes. Lovely, isn't she?'

Abe nodded. He'd done some test flying for Curtiss once, only got out once things had proceeded a little too far with a girl that lived nearby. But he said nothing about that, just, 'Beautiful. Nobody makes 'em better.'

'I'm lucky.'

Abe looked at the plane again. It was a hellishly serious

111

machine, fiercely fast, a machine which demanded speed, strength and decision from its pilot.

'You fly her for fun, or . . .?'

'For fun, yes, I guess. I race her.'

'Pylon racing? Competitively?'

'I race her anywhere I can. The Arberry Cup once. The Burlington Medal. The Conway.'

There was a tiny flicker around her eyes when she named the last race. The flicker jogged a memory for Abe. He didn't follow aviation gossip much, but he'd raced a little right after the war and had kept an interest in the major events. Her name, Hamilton, rang a bell . . .

'The Conway? Hold on, you didn't just fly in that.'

The flicker transferred from eyes to mouth, where it broke out into a smile. 'Last year. Bertie Acosta had to drop out with engine trouble. I was able to take advantage.'

Abe smiled and shook his head. 'No, Pen, a win's a win. Nothing to do with another guy's engine. Any case, the Conway's the only one to win, right?'

She returned his smile. The Conway Cup had been inaugurated in September 1920. The first name engraved on the silverware was 'Captain A. Rockwell.'

They laughed together. Their eyes touched and didn't move away. The moment didn't last long, but it lasted long enough for them both to feel something. Something shared, something mutual.

Abe held Pen's gaze a moment longer, then felt suddenly uncomfortable. He stood up abruptly and went to make coffee, suddenly angry at his spartan accommodation. Almost deliberately, he made the coffee too strong, too gritty. He made it so nobody could possibly like it, probably not even drink it. Pen attempted more conversation, but Abe had closed up. Some women would have needed to talk into the vacuum, but not Pen. Quietness didn't bother her, nor the coffee. She seemed relaxed. But time was running by. She would need to find accommodation in town.

Abe offered the name of a couple of hotels that weren't too dear. Pen took the information like she didn't need it, but was too polite to say so.

'I'll send a truck,' she said.

'Huh?'

'A truck. For the plane.'

Abe was puzzled. 'Why?'

'You said there was a problem with distributing something. The blocks? I thought . . .'

Abe was annoyed again, but tried not to show it. 'Pen, the blocks need cleaning, nothing else. It'll take twenty minutes at the outside.'

'Oh.' There was a pause. 'I guess I ought to know that.'

'I can show you how if you want.'

She hesitated. 'I . . .'

'Yes?'

'Captain, I can fly 'em, I can't fix 'em. I'm not about to try.'

Abe's annoyance fluctuated uncertainly. On the one hand, her attitude was something he hated. On the other hand, there was something amazingly uncomplicated about her. And she could fly. She could certainly fly.

'Listen,' he said, 'I've been wanting the City to move that damn telegraph wire for some time. I'll call 'em. Tell 'em they almost got themselves a fatal accident. If they don't move the wire, then I will. I'll fly your plane back for you. Just let me know where to bring her.'

'Oh, no, I couldn't ask you to do that. If you tell me when the wire's gone, I can come by and –'

'Pen, I hope you're not going to stop me flying her.'

'You want to?'

'Wouldn't you?'

She grinned. When she wasn't smiling, her face was withdrawn, quiet, thoughtful. It was the sort of face you could easily overlook, glance at and not properly notice. But when she smiled, she changed. Everything in her face became open

113

and welcoming. When she smiled, her face called out to you like a bonfire of straw on an autumn day. She put a hand inside a shirt pocket and pulled out a simple white calling card. It bore her name and an address in South Carolina.

'Thanks,' she said, and walked away.

24

Willard waved goodbye and watched his guests go volubly down the hall. They'd enjoyed martinis with Willard, now were going on to the Algonquin for dinner and would be off to a jazz club in Greenwich Village before eventually rolling into bed.

Not Willard.

The pressure of work never let up. Willard spent his day chasing shipments, checking freight manifests, sending confirmations, arranging fund transfers. He needed the evenings to catch up with the days. Every time he felt he was getting on top of things, Annie would hit him with a stack of new files, crammed with deadlines and vicious complications.

But it wasn't only that. Willard's friends were big-drinking, free-spending. They had no idea of Willard's impending poverty. Willard still had a little money, but it was running out fast and he had already borrowed two thousand bucks from Lucinda, his eldest sister. An evening spent working alone was a cheap one at least.

But that was small consolation. Because, so far, twelve weeks in, all his hard work had been for nothing. The loan wasn't getting smaller. How could it? On Willard's first day, Powell had said, 'If you are ever to pay it off, it will be through your ability to earn exceptional returns on assets entrusted to you by the firm.' But the company never entrusted him with money. Not a dollar. Powell hardly seemed to remember he still existed. Willard felt locked in a cell whose key had long since been thrown away.

The corridor fell silent. Willard went back into his apartment.

He took some cold chicken from the refrigerator and ate it in front of the open door, letting the clear, precise light fall in a block across the white tiled floor. A burr of traffic from Madison Avenue rolled down the canyon of East 60th Street and in through Willard's kitchen window. He drank a glass of milk, rinsed it, and decided to clear his head with a shower before resuming work. He walked through to his bedroom and began to undress. He was sitting there, untying his shoe laces, when he heard the metallic click of a latch. *His* latch. For a moment there was silence, then the sound of feet moving quietly over the carpeted floor.

Willard eased his shoes off, then crept noiselessly to the bedroom door. There were more footsteps and the sound of a chair being moved. At his feet, there was a heavy brass weight used for a doorstop. Willard picked it up and hefted it. It would be a clumsy but effective weapon. He put his hand to the door and jerked it open.

There, in the middle of his living room, was Willard's intruder, caught in the act.

His intruder was slim, pretty, stylishly dressed in a knee-length low-waisted blue evening gown in an ultra-fashionable artificial silk. On her face was a look of total surprise. Willard's face was the same.

He was first to recover.

'Good evening,' he said.

The woman let go of the chair and swallowed. Her eyes fluttered quickly all over Willard, trying to assess the nature of the threat he presented. She must have seen something which calmed her down a little. 'Good evening,' she responded gravely.

Willard showed her his brass doorstop. 'I picked this up

116

to hit you with, in case I needed to. Do you think I'm going to need to?'

A smile plucked at the corners of the woman's mouth. 'Probably not, but you'd be wise to keep it handy.'

Willard set the weight down on a side table. 'I'm not quite certain of the correct etiquette with burglars, so you'll have to forgive me if I get it wrong – but would you like a drink?'

'I think your manners are simply perfect. And yes, burglars always like to be offered a drink.'

'What can I get you?'

There was a moment's awkward pause. The awkwardness arose not because of their peculiar situation but because of Prohibition. Nearly everybody drank alcohol – but not absolutely everyone. It was still an illegal substance and it could be awkward to ask for it from somebody you'd never met before. Willard recognised the familiar embarrassment and said, 'I intend to have a large glass of brandy. If I do have to batter you, I should like to be well primed for the job.'

'And if I'm to be battered, I'd certainly like some brandy first.'

Willard tapped his bare chest (pleased that his intruder should have had the chance to see it). 'I was just about to have a shower when you began burgling me. If you'll excuse me . . .'

He went back to his bedroom, and dressed quickly in dinner jacket and tie. When he emerged, his burglar was politely standing by a bookshelf, pretending to be interested in the books. Willard poured them drinks. His burglar was medium-height, hair of dark gold, dove grey eyes and a pretty, darting smile. Willard felt the quick frisson of attraction.

'Tell me, do you burglarise places professionally or is it more of a recreational activity?'

She pulled an apologetic face. 'I'm terribly sorry. I

117

thought the apartment was empty. There were some things here that someone I know had left behind. I was passing. I thought I'd just pop in and take a look for them.' She dangled a key in the air. 'I guess you should have this really.' She tossed the key over.

'You lived here before me? I thought . . .'

'Not exactly.' She sighed, and Willard saw something else in her face: something grim and unhappy. 'The apartment was occupied by my sister's fiancé, Arthur Martin. It's my sister's key.'

'I'm so sorry, I don't know your name. I'm Willard Thornton, by the way.'

'Rosalind Sherston. My sister's name is Susan. It would have been a little bit less embarrassing if she had come, but she was too upset, what with everything.'

'I do understand. I'm at Powell Lambert myself, of course. I never met Mr Martin, but I've heard a lot about him. Only good things, naturally.' This was quite untrue, incidentally. Nobody at Powell Lambert ever seemed to mention the name. 'What a terrible shock it must have been.'

'You never met him?'

'I'm still very new. I've only been at the bank a few weeks.'

'A few? How few?'

Sherston's voice went suddenly weak, though she didn't at all strike Willard as the weak-voiced sort of woman. Willard realised that she was shocked to find the dead man's apartment so quickly reoccupied. He told her when he'd joined, but adjusted the date by two weeks, so the bank's callousness seemed less extreme.

'I see.' Sherston gulped her brandy, suddenly anxious to be off. The mood, which had been sunny, had darkened for no reason Willard could explain. 'Thank you for not battering me. You would have been within your rights.'

Willard shrugged apologetically and pointed to the carpet

118

which was quite new and pale cream. 'It's not the battering, it's the cleaning up.'

She got up to go. 'You've been very sweet.'

'Wait a moment,' said Willard, anxious to extend her visit. 'Your sister's things. I haven't come across anything, but if you know where they might be you're welcome to take a look.'

Rosalind hesitated. The chair was still out where she'd left it. Willard remembered how Rosalind had been dragging it when he'd burst in on her.

'The cupboard? Did your sister mention that cupboard?'

Again that momentary hesitation. Then a nod. 'Yes. It was the cupboard she mentioned.'

The cupboard in question was a large built-in affair, flush-fitted to the alcove next to the doorway. The bottom half was mostly full of bed and table linens. The upper half was full of Willard's collection of flying and movie memorabilia. He wasn't at all unhappy to have to root through it with Rosalind watching. He began pulling stuff out: movie posters, photographs, a medal, a leather flying helmet scored along its outer edge by a German bullet.

'Oh, Willard Thornton,' she said. 'Gosh! Aren't you . . .? Of course, you are. Silly me. I suppose I should have recognised you.'

'Not at all, not at all.'

Willard knew for a fact that the cupboard had been bare on his arrival, but wasn't going to let that stop him emptying it under Rosalind's inspection. Selecting carefully, but appearing casual, he made sure that the choicest artefacts ended up in the pile closest to Rosalind: a condensed history in objects of his life as he liked to think of it. She picked up a model Nieuport, made in silver, a gift from his father to mark Willard's first aerial victory. 'They seem so fragile.'

'Not really,' he answered, with studied casualness. 'Good plane the Nieuport. Wing struts had a tendency to come apart in a dive, but it wasn't a danger if you knew what you were doing.'

'Do you mind me looking?'

'Not at all. It's junk, really. I ought to throw it away.'

She shook her head. The cupboard was obviously empty. Willard swept the back with his hand.

'Your sister's things aren't here, but I'll keep an eye out. What should I be looking for?'

'Oh . . . I'm not sure. Some papers, I think. It doesn't matter. I shouldn't have come. Sorry.' She opened the apartment door. 'Goodbye. Thank you.'

'Wait!'

Rosalind stopped.

'If I find anything, how do I get in touch with you?'

'Oh, yes, of course. You can call me.' She gave him a Manhattan phone number. 'But don't worry about it. Really.'

Her eyes flicked around the apartment, back to the cupboard, then to the mess on the floor.

'And now I've put you out. I'm so sorry. Thank you. Goodbye.'

25

The shadow of Poll's upper wing shifted slowly with the sun. At the moment, most of the shadow fell on the ground, but there was still a long bar of shade lying down the trailing edge of the lower wing. Abe lay with a cigarette in his mouth, his back warm against the fuselage. The Cuban boy who brought the mailbag for Miami was late again. Abe decided that, bag or no bag, he'd leave as soon as the shadow of the upper wing had left the lower wing completely.

The sun slid slowly down the sky. The shadow moved. Abe finished his cigarette and stubbed it out.

Another minute passed. The shadow had almost completely shifted now. Abe got up, ready to leave, when a big black American car drew up outside the airfield gates. A dark-suited man climbed out, leaving one man at the wheel and a second one in the passenger seat behind. The man who got out was bulky, jowly, tough, but also friendly. Abe recognised him as an occasional passenger with the Marion bootleggers – and their obvious superior. The big man came over.

'You Rockwell?'

Abe nodded.

'Hi. Bob Mason.' The man pointed at his chest, as though he might have meant someone else.

Abe shrugged.

'You going back to Miami?'

'Uh-huh.'

'I need a ride.'

Abe shrugged again.

'I'll pay. How much d'you charge?'

'Can't. I'm full. Sorry.'

'Full? With a packet of letters?' Mason snorted. 'Say fifty bucks? I never taken a plane ride before.'

'I thought you went by boat. You'd be more comfortable.'

'Fool sailors left the choke wide open. Engine flooded. In this heat, too.'

Abe shrugged. Since he'd swum out to the boat that lunch-time and opened the choke himself, the news wasn't a big surprise. He'd also undone the nut holding the propeller blade, so if the Marion folk had got the engine started, it would have lost its blade within seconds.

'Too bad.'

Just then the Cuban kid came at a slow trot with the mailbag. Abe took the bag and buckled it behind his seat in the rear cockpit. The American came closer, tilting his head up to speak.

'Fifty bucks. We got a deal, right? Where do I get in? Here?' He made as if to climb into the front cockpit.

'Hey! Out of there. I'm full, I told you. I'm not some kind of railroad service.'

Mason stopped where he was, half-in, half-out of the cockpit. He held Abe's gaze square on.

'A hundred bucks.'

'I'm full. That's the last time I'm telling you.' Abe checked his instruments, before jumping out of the plane to swing the propeller a couple of times. On a cold day, it could take a few turns to bring enough fuel into the piston heads. But in the heat, Abe could tell by the smell that the pistons were already primed. He walked back to the cockpit.

'Bullshit, that's bullshit.'

Abe shrugged. 'My machine, my route.'

He reached inside his cockpit, flipped the ignition, and set the throttle low enough that it would keep the engine turning without sending Poll skittering out across the field. Then he went back to the propellers, ready to spin the blades into action.

Mason let Abe pass him, then said in the same low voice, 'Fuck you.' He picked a hundred dollars from his wallet and threw them into the rear cockpit. Then he grasped the edge of the front cockpit with both hands and jumped up, before swinging his legs down and into the plane. A grimy blue curtain would have blocked his view of anything lying forward from the seat. Expecting empty space, he moved too fast and barked out loud in pain as his feet struck something hard and solid. He swore loudly, then grabbed at the curtain to pull it aside.

And saw it. Six cases of booze, Gordon's Gin still in the original boxes, strapped tight against Poll's wood and fabric hull.

Mason stared – stared – then began to roar with laughter.

'Full! Ha! I'll say you are. That's a sweet little business you got yourself there.'

'Right. So as you see, I got no space for you. Now scram.'

Mason shook his head. His eyes smiled but there was an unruffled confidence in his manner which hinted at something a whole lot tougher. 'I'll squeeze up. I promise not to snitch a drink on the way.'

'It's not a question of squeezing, it's a question of weight. The plane won't take off overloaded.'

'Then lose the booze.'

'I'd sooner lose you.'

Mason paused. His manner was still very easy, very calm. He looked inside the curtain and counted the cases. 'Six cases. And twenty, twenty-five bucks turn on each one. I was underpaying. One fifty.' He counted out another fifty bucks and handed them down to Abe, who didn't reach to take them.

'Sorry, pal. I'm not in the passenger business.'

'My men will get you unloaded.'

Mason glanced over at the car which had brought him and made a gesture. Two men stepped out, not exactly threatening, but not exactly meek either. Abe watched them come.

'Where do you store it?' said Mason.

'If I take you this time, it's the last time, OK? I got people who rely on me.'

'I get it.'

'And it's two hundred.'

'OK.'

Abe spun his reluctance out another second or two, before pointing at the little locked shed, where he kept the bits and pieces he needed to service Poll. 'In there. And your guys had better break a sweat, unless you want to try a landing by moonlight.'

'OK.'

Mason handed over a further fifty dollars, gave brief, precise instructions to his men, then chuckled to himself as the booze was unloaded. And it was true: ever since beginning the mail flight, Abe had been transporting six cases of alcohol a flight, every flight. He bought the stuff from a wholesaler in Havana. He sold the stuff to a poxy little Miami bootlegger, named De Freitas. The booze came in wooden cases, nailed shut and sealed with the manufacturer's mark. To begin with De Freitas hadn't believed the stuff was unadulterated, but as time had gone by, he'd changed his mind. De Freitas paid good prices. Abe's costs, gasoline mostly, were low. Each and every trip he cleared around a hundred bucks' profit.

Mason supervised his men, but didn't help. He jigged up and down, enjoying himself.

'You got Gordon's on the box. I like that. Booze you can trust.'

Abe said nothing.

'You ain't worried about the good folks from customs?'

Abe jerked his thumb at Poll's fuselage, with its sten-cilled mail logo. 'Interference with the mails. It's a federal crime. Besides, why would Uncle Sam want to stop his own airplanes?'

Mason stared at the logo an instant, transfixed by the sight. Then his face creased into a bellow of laughter. 'Ha! You got it figured out there, pal! Good ol' Uncle Sam, huh? Looks after his own, hey?' He laughed some more and shared the joke with his two pals, who had got the last case unloaded. They laughed too, but were sweating too hard to laugh loudly.

'OK, hurry it up,' said Abe tetchily. 'You want to go to the can, go now. Otherwise, get in. There's a helmet and goggles behind the seat. Put 'em on. Keep 'em on. Sit still. Don't touch anything. Miami in three hours. Got it?'

Mason nodded, still chuckling, and complied. Abe got Poll started, and bumped across the airfield until he was downwind of the sea breeze. Then he opened the throttle and let her roar into flight. Abe pushed her upwards at two hundred feet a minute, until he hit her ceiling, seven thousand feet or so. He kept her pushed up against the ceiling all the way to the Florida coast, raising the altitude as the fuel load lightened. Up at those heights, the air was icy, the cold multiplied by the hundred-mile-an-hour wind.

By the time Abe set Poll down in Miami, Mason was half blue with cold, his hands shaking, his face pinched and tight.

'You have to fly her as high as that?'

'Nope.'

'Then why the hell did you?'

'I run a business, but it's not a passenger business. Next time take the boat.'

Mason left, heading off towards town, flexing his fingers to get them warm.

Abe watched him go. It was his first serious contact with

the gangsters of Marion. But it wasn't too late to quit. He was committed to nothing, he had promised less. Few people knew where he was, and no one knew what he was doing. Abe stood watching, 'til Mason had long passed out of sight. But the hesitation that had gripped him since the moment when a lanky storekeeper in Independence had asked him for help still gnawed inside. Should he fight or quit, stay or run?

He didn't know. He still hadn't made up his mind.

26

One Friday afternoon, Willard had had business with the bank's archive on the twentieth floor. He'd deposited one file, collected another and was just about to leave, when he happened to see Leo McVeigh and Charlie Hughes through the glass-paned door. McVeigh had Hughes pushed up against the wall. Hughes was white, obviously terrified. McVeigh was standing too close, speaking intently, his big hands half-curled into fists.

Willard stared for a second, then banged the door open. McVeigh stepped back. Charlie Hughes put his hand to his face, checked his tie, began muttering nervous hellos. Willard already loathed McVeigh and was angry enough to welcome a confrontation.

'Hello, McVeigh,' he said icily, before turning to Hughes. 'You all right, old chap? You're looking rather blue.'

'I'm fine, honestly, Will, please don't worry.'

'I do worry. You're not looking at all well.'

'Spot of tummy trouble. Maybe something I ate. I'll be OK.'

'Have you drunk some water?'

'Water?' Hughes repeated the word as though unfamiliar with the substance.

'Water. You ought to drink something. Maybe go home and lie down.'

Hughes caught McVeigh with his eyes. *He's asking that bastard for permission*, thought Willard angrily.

McVeigh nodded slightly and stepped away.

'Yes, good idea,' said Hughes. 'I'll drink something. That should help.'

He made no move to come with Willard, as though still spellbound by McVeigh's presence. The big one-time football player stood a pace or two back, kneading his hands and breathing silently through his mouth.

'Good. I'll walk you to the bathroom,' said Willard firmly. He put a hand on Hughes' shoulder and steered him away. In a deliberately loud voice – loud enough that McVeigh would be sure to hear it – he said, 'You always feel free to come to me if you need help, anything at all.'

'Yes, of course, thanks, Will-o.'

Feeling distaste for the man he'd just rescued, Willard turned and stared McVeigh straight in the face. For a second or two, their gazes locked. Hostility flickered in the air. Then Willard, pulling some of his Hollywood moves, curled his lip, turned on his heel, and stalked off.

Speaking about it later with Larry Ronson, Willard said, 'I'd swear he was threatening Hughes. The poor chap looked white as a sheet.'

Ronson was sympathetic. 'He's an ugly sort, McVeigh. He's never even attempted to join in with things. I mean, at least Hughes *tries*.'

'Yes . . . Look, you probably think I'm being absurd, but you don't think . . . Look, I don't even know what *I* think, but have you ever wondered if there's anything strange going on at times? You remember that business with the Orthodox Synagogues?'

'Irish rabbis. That'd be something.'

'McVeigh threatened me in the elevator. Told me not to ask questions.'

'He did? He did that? Jesus! Have you told anyone else?'

'No. I'm not quite sure who I would tell.'

'There's Grainger, I suppose. Or Barker.'

'Yes, but what if they're in on it too?'

'In on what?'

'I've no idea. None at all.'

'Look, you know Powell a little, don't you? Or at least your pa does?'

'Father and Powell are Yacht Club buddies, that sort of thing. Trouble is, I don't really know the man and, in any event, I wouldn't know what to say.'

Ronson looked at his watch. It was four thirty-five. 'I trust you're intending to keep New York's bootlegging community in proper employment tonight?'

'Love to, but I'm bursting to get out of the city, to tell the truth. Take a weekend in the country.'

'The delights of Martha's Vineyard, eh? Lucky dog.'

Willard smiled. His father owned a thumping big estate facing south over the ocean. What was more, Willard's four sisters were all going to be there this weekend, with girl-friends in tow. Willard had enjoyed happy hunting with his sisters' friends in the past, and could think of nothing more welcome in the present. Willard stared at his desk and its cargo of detested manila files.

'To hell with it,' he said, feelingly. 'To hell with every-thing. If Messrs Grainger, Barker, McVeigh or Powell want me, please tell them to go to hell too.'

Grabbing coat, hat and briefcase, Willard strode for the door.

27

The shop was dim compared with the street outside, but then again since the street outside was a blaze of white dust and air so hot it practically buckled, dim wasn't a bad way to be.

The kid kicked around at the back of the store, waiting while Hennessey finished serving an old lady customer at the front. The kid was down in the hardware section, fingering the metal pans full of nails, weighing the hammerheads and axe handles. The old lady left the shop. Lundmark approached.

'Afternoon, Mr Hennessey.'

'Hey, Brad. Fancy some candy?'

The storekeeper pulled a jar of Brad's favourite candy from the shelf behind him. The kid looked embarrassed, sticking his hands in his pockets.

'Oh, gee, no, it's OK, I didn't mean to – I didn't come out with any –'

'This candy's a treat between friends. I didn't mean for you to pay.'

'Oh, gosh, Mr Hennessey, thanks.'

The old man and the young one went silent as they chewed on the pink and white candy. Brad was still of school age and his mom's blind eyes didn't let her earn a living. The two of them lived off the town's charity and the poorer the town got, the poorer the Lundmarks became.

'Good candy.'

'Yeah.'

Hennessey could tell the boy wanted to ask something, but wasn't sure about doing so. The older man let him take his time. Another customer came in, asked for a bolt of cloth, was told it hadn't come in yet. The customer left.

'Say,' said Brad, who had plucked up his courage, 'I keep telling Mom it's time she let me earn a little money. Schooling don't bother me none, only it don't pay nothing either.'

'That's a problem with it,' said Hennessey, hoping the boy wasn't going to ask him for a position.

'She thinks I ought to become a carpenter like my pa.'

'He was good with his hands, your pa.'

'Yeah . . .'

'And sometimes you know those things run in the blood.'

'Yeah . . .'

'Only if I'm guessing right, you don't fancy the carpenting line of work over much.'

'Not so much.'

Hennessey was more sure now that the boy was going to ask for a job – a request which Hennessey would absolutely have to refuse – and his manner stiffened as he waited.

'But I reckon you're right about them things running in the blood, though.'

'Yes?'

The boy looked up, suddenly bold. 'Oh say, Mr Hennessey, it ain't carpenting work I want, it's mechanics. I *am* good with my hands, even Captain Rockwell said so. It's all I've ever wanted to do, really. There are four auto shops in Brunswick now. I'll bet one of them needs an apprentice around the place. I could come home every Sunday. I wouldn't need hardly nothing to live off and Ma could have everything else.'

He stopped abruptly and the storekeeper finished for him. 'Only your ma wants you to stay at home. She doesn't like the thought of you heading off to Brunswick.'

The kid didn't answer, but he didn't have to. It was the same all over Independence. Ever since Marion had begun its war of attrition against their neighbours up the hill, the town had been dying. Kids left, not to come back. Businesses folded. Farms went under. Hennessey was an Independence man born and bred, but he couldn't deny that the kid spoke sense. There was no use in trying to hold the youngsters back. They had their own lives to live.

'I'll speak to Sal,' said Hennessey. 'I expect I can talk her round.'

'Gee, would you? Gosh, thanks! And I promise –'

Hennessey raised a hand. 'No promises, Brad.' He hesitated. Under the counter, he'd kept a newspaper from a couple of months back. The newspaper had contained an item about the inaugural Miami–Havana mail flight, about Captain Rockwell and his new airfield in the south.

'Autos. That's your thing, huh?'

'Oh sure. You know Captain Rockwell started out as a racing car mechanic. One day, I'd love to do that, but meantime –'

'How 'bout airplanes, Brad?'

'Airplanes?'

The air turned still. The silence turned holy.

Hennessey produced the paper. 'Now don't you dare tell your ma I showed you this. It ain't autos, Brad, but if you don't mind slumming it, there's a guy working down in Miami who might have a job for the likes of you.'

He handed over the newspaper. The kid read the article, his eyes shining.

'Gee, Mr Hennessey, do you really think he'd –?'

'I've no idea. You'd best ask him that yourself. And, listen up, Brad, mind you don't tell him I said you go see him.'

'I shouldn't?'

'No, son, better not.'

The kid looked back at the newspaper, doubtfully. 'But,

you know Mr Hennessey, Miami's a whole lot further than Brunswick . . .'

Hennessey suddenly felt bad about doing what he'd just done. He couldn't have said why, but he felt like he was a man betraying a trust. He grabbed the tall glass jar of candy, tipped some out into a brown paper bag and thrust the bag over the counter, restoring the jar to its place on the shelf with his free hand.

'I'll speak to your ma. I'll ask her about Brunswick. I won't say anything about Miami, let alone airplanes. If you choose to jump on the eight o'clock freight train when it slows down just this side of Williams Point and ride it all the way down to Miami, then that wouldn't really be my business now, would it?'

A couple more customers came into the shop, one of them Jeb Gibbs, a seventy-five-year-old man whose sweet-tempered moonshine whiskey had kept him one of the wealthiest men in town for as long as anyone could remember. Gibbs was a customer Hennessey did a lot to keep sweet. The storekeeper greeted the newcomers and flashed a last glance at Lundmark. The kid had grabbed his bag of candy and stood with it held against his chest like something precious.

'Williams Point, huh?' he breathed.

'I'll talk to her,' said the storeman, 'but no promises.'

The kid left. Hennessey watched him all the way into the dazzle of the street and the deep indigo shadows of the further side. He hadn't done anything so bad, had he? And if he hadn't, then how come he felt like such a louse for doing it?

28

The weekend was everything that Willard's life once used to be and now wasn't.

Although he carried twelve hours' worth of paperwork in his briefcase, he touched none of it. Deliberately choosing to ignore the difficulties that hemmed him in, he didn't think about his debts, didn't think about Powell Lambert, didn't think about his future. Instead, he did all those things he had once taken for granted. He played tennis, sailed and swam. He was outgoing, charming and easy. He didn't 'score a confirmed hit', as he expressed it to his eldest sister, Lucinda, but he 'winged one or two machines, for sure' – his phrase for petting that stopped just short of the bedroom door.

'One or two?' she teased him. 'You don't know?'

'Two then.'

'Must have been some very slow machines then. Slow and ugly.'

He laughed. 'Fast and pretty. And exceptionally keen for me to call on them in New York.'

But all too soon the weekend ended. On Sunday evening, as the light began to ebb, Willard found himself on the station platform with his father. The train, headed by a steam locomotive painted a sombre black and purple, groaned its way into the station. The two men, travelling first class, found a compartment empty but for one other traveller, a man absorbed in his leather-bound Bible.

Willard, who always found time alone with his father awkward, was relieved at the third man's presence. The two Thorntons settled into seats opposite each other. The older man produced some business papers, and began to read. Willard, loathing the thought of touching any of his hated paperwork, reached his bag down and did so anyway. The train lurched off into the twilight.

The silence in the compartment and the clattering darkness outside began to knit together in one clotted mass. The thoughts Willard had kept at bay all weekend began to swarm in on him: his debts; his lack of prospects; the hopelessness of his situation. He also thought about those other things: the man whose death had been so conveniently timed, the Irish rabbis, Willard's strange but beautiful burglar. Without premeditating his action, he dropped his papers and said, 'Father?'

Junius Thornton and the other traveller lowered their reading matter at the interruption. Then the Bible-reader rose, claimed his bag from the rack, and left the compartment. On the way out, he gave Willard a look which implied that if speaking on a Sunday weren't illegal, then it certainly ought to be. Junius Thornton stacked and bookmarked his papers, but didn't put them away, as though to suggest that any break in the silence were only provisional.

'Yes?'

Willard didn't know what he intended to say. If he could have undone his first impulsive exclamation, he would have. But since he had now to say something, he said the first thing that came into his head.

'You know Powell fairly well, I think.'

'Certainly.'

'And you'd trust him, of course? I mean, you don't believe he'd do anything that a gentlemen shouldn't?'

Junius Thornton stared at his son. The older man's thick features were hard to read at the best of times; still harder in the moving carriage and the uncertain light. 'I believe

Powell to be a reliable man, yes. Am I to know what makes you ask such a peculiar question?'

'Oh nothing!' Willard threw himself back in his seat, annoyed at himself for asking. 'Just one or two odd things have happened lately. Things Powell might not have liked if he'd known about them.'

Junius Thornton continued to examine his son, waiting to see if any further explanation was forthcoming. It wasn't. The old man shrugged slightly. 'Powell likes money. He likes it very much. As far as I know, that's the only thing he likes.'

Willard stared sulkily from the window. 'Well, it's a good job he runs a bank then.'

'Yes,' said his father, deliberately mishearing, 'he does a good job.'

'And do you think . . .?'

His father, impassive, waited for Willard to finish his sentence. Willard made no attempt to do so, and the older man let his glance stray back to the documents he'd abandoned. The glance prompted Willard to continue.

'Well, I must say, I'm not at all sure he's playing quite fair with me.'

'Oh?'

'I mean it was understood – quite plainly – I mean, that was the point of the whole arrangement – that I'd work off the loan. Not just pay interest for the rest of my life.'

'I see. You were clear about the matter with him, of course?'

'He said . . .' Willard struggled to remember what Powell had said exactly. It had been vague and general, for sure, but the tone had been optimistic and reassuring. 'He said there was money to be made on Wall Street. Plenty of it. He said those with the gift would always make money.'

'Indeed. Those propositions seem true enough.'

Willard said nothing, just sat back, petulantly folding his arms and jerking his chin. His father stared for a moment, then tried a different tack.

'And what was stipulated in the contract?'

'Oh nothing – nothing that helps. But it's not just about contracts. It's about – I don't know – I thought he was a gentleman, that's all.'

The older man's expression was never easy to read. Sometimes, Willard thought, it was because he didn't have an expression. Just because somebody owns two eyes and a mouth doesn't mean they register emotions in the normal human way. But that wasn't the case now. There was something alive in the businessman's face. There was a flicker of something in his mouth, some fleeting look in the shadows of his eyes. But the moment didn't last. The older man didn't let it. He clamped his lips and picked up the waiting stack of papers. But before he closed the discussion, he looked squarely at his son and said, 'You ought to know that Powell is pleased with you. He tells me you're doing good work. Well done.'

'Gosh! Thank you, Father.'

Willard was astonished that Powell had noticed his presence in the bank, let alone found favour with it. But his astonishment was doubled by his father's rare administration of praise. Hope leaped unreasonably up. Willard thought about the Firm; renewed the strength of his desire to live up to the family name, to claim the family crown. He felt elated and clasped the feeling in silence all the way to New York City.

His mood lasted until eight twenty-seven on Monday morning. When he arrived at work, he found everyone already there, except Charlie Hughes. The atmosphere was silent and heavy. Willard tried to lighten it. He stood by the hat stand.

'What's this revolting object?' he said, picking up Claverty's pale grey fedora. 'Miss Hooper, kindly dispose of it.' He threw Claverty's hat across the room and hung his own in its place. Nobody smiled, nobody laughed. Annie Hooper picked up the fallen hat and came over.

'Haven't you heard?'

'Heard what?'

'Charlie Hughes. He was arrested last night.' Her voice trembled. 'It seems he was found with sixteen cases of gin in his apartment. They're charging him under the Volstead Act. Oh, Willard! He's going to prison . . .'

Her tears burst forth. Willard put his arm around her and felt her nestle in like a little, lost bird. He wanted to press his lips to the top of her head, but didn't. He held her as she cried. Charlie Hughes! A bootlegger! It was impossible.

When Willard looked up, he found Leo McVeigh staring at him: dark, brutal, intimidating, fierce.

29

You want to check a person out? Start from the air. From up there, you see the whole thing for what it is: for better or for worse.

And Abe saw. From two thousand feet and travelling at a hundred and fifty miles an hour, he saw. He saw Pen Hamilton's home: a vast white house, maybe twenty bedrooms, maybe forty. Plus there were a number of cottages sprinkled around the grounds. And stable blocks. And servants' quarters. And English-style lawns and rose gardens. And well-established stands of timber. And a lake, artificial but beautiful. And thousands of acres of plantation land. And, of course, an airfield, Pen's own private paradise.

'Jesus Christ!'

Abe didn't actually speak the words, but he certainly mouthed them. Although it was early, Abe had intended to land the plane, clean up, then go up to the house, to say 'hi'. But plans change.

A bunch of roses lay squashed in the racer's cramped cockpit. The blooms were pale pink and had looked nice in the florist's shop, only when he had been in the florist's shop, he hadn't seen the one acre rose garden or the glittering curves of glasshouses beyond.

His face moved in a hard-to-interpret expression. Regret? Uncertainty? Loneliness? Even fear? Abe let the plane fly itself, letting the perfectly tuned controls find their own balance, and looked at the roses. The colours were pretty, but an open-air cockpit is a tough place for roses. The blooms weren't at their best and there was already a scatter of petals on the cockpit floor.

Abe's face moved again: the same expression as before, only stronger. He took the flowers and held them out of the cockpit. As he did so, he slammed the throttle open and the control stick down. The hundred-and-fifty-mile-an-hour wind rose into a two-hundred-and-forty-mile-an-hour roar. The wind took one look at the roses, then tore their pretty pink heads off. The leaves snickered, then shredded. Abe levelled off. The roses were now just green sticks dotted with thorns.

He felt a stab of regret. Maybe if he had the last minute over again he wouldn't have done it. But maybe he would. And minutes never come again. He glanced out of the cockpit and threw the sticks away.

Some people have money. Some people have none. The two sorts of people sometimes look like they live in the same place, but they don't. They live in different countries, different planets.

30

The prison smelled bad, looked worse. The cells were big steel-barred affairs, with prisoners four to a cell. Bright lights hung from steel chains in the roof. The long hall rang with noise, obscenity and the smell of violence.

Willard watched as Charlie Hughes was picked from his cell and marched up to the visitors' room. The room was cream with a dark-green band around the base. A single electric lamp hung from a wire in the ceiling. Hughes was brought in and sat down at the table. A smell of vomit entered with him. Willard waited for the guard to leave, then realised he wasn't going to. He loathed having the guard there – it was like having a servant present while seducing a girl – but there was no choice.

'Lord, Charlie, are you all right?'

'Oh, Will-o, yes! Thanks for coming. Shouldn't have, but, gosh, really, thanks!'

There was a pause. Hughes stank. Willard was wearing a new suit, hand-made in a lightweight charcoal-grey worsted, and he worried that Hughes' smell would penetrate the cloth and infect it. He inched his chair back and, for a moment, was too overwhelmed with the awfulness of the place to know what to say.

'I probably smell, do I? An Irishman chucked up on me last night. It's kind of hard cleaning up in here. But, you know . . .' He shrugged, as though being puked on by Irishmen was one of the inconveniences of city life.

'God, Charlie! Isn't it awful! You've got a lawyer, of course?'

'Awful?' Hughes sounded genuinely surprised. 'Well, you know, I'm out of it now. I probably won't get more than a year or so. And you know, I've got two sisters. It's rather a relief really. It could have been worse.'

'What have your sisters got to do with it? How could it have been worse?'

'Well, you know . . .' Hughes made a vague gesture, which Willard couldn't interpret. But he suddenly remembered Arthur Martin, the car-crash victim whose death seemed to have been so conveniently timed.

'Look, I've got the name of a chap if you need one,' said Willard. 'I don't know him myself, but I know my father uses him.'

'Pardon?'

'An attorney. Someone to get you out of here. I can't see them giving you a year, not for your first offence and everything.'

'Oh, no! No, that's quite all right. I don't want to cause a fuss. I mean, it's quite a let-off really.'

'Charlie, can I ask you something?'

''Course, Will-o, anything.'

'Were you really selling booze? They said you had sixteen cases in your apartment.'

Hughes laughed. 'Sixteen cases! Gosh! Was it really that many? But, no, I mean, of course not. Can you see me bootlegging the old hoochino for a living? Not really my type of thing, that.'

Willard felt his familiar sense of distaste where Hughes was concerned. This stupid little man had allowed himself to be framed for something he couldn't possibly be guilty of, then refused to make a fuss about it. Quite the opposite. If anything, Hughes appeared grateful.

'Well, look, Charlie, I can't stay long. If there's anything I can do . . .'

'Oh, I'm OK. I'll be OK.'

'Yes.' Willard hardly bothered to conceal his dislike for anyone who could be OK in a place populated by puking Irishmen.

'Thanks awfully for coming, Will-o. You will be careful, won't you?'

'What do you mean, careful?'

'You know, the best thing would be to leave. I mean, they couldn't do anything to you. It's not as though you know too much, and your father being a pal of Ted Powell's and all that.'

'What the hell do you mean?'

Willard's question was brutally frank and Hughes looked a little shocked. Willard could see he wanted to answer, but he kept shooting suspicious glances at the guard who was standing painfully close. Hughes bent forward and said in a low whisper, 'Get out, Will-o.'

The guard stepped even closer and clattered the table with his night stick. 'No whispering. Sit back. Hands on the table. And wind it up. You've got a minute.'

'I can't quit. I owe Powell two hundred thousand dollars.'

'What!'

'You heard. He financed a movie I made. We had problems with distributors.'

'Jesus, Will-o! Jeez! You got a . . . you . . . Heck, I thought *I* had a problem!'

Hughes began laughing nervously. Willard stood up angrily. Suddenly he loathed the little man.

'If there's a problem with Powell Lambert, I think you ought to tell me what it is. If there isn't, I'll ask you not to make insinuations.' He stood over Hughes, demanding an answer. 'Well?'

Hughes looked anxiously at Willard, anxiously at the guard.

'I can't, Will-o. Not now. Not now that I'm out of it. I'm sorry.'

Willard said nothing. Hughes stayed quiet. The guard moved impatiently. 'OK, let's break it up.' He pushed Hughes on the shoulder. 'Time to go, buddy-boy.'

Hughes stood up and let himself be hustled back to his cell: a small man with bookish glasses, trailing a stink of body odour, vomit and fear. Willard watched him go. Arthur Martin: dead. Charlie Hughes: imprisoned. Who would be next? And why? That was the worst of it.

Willard still hadn't the slightest idea of why.

31

There have always been folks that like to boast the New World has always been precisely that. No kings, no aristocrats, nothing to stop a guy starting with nothing and ending with the world. It's a good theory. One with plenty of truth. But also some holes. And Miss Penelope Marie Corinna Anne DeMontfort Hamilton was one of them.

Her family could trace its American lineage back to one Sir Christopher Hamilton, an aristocratic adventurer from the court of Charles II. The family had bought land, bought slaves, got lucky, stayed smart, made money. They'd ridden out good times and bad times. On their estates, blacks came to be treated, not well exactly, but not as badly as most places. And, by the time Penelope Hamilton landed her plane in Captain Rockwell's backyard, the family was one of the most prosperous, respected and influential families in the old Confederate South.

But that type of family brings its own problems.

Pen Hamilton was expected to dance well, dress well, ride well – and above all marry well. Her dancing was OK. Her riding was good. But now, at the age of twenty-four, she had so far shown no interest at all in hitching herself to any of the eligible young men who came marching through her parents' Charleston mansion like so many well-scrubbed soldiers.

Where other girls fell in love with men, Pen had fallen in love with planes. She flew competitively. She flew for fun. She flew because being alone in a cockpit made more sense to her than any other way of being alive. So far, as one of the few female fliers in America and the world, she had set the women's altitude record, the women's speed record, and a clutch of long-distance firsts. And so far, despite her impressive haul of records, she had never encountered a male aviator who had treated her as anything other than a curiosity. At best, she was a novelty. At worst, some kind of gender-twisting freak.

Until she'd met Rockwell.

He'd been surprised, of course. Anyone would have been. But he'd treated her just as a regular flier. He'd admired her landing and said so. He'd admired her plane and said so. He'd been unimpressed with her ignorance of her engine and come pretty close to saying that too. In the short time they'd spent together, Pen had felt connected with Rockwell in a way she'd never felt connected with any flier or any man before.

Which was why she was in a state of shock, when she strolled down to her own private airfield one morning to find her favourite plane, the Curtiss racer, sitting idly on the grass.

'How come this is here? You sent a truck? I thought I said –'

'No, ma'am,' said the mechanic. 'Guy brought it in. This morning. I figured you knew.'

'A man, your height, blue eyes, blond hair cut very short?'

'Uh-huh.'

'What time? When did he leave?'

'Came in eight o'clock, thereabouts. Left again right after.'

'You didn't tell him to come up to the house? He didn't ask to come?'

'Guy seemed in a hurry to leave, ma'am. Asked for a ride to the railroad.'

Pen looked at her watch. It was after ten now. The train

146

out had left at nine. She bit her lip, unreasonably upset. She'd made a connection with Abe. She'd been sure of it. She didn't mean that Abe had to go falling in love with her . . . but not even to call in and say hello? Not even to spend ten minutes chatting about his flight? It was rude, downright rude.

'Ma'am . . .'

The mechanic looked awkward, keen to avoid Pen's direct look.

'Yes?'

'You just might want to check the airplane over.'

'Why? There's nothing wrong with it, is there?'

'Oh no, nothing like that. She seems in good shape and all . . .'

He trailed off and Pen, keen to be on her own anyway, left the shade at the edge of the hangar and walked over the clipped grass to the little racer.

For a second, she didn't know why she was there. The plane had just flown up from Miami. Its little raked-back windscreen needed wiping down. No doubt the great Captain Rockwell would want her to fuss over the distributor blocks, whatever they were. But there was nothing unusual.

Nothing, until she happened to glance into the cockpit, into the angle of the rudder bar.

There lay a little tumble of rose petals, pale pink, pretty. She moved to touch them: they were still soft, but already beginning to wilt.

He'd come with roses. Seen the house. Ditched the roses. Run.

Pen felt suddenly angry. In the end, the great war hero had proved himself as small as any other man. A hero in the cockpit, he was a coward in matters of the heart. Men were men. Planes were planes. Pen knew which she liked the best.

32

The newspaper which Willard wanted to check was filed in a high mahogany bureau slotted with a dozen low drawers. In front of the bureau was a tall thin man with a thin greyhound face. The man wasn't reading a newspaper or looking for one. He didn't look like he could read one without moving his lips.

'Excuse me, please,' said Willard.

The man said nothing.

'I said excuse me.'

The man's deep brown greyhound eyes looked slowly up into Willard's and there was a half-second of pointless, meaningless confrontation. Then the man produced a matchstick, held it up like a conjuror, then placed it with exaggerated care in the side of his mouth. He moved away. About sixteen inches, just enough for Willard to open the drawer.

Willard opened the drawer, got the paper, ignored the man.

The brief newspaper report confirmed what he'd already learned from the coroner's report. The day that he died, Arthur Martin had been driving alone. There were no witnesses as to his speed or manner of driving. What was clear, however, was that the driver had lost control of his vehicle and crashed into a road-side tree. The *Times* report contained a photo showing the car buried in the trunk of a substantial maple tree. The driver's head had been struck by the steel bar across the top of his windshield. The blow had been fatal. Verdict: death by motor accident.

Willard's anxieties began to subside, but there was one further check he had to make. He surreptitiously clipped the photo, then drove up into Connecticut towards New Haven. His big Packard flew along, its tyres humming a private tune of satisfaction. Birds sang. The air was sweet.

He found the road where the accident had happened: tree lined, rural, quiet. The tree which had claimed Arthur Martin's life was easy to pick out: a big old maple, split by lightning. A car had rammed the tree. Its driver had died. The story was sad but simple.

Willard began to relax. The tension that had been gathering in his back, legs and head for longer than he cared to remember began suddenly to release. He pulled the photo from his pocket to check his memory one last time. He stared at it, then was about to put it away, when a leap of horror jumped to engulf him.

The newspaper photo showed Martin's Studebaker jammed up against the trunk of the tree. But the tree stood just fifteen feet back from the road. Given the angle at which the car had struck it, Arthur Martin must have left the road *at right angles*. For his death to have been an accident, one would have to believe that Martin had tugged his car around a full ninety degrees without loss of speed and accelerated at top speed into the trunk.

Willard went cold. His back tightened. The birdsong died.

Willard climbed into his Packard and, on an open stretch of road, Willard tried the manoeuvre himself. He couldn't do it. The thing was impossible. To turn the full ninety degrees, Willard had to bring his automobile down to just fifteen miles an hour. At that speed, Martin could have damaged his fender, but not a lot else. If, on the other hand, Martin had been dead before his car went anywhere, somebody could have put his body in the car, put the car in the field opposite the maple tree and driven it full tilt across the field, over the road and into the tree.

And that was when Willard knew it. Arthur Martin hadn't died in a car accident. He'd been murdered.

33

Abe snapped awake.

He was lying under a single blanket on the hangar camp bed. Something had woken him, but he wasn't sure what. He listened in the darkness. The tin roof around him was noisy in any sort of breeze, but the air outside was still and, aside from a few creaks and aches, the hangar was quiet. He sniffed the air. He could smell gasoline and castor oil; airplane dope and the smell of paint; yesterday's bacon and tomorrow's coffee.

Perhaps it had been nothing. In his dreams, Abe had been flying over Pen's house again. He remembered the masculine stiffness of the controls. She must be strong to fly a plane like that. But in the dream, the whole episode had got muddled up. The roses, the plane, the girl, the mansion. Abe had had the feeling of searching for something and not finding it.

He was about to lie down again when he heard a sound from outside. Something metallic, the click of a car door maybe. Abe felt for his boots and flying jacket and pulled them on over his nightshirt. He found a flashlight and slipped it into a pocket. Then, groping along the workbench, he found a crowbar, four feet long, claw-headed and heavy. He picked it up and crept around Poll's oustretched wings to the hangar door.

Another car door opened and closed. There was a low muttering of voices. In places where the overlaps on the tin roof were inadequate, Abe caught glimpses of a flashlight. On just the other side of the door, the voices gathered and stopped.

'We knock first?'

A second voice said, 'We don't need to. We're friends, ain't we?'

The door pushed open. Abe held his bar back, ready to swing. There were two flashlights outside, prodding the ground. Abe saw legs: two or three pairs, dark shoes, dark pants. The door into the hangar had just been punched straight through the wall. The front arch of the hangar was braced by a solid steel girder. In the centre of the arch, a gently sloping ramp made it easy for Poll to climb in and out, but here at the side, the girder formed a hurdle a full five inches high. One of the men moved forwards, caught his foot, and began to topple. Abe kicked hard at the pair of legs still standing, grabbed a handful of coat and jerked. The second man crashed forwards onto the first. Abe raised his crowbar and flicked his flashlight on.

The first face he lit up belonged to Bob Mason, who was lying on the ground, trapped under the second man's body. Everyone was swearing at everyone. Abe lowered his bar.

'Evening, Mason. You should have said you were coming.'

He turned on the electric light. There were four bulbs in the hangar, none of them shaded, but it was a big space and the light was dim and heavy with shadows.

'Christ, Rockwell. That any way to treat a pal?'

Abe shrugged. He turned his back on his visitors and made for the little wooden table by his bed. He got out a bottle of whisky and two glasses. He poured one for himself and one for Mason.

'Nice place,' said Mason, pulling out a cigarette.

Abe waited till Mason's cigarette was lit, then pulled it from his mouth, dropped it on the floor, and stamped it out. He jerked his thumb at the aircraft and the barrels of gasoline and oil.

'Not here.'

Mason picked up his whisky glass and turned to the two other men who were hovering silently behind him.

'What are you boys drinking?'

The goons spread their hands and looked pained by the unrehearsed difficulty of the question.

'They're not drinking here,' said Abe.

Mason pulled a face and leaned forwards, speaking confidentially. 'All right, I'll level. It's a shithole you've got yourself here. A shithole, but a nice business.'

'Wrong. Not *a* nice business. *My* nice business.'

'I got some friends who are interested in it.'

'Mason, did your mom never teach you the word "no"?'

'Very interested. I should have said very.'

'These guys?' said Abe, pointing to the goons. 'They're interested?'

'Not them exactly.'

'Then they can get lost.'

Mason hesitated. Abe pulled his jacket open, revealing his nightshirt and nothing else. No gun.

'OK.' Mason turned to the goons. 'Outside.'

'In the car,' said Abe.

Mason nodded. The goons left.

When the hangar door clanged shut, Abe said, 'I don't care what business you're in. I've got a business I'm happy with. I don't want partners. I don't want money. I don't want help. I don't want you.'

Mason shook his head and rolled his whisky around his glass. 'Maybe we've got things you need. Maybe things you don't even know you need.'

'Yeah. Maybe. Only not.'

'You sell your hooch to a guy named De Freitas. Bootlegger to the speakeasies on the north side of town.'

Abe shrugged. It was true. So what?

153

'I wonder how much you know about De Freitas's business. He has to pay a cut to the cops, of course. But that's not the payment which matters.' Mason waited for a response but didn't get one. He continued anyway. 'He has to pay for his patch. He pays us. My friends and me. That way, De Freitas has all the trouble of selling hooch. Trouble and the occasional inconvenience when the cops forget what a nice guy he is. Meantime, my friends and I enjoy the profit.'

Abe rubbed his hand over his face. Even with the electric bulbs, the room was too gloomy to see Mason's face properly. Abe dug out an oil lamp and lit it. Mason smiled.

'Maybe I will have that cigarette. If I promise not to drop it on your nice shiny airplane.'

He lit up and watched Abe's face for a second or two. Abe was listening.

'So just suppose that we got tired of making room for De Freitas, then you wouldn't have much of a business now, would you?'

'He's not the only whisky seller in America.'

'No, but the way I figure it, you know plenty about flying planes. You probably don't know a whole heap about the way liquor is sold in this fine country of ours. There are plenty of De Freitases, but not many with liberty to pick their suppliers.'

There was a moment's long silence.

The two men stared at each other. Mason pulled on his cigarette, then held it up for Abe's inspection. The cigarette was only a quarter-burned. Mason drew on it one more time, so the tip glowed orange, then flicked it deliberately towards the aircraft. Abe got up, stamped out the butt and returned to the table.

'America's bigger than you are, Mason. I know people who are flying the border from Mexico. There's plenty of border with Canada. Every inch of it flyable.'

Mason blew a puff of air from his mouth, like a deaf-

and-dumb imitation of a laugh. 'Mexico? It's too hot and the food gives you the trots. Canada? It's too cold and you have to sing *God Save the King*.'

'I won't be threatened.'

'Who's threatening you, Captain? I'm not threatening you, I'm sharing a drink.' Mason waved his glass. 'I told you my friends and I like your business. We'd like to see if we can work something out. Think of it like a partnership.'

There was a long silence. Nowhere fills with silence like an aircraft hangar, no matter how many creaks may hide in the roof. Eventually Abe leaned forwards and pulled aside Mason's jacket. Snug in a holster beneath his armpit, lay a gun, black and squat. Mason pulled it out between finger and thumb and dropped it on the table equidistant between himself and Abe. 'I mean it. A partnership.'

And then, and only then, did Abe relax.

'No promises,' he said, 'but I'll hear you out.'

34

Monday evening, six o'clock, and Willard had already left work, feeling reckless. Through fast-fading sun, he walked quickly uptown to the edge of Central Park. Passing a drug-store, he stepped inside. He asked for a phone and a sad Italian nodded him to a dark corner booth, lined with dirty red cotton. Willard entered and asked the operator for a local number. In the short delay, Willard could hear the operator complaining in the background. He had sudden doubts.

Too late.

The call came through, and Willard was already speaking.

'Good evening. My name is Thornton, Willard Thornton. I was hoping to be able to speak to Miss Rosalind Sherston.'

Willard held the line as Miss Sherston was sought. His doubts increased and only the unbreakable code of East Coast politeness kept him holding. Then a woman's voice: 'Rosalind Sherston speaking.'

'Rosalind? Willard Thornton. I'm the gentleman whom you attempted to burglarise the other day.'

'Yes. I know who you are.' She sounded embarrassed. 'Thank you for calling. Did you find anything?'

'Your sister's things? No, I'm afraid not. They must have been cleared before I came.'

'Yes, I suppose they must. Well, thank you for letting me know.'

'Listen, I was wondering if you were free any time.'

'Free . . .?'

'Yes. To go out somewhere. I thought maybe we could stroll down Park Avenue and see if we could bust our way into one of those big modern duplexes. You could handle the jewellery, I'd take care of fine art and antiques. Cash and securities we'd split down the middle.'

'I suppose you know you're sounding a bit peculiar. I don't just mean about your proposed entertainment.'

'Am I? I *am* a little light-headed actually. They shouldn't let me out of the office so early.'

'Have you been drinking?'

'No. Coffee and water. Nothing else all day. I'm pretty much of a monk in that way.'

There was a long pause. Willard almost thought he had lost the line, except that the crackle was still there. Eventually Rosalind spoke again.

'Listen, Willard, I think you may be a very sweet man, but I think perhaps it would be better if we didn't meet. I'm not over-fond of your employer.'

'Well, perhaps it would be better if we did meet. I'm not sure *I'm* over-fond of my employer.'

There was another long pause, only this time Willard was very sure that Rosalind was still there, still listening. Speaking very intently now, he added, 'I went for a drive in the country the other day. Up towards New Haven. I found a long straight road. It looked like a very safe one to me.'

Rosalind's voice slowed right down. 'Yes. It was a safe one, I believe.'

'Rosalind, I have no idea what happened to your sister's fiancé, or why. I also have no idea what happened to a former colleague of mine, who is currently in prison on a false charge of bootlegging. It really isn't any of my business, except that I'm not marvellously keen to follow in their footsteps. On top of which –' he paused. He wanted to say something about his debt, about his desire to join the family Firm, about the sort of life he thought he deserved and the sort of life he actually had.

'On top of which?' she prompted, the soft warm tones of her voice losing nothing over the wire.

'On top of which, I would like to take you out to dinner.'

Sometimes you can hear an expression. A smile. A look of sadness. A hint of attraction. Willard heard it now.

'How soon can you get here?' she asked.

'How soon can you get downstairs?'

35

That afternoon, Abe dug an oblong trench, slip-sided in the sandy soil. He mixed concrete by hand in the heat of the sun and filled the trench. The globby grey mixture, already beginning to dry, would form the foundations of his new house. The next task was to lay a floor and Abe began work on the shuttering, ready for the following day.

The sun was just flirting with the tree-tops in the western sky, when a dirty truck with blue canvas sides bumped off the Tarmac beach road and swung across the airfield. The truck's canvas sides were marked 'Peterson's Pies – My, How Delicious!'. Abe dropped his handsaw and wiped his hands free of sweat, though not the spatters of grey concrete. The hangar had a tap on its back wall and Abe drank thirstily before walking around to meet his visitors. The sloping metal roof caught the heat and radiated it, so the warm air in its shadow had the glow of an oven door.

'Hey, Birdman!'

The man leaning out of the passenger window was Bob Mason, an unlit cigarette in his mouth and a box of matches in his hand.

'Mason.' Abe nodded.

Mason slid out of the cab, lit his cigarette. He put out a hand to Abe, but Abe showed the muck on his hands and declined the shake.

'Been working?'

'Building. Poll's getting too old to share her bedroom.'

'You want a builder? I know some people.'

'I like building.'

'Then you build away. You build the Eiffel Tower for all I care – that *is* a building, right?'

'Kind of. Its walls aren't too good and I don't remember it having a whole lot of roof.'

'That don't sound like much of a building.'

'It looks pretty.'

'What's it for?'

'It's for looking pretty.'

'Then I guess it works just fine.'

As they were having this dumb conversation, Mason walked through into the hangar, without asking or getting Abe's permission. Abe kept pace. The truck driver, a huge silent man in blue overalls, followed a couple of steps behind. In the darkest corner of the hangar, tucked out of sight of Poll's looming wingblades, a pile of boxes was stacked under a dirty cotton sheet. Mason pulled the sheet aside and counted the boxes: nearly forty cases of booze. It was the haul of booze from one week's flying.

Abe's flying, Mason's booze.

Because Abe had done it. He'd cut the deal, made the trade. He carried booze and not only that. Smuggling was smuggling, after all, and Abe was entrusted with the most valuable items coming through Mason's pipeline: securities, jewellery, gold, cash, even boxes of women's dresses all the way from Paris. In exchange, Abe got a quiet life, plus four hundred bucks a week cash.

The money was welcome. Except for a short while on the racing circuit, Abe had never earned a whole lot. The income he'd been receiving from booze – first from De Freitas, now from Mason – was the best he'd ever earned. Most of it he was sending to his parents, whose Kentucky farm had been sliding inexorably into the hands of the bank. Digging them out of debt would be the best possible way of spending his cash.

And yet, the whole thing nevertheless left him uneasy. He was taking Mason's money. He was allying himself with an organisation for whom bullying, thuggishness and murder were a regular part of business. And that would be fine, if Abe were certain that he meant to do what he could to smash Marion and save Independence. But he wasn't.

He hadn't been before, when he'd said goodbye to Brad Lundmark on the beach outside Brunswick. He wasn't now that he was already halfway inside the organisation. Most of him still wanted to quit. One small but stubborn part of him refused to let go of the picture of Brad Lundmark's pile of flying souvenirs, and of the boy's mother, burned, blinded and widowed. Silently to himself, and not for the first time, Abe cursed the storekeeper's shrewdness and persistence.

Mason inspected the pile of booze, then nodded approval. He handed four hundred bucks to Abe and growled 'Load up,' to the driver. Then he strolled over to Abe's living area to find himself a glass of water. On the small wooden table which served as Abe's dining table, there was a deck of cards lying face down.

'You a card player?' he asked brightly, as though hoping to have located a normal human characteristic in the airman.

'Not really.'

Abe picked up the deck, fanned it open, picked out the ace of spades. He held the card up, then flicked his hand and made the card disappear. It reappeared again, then vanished, then appeared in the other hand, then, just as Mason was sure he'd seen the card transfer back to Abe's right hand, the ace reappeared on top of the deck.

'Sheez!'

'It's all hokum,' said Abe, inserting the ace back in the deck and shuffling. 'As a kid, I always knew I wanted to work on engines. I worried maybe I was clumsy, so I bought a book of card tricks and made myself practise until I figured I had enough dexterity.'

'Jeez, you take life kinda seriously, buddy.'

Abe shrugged. He fanned the pack open, holding the cards face up towards Mason. The mobster glanced, then stared. He took the pack and leafed through it one by one. The ace of spades had disappeared.

'Where's it gone?'

Abe ignored him. 'Later on, I discovered that card tricks weren't a bad way of understanding war in the air. Trickery, misdirection, concealment, deceit. They're all transferable techniques. There were other commanders who thought that type of thing not quite "sporting".' Abe spoke the word in a British accent, then dropped it instantly. 'I wouldn't know. I never played those type of sports.'

'Misdirection?' queried Mason.

'Listen, I've got something for you.'

He went to the office at the side of the hangar. The door, little used, had begun to stick and warp. He kicked at it, opened the door, picked a newspaper off the desk. A colony of brown-legged spiders had extended itself from an out-of-date Cuban calendar to the light fittings. Abe ignored the spiders and came out, passing the newspaper to Mason.

'Army Air Service Gazette, huh? You think you could cut it in the army?'

Abe shrugged. 'They still send it.' He tapped a small news item at the bottom of the page, circled in blue. The item was a short report indicating that the army was about to sell some of its war-surplus fighter-bombers. 'DH-4. Good plane. We'd be getting it cheap.'

'A DH-4. They sure think up some swell names.'

'It's a de Havilland. A British plane, built here under licence. It's a bomber. Fourteen thousand pound load capacity.'

'A bomber, huh? If we ever want to drop bombs on somebody, that'd be a real good idea.'

'Allowing for my weight and the weight of fuel, I calculate we could carry thirty-five cases of booze every day. That'd be nearly six times as much as now.'

'Booze?' Mason's face looked wide-eyed and innocent. 'Booze? No booze here I hope.'

'You talked about a partnership. I'm not too keen on being treated like a junior employee.'

'Junior, buddy? No way. Believe me, we think highly of you. We ain't never had a real live fighter ace working for us before.'

'The plane, Mason. What do you say?'

'Say? Say to what?' Mason raised his eyebrows. The truck driver had got the booze loaded up and was sitting in the cab, with the engine turning noisily over.

'We buy a plane. We load her with booze. I bring her in.'

'Booze, you're always going on about booze.' Mason climbed inside the truck, grabbed one of his meat pies and took a gigantic bite. 'Peterson's Pies,' he mumbled. 'Oh my, how delicious!'

The driver had the truck in gear and the clutch down. The engine was in need of tuning, and it ran too fast and too heavily.

'Misdirection,' said Abe. 'It's the art of making a person look one way when they ought to be looking the other.'

'Huh? Back to conjuring tricks, right?'

Abe didn't answer directly, but stood tapping the shirt pocket over his heart. Mason didn't figure it out immediately, but then he did. His gaze dropped down to his own jacket pocket. 'Aw, shit,' he said, then pulled out a playing card: the ace of spades. He passed it out of the cab window and was still chuckling as the truck bounded away in a kick-back of sandy dust.

36

The mirror reflected this: a sandy-haired man, strong-jawed, very handsome, very carefully turned out in immaculate evening dress; a woman, dark-gold bobbed hair, aquamarine gown dropping hardly any distance below the knee; and in the background, a single black jazz singer, with a battered, southern, bluesy face, his eyes half-closed as he bobbed hypnotically on the melodic disorder of the four-piece band behind him. Willard paused to relish the sight, his gaze returning three times to his face for every two times it touched on Rosalind's.

'Best cocktails in midtown,' he murmured, still looking in the mirror. 'The music's good too, you know. Don't worry if you don't like it at first. It's the sort of thing –'

'Oh, I love jazz. I listen to it whenever I can. Did you catch Mo Johnson at the Alabama Club last week? I thought –'

Rosalind's enthusiasm turned Willard quickly off the subject.

'Your coat,' he said, 'we need to check it.'

He checked her coat then steered her to a table in the dim room. He liked things modern, and how much better could it get? Himself: as handsome as anything, a beautiful woman at his side, the thrill of a speakeasy, the illegal taste of alcohol, the strange, clashing rhythms of jazz. They sat down. While Willard fussed over getting seated just right – he hated it when the chair back interfered with the proper fall of his jacket – Rosalind sat easily, cocking her head to the music. Willard got things arranged as he wanted, ordered cocktails and pretended to listen too.

California had been brash, he'd decided. The girls there had lacked class. Too much sunshine, too little sophistication. Rosalind, now, was sophisticated. She had class. She knew how to dress, how to drink, how to talk, how to act, how to move . . .

He'd been thinking this, half daydreaming, before realising she had turned towards him. Earlier, over dinner, they'd started a conversation, but hadn't finished it. He'd told her about Charlie Hughes and asked her to tell him what she knew about Arthur Martin.

'Not much, I'm afraid,' she'd answered. 'Susan says that Arthur began acting strangely about a month before he died. Jumpy. Nervous. On one occasion, he told her that Powell Lambert was up to no good. He seemed to have a grudge against the place.'

'What sort of no good?'

'Don't know. He wouldn't say. Just before he died, he told Susan that he was collecting some documents. Incriminating, so he said. He seemed on the lookout for foul play. Almost expected it. Then the auto wreck. It wasn't an accident. It was almost an insult, the way they staged it.'

'And the documents?'

'We couldn't find them. We went through all his personal possessions as soon as we could. That was why I came back to the apartment. To see if I could find them there.'

'I've made a really thorough search. The place was cleaned out before I arrived.'

They'd left it there, but both knew the conversation was unfinished. A black waiter, his head nodding with the jazz, brought them cocktails and a bowl of roasted nuts. The song finished. Rosalind let out an 'Ah!' of appreciation and began to clap. The waiter, speaking to Rosalind not to

Willard, said, 'They sure good, these fellers.' Rosalind beamed at him, still clapping.

'Excellent,' said Willard, clapping hard. 'Excellent.'

The waiter left. Rosalind turned back to the table.

'You'll quit, I imagine?'

'I want to, yes.'

'*Want* to?'

'I can't. I made a movie in Hollywood before I left. You know. Wrote it. Acted. Directed. Produced. Ted Powell financed it. The movie didn't do what everyone expected. It's a difficult business, you know. Lots of angles. It's not enough to make a quality film, the distributors are like sharks, really.'

'You owe Powell money?'

'Two hundred thousand dollars.'

'Oh my goodness!' Rosalind's hand flew to her mouth and stayed there for a while, as her grey eyes flickered over his face. 'You'll be careful, then?'

Willard gestured helplessly. 'Yes, but of what? At least in the war I knew who I was fighting.'

'What are you going to do?'

'Whatever I can. Locating an enemy is the first thing.'

'On your own?'

'I hope not.'

'Then who?' Her voice petered out as she caught Willard's drift. The jazz band had started up again, a faster number than the last one, but neither Willard nor Rosalind were listening now.

'Well?' he said. 'Are you in?'

She swallowed hard. The question wasn't a small one. One man had died, another one had been imprisoned. Now a third man was asking her to join the fight. A man she hardly knew. A man whose presence could mean only danger. She reached automatically for her cocktail, but didn't drink. Her eyes locked on Willard's handsome face, his blue eyes, his strong masculine chin. He seemed to promise something trustworthy. Something resolute. Something dependable.

'Oh my goodness. Yes, all right. I'm in.'

And that was that. A positive end to the evening in every way.

Except for one thing.

As they left, a little drunk, a little excited, Willard collected Rosalind's fur from the coat-check. He dropped a quarter into the girl's discreet little saucer, a stingy tip by his standards, but he was becoming ever more conscious of his ailing bank account. As he did so, he felt a glance hot on the back of his neck and whirled around to meet it.

And there he was. Long-nosed Greyhound-face from the public library. Staring. Eyes empty but confrontational. There was a meaningless pause. Nothing happened. Nothing was said. Then Greyhound-face offered a temporary yellow smile, popped a matchstick into his mouth and left.

A coincidence? Maybe.

But a disconcerting one? Definitely.

37

Gibson Hennessey sat on his porch smoking.

He enjoyed watching the Georgian sun go fizzing down in a cloud of red and gold. He liked the shade of his porch and the way he could hear the night birds and the crickets take over from the sights and sounds of the day. He liked staying out of the house, when his wife was sending his kids bawling up to wash. And he liked the tobacco. Nowhere grows better tobacco than Georgia, and Hennessey got his from a farm which worked a little magic on those precious golden leaves.

He inhaled, relaxed and pondered. And what he pondered was this. One week ago, the kid Lundmark had finally got his mom's permission to get himself apprenticed down in Brunswick. Instead, the kid had ridden a freight train to Miami and headed on to the airfield there.

The kid had pitched up early, but too late to catch Abe. No problem. The kid made himself useful. He sharpened Abe's tools, ground chisels 'til their edges flashed silver, threw sawdust onto oil spills and swept up after. He kicked open the door of the lean-to office and cleaned the place top to bottom. He lingered on the long shelf of castings above the workbench. Each loaf-sized model was perfectly cast, flawless, but also strange, apparently useless. Why would a guy want thirty or forty model airplanes? Not even airplanes, most of them, just airplane parts really. The kid didn't know, but didn't pause long. He'd brought with him the letter to Abe that Willard Thornton had enclosed with the movie poster. Brad left the letter propped by Abe's coffee pot.

And there had been just one final job. In the darkest corner of the hangar, under a light bulb that was broken and not replaced, a filthy cotton sheet had been pulled over a stack of boxes. Brad pulled the sheet away and saw what was underneath. Cases of booze, stacked high.

Abe Rockwell, liquor smuggler. It was impossible to believe and impossible not to.

The kid stared at the huge illegal stack through eyes that pricked with tears. For twenty minutes he drifted around the empty hangar, watching the dust dance in the sun and chewing peanut brittle from a bar gone furry in his pocket. What was there to say? What was there to think?

And when the southern sky began to burr with an approaching engine, the kid took one last look at his hero's home. Then he ran. Away from the hangar, over fifty yards of pockmarked sand to a line of scrubby bushes, then through the bushes and on, not stopping, until he reached the bright city lights. The next day he'd been in Brunswick, looking for work. Back home on Sunday, he'd told his mom nothing and Hennessey everything.

Abe Rockwell, liquor smuggler.

That was what the old storekeeper pondered as he smoked and watched the dying of the sun.

38

Abe saw the changes.

The place was cleaner, tidier, newer, shinier. Floors had been swept, things dusted. Moving slowly, Abe checked out his property. He checked his workbenches, his castings, his sleeping area, the stash of booze. He pushed at the door of the little office, and found the place brightened up, actually clean, no little brown spiders anywhere in sight. Abe continued to check things over, but slowly. The little metal table. The floor. The places in the roof where the sheets of tin overlapped and caused a sharp-edged hazard for anyone who stood too quickly. Abe's eyes narrowed. Reaching towards the low edge of the room, Abe found two hairs, caught in one of the chinks. The hairs were short, about an inch and a quarter long. And red. Just as though they'd come from little Brad Lundmark, the red-headed kid from Independence.

Abe's face tightened for a moment and his expression hardened. Then, as though to shake away the feeling, he rubbed his face, washed, and ate, making supper from a loaf of bread, a tin of meat, a mango. It was only when he came to make coffee that he found the letter which Lundmark had left. The letter was from Willard Thornton. Only a few lines long, it attempted a curious mixture of warmth and independence, boastfulness and humility. Abe's one-time lieutenant, it seemed, had given up the movie business in favour of Wall Street, 'Trade finance, would you believe it!' The letter ended with the vaguest of invitations to look him up should Abe ever be in New York. Abe read the letter a couple of times, smiled, then put it away. He wasn't planning on being in New York any time soon. Even if he was, he wasn't too sure Willard would be happy to see his old commander. But he was pleased the guy was getting on with his life. Finance seemed like a better career than making movies.

Meantime, Abe had other things to think about. Dressing in dark, inconspicuous city clothes, he left the airfield. He walked into town and found an anonymous all-night café with a phone booth.

'Your party, please?' said the operator brusquely, like she had better things to do than handle callers. Abe gave her a number. A dim chatter on the line lasted a few seconds. Then a man's voice, sounding loud and close. 'US Coastguard.'

'Good evening. I have some information for you.'

'Who's calling please?'

'Two launches, forty feet long, painted green, maximum speed twenty-seven knots, will enter the Okefenokee River in Okinochee County, Georgia at between midnight and two a.m., Monday. The boats will each be carrying one hundred fifty cases of hard liquor.'

The man's voice at the other end of the line changed. It became hard and direct. 'Please. Who's calling? You must identify yourself.'

'Each boat is manned by two men, armed with hand-guns and rifles. There is a bow-mounted searchlight on each boat. There is no automatic weaponry.'

'Who is providing this information, please?'

'You be sure to have a good evening now,' said Abe, and hung up.

Another step taken. Another step forward. Another step closer to a place he didn't want to go.

39

There was a ring outside the door.

Literally. Not a knock or a ring on the electric doorbell, but a strong, bright ringing sound. Willard was due to meet Rosalind around now – but the bell, what the hell was that about?

Willard crept up to the door and listened. The sound of the bell was dying away, but he could hear breathing and a floorboard creaking under someone's weight. Willard now kept a gun in his bedside drawer. He thought about fetching it, but decided against. All the time now, he felt under strain. There was the pressure of work, the pressure of his almost empty bank account, the pressure of his vanished future. And now, too, the pressure of danger, red-tinted, dragon-toothed.

Squeezing his fear and self-pity to one side, he flung the door open. Outside stood a woman dressed in a black coat, black hat and a broad scarlet sash with *Temperance Army* embroidered on it in white. Seeing Willard, Rosalind grinned, pulled off her hat and let her dark gold hair tumble down.

'Temperance Army,' she said huskily. 'We have reports of some terrible sinning taking place at this address.'

Willard felt angry and relieved at the same time, but was careful to let only the relief show. 'Gosh, it's you. Come right on in. I believe some sinning was just about to commence.' He led her in, to a jug of iced martini. 'Well? How d'you get on?'

'I'm not sure,' she said, removing her sash and coat. 'The first problem was how to spend time in the neighbourhood without looking out of place. I thought about borrowing one of my maid's dresses, but then what was I meant to be doing hanging around an intersection on the Lower East Side all day? Then it came to me. If I was going to be out of place, I might as well be *really* out of place. So I signed up with the Temperance Army and told them I wanted to bring in sinners. I've been there for two days, ringing my bell and shouting myself hoarse. Nobody took a second look at me. A few folks felt sorry for me and took some of my leaflets, bless them.'

'And?'

'Not a rabbi in sight. Not even Jews, really, certainly not the religious types. I'd bet my life that there's no Jewish religious organisation anywhere close.'

Willard nodded slowly. 'But Powell Lambert finances everything they need. Holy books, vestments, furnishings for the synagogues. Everything. Twenty-nine thousand dollars' worth of materials in the last year alone.'

'All to that address?'

'Yes.'

'A mistake maybe?'

'No. It's not just a single bit of paper, you see. There's insurance, transportation, certification, billing, all kinds of things. It's an amazingly complex business, this trade finance game.'

'Yes, I see.' Rosalind sipped her martini thoughtfully. She had an odd way of doing it: lowering her mouth to the glass before tipping it, like a churchgoer at communion.

'Storage?' asked Willard suddenly.

'I'm sorry?'

'Storage? Was there any place to store goods if they did arrive? A warehouse or something?'

'Not a warehouse, but there was a garage at the back. Big double doors, always locked. I couldn't get in or see in.'

'Hmm.' Willard swigged his martini and put it down. In the past, he'd never thought of himself as an intelligent man. Beyond a certain point, in fact, Willard thought of intelligence as a social failing: like not being able to hold drink or being no good at sport. But times had changed. Willard was facing a new kind of enemy and only thinking could help. He frowned. 'It's a shame we aren't able to see the documents that Arthur Martin collected.'

'Yes.'

'But, you know, if I had been Arthur, worried that somebody was going to start cutting up rough, I'm not sure I'd have left anything important just laying around. Especially not here.'

'I agree.' Something in Rosalind's tone of voice made Willard look sharply at her.

'You think so too? You thought so that time you came to burglarise me?'

'Yes. Sorry.'

'Why didn't you say so?'

'This is a whole new game. I'm not sure what the rules are.'

Willard bit his lip, not happy with Rosalind's reticence. There were times when she seemed very warm and friendly, other times when he felt almost patronised. 'Well, I think you might have said something,' he muttered sulkily. 'I mean, we're either in this together or we're not.'

'Sorry.' She hung her head, like a repentant child.

'But still, the cupboard . . .'

Willard opened the cupboard, which, as before, contained linen in the lower half, movie and war mementoes above. Willard cleared things out, while Rosalind made a pile on the floor.

'You're the first living breathing war hero I've met,' she said, after a pause. 'Most of the men I meet either never went to France, or talk a lot about it and it turns out they

174

never got beyond a training camp or five days at the front the week before armistice.'

'I'm not really a hero, though. I know men who were, served under one in fact. Captain Rockwell.'

'Captain Rockwell? As in . . . ?'

'The Glory Boys. Yes.' Willard pulled the original *Times* article from the pile in front of Rosalind and spread it out. The main photo was of Rockwell himself, but there was a subsidiary photo showing every pilot in the squadron, including a very young Willard. He looked at the photo with mixed emotions. *The Glory Boys*. He had taken intense pride in being one of that select band, but now, alongside the pride, there was something else, some impulse of honesty that struggled to come out. 'We were a very good unit, perhaps even the best. But we others didn't have what Rockwell had. He was . . . unique. It took a special sort of thing to fight that well and we didn't have it. I didn't. I fought well. But that's all. I wasn't a hero.'

Rosalind stared at him. She had a captured German flying helmet in her hands, which she held as one might hold an injured bird. 'That's the first time I've ever heard you talk like that. Normally, you try to sound modest, but you look as if you'd die if anyone took you seriously.'

'Yes, well, of course it isn't everybody that shoots down five of the enemy's aircraft. It isn't as though I didn't see action.' Willard spoke quickly, covering up his earlier moment of truthfulness, not sure why he'd said it. He folded the article again, then emptied the cupboard at double speed until it was bare. 'There!'

'Now what?'

Willard didn't know. He hadn't had a plan, just an impulse. He tapped at the back of the cupboard, pulled at the architrave, jiggled the shelves, ran his hand over every surface. He found nothing. 'It was this cupboard? You're sure?'

'The built-in cupboard left of the door. It must be.'

Willard jiggled at the shelves again: nothing. Behind him, Rosalind stirred. The movement probably meant nothing. Maybe her legs were cramping. But Willard was feeling sensitive. He didn't like the occasional impression that Rosalind was less than entirely awed by him.

'Hold on.'

He left the apartment and ran downstairs to the janitor's store cupboard in the basement, where he found a box of tools. He took the tools and went back up.

Using hammer and screwdriver, he began tapping at the back and sides of the cupboard. To left and right, he hit brickwork right away. At the back of the cupboard, the screwdriver tip bounced instantly off solid board, which had been covered with lining paper, then painted. Willard pulled his head out, banged it, swore and rubbed it. As he did so, he caught sight of something: a dog-eared scrap of lining paper in the top left-hand corner. The other corner had the same thing.

'Ha!'

Beneath the dog-eared paper on both sides, was a screw-head, painted white, hardly visible. Willard unscrewed them both, looked further down, found two more, and unscrewed those too. As the last screw eased from its hole, the entire cupboard back began to come away from the wall. Sheets of newspaper had been used to plug the gap between the board and the wall. And gummed to the back of the board was a flat canvas pouch, bulging with documents.

40

Out to sea, a typhoon smashed its way northwards. Huge waves thundered on the beach. Coconut palms tugged and screamed in the wind. Poll was snug inside, but even so her timbers rocked and groaned in the eddying draughts.

The cops used the wind.

The noise allowed them to drive up to the hangar and enter without Abe hearing a thing. The first he knew of anything was a flashlight in his face, a gun at his temple, and the tearing metallic snap of handcuffs slamming into position. Once he was cuffed, the cops put the electric light on. One cop strolled idly down Abe's workbenches, sweeping all the tools, parts, castings, and models to the floor with repeated sweeps of his arm. 'Whoops. Damn. Woah – it happened again.' Another cop looked at Poll and gave her a kick on her tail cone that ripped right through her fabric shell. Over in the corner, under the broken bulb, a third cop pulled the sheet off the boxes of booze. 'Hey Captain, this ain't legal, is it?'

They hauled Abe downtown.

They searched him, photographed him, threw him into a tiny windowless cell, which contained an iron bed, no mattress and a can that seeped water and urine across the concrete floor. He had no food or water. He was permitted one phone call, which he made to a lawyer whose name he picked out of the phone book. The phone rang eight times without answer. 'That's tough shit,' said the cop. 'That's your call over.'

At one in the morning, he was hauled into another room, this one containing a metal desk and two chairs. Abe stood, while two cops lounged in the chairs and interrogated him.

Did he admit to using the federal mails to transport alcohol? Did the cases of alcohol found in the hangar belong to him? If not, to whom did they belong and what were they doing there? How long had he been carrying booze? Who bought it? How much did he sell it for? How much money had he been making from the enterprise?

But aside from confirming his name and residence, Abe answered nothing. At one point, one of the two cops got bored. He got up from his seat, walked around the desk and punched Abe as hard as he could in the stomach.

The blow was shockingly hard. Abe felt the smashing force of the punch, the sudden lurch of the room around him, a sharp knock where his falling head cracked up against the concrete floor. For a second or two, the pain was so strong, Abe didn't even quite know which part of him had been hit. It felt like someone had just picked up the wall and hit him with it. His belly contracted in a series of dry, acidic retches that left him gasping for breath. The cop who'd hit him stood over him for a second or two, then strolled back to his original position. Abe stopped retching, hauled himself first to his knees, then his feet, and stood again, facing forward, swaying slightly.

'You wanna talk?'

Abe shook his head.

The cop exchanged a pale grin with his colleague, as though he'd just got the answer he wanted. The interrogation continued.

Abe was kept standing until four in the morning. He was then left alone for forty minutes, until his next interrogation started shortly before five. This time he had a new pair of cops, tougher than the first two. He had a cup of hot coffee thrown in his face. He was punched and kicked. The cops were innovators, artists and athletes combined. They came up with ideas that Abe would never have thought of, like prostrating Abe on the floor, so one of them could stamp hard down on Abe's ankle, as the second one kicked hard at his knee joint. Abe's legs swelled so he could hardly stand, but if he didn't, he was punched and kicked until he did. He wasn't allowed to sit or lie. He wasn't allowed to eat or drink.

After four hours, he was taken back to his cell. Abe fell almost instantly asleep, but his rest lasted only fifteen minutes. At a quarter past nine, the police captain who'd arrested him came into the cell holding two cups of coffee and a packet of cigarettes. Abe took the coffee and a cigarette. His lips were so badly injured that the coffee stung and he had to pull his gashed bottom lip down to make a place to hold the cigarette. The police captain lit up for both of them.

'Looks like they've been treating you pretty rough.'

'I guess.'

'You know, it's tough being a law officer in this town. The hoodlums mostly own the place. It ain't making the arrests which is tough, it's getting anything to stick.'

'I could use some water.'

'Sure, looks like you could.' The captain opened the cell door and yelled down the hall. 'Flaherty, you ape, go get some water. And find a cookie or something. We could all use something to eat.' He closed the door. 'You know how many speakeasies there are in Miami?'

Abe shook his head.

'More than two hundred. In a town of forty thousand people. Bootleg whiskey is so easy to get a hold of, you can buy it as cheap now as you could during the war. Almost. Almost as cheap. You bootleggers have got to make your turn, right?'

Abe said nothing.

'But you know, I could make two arrests a day every day for a year and still get no place. You know why? First, I wouldn't get convictions. Not here. Not in this town. And even if I did, every day I closed down a speakeasy, there'd be another one back in the same place next day. Same with you guys. Bootleggers are like ants. You can poison 'em one day, but they'll be back the next day, probably more than ever. You see my problem?'

Abe nodded.

There was a knock at the door, a big policeman, one of the pair that had been assigned to kicking the crap out of Abe, arrived with a glass of water and two pecan cookies on a small white plate. Abe drank the water and ate one of the cookies. Everything inside him hurt. Everything outside hurt worse. He wanted to drink, sleep and eat in that order.

'But then again,' continued the captain, 'there's your side of things to look at. It's real sad, in a way. Hero of the United States and all, running booze like a two-bit bootlegger. If the newspaper folks ever got hold of a story like that, it'd be all over. Not just Florida, I mean all over. The great Captain Rockwell bringing in liquor through the federal mails. That's sad. Real sad. Me, I'd get a lot of credit. The guy who brought in Captain Rockwell. Imagine the ballyhoo. Can you imagine?'

Abe shrugged.

'You're not very talkative, are you? I've seen crabs talk more than you.' The policeman paused and lit up another cigarette, inhaling deeply a couple of times before resuming. 'Now what I'd like to do is cut a deal. You tell me who you sell to. You give me names. You help me bust the guys who operate the racket. And that's it. We don't make a fuss. We don't ask you to testify. We don't tell the newspapers. You either clean up your business here, or you go to another state and do whatever the hell you got to do.' The policeman leaned intently forward, so his face was only twelve inches from Abe's. 'Let's nail these bastards. There's no point the little guys taking the fall. Huh? How about it? What d'you say?'

Abe groaned.

Not out loud, but to himself. And not because of his bruised and battered body, but because of the captain's question. He could still quit. He was still free to get out.

'Huh, buddy? What d'you say?'

'I say . . .'

Sensing victory, the policeman leaned in again. 'Yeah?'

'I say that you're a horse's ass.'

41

Trade finance documents.

The hidden papers were trade finance documents, nothing else. Insurance forms. Delivery receipts. Letters of credit. Transportation acceptances. Correspondence.

Both Willard and Rosalind had snatched eagerly for the pile, glanced at the first few papers with breathless expectancy – then sank back, baffled and disappointed. They went through the pile slowly and carefully. Nothing. Rosalind put down the last tedious letter with a puff of frustration. She pulled off her shoes and let her stockinged feet dig into the thick cream-coloured carpet.

'I feel rotten saying it, but this seems awfully dull.'

'You know what this is, I suppose? This is trade finance work. The sort of thing I spend my days sorting out. The sort of thing Arthur did too.'

Rosalind picked up a sheet of paper. 'Six thousand dollars' worth of tanned hides. Received by New Orleans Leather Goods, Inc, in good condition, April 27, 1926. That sounds like an awful lot of cow hide, but nothing to get excited about. Nothing that would be worth . . .'

'. . . worth losing your life over. No.'

The documents related to four separate transactions. The first one dealt with a shipment of paint from a paint factory down in St Louis. Another had to do with fifteen thousand dollars' worth of furs from Canada. The third was the Detroit hides. The final deal related to five shipments of household ceramics from a New Hampshire pottery manu-facturer.

They sorted the papers into piles, then sat back. Rosalind rocked back on her ankles. She was wearing a grey-green day-dress that did terrific things for her eyes. Out of an absent-minded desire to fiddle with something, she had picked up her scarlet Temperance Army sash and was wearing it across her chest, fiddling with the long tails of the rosette. Without thinking out his move in advance, Willard reached out and stroked her cheek.

She looked up, surprised. Willard was about to with-draw his hand, when she moved her shoulder up to her cheek, gently trapping his hand. She held it there for a moment, then released it. He smiled. She smiled back, then changed her expression to signify that the moment had ended.

'Well, Sherlock?'

Willard shook his head, puzzled. 'These seem like four completely regular trade finance transactions. We do deals like this all the time. This Canadian outfit, Northern Furs, I've worked on one of their deals myself. Animal furs. Twelve thousand bucks. East Coast buyer. It was a different delivery address, that's all.'

'So either my sister's fiancé went crazy before he died . . .'

'. . . or else these things stink and we need to find out why.'

There was a pause. Neither of them thought that Arthur Martin had been a nut, but nor could they guess why someone had killed him over some tedious trade finance deals. She gazed at him. There was an intelligence and seri-ousness in her eyes which searched his face for an answer to a question he couldn't guess.

'Aren't you scared?' she said at last.

'Scared? Well, maybe a little.'

'And do you have any ideas? What to do, I mean?'

'Maybe, yes, if you're still happy to help.'

She nodded gravely. 'And you'll be careful, won't you? I wouldn't want . . .'

'Of course. You too. Lord, I should say we had plenty of reason to tread carefully.'

'And you won't . . . you won't . . .?' She trailed off.

'Won't what?'

'Look, this probably sounds mean, but I can't quite stop remembering that you work for Powell Lambert. I don't know if the whole organisation is rotten or just part of it. But, whatever happens, whatever we find – you won't join its rottenness, will you? You'd never do that?'

Willard jutted his chin and looked hurt. 'Gosh, Ros, I hope you don't really need to ask. I mean, there's your Arthur Martin to think of, not to mention my Charlie Hughes. I mean, he was a silly little man really, but you can't just go sticking people in prison because they don't understand how a fellow ought to behave. I mean, there are things one has to stand and fight for.'

'Oh, Willard! I do so love a man who can't act!'

Her statement burst out before she'd realised what she'd said. But Willard was immediately affronted. He jerked backwards, chin and nose up, his voice high and sniffy.

'What? You know, I wasn't at all bad, actually. Rather good, in fact. Put me in front of a camera, with costume and lights and everything . . .'

Rosalind, contrite and apologetic, came and knelt in front of him, putting her long bare arms around his neck. 'I didn't mean that. I didn't mean anything. I bet you acted a dream. I think the studio was crazy to let you go.'

She didn't let go. Her arms continued to hold his neck. He remembered that when he'd touched her cheek, she had held his hand there instead of letting it go. He moved forwards to kiss her, but a slight movement of her head deflected him from her lips to her cheek. She had lovely skin. Soft. That lovely peachy-gold colour that comes naturally to only a few. Her tiny blonde hairs formed a portable soft-focus effect. But she had deflected him. That was the point.

She leaned back and they smiled like nothing had happened. And there it was again. That doubt. That uncertainty. Was he a friend, almost close enough to pet her? Or was he just a colleague? The sort of man you could patronise, as long as you made up with a kiss?

Willard didn't know, but he didn't stay thinking about it for long. His eyes fell on the stack of documents. He already knew what to do next. A thrill of excitement and fear wormed in his belly.

42

Abe's ordeal continued for another forty-nine hours. He was kept short of sleep, food and water. He was knocked around, yelled at, interrogated, threatened.

And he was utterly unused to it. People sometimes thought that, because he was the great war hero, he must be a tough guy. But toughness, physical toughness, played little part in flying. Among army pursuit pilots, the death rate had been horrific: greater even than the death rate on the ground. But though the danger had been extreme, life itself had been cushy. The accommodation had been first-rate, the meals excellent, sleep plentiful, duties unburdensome, leave easily obtained. Although Abe was no lover of luxury, he appreciated comfort. He had never had any reason to become accustomed to pain. For those forty-nine hours and the eight hours that had preceded them, that changed. When he was kicked, he felt it. When he was hit, it hurt.

But through it all, he said nothing. And then, at ten-forty on Monday morning, everything changed.

A cop came into Abe's cell. 'OK, buster, you made bail. Jesus, you look a wreck.'

That was an understatement. Abe's lips were cut, bruised and swollen. One of his eyes had mushroomed black and purple. There was dried blood in his hair. His legs, arms, neck and body were fused into one solid ache. He was swaying with tiredness and his mouth had turned to gum.

He was so far gone, he wouldn't have made it upstairs, if it hadn't been for the cop helping.

In the lobby of the police station, a man in a dark suit and red shirt jiggled impatiently. Abe recognised him as one of the goons who had accompanied Mason the night of their first visit to the hangar. The man saw Abe and whistled.

'Jeez! They sure messed you up. Here, I got your things. It's OK to go. I got a car.'

The goon carried Abe back to the airfield and dropped him there.

'You want anything? You're looking pretty rough, you know.'

'I'm OK. Thanks.'

'Don't thank me, thank the boss.' The goon climbed back into his car. 'You sure you're OK?'

Abe nodded. The goon left. Abe entered the hangar.

Poll stood, her wings looming huge in the semi-darkness. The familiar smells of oil and airplane dope, dust and sunshine closed over Abe like a warm bath.

'Hey, old girl,' he murmured, running his hands down her fuselage.

Poll said nothing, but her solid presence was reassurance in itself. While he'd been downtown having his kidneys rearranged, he'd been worried about her. He needn't have done. She was fine. The cops had thrown Abe's tools around a bit, messed up his workbenches, but a couple of hours should get the place tidy. The only real damage was the hole kicked in Poll's tail end, plus a few of Abe's precious castings had broken in their journey from wooden shelf to concrete floor.

Outside the hangar, Abe checked out his little construction site. That was fine too. Abe had his walls up to four feet now. Wooden frames marked out the future position of doors and windows. The cops could have smashed things if they'd wanted, but they hadn't. The hangar was OK. Poll was OK. The little cement rectangle which might one day become a home, that was OK too.

But he didn't feel OK. He felt awful.

He sat down on his camp bed, feeling far older than his age. He was beaten-up, on his own, lonely. He thought of all kinds of things he shouldn't have thought of. He thought of the little red-headed kid, Brad Lundmark. He thought of Gibson Hennessey, the old fox of Independence. He thought about his mother and father, growing old together on their Kentucky farm. And he thought about Pen, the woman flier he hadn't had the balls to say 'hi' to.

The thoughts gathered into a solid, darkening gloom. Mostly, when he felt low, he got up and did something. He'd tinker with Poll, or sharpen tools, or get out some of his books on airplane engineering, all of them heavy with math that made his head ache. But he wasn't up to any of that now. His body stiffened as he sat, until even small movements caused him pain.

He forced himself up, tried to stretch a little, this way and that, but each movement caused a wound to open or a bruise to shriek. Gingerly, he made his way over to the workshop sink. He drank a quart of water, then tried to wash. The water pipe must have been contaminated by seawater, because the tap ran salty and sharp. The cuts on his face, scalp and body hissed angrily as he tried to clean up. He washed anyway, scrubbing at himself with a cold, masochistic fury. He normally liked to dry off after washing, but the towel was on the floor over on the far side of the hangar where the cops had been throwing things around. It felt too far to go and get it. Instead, he crept back to his camp bed, fell into it, and dragged the blanket halfway up his torso. He was asleep within fifteen seconds.

The sleep didn't last as long as it should have done. A sense of hopelessness and a huge, empty feeling that was probably loneliness forced him out of sleep. The acute pains in his body were better, but the overall ache, the solid, dark bruise of him, was worse. He drank more, used the can, found some stale bread and a packet of biscuits and ate.

He was just about to root around in the debris on the floor for something more to eat, when he heard the sound of a car outside and Mason's cheerfully thuggish face appeared in the doorway. He stepped through, and looked around at the mess. 'Jesus!' he said. He picked his way through the litter until he was near enough to see Abe up close. 'Holy shit!'

Abe pointed to the kettle. 'Coffee?'

'Uh-huh. If there's more whisky than coffee in it.'

'No whisky. The cops cleared me out.'

'Yeah. They're probably down on the beach flogging it right now.' Mason looked disgusted.

Abe made coffee, economising on every movement.

'They hurt you bad?'

Abe gestured at his face. 'What you see.'

Mason stared as though he were a connoisseur of grievous bodily harm, which maybe, Abe reflected, he was. 'I expect you're not too pretty with your shirt off either.'

'Not so pretty.'

Mason lifted Abe's shirt, stared for a moment, then dropped it again without comment.

'They let you sleep?'

'Not a lot.'

'Food and drink?'

'It wasn't a holiday camp. But thanks for springing me. I was just about done enjoying myself.'

'You're welcome.' Mason took his coffee and stirred it solemnly. 'You know, we generally have good relations with our cousins in the police force. We don't usually have a problem.'

'I've noticed.'

'Someone somewhere forgot to make a payment. Our mistake. We're a big organisation, and sometimes things go wrong. This was the cops' way of reminding us not to forget them twice.'

'Next time maybe they could send a postcard.'

'We've let them know we're not too happy. There are ways of doing things and as far as we're concerned they broke the rules.'

'Great.'

'But that's not the main point. Not as far as your connection with us is concerned.'

'Oh?'

'We know you didn't say anything. Not a squeak. The whole time you were in there. I appreciate that kind of loyalty.'

'Maybe I just don't like helping folks who are swinging a boot into my kidneys.'

'Maybe. Or maybe you're just a stubborn-assed son-of-a-Kentucky-mule. You weren't very friendly with me the first time I met you.'

Abe tried a grin, but all he achieved was to shift the yellow and purple blotches around his face a little.

'A little while back, you talked about buying up some second-hand piece of flying junk. A D-something.'

'A DH-4. A de Havilland. Good plane.'

'You still keen?'

Abe nodded.

'We could work something out maybe. Kind of a thank you.' Mason drummed with his spoon on the wooden packing case they were using as a table. 'You don't spend a lot, do you?'

'My parents' farm had pretty much fallen into the hands of the bank. I'm still digging them clear. That's part of it.'

'And the other part?'

'Is none of your business.'

Mason shook his head. 'You are my business.'

Abe held the other man's gaze for a second or two, then answered. 'I'm not a big spending type. I'll make my money. When I've got enough, I'll quit.'

'Enough for what?'

'That's none of your business, Mason.'

The two men locked gazes. Abe's eyes never flickered, but some intuition made Mason look around to the shelves containing Abe's castings of aircraft parts. Mason stared as though to find the answer there, then gave up. He dropped his eyes.

'Maybe you're right. I spend too much time with lowlife. When I meet a straight guy, I don't know what to do with him. OK. A question.'

'Sure.'

'Suppose I told you we'd buy you a plane. Nice modern machine. Big carrying capacity. Reliable. Everything nice.'

'I'd say great.'

'You'd carry more booze for us. Because you're carrying more, your pay goes up.'

Abe nodded.

'But one other thing. We'd like it if the plane could run up the coast every now and then.'

Abe nodded, slower this time.

'The way I figure it, you'd get a good view from a plane. You'd see plenty.'

Abe nodded again, even slower. 'People forget,' he said, his voice a little mushy from the bruising. 'People forget that during the war, the only reason for having planes was observation. Our bombing raids were virtually useless. Attacks on ground troops looked impressive, but had no real military value. What mattered was observation. We wanted to get over their lines so we could report back to our guys. They tried to do the same with us. The only reason we even had pursuit aircraft was because we wanted to stop them looking at us, they wanted to stop us looking at them. But it all started with observation. That was the only thing that ever mattered.'

Mason, who had been picking his teeth with a matchstick, put it away and grinned. 'I like you. I always knew you'd be a good guy to know.'

Abe relapsed into silence, reached for his cold coffee.

'Boats,' said Mason. 'The Coastguard have been picking up a few of our boats recently. Don't know how, but somebody's been tipping them off. You get that with a big outfit. Somebody doesn't like the pay they're getting, they try to supplement it. It's not right, but it's how it is. Anyhow, we've lost three entire consignments, plus the boats, plus we've got a few of our men in federal courts. We'll be able to spring them, but it'll cost us.'

'Boats are easy. Nothing easier than looking out for boats.'

'Really? Good. You need an observer with you or . . .?'

'I fly alone.'

'So what type of plane?'

'You're asking me to choose?'

'Uh-huh.'

'New or second-hand?'

'Whatever. The best. Doesn't have to be the biggest, just the best. Let me know.' Mason stood up. 'I ought to let you sleep, I guess.'

Abe looked at his watch and nodded. 'Yeah, we got to leave in eight hours. And she can't leave with that hole in her tail.'

'We?'

'Poll. Me and Poll.'

Mason stared. 'You're flying? Tomorrow? Have you seen how you look?'

Abe shrugged. 'It's not a beauty pageant, Mason. I've got the mails to fly.'

Mason paused for a moment with real concern visible on his face, then he laughed and shook his head. He stuck a cigarette in his mouth, ready to light when he left the hangar. 'Sleep well, Captain.'

'I plan to.'

'And let me know. The best, OK? Just let me know.'

Abe nodded and sat on his bed as Mason left. Poll could

be patched with a tight cotton bandage. A proper repair would take longer, but she could fly with just the patch.

But he wasn't thinking about that, or whether he was sane to contemplate flying in a few hours' time, or about any of the messages of complaint that his various body parts were now submitting. Instead he thought about that huge and empty loneliness that had forced him awake. He felt now as though he'd always been lonely; that his whole life had been a version of escape; that he'd achieved nothing that had ever meant anything.

He sat with his legs dangling from his cheap metal bed, looking down at the floor, doing nothing at all.

43

Exhaustion, fear, hard work, poverty, tension, danger.

Those were the ingredients of Willard's life, the flour, yeast, salt and water of his daily bread.

Charlie Hughes had gone. He hadn't been replaced. No replacement had been spoken of. And all the time those hateful files came flooding in. More than before. Powell Lambert's business was increasing and the poor saps in the engine room had to keep the great machinery moving.

Weekends disappeared. Saturday was no longer a day off, a day to spend in the country or at the races or playing tennis or at the shops. Saturday was a regular working day. In the office by seven-thirty. Out again twelve or thirteen hours later with a briefcase still bulging.

But the long working hours were a relief. Because Willard's money had run out. His bank account had emptied, and then some. Lucinda and Laura, his two elder sisters, were beginning to make difficulties over lending him still more money. To his acute and unrelenting shame, Willard had sought to pawn or sell items for which he'd paid collectively thousands, and for which he seemed set to receive a few meagre hundreds. His long hours at least gave him an excuse for tight-fistedness. He began to walk sooner than go by cab. He refused invitations. For the first time in his life, he counted his change.

But while Willard felt besieged, he was also frightened. For one thing, his fears had become more tangible. Long-nosed, brown-eyed, yellow-toothed Greyhound-face was tracking Willard's movements. Willard had now seen the man five times, five different locations. And it wasn't only Greyhound-face. Willard thought he'd identified one or two others, only he'd become so jumpy and suspicious, he couldn't be sure.

And not only that. He was now certain that his phone was listened to. One day, he'd made a date with Rosalind by phone, then made his way there, changing cabs, running the wrong way down one-way streets, ducking into alleys, waiting in doorways. At the end of it all, he'd have sworn that nobody could have kept pace with him, not even a team of pursuers. But when he'd got to the restaurant, to join his beautiful Rosalind, there was Greyhound-face, chomping his matchstick and training his mournful brown eyes on Willard. Willard hadn't yet mentioned any of this to Rosalind, but would of course, some day soon.

Meanwhile, on top of his regular work, he'd started to add his own.

The files. Arthur Martin had collected four files then died before he could use them. Why those? What was the riddle of those bland and tedious documents? It was possible that Willard's life depended on his ability to find out.

So he went to work. Every two or three days Willard went to the bank archive. He needed archive files for his work downstairs and the archivists already knew Willard well. But as well as asking for the files he needed for work, he slipped in additional request slips for files relating to the ones that Arthur Martin had died to collect.

He was interested in any transactions where either the buyer or the seller had been the same as the ones in Martin's collection. That amounted to a lot of deals: forty-five where the manufacturers were the same as Martin's; sixty-two where the customers were identical.

So day by day, week by week, Willard filled in his little pink request slips and collected his precious files. Day by day, week by week, Willard carried these files out of the bank and took them to Rosalind. Together they copied them, trusting no one else to share the work. Page by page the information accumulated, its owners not knowing what was precious and what wasn't. Once each file had been copied, Willard returned it, innocent as the first day of spring.

But Willard's mammoth hours on Wall Street left Rosalind with plenty of time. And she had calls to place, trips to make.

Today, for instance. She'd just come back from the New Hampshire porcelain factory. The place had looked like a sweet little ceramics manufacturer, as sweet and bright as its candy-soft advertising. But the business was also the seller in one of Arthur Martin's deals. It was nine-thirty in the evening. Willard had just got home, exhausted and low. They kissed cheek to cheek. Rosalind had martinis already mixed and offered him a glass.

He shook his head. 'Sorry, no. D'you mind? I thought I'd shower first. Then eat.'

She looked at his briefcase. 'I'm growing to hate that thing. Do you have . . .?'

'Yes. More tonight. Another hour or two, if the papers are OK.'

Rosalind said nothing, but put her hand to his face, to the soft area beneath his eyes where the skin was puffy and dark. 'If I can help . . .'

He showered. Hot for two minutes, as hot as he could stand. Then cold, half a minute under the full stream. He jumped out gasping and shivered on the bed holding a towel. The door to the living room was open a few inches and Rosalind spoke to him from outside.

'Do you want to hear about my trip? New England Porcelain, Inc.'

'Oh yes? That was today was it?'

'Yes.'

'And?'

'And – I found a pottery factory.'

Willard rubbed his legs with a towel. He was getting no exercise now. He wasn't exactly out of shape. He'd always been blessed with the kind of body that looked good no matter how little he attended to it. All the same, sitting on his butt all day long was no help. Willard wondered if his calves were getting thinner, and decided they were. Outside the door, Rosalind shifted her weight. Willard realised some further question was expected.

'A pottery factory, huh? Bona fide, you think?'

'Think? They offer tours for visitors. They whizz you around a couple of kilns, show you the plates and things being made. It's all surprisingly smelly. The dyes and glazes, that sort of thing. I hadn't realised. Then you wind up in the factory shop where a greasy little salesman tries to sell you some kitchenware you don't want. Succeeds, actually, in my case. I spent forty dollars.'

'Get anything nice?'

'You're eating off it tonight.'

'Hmm.'

In his better days, one of Willard's greatest gifts had been charm. It wasn't just that he was good-looking. Looks could get you to first base, but if the rest of the package was missing, no looks in the world would get you further. But Willard had been charming. He could make women laugh. His own laugh, insincere but easy, made everyone around him feel like they were being funny too. But that had been then. A tired man isn't charming, or if he is, it's something that flickers on and off like power in a thunderstorm. He rubbed his legs again and tried another question.

'So we strike out again, I guess?'

'Well . . . It was a big site and I only toured a piece of it. Maybe there was a room somewhere where red anarchists were plotting to blow up the President, but if so, I didn't see it.'

'Still, they make pottery. That's the point.'

So far, every time they'd attempted to test Arthur Martin's files or any of the sister files they'd collected, things seemed to check out. They'd found porcelain companies which made porcelain. They'd found engineering companies which engineered things. They'd found paint companies which asked you how many gallons you wanted. Willard lay back on the bed, completely naked except for the towel. He stared at the ceiling, tired and defeated.

A moment passed, then another.

Rosalind was silent. So was Willard.

Then he began to lever himself up, when he stopped dead. Rosalind had come into the room and was standing, staring down at him. They looked at each other in silence.

Willard was very conscious of his nudity – his private parts were covered, even if only just – but something in the way Rosalind looked at him made him say and do nothing.

'Maybe it's too much,' she said at last.

'What is?'

'This. All of it. Everything. There's a limit to how much one person can manage.'

Willard managed a smile. 'I'm not one person, though, am I? I've got you.'

'You could quit.'

'The loan, Ros, the loan.'

'Your father? If you explained everything?'

'You don't know my father. He wouldn't help.'

'You haven't asked.'

'He wouldn't help. I won't ask.' Willard spoke sharply.

'You know, that's not the only way out.'

'Oh?'

'You could . . .'

'Could what?'

'You know . . . declare yourself bankrupt.'

That word raised Willard's anger like a storm cloud. In his social circle, a man could get by with leprosy more

198

easily than with bankruptcy. He'd be an outcast. A nobody. 'Never.' His anger forced the word out like a fat little bullet.

Then Rosalind did something unexpected. She was wearing an evening dress in soft blue. Her hair was combed and bobbed and gleaming gold in the lamplight. She kicked her shoes off and bent down, close to Willard, holding his knees. Her touch was so sudden, so unexpected, that Willard's member stirred under the towel. He twitched the towel back into position, excited.

'Why?' she asked.

Something in the atomsphere of the room guided Willard's answer. If his anger had had its way, the answer would have been something short, rude, unkind, petulant. But that wasn't how he answered. Instead he said simply, 'We've got a job to do. We're not finished. Think of Arthur Martin. Think of Charlie Hughes.'

'Oh.'

There was another moment of stillness. Willard's erection stirred again and he began to sit to hide it better. But Rosalind stopped him. She put her hand to his chest and pushed him softly back down. He was lying flat, breathing fast.

For one moment longer, Rosalind stood, some decision taking shape in the shadows of her face. Then she bent down and lifted the towel. Willard's erection, not that small to begin with, jumped out like a minor lighthouse. His penis was good-sized. He liked her looking at it.

Rosalind hesitated for a moment longer, then put her hands to her dress. She slid off her dress, her slip, her stockings, her pearls, her panties. Her body was cream and gold, with nipples as dark as raspberries. Willard began to sit up again, ready to lead her down into his arms, but once again she motioned him back.

He lay down. Climbing onto the bed, she squatted over him, lowering herself slowly onto him. Aside from a little 'Ah!' as he entered her, both he and she were silent. She began to move, but slowly. Willard hadn't made love for longer than he liked to remember and tiredness and lack of practice made him ready to burst almost straight away.

But she didn't let him. Each time she rode him almost to climax, she stopped. She let the feeling dwindle until Willard, still lying, was ready for more. Her own face looked quiet, introspective, except that her lips never quite closed, her eyes were only half-open. She let Willard touch her wherever he wanted, but after a while his hands came to rest on her hips.

For a while longer, they moved together. Willard had never been in this position. He'd always been the master in bed, the one on top, the one in charge. This position felt new but just right. He let Rosalind have things her way until it was time to take control. Then, with his hands on her hips, he began to move her himself. He rocked her up and down, until she understood his intention and let herself be rocked.

Her head, which had been tilting down, began to arch backwards, exposing the long lines of her throat. Her panting came faster. Her outbreaths had a low moan, then not so low, then not low at all.

They climaxed together: Willard in one, long, starburst of colour; Rosalind in a long, dim, greenish-gold heave of pleasure. And from that moment, it was all different.

Before: something had been missing. Not just sex, but something more than sex.

And after? Well, it was different. The gap that had existed between them either vanished or (what was just as good) seemed to have vanished. Rosalind accepted Willard's charm for what it was. She laughed at his jokes. She nestled into his caresses. She began to look at Willard the way he expected a girl to look at him: trusting, fond, adoring, his.

44

Atlanta, Georgia.

A rainstorm had just passed through and the air shone clean and brilliant. Gibson Hennessey, the storekeeper from Independence, walked quickly downtown from the station. He'd come by train, but a Southern Express locomotive had derailed just north of Macon and Hennessey was running late. He walked fast. His old black suit had too many shiny patches. Elbows, knees, seat and shoulders shone in the sun. The cuffs of his shirt were fluffy and soft.

The Southern Pride Restaurant was a pompous affair with big arched windows overlooking the burning sidewalk. Hennessey entered. Just inside, a girl sat at an over-sized mahogany hat-check kiosk. The girl was blonde-haired and blue-eyed, and taller than Hennessey when she stood. A painted board just behind her right ear said 'HAT CHECK – ZARAH HARRISON' in big capital letters, as though the fact was too important to be ignored.

'Good afternoon,' said the girl, in an accent which placed her birthplace closer to Cork, Ireland, than to Atlanta, Georgia.

'Good afternoon,' said Hennessey.

The girl gestured at the book like Hennessey should know what to do next. He didn't. The girl had a plate of cheese – no biscuits, no butter, just cheese – beside her. Hennessey found himself staring at it because he didn't know what he was supposed to do or say. She twitched the plate away with an elbow, but managed to look longingly at it at the same time, as though she'd rather be eating cheese than talking to Hennessey.

'Your name, please? You have a reservation?'

'My name's Hennessey. I don't exactly have a reservation, though the person I'm meeting might do.'

'Their name?' Zarah Harrison persisted patiently.

'You don't have anyone in there calling themselves Aunt Polly, do you? This is going to sound a little strange, but the party I'm meeting may be a man.'

The girl looked at him like he was a freak, but a freak within her job description.

'You'll find your aunt at the corner table inside.' She made a face, as though to indicate that whatever Hennessey might be up to was OK with her, as long as she had no further part in it.

'Thank you.'

'Your hat.'

'Huh?'

'Your hat. You can leave it with me.'

'That's OK, I don't mind . . .' Hennessey tailed off. The girl took names and collected hats. That was her job and she had a signboard to prove it. He took off his hat and handed it over.

Abe watched the storekeeper enter the restaurant.

'Hey, Hen,' said the airman.

'Hey, Captain. Real nice to see you again. Unexpected, but nice.'

Abe nodded. 'You want to eat?'

'Uh, I'm fine really.'

'You're going to need to eat. I've been here a while and I've had all the food I can get down.'

'Yeah, sorry. Train was late.'

'I know.'

A waiter came over and Hennessey ordered. The waiter left.

'Well?' It was the storekeeper who spoke.

'I'm in.'

'I'm sorry?'

'I'm in, Hen. They've taken me in.'

'They? You mean . . .?'

Abe nodded. 'I'm flying booze for them. I'm about to start guarding their shipping fleet against the Coastguard. They're buying me a plane. A big one. A twenty-thousand-dollar one. They trust me. I'm in.'

He spoke clearly, but there was a flicker in his face. He'd never been sure about doing as Hennessey had asked, but this was his most decisive step yet. Not even his two and a half days in a Miami police cell had the significance of what he was doing now. The storekeeper heard the words, but he read the flicker too. He leaned in for confirmation.

'You're in and you're on our side?'

'Yes. I didn't want to promise anything earlier, because I didn't know if I'd even get this far. Not only that, it was better if you and everyone in Independence forgot about me, or at least thought I was a bum.'

'Brad Lundmark told me about the booze. I didn't know what to think.'

'That I was a liquor smuggler. How come you didn't think that?'

'I couldn't see it, Captain. I just couldn't see it.'

'Yeah . . . good old Brad. Nobody else has quite the same thirst for getting a place tidy.'

Hennessey stared at the airman. Even now, ten days on, Abe's face bore the marks of his beating in the police cells. His cheeks and forehead had mostly healed, but they were still puckered in small white and red scars and his upper lip was still decorated in tints of black, purple and yellow.

203

'You say they trust you. What did it take to get them to do that?'

'It was harder than I thought. I started out flying booze for them, but that was it. I saw no distance into the organisation and as far as I could see they intended to keep things that way. So then I started telling the Coastguard where they could pick up some boats, and things changed. They got their police friends to kick me around a bit, to see if I'd squeal. I didn't. And that was that. They needed me. They'd tested me. They decided to trust me.'

Hennessey whistled softly out, but kept quiet as a waiter brought him crab-cakes and a plateful of fried potatoes.

'You couldn't have been sure the police were in their pay.'

'No, not sure.'

'It was Brad Lundmark who persuaded us to come to you. He was right. We were lucky.'

'He's a good kid.'

'Do you know what you hope to accomplish? One man against an outfit the size of Marion?'

'No, but they think I'm on their side. That makes them vulnerable. And it's like combat. It's all a question of positioning. Positioning and aim. We hold fire until we find their weak spot. Then we hit it. Always the same thing in the same order. Prepare. Observe. Manoeuvre. Destroy.'

'And their weak spot?'

Abe grinned. 'They're criminals. They're operating one giant criminal conspiracy. That's against the law, Hen.'

Hennessey sounded disappointed. 'They've bought the cops, Captain. County and state. Federal enforcement is the same. Just as bad or worse. The Coastguard seems to be clean, though they have their rotten crews of course. But however many boats they intercept, there are always more coming. And the Coastguard have no jurisdiction inland.'

'OK. What d'you say we use a law enforcement organisation which is totally untouched by their money? A federal

204

organisation which is one hundred per cent clean. Which has the resources and the competence and the will to root out and destroy every element of the conspiracy?'

Hen shook his head. 'It doesn't exist. We've tried. We've done everything, we –'

Abe interrupted him by slipping a newspaper clipping across the table. 'While I was making up my mind whether to help, one of the main difficulties I saw was how we could ever win if the law was rotten. Then I saw this. I've checked it out, Hen. From what I can make out, this thing looks like it'll go all the way.'

The storekeeper read the clipping, then read it again. As he read, he smiled. The smile grew wider and wider, bigger and bigger, until it broke out into a deep contented chuckle.

'It's a crazy idea, Captain. But beautiful-crazy not dumb-crazy.'

Abe took the clipping and tore it into pieces.

'Needs must when the devil rides,' he said, 'according to my grandma anyway.'

'You don't set yourself easy targets do you, Captain?'

'I don't think it was me who set this one, Hen,' Abe reminded him.

'D'you know what happens next?'

'Not really. But I do know I'm going to be airborne a lot. Not only that, but even with the new plane and all, I don't think they trust me absolutely. I'm not exactly their regular type of hoodlum. I'm making money now, but I don't throw it around. I don't drink much. I don't gamble. I don't go with girls. At least . . .'

'Yes?' The storekeeper raised an eyebrow.

'I don't go with girls unless they're very pretty and have nice long wings.' Abe made his habitual joke, but it sounded, even to him, more forced than usual. He remembered a female flier, a bunch of roses, and the way he'd chosen to slice their pretty pink heads off. The ghosts of loneliness hung around that thought too.

'You need someone on the ground, right?'

'Right.'

'You think Brad . . .?'

'Heck, he's kind of connected in to Independence. If it wasn't for his pa and all . . .'

'He worships you, Captain. You'd have loyalty.'

'He's too close to Independence, Hen, sorry.'

'OK, you got any ideas?'

'Yeah, a couple.'

'Go ahead. Shoot.'

'I'm going to need a mechanic. So far, I've been looking after Poll and flying at the same time. If I'm airborne more, and I'm flying a bigger, more complex plane, I'm gonna need help. I figure the grease monkey may as well be a guy we can both of us trust.'

'You want me to find you an airplane mechanic?' Hennessey's voice rose in alarm.

'No, a regular auto mechanic is fine. I'll teach him what he needs to know. Just make sure he's up to the job where engines are concerned.'

'I know a couple of people, maybe. I'll check them out.'

'OK. I'm going to advertise in Jacksonville. Whoever you get, make sure they answer the ad.'

'You want me to let you know who I'm sending?'

Abe shook his head. 'Before Poll, I had a Thomas Morse airplane, called Sweet Jemima. She wasn't so sweet, actually, an ornery little miss who tried to kill me a couple of times. I usually called her Jemmy. Whoever you send, just make sure they mention their Aunt Jemmy.'

'OK.'

'And last thing. If I need to get hold of you, I'll be your Aunt Polly. Just do whatever the old bird asks. Also, you might want to check your yard from time to time. Your aunt might take it into her head to drop messages there.'

'I'll look out.'

'And you need to be able to reach me, but I don't want you to use the mail or, assuming I get one, the phone.'

'It's a long way to holler, Captain.'

'Where does Mrs Hennessey dry her washing?'

'Huh? Her laundry? Out in the yard. She's got a line.'

'OK, good.' Abe gave Hennessey instructions about what to do if he needed Abe's help. 'And remember, we need to assume that they don't trust me, they don't trust you, and that they're gonna be watching us both.'

'I got it. You take care, Captain.'

'Both of us, Hen. We must both of us take care.'

45

'Miss Hooper,' proclaimed Larry Ronson, holding up one of the group's detested files, 'thou hast erred. Erred greatly. Or, to put it another way, please remove this thing.'

He handed the file back to her.

'No, Larry. No mistake. It's your turn. The others are snowed under.'

'The snow it snoweth every day. I don't mind taking another of your filthy files, my dear lady. But this one belongs to that man there.'

He pointed to Willard, who looked up.

'Oh?'

Larry took back the file from Annie and dropped it on Willard's desk.

'The well-known and highly religious Association of Irish Rabbis is buying ever more . . . I don't know. Torahs. Skullcaps. Candles. Dried fish. Whatever makes an Irish rabbi jump for joy.'

Willard opened the file. It was his old friends at the Association of Orthodox Synagogues. They had another large order for religious materials, the first part of which was due to be shipped soon. He hesitated. The file was dodgy and it was Ronson's file. What's more, Willard had a sense that, by bad luck or by some malevolent design, the tough files always came his way. The files with errors in, the files with incompetent counterparts, the ones with documents missing. Perhaps he was wrong about that. But what was certainly true was that, although everyone in the trade finance team worked long hours, Willard's hours were the longest, the most brutal.

Annie picked up the file and was about to pass it back to Larry, telling him to stop ducking work. But Willard stopped her.

'No, Annie, that's all right. I've become rather fond of my invisible rabbis. I don't mind taking this one. You give Larry the next one you've got lined up for me.'

Annie frowned, feeling that Ronson had somehow pulled a fast one.

'You've got plenty to do already.'

'I must be a saint.'

'Saint Willard of Wall Street,' said Ronson. 'I'll light a candle.'

Willard sat back down, his blood already beating faster in his veins. He knew the feeling. It wasn't the sudden, explosive excitement of combat, but the moment of silence beforehand. It was the first sight of specks in the sky: the glimpse of a target, a hint of battle.

46

'He's a good guy, Captain. Jesus!' Mason spat on the hangar floor, then brushed the mark into the dirt with his toe. 'I had a real sweet Lincoln. Wouldn't start no matter what I did. This guy comes in and fixes it, sweet as a nut.'

'I'm flying an airplane, not a nut tree.'

Mason wouldn't quit. 'It makes a lot of sense to pick someone from the organisation. We like keeping things among friends, especially our most important things. And that includes you, buddy, like it or not.'

Abe said nothing, just turned to the mechanic that Mason had brought. 'Take your coat off.'

'Huh?'

'If you don't want to get your coat covered in oil, take it off.'

The mechanic, a man with eyes that scraped the ground and big hands twisting uncomfortably in his lap, took his coat off. He wasn't carrying a gun now, but Abe could see the lines of sweat where a gun-harness had been not so long ago. Abe threw the man an overall.

'I've got an engine here that's not sounding right. I want you to tell me what's wrong.'

'Yah! OK. Sure.' The mechanic threw Mason a look, which Mason refused to acknowledge.

Abe started up Poll's engine and let her run. Alongside the regular thunder of her pistons firing, there was a tell-tale noise of something loose and a perceptible vibration in the engine cowling, different from the normal vibration.

'OK,' said Abe. 'Any ideas?'

'Huh?'

'I want you to tell me what's wrong with the engine.'

The man gestured helplessly. 'You got it running. You want me to look, you better switch off.'

Abe switched off. The mechanic struggled into the overall which was a couple of sizes too small. He removed the engine cowling quickly enough, then spent fifteen minutes rooting around inside. Abe hated the idea of anyone he didn't trust with his hands inside Poll's most personal space, but he forced himself to wait.

'He's doing good, huh?' said Mason. 'Thorough.'

'We'll see.'

Eventually, the mechanic finished. He brought the engine cowling down too hard and it echoed through the hangar with a hollow boom.

'I reckon you got a problem with your oil. Dirty filter. Here, I took it out.' He held it out, dripping oil onto the concrete floor.

'OK, wait outside.'

The man went.

'Well?' said Mason.

'The filter's clean. I cleaned it this morning.'

'Cut the guy slack. He's never even seen an airplane before.'

'He should have seen an oil filter.' There was an ugly pause. 'I need a mechanic, Mason, not one of your heavies holding a monkey wrench instead of a gun.'

'It's true though, he fixed my car.'

'I need a mechanic. A guy who understands engines. You need him too. I can't fly for you, if my plane isn't flyable.'

Mason wanted to spit again, but knew Abe didn't like it. He pursed up his lips and scowled. 'Who's next?'

Arnold Hueffer was next. A lean, dark man, with a shock

of hair that fell across his eyes like a raven's wing. He had an olive complexion and quick brown eyes, that suggested his mother wasn't as Germanic as his surname.

Abe went through the same question and answer routine with Hueffer. Name. Previous employers. Experience. Engines previously worked on. Responsible positions held. Hueffer didn't have much to boast of. He worked in a small garage in Brunswick. When the owner had retired, Hueffer had bought him out. He worked on any type of engine that drove in through the door. He'd answered the ad because he'd always liked airplanes, the idea of them anyway.

'OK, Mr Hueffer. I've got a problem. Poll here isn't working quite right. I want you to tell me what's the matter.' He threw the overall across to Hueffer, then went over to Poll and started the engine. Hueffer sat in his seat, holding the overall across his lap and listening. After a while, he went up to Poll and listened closer to, keeping the finger-tips of his left hand pressed lightly against the cowling. He had left the overalls lying across his seat.

'I don't know anything about airplanes. I don't even know what type of plane this is.'

'She's a Curtiss JN-4D-2. You'll have heard of her type as a Curtiss Jenny.'

'A Jenny. Sure.' He listened some more. 'Four cylinders, right?'

'Right.'

'They're firing OK, nothing wrong there.' He moved his hands further down the engine cowling, then up again, like a doctor feeling for a pulse. 'I'm getting a kind of metallic knocking sound. There . . . there . . . there.' He beat time with his spare hand in time to the knocking. 'That normal?'

'No.'

'And I could be wrong about this, I ain't never seen an airplane engine before – still haven't actually – but I don't quite like the feeling I'm getting. She always shake this way?'

'No.'

'You happy with the crankshaft bearings?'

'It's not the crankshaft.'

Hueffer listened a little more, then removed his hand and came back to his seat.

'You started out kinda simple, didn't you? I was expecting something tougher.'

Abe looked at Mason, who looked back at Abe. 'Well?' said Mason. 'Aren't you gonna take a look?'

'Don't need to,' said Hueffer. 'My Aunt Jemmy could tell you that that engine needs its connecting-rod bolts tightened.'

Abe smiled

'It sure does.'

He threw Mason a glance. Mason grimaced, but he nodded as well.

'OK, buddy, you won the prize.'

47

It was a dark night on the Lower East Side.

A few drunks rolled by. Every now and then a car or truck. Down the block, steam curled upwards from a broken Conn Ed pipe, but no one paid it any attention. The street was quiet. Willard sat in a borrowed sedan, blinking to stay awake.

Earlier that evening, he'd called his mother from the office to let her know he was planning to visit that weekend. He'd given the times of his train, speaking slow and clear. Later on, at Grand Central, his ever reliable buddy, Greyhound-face, had been already there, lounging up against a hamburger stall, reading a racing paper, picking his yellow teeth. Willard had done everything as expected. He'd bought a ticket, bought some candy, strolled onto the platform, boarded his train. But then, instead of sitting down, Willard had run up the train, and changed his pale coat and hat for dark ones from his bag. Then he'd jumped off and hidden behind a pillar until he was able to leave the platform in the rush of disembarking passengers from the next incoming train.

He'd made his way here, unseen, unfollowed, to a place he already knew. He was parked outside the locked garage doors which might or might not belong to the Association of Orthodox Synagogues. According to the office paperwork, his precious Irish rabbis were expecting a delivery that very night – and Willard was painfully keen to see if the deliveries were any less fictitious than the organisation they served.

So he waited.

His eyelids ached to close. Sleep called. He opened the car window, first on one side only, then both. He drummed his feet. He hummed every tune he could remember. He took off his shoes and socks, so he could feel the cold metal of the pedals on his bare feet.

He thought about Rosalind. They were having sex all the time now, fantastic sex, marred only by the thick yellow condoms which he hated and she insisted on. And, though it had been slow progress, she was tipping over into love with him. He knew it. He could tell from her smile, her lips open in orgasm, the way she found his jokes funnier than before, the way she followed his lead, admired his example. Once, they'd been walking down the street, when they passed a bridal outfitters. There was a dress in the window: slim, lacy, straight. The sort of dress that would look a million dollars given the right girl. Rosalind hadn't exactly stopped to look at it, but her gaze was caught and she had checked her stride. Willard stopped to let her view it. Rosalind looked in the window for another couple of seconds, then blushed. He laughed, made some light remark, let her laugh away the tension. But the point was there. Rosalind could at least consider the possibility that she would one day marry Willard.

And Willard? He didn't rule it out either. He wasn't a great one for falling in love. He enjoyed sex and he enjoyed being adored. Of course, one day, he'd marry and when he did, he hoped it would be with a girl like Rosalind. In the meantime, her slow tumble into love was like a rosy background glow that compensated a little for all the other things in his life he didn't like.

Willard drummed his feet, yawned, fought to stay awake. It was three in the morning.

Down the street, a bakery store window lit up. Willard

pulled his shoes and socks back on, and went to bang on the bakery door, which was yanked open by a sour-looking Brooklyner. From the kitchens behind there was a press of heat, white tiled walls, white dough, and clouds of white flour rising into the bright overhead light.

Willard asked for a couple of rolls. 'Five minutes, maybe ten,' said the Brooklyn man, but instead of heading back to the clatter of ovens, the guy stayed at the counter, cracking wise and talking about the movies.

Willard was about to launch into his 'do you know who I am' spiel, when he remembered that he needed to be anonymous. The guy preferred the slapstick stuff anyhow. Buster Keaton, Charlie Chaplin, the Keystone Cops. Although Willard had once got drunk with Keaton and swum in Chaplin's swimming pool, he said nothing. And it was kind of nice. Odd but nice. Regular guy talk, man to man.

The rolls came. The Brooklyner asked if Willard wanted coffee, which he did. He ate the rolls, drank the coffee, and paid for it all with some coins he'd found rolling on the floor of his friend's car.

He resumed his post and waited some more. Day broke. The streets grew busy.

Then, just as Willard worried he'd wasted his night, it happened. At eight-fifteen sharp, a canvas-sided truck came down the street. The truck had no markings, looked neither new nor old, and had two men sitting up in the cab. Outside the garage, the truck stopped. One of the men jumped out, unlocked a padlock, and swung the double doors open. The truck drove on inside. The double doors were closed again and locked.

That was it.

As the man had pushed open the garage doors, his coat had swung open. Willard thought maybe he'd caught a glimpse of a shoulder holster. Before the doors had swung shut, Willard had driven slowly by. Inside, he'd seen a concrete yard, the truck, some fuel cans, some wooden boxes. Nothing else.

On Monday morning, he placed a call to the Association of Orthodox Synagogues.

'Hello?' The voice on the other end of the line was as Jewish as the Blarney Stone and as orthodox as a plateful of pork.

'Willard Thornton here from Powell Lambert. Some confusion in the paperwork, I'm afraid. It looks as though you won't be getting your first delivery until a week from now.'

'It's already arrived, mister. Arrived and unloaded.'

'It's arrived? That can't be right. According to my papers –'

'Forget your papers. We got the stuff. Saturday morning, no problems.'

'Really? What time? If you have an arrival time, I can check back with the transport people.'

'Jay-sus . . . Eight o'clock. Half past. How would I know? Any case, we got it. Forget about it.'

A Jewish religious association which didn't exist. A stream of deliveries which definitely did. Bugged phone calls and secret watchers. One man dead and a second man jailed.

The one thing Willard couldn't do was to forget about it.

48

Arnie Hueffer pulled his head out of the cowling, his olive skin blotted and smudged with oil.

'Done!'

Not for the first time, Abe was impressed. Hueffer had stripped, cleaned and reassembled an engine he'd never seen before in little longer than Abe would have taken himself. Hueffer turned on the ignition and let the engine build up power. He listened to her like a maestro, his fingertips delicately pressed against its metal skin. After a minute, his startling grin returned.

'Sweet,' he commented.

Abe nodded. 'Sounds good. You want to take a ride?'

'Take a ride?'

'You been up in an airplane before?'

'Motherogod, no!'

'You want to try?'

Hueffer shook his head with unnecessary force. 'Not for a million dollars. I don't like heights.'

'How d'you know? There's nothing in Brunswick higher than two storeys.'

'That's why I like Brunswick.'

'Try it. You might like it.'

'I might hate it.'

'Sure?'

'Positive.'

Abe shook his head in bafflement. 'Suit yourself.'

The aircraft in question was no longer Poll, but the new first lady of the hangar, *Havana Sue*. Sue was a converted de Havilland bomber, the DH-4. As promised, Mason had left the choice up to Abe, and – after the long and exquisite pain of choosing – he'd opted for the plane he'd first thought of. There were bigger planes on the market, but no better ones.

And Abe was pleased for a wider reason. The team was beginning to come together. Hueffer was a first-class mechanic, but not only that. He was also a man who'd lost his best friend, a fisherman, in an argument out at sea. A boat belonging to some bootleggers had snared this man's nets. He yelled at them. They yelled at him. He yelled some more. Then they shot him five times in the head at close range. Hueffer didn't just dislike mobsters, he hated them.

Abe had the plane. He had the mechanic. He had Bob, Mason's trust.

Only one thing bothered him. Mason wanted his boats tracked and guarded from Havana all the way to Marion. That was more than one man could do on his own. Abe needed help not only on the ground, but in the air as well.

Reluctantly, Mason had agreed to let Abe find another pilot. That, in itself, should be simple. At four hundred bucks a week, better than twenty grand a year, Abe could have filled a flying vacancy a hundred times over. But it wasn't that simple. Abe needed a first-class pilot. He needed someone who could take Mason's money but still be loyal to Abe. And Abe was a realist. He knew that the flying was dangerous and the Marion mob more dangerous still. So, on top of his other requirements, Abe added one more. He needed a man without family, without ties.

Abe had drawn up a list of all the pilots whose flying he trusted. One by one, he went through his list. Without success. Most of the guys had families. Those who didn't were over-fond of liquor, girls or gambling. One by one, Abe crossed off every name. Every name bar one.

And Abe was just thinking about that one last improbable name, when he heard it.

An engine whine pushing down against the wind. A low note, but clear, soon followed by the plane itself. The stubby little shape. The curled-up power. The perfect beautiful streamlined monster. And in its cockpit, helmeted and goggled, sat a slim boyish confident figure – the last pilot left on Abe's list.

49

Willard replaced the phone and stood up. He felt ridiculously nervous. He ran his hands over his smoothly parted hair, checked his collar, his already straight tie. Annie Hooper spotted his anxiety and came over.

'Is there a problem?'

'Oh no, of course not. Just Powell, you know.' He said the last bit like he didn't give a damn about Powell.

'He wants you to see him?'

'Yes. Right away, it seems.'

'What about?'

'No idea. It wouldn't be very like him to bother telling me.'

'No.' Annie put her hands to his tie as though it needed adjustment, which it didn't. She let the backs of her hands rest against his chest as she fiddled with the knot. 'You'll be fine.'

Willard let her fiddle. Willard realised with sudden pleasure that his almost automatic showing off had achieved its objective. Without particularly wanting to, he had won Annie's tender heart. He smiled his movie-star smile and put his hand on her arm.

'Oh, it's all mouth with Powell. I'd tell him what I think of him, except for the damn loan.'

Annie looked away and moved her arm. 'Good luck anyway.'

Feeling foolishly buoyed by his triumph, Willard bounded up the stairs to Powell's office.

'Thornton! Excellent! Come in. Listen, how long have you been with us now?'

'Getting on for five months, sir.'

'Hell, as long as that? I haven't been looking after you properly. Your papa will probably want to kill me.'

A bottle of French champagne sat openly in a bucket of ice. Powell grabbed the bottle and began tearing at the foil and the wire cage. Willard stared at the bottle.

'Is there something to celebrate, sir? My move into investments perhaps?'

'Why d'we need a reason? I just wanted to offer a drink to the son of one of my pals. Here.'

Powell had torn the wire off the bottle and jammed a glass into Willard's hand. He ripped the cork out of the bottle and held the bottle over Willard's glass, not caring that the champagne splurged out everywhere, over-filling the glass, pouring down onto the expensive carpet and Willard's hand-made shoes. Willard reflected, not for the first time, that there was something coarse in everything Powell was or did. Coarse and brutal. The wire cage from the bottle lay on the floor in the middle of the champagne spill. Powell let it lie there and just trampled it underfoot, as though unaware that the carpet was a pure wool, deep pile affair that probably came in at ten bucks the square yard.

'How you getting on downstairs? Ronson looking after you? McVeigh? Claverty?'

'Yes, indeed. Thank you. I've been made most welcome.'

'Come on, Thornton, you don't have to talk like you've got a stick up your ass. Really, how are you getting on?'

'Fine, honestly. A lot of hard work, of course, only . . .'

'Yeah? Only what?'

'Well, sir, I don't mind the hard work.' Willard's voice jerked petulantly as he spoke. As a matter of fact, though the hard work itself was OK, he did mind the fact that there seemed to be a conspiracy which passed the hardest files to him. He was sure now that his workload was the highest in the group's, a fact he resented bitterly. But he steadied his voice as he continued. 'What concerns me is my financial obligation to you. When you introduced me to the bank, you mentioned that if I were to repay the loan, it would be through my ability to earn exceptional returns on the bank's money. I'd like to be given a chance, sir. I'm keen to start.'

Keen to start, keen to pay off the loan, keen to watch the whole of Powell Lambert sink into the ocean.

'Maybe you have started, had you thought of that?'

'Of course in a way I have, and every man has to start somewhere, naturally, only . . .'

Powell interrupted, refilling Willard's glass until it brimmed over.

'Only, horseshit, Thornton. Tell me, if you were going to invest some money, where would you invest it? Not a motion picture, I hope?'

Willard's chin jerked upwards automatically at the jibe. 'No sir. I believe the electrical traction industry is of interest. I believe there are opportunities on the stock market that deserve further research. I'd be very happy to compile a report and –'

'Electrical traction? That a fancy name for streetcars?'

'Yes sir.'

'Tell me, what do you know about the streetcar industry that nobody else in the world knows?'

'I beg your pardon? Nothing. But the purpose of my research would be –'

'Don't waste your time!' Powell spoke with such aggression that Willard was jolted. Powell had a cigar in his hand. He looked around for his silver cigar cutter, couldn't find it, and bit the end off instead. He rolled the bitten tobacco into a ball and threw it away. 'The stock market is a crap shoot where half the players have loaded dice. Are your dice loaded, Thornton?'

'No, sir, I should hope not.'

'Then don't waste your time. Yours or mine.'

Willard paled with anger. 'I owe you two hundred thousand dollars, sir. It was my understanding that I should get a chance to repay it.'

'Right.'

Powell's face, though smiling, had been hard and unpleasant. At this point, and for no obvious reason, it softened. His grin widened, extending for the first time to his eyes.

'You know, Thornton, last year your father made more money from guns and bombs than he did in either nineteen seventeen or nineteen eighteen, during the bloodiest war in human history.'

'I believe he did, yes.'

'Money. He has the gift. More than anyone I know, your father has the gift.'

'He works hard for his success. He deserves it.'

Powell rose from his seat and gave Willard's shoulder a couple of good-natured thumps. 'He does indeed. And if you have the gift, you'll make money too. Plenty of it. Enough for the loan. Enough for us. Enough for you. And you have your chance, Thornton, you have it now.'

Willard would have answered, but Powell's expression told him not to bother. Powell puffed at his cigar with one hand, drank champagne rapidly with the other, kept up a stream of conversation in between. Willard drank less than Powell, but a second bottle soon appeared and he grew light-headed all the same.

'I'm surprised you do this,' he commented.

'Do what?'

'The champagne. You're not worried about Volstead?'

'Yah!' Powell made a gesture of contempt. 'This was all in our cellar before Prohibition. No rule against drinking up. Me, I'm the driest of the dries. But you got to understand. Volstead was all about protecting the American working man. He was never against hospitality. He was never against a man giving a good time to his pals. That's all we're doing. You think that's wrong?'

'No, I guess . . .'

They drank more. Willard disliked Powell and wanted to get away. He put his glass down and muttered about returning to work.

'Huh? What's that?' Powell had a habit of simply not hearing things when he wasn't in the mood. 'Oh, and that reminds me, I've got a gift for you.'

'A gift?'

'A gift.' Powell yelled through the door to his secretary, who came in, pushing a little trolley of the sort that restaurants use to display their puddings. Just beyond the door, there was a short man in a dark suit. The man was standing, looking in through Powell's door as it opened, staring straight at Willard. Willard couldn't help but stare back. The man was short, maybe five-foot-six, but with a compact and powerful upper body that gave him the look of someone larger. The man's face was intent, a little ugly, but somehow powerful, authoritative. The man was examining Willard; seemed to have come in order to look at him. Willard turned away feeling uncomfortable, then the secretary left and closed the door. Willard turned his attention to the trolley, which was laden with beige files tied off with pale green tape.

'A gift,' repeated Powell. 'You like it?'

'Files? That's the gift?'

'Go on. Take a look. You'll like it.' Powell was almost hopping with glee. Champagne slopped over the side of the glass and fell foaming onto the carpet.

Willard looked.

There were around forty files on the trolley. The pale green ribbons that bound them indicated they were completed transactions – archive files. White cards gummed to the front of each file marked their contents. Each card

225

identified the transaction by buyer, seller and completion date. For a second, Willard looked blankly at the stack.

Then it clicked, and his belly dropped away in sudden terror. *The sellers.* There were around forty transactions on the trolley, but only four different sellers: the same four companies whose documents had been concealed by Arthur Martin behind the cupboard in Willard's apartment. Willard staggered back, his face pale. Powell's mouth was champing with delight, but his eyes were cold.

'You like it? Go on. Tell me. You must be pleased, right? The archivist tells me you're very interested in these clients of ours, but haven't yet had a chance to look at these files.'

Willard shrank away. 'It's OK. It's nothing. I just wanted to follow something up. I don't need all this. Honestly, I . . .'

He fell silent, choked by a rising tide of nausea. *Arthur Martin had been killed for the sake of just four of these files.* What in hell's name did Powell mean by shoving forty of them at him? It felt like some coded Mafia communication. Willard didn't understand the code, but whatever it meant, it could hardly be a healthy sign. His face was numb. He put down his glass, backed away, went almost running down the hall.

50

Pen's plane touched down. Abe went to greet it. The thing about a coastal airfield is that it's nearly always windy: the wind pulling off the ocean during the day, blowing out from land at night. The wind today wasn't strong, but it made itself felt. It scuffed at the sand, dragged at the palms, tugged and snapped at clothing.

Abe – in shirtsleeves only, no coat or tie – met Pen, who discarded her heavy jacket to reveal a plain white shirt beneath.

They said hi, said nothing about the way he'd returned her plane, said nothing about the pretty pink roses which Abe had so brutally decapitated. Then Pen, in that direct way of hers, made her request. She wanted a job flying the mails. He thought about it for a second, maybe less.

'No.'

'Why not?'

'I know you can fly, but this is different. There's the ocean for one thing.'

'I've flown the ocean plenty.'

'Yeah, but twice a day, every day? It won't be long before we have a forced landing.'

'So? You carry a raft, right? A flare pistol? Food?'

'Then there's the weather. These tropical storms can kick up bad, as foul as I've known it. And I used to fly up near the Canadian border, with blizzards coming over the mountains and no place safe to land.'

'You aim to fly the storms or avoid them?'

'Avoid them.'

'So.'

Pen let a long pause open between them. It was quiet, except for the buzz of distant traffic and the sound of the seabreeze scraping its salt off on the coconut palms. Abe felt jerked around by his feelings.

Mostly he didn't want her. Women on an airfield were like a vapour lock in the fuel pipe: unpredictable at best, dangerous at worst. The not wanting part had made him curt, almost rude in his answers just now.

And yet, and yet . . . Pen wasn't like other women. Her flying was excellent. The landing she'd made that first time had been nerveless and impeccably accurate. Nor did she seem to carry with her that storm of emotional complexity that Abe associated with other women he'd known. And then again, there was Abe's new sense of the darker side of his life: the shadows of loneliness that had come to seem as spacious and unlimited as the sky itself.

So he didn't know what to say. He just literally stood there, scratching his scalp, lost for words.

She pursued him. 'Listen, I know I'm a woman and a woman isn't supposed to like flying airplanes. But I must have been put together wrong. I do like flying them. More than anything else. I've flown a few competitions, but there aren't many left which'll take me now. And in any case, pylon racing is just a type of stunting. I want to fly for a serious purpose. I want to because I'd like to teach the world something about women and planes. Is that wrong?'

'No.'

'And you've got a mail route. You must need help. I can provide my own plane. I'd live in town, not here on the airfield. I don't need payment. If you want, we can try it out for a while. If the arrangement works, we'll go ahead. If it doesn't, it doesn't.'

She finished speaking and she looked him full in the face

228

before dropping her eyes. Her eyes were as clear a blue as Abe's own, and once again he got a sudden, disconcerting sense of the person lying behind them: unfussy, direct, honest, straight.

'Pen, when I flew your plane back to your place outside of Charleston, I'd been planning to stop off and say hello. But then I saw the place you came from. And I came over all yellow. I ran home without saying hi. And the reason I'm telling you this is because I can't believe that your folks are going to be too happy with their little girl serving as a mail pilot.'

'So?'

'I don't want to cause trouble.'

'My mother and father hate the idea of me flying. But I fly anyway. And in any case, I don't see how that's any of your business.'

Abe let out a long breath. Even for a Kentucky-born man like himself, there was something disconcerting in the full strength of the Florida sun. There was something bright, dazzling in the situation: the hot sun, the tugging breeze, Pen's shirt flapping and snapping in the wind.

'Heck,' he said, feeling dizzy, making a decision in the worst way of all, unthought-out, unclear, in a daze. 'Look, you're right. Why not? Only one thing. Can you keep a secret?'

She didn't make any direct answer, but when he turned and walked towards the hangar, she followed. And when he led her to a gloomy corner and pulled away the sheet which covered that week's haul of booze, she gasped in amazement. For about three seconds, she stared at the whole illegal pile, then turned away, shocked.

'I guess flying the mail doesn't pay a lot.'

'I fly it for free. This is what brings in the money.'

'That's why no passengers, no advertising.'

'Right.'

'I'm sorry, I've been very stupid. I'd never really thought about the financial aspect of things.'

'The job's yours, if you want it.'

Pen continued to back away. The light in the hangar was always gloomy, and against the brilliant sunshine flooding the doorway, all Abe could see was her silhouette, tall as his own, but graceful, the way only a woman can be graceful.

'In answer to your question, yes, I can keep a secret. I won't tell anyone about this and I guess I hope no one finds out. But there's more of a difference between us than I'd thought. I don't know that I think too much of Prohibition, but I do know that the constitution isn't there to be made a fool of. Sorry, Captain. Goodbye.'

She turned on her heel and left, back to the brilliant sunshine and dizzying wind.

Abe caught sight of Arnie Hueffer. The mechanic's olive face was split by a grin wide enough to park a plane in. Abe began to say something, but couldn't. He realised he was grinning like an imbecile too. He felt the same way: part happy, part imbecile. There was a starburst of sunshine expanding in his belly as though the best thing in the world was just about to happen. He went skipping out of the hangar after Pen.

'Hey, Pen, hey there! Wait up!'

Her boot-heels, crunching across the sandy grass, hesitated, stopped and turned. She looked back at Abe, the wind still tugging at the dazzling brightness of her shirt.

'Yes, Captain?'

51

Willard burst out of Powell's office, down the hall, past the elevator bank to the firestairs. Taking the stairs three at a time, he completed each flight down in four bounds: leap, leap, leap, leap-and-turn. In just two and a quarter minutes, he arrived on the ground floor, and was running outside onto Wall Street, downhill, around the corner and away.

'*You like it? Go on. Tell me. You like it?*'

Powell's sarcastic question drilled in his head. Arthur Martin had stolen four files and had been killed for it. Today, over champagne and smiles, Ted Powell had thrust a further forty at Willard. What in hell's name was going on?

Willard walked, without plan, without direction, without purpose. He just walked and let the city fold itself around him, smelling of fried food, car exhausts, sea wind, coffee, steam, rain, gasoline.

And in the midst of the city, he did something he hadn't done before. He held up his life and looked at it, as though from a distance, as though he were an art gallery connoisseur looking at an exhibition by an unknown artist. And he saw for the first time various truths that he'd either never known, or sought to avoid knowing.

His movie, for one thing. *Heaven's Beloved* hadn't just been bad, it had been awful. And it had been awful because of him. He hadn't been good enough as writer, director, or (especially) producer. He hadn't even been good enough as an actor. Powell had been right: the picture had been a stinker.

For another thing, he saw that his father had been right about something. He saw that his relationship to money had been skewed, was lopsided. He could spend money like a millionaire, but only now at Powell Lambert had he come remotely close to earning it. What was it his father had said to him? *'The Firm is a very demanding organism. It turns a profit because I compel it to turn a profit. Making money is never just a question of holding your hat out.'* Willard saw that now. He saw how hard it was to make money. If men like Ted Powell and Willard's own father succeeded better than their fellow men, it was because they had a rare and precious gift – a gift that was, in Willard's case, absolutely unproven.

And finally he saw one last thing. Or rather, it was as though he'd always seen it and never acknowledged it. The feeling wasn't one of discovery but of unburying. The insight was this. That the Firm was everything. Here and now, in his place of danger, poverty and over-work, Willard saw the Firm at its true worth. A beautiful complex organism which produced wealth, status and security in a world terribly short of all those commodities. Willard felt a burning eagerness to renew his life, to begin work at the Firm, learning steadily under his father's relentless eye.

And all the time he walked. By eight that evening, he'd been wandering for almost five hours. His feet were sore. A light rain had been blowing and he had left the office hatless and coatless.

He looked around him, so distracted that he had hardly any idea where he was. He found himself in a poor part of town: East Twenty-Second and First. There were no cabs on the street, not even many cars. A vague air of poverty and menace hung like steam in the dirty alleyways, the badly lit sidewalks. He shivered, suddenly cold. He was about to strike out for Fifth Avenue and the certainty of finding a cab, when he suddenly noticed that his surroundings were familiar.

He didn't understand why – then did. Annie Hooper lived near here. He knew this because, in the days before Rosalind, he'd dropped her home after boozy nights out with Ronson and Claverty. His feet led him to her apartment block – a tenement rich with the smell of fried food and boiled laundry.

He hesitated. He had no reason to be here. But an impulse he couldn't define carried him up the cracked concrete steps to the door. He rang her bell. He shivered again, thought about leaving, but was too late. The door opened and there – startled and out of breath – was Annie.

'Willard? Is that . . .? Come in! You're soaked.'

'Annie, you are sweet. I left my coat somewhere. I couldn't find a cab. Good job you were in.'

'Yes, isn't it? What on earth . . .?'

'Could I come up? Just until the rain passes.'

'Of course.'

They went up. The stairs and corridors smelled of detergent and the bare electric bulbs were spaced wide apart by a stingy apartment manager. Annie let Willard into her apartment.

'I'm sorry. It's not exactly . . .'

She didn't finish, but her meaning was obvious. She didn't earn much and, from what little she did, she sent money to her parents in Kansas. There was enough left over for one small apartment: a bedroom which Willard didn't see, a tiny kitchen, a sitting room just eight foot wide with an almost twelve-foot ceiling. A wide damp patch on the wall had been inadequately painted over and the room smelled strongly of old damp and new paint.

Willard sat on the only couch. There was one other chair, also a table, a radio, and (to their shared embarrassment) a washing rack with Annie's clothes spread out on it. She cleaned them away in a sudden rush, then turned to him,

233

blushing. The blush set him at his ease. He relaxed and pulled off his wet jacket.

'Do you mind?'

'No, of course not.'

'Sorry, I should have phoned or something, only . . .'

'Oh, don't worry. Sorry about the smell. They've just repainted.'

'The smell's all right . . . You don't maybe have a drop of coffee in that kitchen of yours?'

'Yes, yes, good idea, of course.'

Annie went into the kitchen to make coffee. Willard hung on the door post – the kitchen was far too small for two – and watched. Annie made the coffee, poured two cups, then, with a quick smile, opened a cupboard door and produced a flat pint-bottle of whiskey. She held it up, the fine threads of her eyebrows raised enquiringly.

Willard nodded. 'You bet.'

Annie added the drink to their coffees, a big glug for him, a token one for her.

'Was it all right with Powell? You took off very suddenly afterwards.'

Willard rubbed his face. 'God, he's a brute, isn't he? Not gentlemanlike in the slightest. I wanted to punch him, Annie, I swear to you.'

'Oh good, I was so worried. You just went up, then never came back. I couldn't help thinking about poor Arthur and poor old Charlie and . . . Oh Willard, I am sorry, I'm probably being silly.'

She was crying.

Mostly Willard thought girls made themselves look worse by crying. It messed up their eyes, their skin, the proportions of their face. But Annie was different. Maybe because it wasn't beauty she had, it was prettiness. Her fine brown hair, her delicate complexion, her scattering of freckles, and timid, over-expressive lips – they all somehow benefited from tears. Willard did the only thing he could do. He pulled her towards him, let her nestle against his chest, and let her cry.

'I'm sorry, I'm being silly, I'm sorry.'

It was the signal for her to pull away. It was the signal for Willard to let her. But she didn't move and neither did he. He just held her, by the window, near the dirty yellow light from the street, near the thin curtains and the damp walls. They stood in silence, listening to the rain.

PART THREE

Thrust

Sir George Cayley might have worked out what an airplane would look like, but he'd never got further than building a glider. Where would the power come from? In Sir George's day, there were two main sources of power: horses and steam engines. Horses mostly didn't fly. Steam engines were so huge and heavy, you could wrench your back just looking at them.

But that didn't stop folk trying. In 1843, William Henson used Cayley's research to build his Aerial Steam Carriage. The carriage looked in most respects like a modern airplane. In layout, the carriage had a fuselage slung below a monoplane wing. It had a movable tail unit, an undercarriage, a pair of wing-mounted propellers. It was, in short, an airplane. But it didn't fly and couldn't. Steam engines were too heavy, and there was nothing else around.

Throughout the nineteenth century, experiments continued. The first powered flight in history came about thanks to a twenty-one-year-old Frenchman, Alphonse Penaud. The aircraft in question had a wingspan of eighteen inches. Its propeller was a pair of feathers and the engine was a rubber band. On its first flight, the model plane flew a hundred and thirty feet in eleven seconds. The year was 1871.

Meantime, Cayley's gliders were developed and improved. Stronger, lighter steam engines were built. Airplanes were constructed that could just about haul themselves from the ground. But nothing yet looked likely to crack the secret of flight.

The invention of the internal combustion engine changed all that. The petrol engine offered more horsepower for less weight. For the first time in history, thrust, the second ingredient of flight, was available on tap.

But there was no use lifting something into the air at speed, for the machine only to spin out of control and smash up. Everything now depended on the third ingredient of flight: how to control the aircraft in the air.

Across the industrialised world, in England and Germany, France and America, the race was on.

52

The man wore a dark city suit, heavy and good quality, a navy silk tie, clean shirt, good shoes. He was also young, had hair the colour of dark oak and a chin you could use for the backboard of a basketball hoop. He jabbed himself twice in the chest.

'Now I don't know how much you folks know about me and what I do, but I figured I oughta give myself a little bit of an introduction. My name's Jim Bosse. I'm a Senior Investigator with the Special Investigations Unit of the Internal Revenue Service. That's a bit of a mouthful, but perhaps you'll understand me better if I tell you I'm a policeman, dedicated to the investigation of tax fraud against the Government of the United States. Our unit is small and it's new. But good. And keen. And clean. Absolutely clean. We're uncorrupted and uncorruptable.'

He stopped, then laughed. He laughed easily and when he did so, he looked more like an easy-going farmboy than a taxman. But though his eyes didn't exactly contradict the picture, they certainly added to it. Easy-going he might be, but if so he was also determined, also implacable.

Pen looked around to sense her companions' reactions. She was out here – a creek-bed running by a dilapidated farmhouse in mid-Georgia, nine miles from the nearest buggy stop – with Abe and Hennessey, whom she was meeting for the first time. She felt strange being here like this. Strange to be in the presence of men who apparently couldn't care less about her gender, only about her competence. Strange to be here in secret. Stranger still to be in the midst of a real conspiracy, a conspiracy which would kill her if it ever leaked. But neither Abe nor Hennessey showed any reaction to Bosse's words. Was it because, as men, they were in some way accustomed to situations like this? Or was it that they felt as much as she did, but simply didn't show it?

Bosse continued to speak.

'Now, I'm sorry to drag y'all out here. But I figured the quieter the better, right? And the folks that own this place,' he nodded towards the creaking, dilapidated farm, 'are close relatives of a person I trust. They won't gossip, won't talk.

'Now three or four weeks back I got a call from Captain Rockwell here. He told me what he was up to, asked if I was interested in helping. I was. Not just interested, neither. I'd say I was as eager as a gundog in a duck farm. That applies to me. It applies to one, maybe two of my colleagues. And that's it. No one else knows. No one else will until we're ready to move. Captain Rockwell has asked for the highest possible level of secrecy, and you fellers – and you too, ma'am – are gonna get it. You've got the guts to go bear-hunting, I'm gonna honour that.'

Bosse stopped, and let the silence step in. Pen glanced at Abe, who was stretched out against a fallen tree trunk, his feet warming in the sun, his face in the shade. He looked comfortable, but impassive. She could read literally nothing in his expression.

'Now it's probably just as well to give you folks a history lesson. A coupla years back, we noticed a guy over in South Carolina who hadn't declared his income for the purposes of income tax. Guy name of Sullivan. We knew Sullivan made plenty of money and he sure hadn't told us about it. Way we saw it, that was a crime.'

'Right,' said Pen. 'Of course.'

240

He grinned at her. 'Of course. Only Sullivan was a boot-legger. Was. Is. That's how he makes his money.'

'Oh!'

'But the law says you pay tax on your income. We don't care how he makes his money, we just care he pays us tax on it.'

'But if he declares his income, isn't that just like admitting his crimes? Doesn't he have a Fifth Amendment right not to incriminate himself?' Pen spoke slowly, thinking hard.

Bosse chuckled. 'That's what he says too, ma'am. That's exactly the case his lawyers have put up. Only we say, phooey. He doesn't have to tell us how he made his dough, he just has to say how much, then pay us tax on it. We don't care if he makes his money selling booze or buttons.'

'The case has gone to court?'

'Not just once. Twice. The first court, the South Carolina District Court, found for us. We were right, Sullivan was wrong. So he appealed.'

'And?'

'Case went up a level, to the Circuit Court of Appeal, Fourth Circuit.'

'And?'

'Sullivan won, so we appealed.'

'And?'

'That's as far as we've got. The Supreme Court hears the case next year, April. We're gonna win.'

'How can you know that? You've already lost one decision. Are you telling me this whole conspiracy depends on –?' Pen stopped. She was stopped by the twinkle in Bosse's eye, by Abe's calm composure to her right. She realised in a flash that Abe wouldn't have pinned his whole plan of action on a fifty-fifty court decision; that Bosse himself would hardly be likely to jump the gun. 'What are you saying? You've spoken with the Supreme Court already? You've had indications from them?'

'Let's just say we're very confident that the highest court in the land will get things right. The law's the law, after all. We don't want no one to incriminate themselves. We just want our tax.'

Pen let the taxman's confidence sink in. The idea was a crazy one, of course, but anyone who still cared about America could see that organised crime was running rampant. Conventional law enforcement had almost totally failed. Despite the unrestrained homicide spree which had guzzled the city of Chicago, for instance, not one single gangster had been successfully prosecuted for murder. If the forces of law and order were to succeed, completely new approaches would need to be found. Prosecutions for tax evasion sounded unlikely but, in a way, the more unlikely the better.

Pen realised that everyone was looking at her: Abe, Hennessey, Bosse. It was as though she was being asked to give a verdict on the plan that had brought them together. She nodded slowly.

'It's good,' she said. 'I like it.'

Bosse grinned like a kid at Christmas. 'Great. I knew you'd love it. OK. Next up. What we plan to do. How we plan to do it. First off, the aim is to gather enough evidence to prosecute all the key players in Marion for tax evasion. That's only the start of course. As soon as everyone sees that the whole organisation is gonna fold, we're gonna start offering deals. Time off in return for confessions. That way we'll start to rake in evidence for the conventional type prosecutions. Liquor offences, assaults, racketeering, homicide. We want a lot of people behind bars for a long time. That's the aim.

'To do all that we need evidence. Hard evidence. Material we can use in court. Original documents. Copies of documents as long as the copies are witnessed and preferably notarised. Witness statements. Photographs. All that type of thing. Everyone follow me?'

242

The tone was getting serious now. Everyone was infected. Pen nodded gravely. So did Abe. So did Hennessey.

'Good. How you get those things is kinda up to you. If you need extra resources, we can supply them. We can supply people to run wire taps. We can supply notaries. I guarantee you that everyone we produce will come straight outa my department. Uncorrupted and uncorruptable. That's the deal.'

Everyone nodded again, but more slowly this time. Bosse's offer was appropriate, of course, but it didn't necessarily amount to a lot. Marion was so remote, so back-of-beyond, that a single stranger would be instantly noticed. This case wasn't going to be about manpower, it would be about guile and invisibility.

Then Abe spoke for the first time. He cleared his throat before speaking, but even then his voice came over hoarse.

'The evidence, Jim. What d'you figure you'll need?'

'We been thinking hard about that, Captain. Everything we need's in a list right here.'

He took an envelope from his pocket, handed it over. The sunshine, filtering through the dappled willow shade, struck the envelope and made it seem implausibly bright and white against the dusty world beyond. Abe took the envelope, opened it, and read slowly. When he was done, he folded the last sheet and put them all back in the envelope. He said nothing.

'Well?' said Bosse. 'What d'you reckon?'

'It's a lot, Jim. It's one heck of a lot you're asking.'

'It is. But you folks are hunting bear. You'd better shoot to kill.'

The taxman was right. Prosecuting the Marion gangsters was dangerous. Prosecuting them without convicting them would be lethal. For a few moments, silence reigned, so absolute that a single cricket chirping near Pen's foot was almost raucous in its intensity.

'You figure you can do it?' asked Bosse.

Abe put the envelope in his pocket. He wasn't smiling, wasn't nodding, wasn't anything.

'I don't know. We'll just have to see.'

53

In July 1918, Willard was halfway through a patrol over German territory when he experienced a small problem with his starboard ailerons. The plane was entirely flyable, but it was a rule of Rockwell's to pull back any plane that wasn't in perfect condition. So, dipping his wings in apology to the formation leader, Willard pulled around and headed for home.

He came close enough to his aerodrome to see its long oval of sun-bleached grass, pale against the surrounding farmland. But, before putting in to land, he saw something else: a clumsy German observation plane, a two-seater Albatross of a 1917 vintage, perhaps even a relic from 1916; fat and easy prey for Willard's modern Spad.

There followed a short but furious chase. But the battle had only one likely outcome. Willard outsped and out-manoeuvred the enemy plane. He locked his nose onto the enemy's tail and pulled his trigger.

Nothing happened. Aside from a dull click, nothing happened. The gun had jammed. Instinctively, Willard pulled out his jam-hammer to knock at the gun barrel. The instinct was an obvious one, but in this instance nearly lethal. The Albatross was close enough to see everything. The jammed gun, the defenceless plane. The German did what any pilot would have done. He pulled his Albatross around in a long loop and made straight for Willard, intending to fire into him at point-blank range. It was the worst moment of Willard's aerial career.

The worst and also the best.

Because Willard cleared his gun with the first blow of his hammer. He was so surprised he sat back in his seat, shocked at his sudden brilliant luck. He waited for the Albatross to get in range, then sent a long three-second burst of bullets straight into the machine's nose. The Albatross folded into a mass of flame. Willard could still remember pulling back hard on the stick to pass above the burning aircraft, feeling the scorch of air and the sudden uprush of black smoke.

And the incident had taught him something. That luck and unluck can be hard to tell apart. That from time to time, disaster is the closest possible thing to victory.

And perhaps it was like that now.

The more Willard thought about it, the more he felt that, far from implying danger, Powell's Mafia-style communication implied something else – maybe something good.

Here was the first point. Whatever it was that had sent Arthur Martin to the grave and Charlie Hughes to jail, the secret reached all the way to Ted Powell.

Here was the second point. Powell had no compunction about murder. If Powell wanted to have Willard murdered, he'd do so without a second thought.

And that led to the good part. Powell didn't want Willard dead. What's more, his gift of the files suggested he didn't even care if Willard succeeded in busting Powell Lambert's secret. He might care a lot about what Willard did with that information, but the information itself was not forbidden.

So Willard acted.

First he went back to the grim state penitentiary where Charlie Hughes was held. Hughes was thinner now. His jaunty carelessness had been replaced by something older, unhappier, more broken.

'Oh, Will-o! Hey there. Gosh, thanks.'

Willard shoved a cake across the steel table. Willard

hadn't really thought about what to bring and the prison guards had had a merry time probing the cake with a screwdriver to check there was nothing concealed within. They'd only stopped once the entire cake had been mashed to a pulp. There was nothing left now but a mass of broken crumbs and browning marzipan.

Willard tried beginning with the usual small talk. Only what the hell do you talk about with a convict? How's the food? Worse than shit. How's the view? Kinda samey. How's the company? Great. Varied. Fun. A little bit violent, to be sure. A wee bit inclined to see the little guy with the glasses as the one to pick on, the one it's fun to punch hard in the stomach for no reason – but, hey, it's new. You live and learn. Hughes tried to grin, but looked as if he was about to cry.

Willard cut things short.

'Listen, Charlie, I came to ask you something.'

'Sure, Will-o. Anything.'

'That day outside the library, when I broke things up between you and McVeigh, I assumed that he was threatening you. Intimidating you.'

Hughes put his hand to his face, as though remembering the past was difficult for him. 'No, not Leo. It was sort of funny that. We laughed about it afterwards.'

'But somebody was threatening you. You already had a hint of . . . of all of this.'

'Not Leo. He was . . . he was protective. He tried to warn you. He thought maybe you took it the wrong way. He can be kind of . . . I don't know . . . heavy with things.'

He can look like a thick-as-shit footballing ape, thought Willard, without quite saying so.

'Then who? I need to know, Charlie.'

Again that gesture. That hand to the face. That look as though the past was a distant country, half forgotten.

Hughes shook his head. 'I can't say. I'm out of it now. I'm sorry.'

But Willard had enough. There were two camps in the trade finance group. There was the Ronson-Claverty axis. And there had been the McVeigh-Hughes axis. If McVeigh wasn't connected with the violence done to Arthur Martin and Charlie Hughes, then Ronson almost certainly was. Willard felt like laughing at his own stupidity.

'Just one last thing, Charlie. The twentieth floor. A part of it is closed off. Do you know why?'

'The twentieth floor?' The little man's eyes expanded as though he was having trouble remembering a world more extensive than a few square yards of concrete, a few square feet of bars. 'The twentieth floor?'

'Yes. It probably doesn't matter. Ted Powell told me it contained lifting machinery to drive the elevators. Only it doesn't. The elevators run all the way to the twenty-fourth and the lifting machinery is operated from the basement. Just a small point, but I went down there to check. I got the maintenance janitor to show me around.'

'You did? Gee. I guess I'd always thought the lifting machinery must be up above. I guess I hadn't thought about it much. The basement. Really!'

Hughes' blank little face plainly had no idea what Willard was talking about. If anything his air of desolate surprise had intensified. Willard concluded that Hughes knew nothing of the twentieth-floor mystery. It was possible that Powell himself had been confused – only Willard doubted it. He doubted that Ted Powell was confused by anything much at all.

He took his leave from Charlie Hughes and went back to work. He had got into the habit of lingering by Annie's desk at around the time she was due to distribute her hated manila files. And one day he got lucky. Of Arthur Martin's four sellers, the largest and busiest was the Canadian company, Northern Furs and Hides. Every few weeks, another shipment of animal pelts came down from the frozen north. However regular the transactions seemed,

Arthur Martin had been suspicious and Willard was determined to find out why. He slipped the file from the stack.

'Bits of dead animal,' he commented. 'Charming.'

'Which one?' said Annie, in her businesslike voice. 'Northern Furs? That's for Iggy, actually.'

Willard undid the tape and looked inside the file. 'Ha! Not just any old dead animal. There's mink here, Annie. Arctic fox. Ermine. What do you fancy?'

'Oh, don't be silly. Anyway, like I say, Iggy –'

'You want your mink from Iggy, not me? I think not. I shall work on this file and, if I possibly can, I shall extract a mink coat for you as my commission.'

And as Willard took the file, he heard Powell's words again, stronger than ever before. '*You have your chance, Thornton, you have it now.*'

54

Abe lost height, until he was skimming just fifty feet over the ocean waves. He throttled down, so his speed was cruising only five or ten miles an hour above stalling speed. The men on the bridge of the ship, the Cuban-flagged SS *Carmen*, were gathered in a tight knot, watching the fly-by.

Abe frowned a little. He needed to communicate directly with the ship's captain. The cluster of men on the bridge made it impossible to tell who was who. But never mind. This was a new procedure; new ships, new lookout system, new codes. They'd learn. Abe unfastened a paddle from its position tied down to the cockpit wall. The paddle was about the size of a tennis racket and had two sides, one green, one red. Abe showed the green side to the group on the bridge, code for All Clear. There was jostling on the bridge, some clapping, some waving, a couple of raised thumbs. They were meant to show an answering signal, a white flag indicating message received, but never mind; things would improve.

Abe flew back to the coast, his DH plane, *Havana Sue*, easily outstripping the slow booze-laden freighter. Abe had already checked out the Okefenokee river, its twisting channels, the sandbanks and the mangroves. The river was clear of the Coastguard; so was the sea beyond; so was the coast north and south for forty miles. But Abe stayed alert. He continued to fly guard as the freighter chugged towards the shore, twisted up the sluggish green Okefenokee, then moored alongside Marion's dirty concrete quay. A dockside crane sprang into action. Pallet-loads of booze began to sway up from the hold.

Up above, Abe let Sue laze around on the thermal updrafts, spiralling like a bird of prey. He loved his new aircraft, which was a pilot's dream, the perfect combination of strength and responsiveness. Even now, as he worked, part of his mind was singing like a bird, with the de Havilland's thumping music providing orchestra and chorus.

But another part of his mind – the more active part – was engaged in an altogether different activity: one that Bob Mason didn't know about and wouldn't have liked much if he had.

Beneath the fuselage was a movable panel about five inches square, stamped OIL VENT DO NOT OBSTRUCT. But the panel wasn't a vent and it had nothing to do with oil. The door of the panel was opened via a lever in the cockpit. Behind the little door was a lens. Behind the lens was a Kodak camera. The first shot on each roll of film was always the same: the front page of the local newspaper. Every other shot was taken by Abe in flight over Marion. He photographed the freighter, the booze, the quayside, the loading of the booze into the railcars.

The first item on Bosse's list of requests for evidence had been the simplest: '*Evidence of alcohol importation activity; dates; quantities, types of liquor; method of importation.*'

When each roll of film was finished, Abe extracted it from the camera, wrapped it in cotton wadding and dropped it in Hennessey's backyard. When Hennessey made his next trip into Brunswick, a man from Bosse's outfit was there to collect it. Each film could therefore be reliably dated to a short period in between the date of the newspaper headline in the first photo and the film's arrival in Brunswick. The dating method was rigorous enough for use in a court of law.

Over in Washington, Bosse was beginning to build quite a collection: day by day, freighter by freighter, flight by flight.

55

Willard was annoyed.

'Look at this,' he complained, laying a new black leather glove on the black fur trim of his brand-new winter overcoat.

'What? It looks all right to me,' said Rosalind.

'Well, all right maybe, but not good. I mean the fur on the coat isn't properly black, is it? It looked black enough in the shop, but really, when you put it together as an outfit . . .'

'I think it looks nice.'

'Well, yes, on its own but, you see, you have to think of the overall effect.'

Willard was in Rosalind's dressing room. In the hall downstairs, his suitcase was packed and ready. In his coat pocket, Willard had train tickets booked all the way through to Montreal. His plan was a bold one – frighteningly bold, in Rosalind's opinion. He was travelling to Canada in order to intercept one of the suspect shipments of furs and hides. Arthur Martin had lost his life investigating the paper trail of one such transaction. Willard was proposing to investigate the shipment itself, all alone, hundreds of miles from the nearest help.

As Willard continued to fuss, Rosalind was quietly astonished. In two days' time, her lover might be fighting for his life, might be dead or dying, and all he cared about was his stupid coat collar.

'Aren't you scared?'

'Scared?' Willard had his collar pulled down so he could scrutinise it better and for a moment didn't understand her question. Then he did. He patted the collar back into place and said, 'Well, I guess. The trick is not to worry too much. Fellows who did that in the war never managed for long. It runs the nerves ragged, you know. Besides, I don't mean to upset things. I certainly don't mean to end up wrapped around a maple tree.'

Something in Rosalind's face flickered. Perhaps this was true courage that she was seeing. Perhaps courage didn't look the way people expected.

'Have you got everything?'

Willard nodded. 'Money. Passport. Clothes.' He paused. Stowed carefully in a silk bag between the shirts in his suitcase, he had packed his old army-issue revolver and half a dozen clips of ammunition. 'Gun.'

'I wish you hadn't spoken to that friend of yours.'

'Hmm?'

'That friend of yours from the bank, Larry Ronson.'

'Oh, Larry!' said Willard dismissively. The other night, the three of them had been taking a late supper together after work. Willard had been drunk and talkative. He'd scared Rosalind with his loose talk. He'd spoken about his upcoming Canadian trip – claiming it was to visit friends. He'd mentioned his travel plans, at least as far as Montreal. He'd even rambled a little about the shipment of furs coming south over the border – a shipment which Larry would have to look after in Willard's absence. 'Don't worry about him.'

She fell silent, stroking the lines of his face with her fingers.

'You will be careful, won't you?'

'Of course. To be honest, I need the holiday.'

She stepped closer. Something liquid moved in her eyes and mouth. Courage wasn't just a characteristic she admired, it was one she loved. One that aroused her. Willard felt bad for a moment. He hadn't told Rosalind about his meeting with Powell. He hadn't told her about the files or the deductions he'd made as a result. It *was* brave what he was doing, but it wasn't as brave as she thought. His conscience flared up, then died back again, under control as usual.

'Your train? When do you have to . . .?'

Willard looked at his watch, then at the invitation in her eyes. Her hands were on his chest. Her mouth was slightly open, her eyes slightly closed.

'Well, not right away, perhaps, not if you wanted . . .'

She wanted.

And twenty-six minutes later, still buttoning his coat, Willard went bursting downstairs, snatching his bag, running for his train. It would carry him north to Canada. He would come back victorious or come back dead.

56

The shower looked good: a huge tin plate with about a million holes nail-punched through it. The shower looked man enough to wash a regiment. Looked, but wasn't.

The shower pipe ended about three feet from the shower head, which was dry enough for a gekko to be warming his belly upside down on it. Pen twizzled the faucet over the basin, with the same dry results. She grimaced and shouted down the hall for the boy to bring water.

There was a delay of about five minutes, then a small boy appeared carrying a huge bowl of tepid water. She thanked him in English and took the bowl. There wasn't a curtain over the window, so Pen stood in the corner, stripped down to her underwear and washed as well as she could. Since she was now in Havana a fair amount, Pen had bought herself a basic wardrobe and she changed into a light cotton summer dress and a pair of pale pink flat-soled pumps.

She tipped the water away and carried the bowl back to the hotel kitchen, where she found herself a glass of lemonade and a packet of biscuits. She took her trophies to the bar, a dim prison-like room, mauve-painted, smelling of male bodies and spilled wine, lit by a couple of windows too high to see out of. A wooden ceiling fan stirred the air with an authentic Cuban dislike of doing anything too fast or effectively. Frank Lambaugh was there, Marion's purchasing agent on the island. So too was Ayling Gann,

256

the freighter captain, plus Raul Jiminez, the Cuban distributor for two of the Jamaican rum distillers.

'Hi.' Pen came in and sat down.

The men were drinking rum and shelling pistachios. Glancing at Pen, they nodded hello, but switched their conversation from English to Spanish.

'This evening. Yes, this evening. It's not my fault if the truck breaks down.'

'It's your truck.'

'OK. You have the rum this evening.'

'All of it?'

'Yes, eighty cases. As agreed. Eighty.'

Lambaugh and Jiminez were arguing over a late delivery. Pen had mostly been brought up by the black servants on her father's plantation, but for six years she'd had a Spanish-speaking nanny from Mexico. She could read, speak and understand Spanish with no more difficulty than she could English – a fact she'd so far kept hidden.

Lambaugh caught Pen's eye.

'Sorry, this must be boring for you.'

'That's OK. Don't worry about it.'

'I wasn't worrying, I was just telling you sorry.' He continued to hold her gaze. *'I'd like to put you across this table and screw you right here, right now.'*

'Mind if I take some nuts?' said Pen, not letting her expression waver. Ever since Abe had introduced her as his newest recruit, she'd experienced a wave of distrust, which in Lambaugh's case had thickened to outright hostility. Booze-smuggling appeared to be a men-only sport. Flying certainly was. The idea of a woman flier escorting freighters up the Florida coast seemed to give everyone involved a severe case of woman-hating. It didn't help that Mason had waved through the purchase of a second DH-4 without so much as a grumble over cost. Lambaugh pushed the nuts at her.

'Help yourself.'

From that point on, Pen had felt Lambaugh's distrust like a belt of high pressure, a problem aggravated by mutual dislike. But she didn't mind. She was happy. For the first time in her entire life, she had work to do, work that mattered. The feeling was an intensely satisfying one. As a flier. As a woman. Her new role in life filled her with a quiet joy that all the Frank Lambaughs in the world wouldn't be able to shake.

And as for the work, she took some photos, of course, but there was nothing illegal about handling booze in Cuba. The photos brought Bosse little or nothing that he could use. But Pen's ears brought plenty.

Like today. Lambaugh and Jiminez were talking again. Jiminez was complaining that payments from Marion were being held up by the banks. Lambaugh's domineering Spanish overrode Jiminez, mowing down his objections. And Pen listened, as she listened to everything. *Names of banks. Names of people. Payment arrangements. Payment amounts. Timetables. Contacts.* She'd write it all down, mail her statement to Bosse. Some days she learned little, other days plenty. But she was making progress.

Week by week. Day by day. Flight by dangerous flight.

57

Ruxion, Alberta.

November in Canada.

Black pines standing around a freezing lake. A tumble of grey rocks. A sprawl of wooden houses hunkered down by the water. A couple of fishing boats, pulled up against the ice. A wind sweeping down off the Rockies. A landing strip squeezed into the grassy margin between the lake and the hills. An aircraft that Willard didn't recognise poking its nose out of a hangar crammed in amongst the pines.

He climbed out of the car, a De Soto that looked ancient, but maybe wasn't. In that climate, it was hard to tell the difference.

'Welcome to Ruxion,' said the driver.

Willard pulled his coat closer and groped in the pocket for gloves. He wore his usual grey felt fedora, but found himself envying the rabbit-skin trapper's hat which the driver wore pushed back on the crown of his head. The driver might have had a decent hat to put on, but he clearly wasn't over-fussed about the cold. His waist-length plaid jacket was open right down the front. His flannel shirt wasn't even buttoned the whole way. The driver noticed Willard fussing.

'It ain't proper cold yet,' he said. 'It don't get real cold for another few weeks yet.'

Aside from a sour look, Willard didn't reply. From Montreal, he'd travelled most of the way across Canada to Calgary, before taking a local train south to a nowhere-

and-nothing stop on a nothing-and-nowhere railroad. The road from the stop had come all the way through Ruxion to the airstrip, where it ended in a big circle of churned dirt and bare grass. A couple of trucks sat, nosing the hangar wall like cattle feeding from a manger.

Willard hurried up the low slope to the grey door at the back of the hangar. A primitive electric generator driven by stream water churned away in the woods somewhere close. A neatly painted sign said, 'Ruxion Trading Corp. Please use bell.' There was no bell. There wasn't even a catch on the door, which was only held shut because it hung crooked from a broken hinge. Willard shoved against the door, the driver close behind.

Inside was a second door, a wooden one, properly hung. Willard passed through into an interior of almost stifling heat. A cast-iron stove squatted burning hot against one wall, leaking red light and wood smoke in exchange for nearly all the available oxygen. There were three men present, one of them stretched out on a camp bed. The other two were playing cards for what seemed like a very small pile of money. A single dim bulb hung from a light cord. A hunting rifle, complete with a leather ammunition pouch, was slung from a couple of pegs over the camp bed.

'Train was late,' said the driver.

'Yah! Figured,' said one of the card players, throwing down his hand.

'My name's Thornton,' said Willard. 'From –'

'Yah. Money man. Never expected to see one out here. 'Course, it ain't cold yet. Not real cold.'

'I wanted to run a quick product inventory. We've been having some problems with our paperwork. Nothing major. Just wanted to check everything was in order.'

In that environment, Willard's words sounded, even to himself, like something from another planet. His confidence in his plan had begun ebbing long before his arrival in Montreal, let alone his journey out here, to a place that seemed like the end of the known world. What if he'd been wrong about Powell's coded message to him? What if Larry Ronson had been too drunk to take on board the information that Willard had been so careful to give him? What if he'd been altogether wrong about Ronson and whose side he was on? If he'd been able to, Willard would have run – but what was there to run to? A two-hundred-thousand-dollar loan. One man dead and another man jailed. A life of hard work, poverty, exhaustion and fear.

The card players exchanged looks with each other and the man on the camp bed. Willard felt a surge of anger. He shouldn't even have to be here. He was frightened now, out of his depth, scared.

'You want to poke around?' The card player who'd spoken before spoke again.

Willard nodded. 'It won't take long.'

The men exchanged glances again. Willard didn't understand the atmosphere and didn't like his lack of understanding.

'Sure,' said the card player, the chatty one. 'You need those?'

There was a stack of papers clipped together in a cardboard carton under the camp bed. The card player, Mr Chatty, as Willard christened him, shoved the carton at Willard, who looked at the bundle of papers inside. The first page was entitled 'Northern Furs & Hides – Loading Bill, Goods in Transit'. There followed five pages of detail. Willard glanced at the uppermost page.

'Hides, tanned, (½ doz) . . . . 4 rolls
Roll (1) . . . . No. 11086
Roll (2) . . . . No. 11087
Roll (3) . . . . No. 11088
Roll (4) . . . . No. 11089
Beaver skins, tanned . . . . 12 Boxes
                              (min 60 lbs, wt net)
Box (1) . . . . No. 1044
. . .'

The paperwork corresponded to the documents that had passed Willard's desk in Wall Street, only here, of course, the detail was much greater, every single box-load itemised and numbered. Willard was no accountant, but he felt pretty sure that the most scrupulous accountant in the world would have liked paperwork like that.

'Looks good,' he said, hearing himself adjust his Princeton rhythms to the monosyllabic speech of the men in the room. 'I ought to check off a couple of boxes, if I can. No need to do 'em all.'

Mr Chatty jerked a finger at a second wooden door, set into the wall that separated the little office space from the hangar proper.

'She's loaded, you know.'

'Loaded? Already?'

Mr Chatty shrugged. 'Your train was late. We didn't sit around crying.'

Willard opened the door. The hangar yawned huge and cold around him. He groped for a light switch and flicked it on. The pale Canadian sky was framed like a wide open mouth by the open wall on the far side of the building. The aircraft, a massive one, dominated the space. Willard estimated her wingspan at more than seventy feet, the upper wing pair a full eight or nine feet above the lower set. Her metal body bulged backwards from her nose. She looked like a submarine had ploughed forward into a set of airplane wings and become lodged. Not exactly nice-looking, thought Willard, but plenty of muscle. Even with fuel on board, she'd carry literally tonnes.

There was no way into the plane except via a wooden stepladder which leaned up against the side. Some gasoline-slopped steps further back showed how the aircraft was refuelled. A row of red ten-gallon fuel cans were ranged along the wall behind.

Willard climbed up into the cockpit. The instruments were more modern than those Willard had been used to, but the main difference from his old Nieuports and Spads was the cockpit itself. On this monster, the cockpit was entirely closed off from the sky. It had a metal-skinned roof and thick glass windows. Willard thought how strange it must be to fly and not feel the wind. But he wasn't here to compare planes. He was here to check boxes.

He clambered back into the hold and looked at his first box. A number chalked on the side corresponded to a number in the loading bill: a consignment of beaver skins. The box was put together from pine boards and nailed shut, but Willard had brought some basic tools up from the hangar, including a crowbar. Willard wrenched the lid of the box open, gashing his palm. He swore and probed the box with a flashlight.

It was beaver skin all right. Or at least, if it wasn't, then some other bunch of small furry animals had died to fill the box. Willard shoved his hand down to the bottom of the crate. He found beaver skin all the way. Fear prickled through Willard's skin, he didn't know why. He assaulted another box. Blood dripped from his open wound first onto the wooden case, then onto Willard's trouser leg. He swore again but got the second box open. This one wasn't dead beavers, it was dead something elses. Willard checked his list. Arctic fox. The silvery fur shone blue in the torchlight. Willard thought of Annie: he'd jokingly promised to bring her back a coat from this trip. Her presence seemed real and close. Rosalind, strangely enough, he could hardly even picture.

Willard swept the light around the metal hold. The light was dim, but he could make out the big rolls of cowhide looming out of the shadows. The hold smelled of fuel oil, leather, pine resins, and the faint but odious smell of the tannery. There were a load more boxes to check. Willard didn't feel like checking them. He felt suddenly nauseous and scrambled out of the hold, out of the cockpit, and too fast down the rickety wooden stepladder.

Tariffs.

A Republican Administration had slapped import tariffs on most things, including Canadian furs. It was fairly obvious – obvious from the moment that Willard had found the tiny dot marked 'Ruxion' on the map – that no Customs official was ever going to catch a glimpse of any US-bound cargo. Of course, somewhere down the way the documents would acquire a 'Tariff Paid' stamp on them, but Willard assumed such things could be either bought or forged. So this was Powell Lambert's game: a smuggling racket dressed with Wall Street flair.

He felt sick and uncertain.

He made his way back to the stifling little room where the four Ruxion men chatted together in the half-darkness.

'That's all I needed. Thank you.'

'It's OK.'

None of the men made any move to get up.

'Is there any chance of a ride back to the railroad? My train out leaves in ninety minutes.'

The driver shook his head. 'No train today.'

'No? I was told in Calgary . . .'

The driver found something he didn't like in his throat and hacked unpleasantly until it was cleared. 'Don't listen to them in Calgary. There's a slip just two, three miles down the line. Won't be another train back up again for a week or two. Depending on the weather. If it snows before then . . .' The driver shrugged.

Willard felt like he'd just been sentenced to a fortnight in hell and the man was shrugging. 'I have to get back out,' he said in a rising voice. 'I simply can't . . . Can I borrow the car? I could buy it.'

'Need the car,' said the driver. 'Need it here.'

Willard blinked in astonishment. Imprisoned in Ruxion of all places! No linen. No hotel. No company. And – great God! – if the snow came early, then there was no telling how long he might be stuck. Willard began to regret the entire venture. The four men in the room exchanged vile, nodding, amused grins. Willard felt like the new kid at school being deliberately intimidated by his elders.

Then the man on the camp bed spoke, the first time Willard had heard him say anything. Most of the man's teeth were either missing or so brown that they were invisible inside his mouth.

'Fly,' he said.

'I beg your pardon?'

'I know who you are.'

'Fly?'

'Willard T. Thornton. America's favourite ace. Huh? I'm right, huh? Guy like you shouldn't need a railroad.'

The suppressed mirth around the room broke out into open chuckles. Willard noticed that none of the men's dentistry was all that great.

'You mean fly that airplane south?'

The man on the camp bed relapsed into silence, except to repeat with a kind of sigh, 'Willard T. Thornton, huh? Willard T. Thornton.'

Mr Chatty indicated his camp bed companion. 'Ben's sick. Chest cold. Been coughing up stuff all morning. He's the pilot around here.'

'I've never flown a thing like that before,' said Willard, fending off the suggestion. 'I was a pursuit pilot, not a . . . not a . . .' He faded out, unable to think of any description other than 'goddamn smuggler'.

'Flies just the same,' said Ben the Pilot. 'Don't fly no different.'

'The plane oughta go out today any road,' said Mr Chatty. 'It's loaded, fuelled, ready to go. No telling how long Ben's gonna be out. If you want to be out before the snows . . .'

Willard was about to snap something expressing his total lack of concern in Ben's wellbeing, but he held himself back. It was fly the plane or sit it out in Ruxion. Neither option seemed great, but one of the two seemed a whole lot worse than the other.

'I don't have maps,' said Willard hoarsely. 'I'm gonna need maps.'

58

The cement block sat in the wall as snug as any of its neighbours, with no more than a thick fingernail's gap showing at any point.

Abe had a flat-bladed decorator's knife in his right hand. The knife had its tip turned down into a little hook. Abe probed around the block, found an opening, then slid the knife home. He fished carefully, then felt the tip of the knife catch. He pulled carefully until the block began to come free. When a clear half-inch of block was exposed, he put his hands to it and lifted it out. Behind the block was a cavity, packed with documents: Bosse's list of information requests and their own list of what had already been accomplished. Abe took both.

Meanwhile, in the hangar, Pen was getting dinner going. In a breach of her normal slacks-and-shirt policy, she was wearing a pretty cream sleeveless dress with matching flat-soled pumps. If she hadn't mussed up her hair within minutes of combing it, she might have been almost smart.

She'd brought food – potted meats, cheeses, salads, olives and bread – and laid it out on a board table covered by a clean white sheet. On a table to the side, stood a gramophone and dance records. Although, strictly speaking, *Sweet Kentucky Poll* was no longer entitled to her own hangarage now that the two DH-4s needed space, Abe hadn't been able to bear the idea of putting her out with nothing to wear. So he'd ordered a canvas canopy from a fisherman's store in Brunswick, but until it came, Poll continued to occupy the hangar, nosing the table like a wolf come to share with the mice.

The men came to join Pen. Both of them were in shirt-sleeves and neither wore a tie. Initially, Arnie was nervous at Pen's sudden air of femininity, but she resolutely refused to acknowledge that anything had changed and he soon acclimatised. He stole a slice of sausage which he ate quickly with his long, bony fingers.

'Nice,' he commented.

'Mason's providing the wine,' said Abe, producing a couple of bottles. 'I hope it's OK.'

Pen turned the bottles into the light. The wine was from one of the great French vineyards, one of the best pre-war vintages. 'Good? This is exceptional.'

'He said it was. I didn't know.'

They sat down and began to eat. Abe's home was ready now. He'd built himself a kitchen, a bathroom, bedroom-cum-living room. Though Arnie was shacking up with Abe for now, he too was getting his own place built on site. But though Abe's new home was more comfortable, the hangar had one overwhelming advantage: its size. With the table in the middle of the floor anyone outside trying to listen in would have been a solid twenty feet from the action. With the gramophone playing as well, any conversation would have been absolutely inaudible.

They got down to business.

'We've made a good start,' said Abe, 'but looking at this list of Bosse's, we've got a lot still to do. We're getting great photographic evidence. Pen, you've given us all we need on where Mason buys his stuff, who he buys it from, that kind of thing. But we've got nothing financial. We can't prove how much money is coming in, what it's spent on, or where the profits go. Bosse needs all of that. We need to figure out our next steps. What to do, how to do it.'

Pen nodded slowly. It was a topic she and the others had

been thinking about for some time. 'Well, one place to start is the mail. All the mail from the United States to Havana comes through us. Arnie reckons he could build me a steam valve . . .'

Arnie nodded. 'Right. Running right off of the engine. Simple one-finger release. Pot of gum concealed in the cockpit side-panel. No problem. It can be ready in a couple of days.'

Abe smiled, but – Pen fancied or was she imagining it? – there was something a little ghostly in his smile. 'Good. Only, Arnie, you might want to put steam valves into both airplanes. I've got a fancy that Mason might start giving us his best stuff to carry.'

'Huh? You mean Mason's just going to hand us all his most crucial documents?'

'Well, not all, just some. And he doesn't know it yet.'

Abe explained his idea: a beautiful one in its way. The length of Bosse's list already seemed less daunting. They ate and drank. They listened to the dance music. The conversation began to drift. Arnie asked Abe about the time before the war when Abe had been a race car driver. It was a world Pen knew nothing of and Abe talked with absorption, passion and colour. He'd obviously loved driving and only the superior thrill of an aircraft engine had been able to lure him away.

'But you don't have a car here,' said Pen. 'You don't miss driving?'

'I've got Poll. I've got Sue. I even get to drive your sweet little Curtiss.'

'That's not the same.'

'I guess I did my time on the racetrack.'

An evasion. Pen was getting used to them. She noted to herself how Abe's involvement with racetracks had come to an abrupt end with the onset of war. His military career had ended with equal sharpness. So had his time with the Post Office, with pylon-racing, with movie-stunting, with test-flying and anything else he'd ever touched. The theme of deep involvement followed by abrupt termination seemed too often repeated to be coincidence. She couldn't explain it. He wouldn't talk about it. Although Pen had been working right alongside Abe for five weeks now, it seemed she knew him less and less with each passing day.

Arnie had gone to get Abe's deck of cards and was persuading him to do tricks. But Pen watched with a sceptical eye. She had never been interested in card tricks and she'd never flown as a pursuit pilot. But some of the patterns of thinking made intuitive sense to her. She could feel Abe trying to steer her eye in one direction and she taught herself to look hard in the other. The more she learned to 'read' the tricks, the less impressive they appeared. They seemed shallow, a distraction from the real world.

The dance music upped its tempo. Pen felt an impulse to release her feelings in movement.

'Arnie, do you dance?'

'Uh, not really, I wouldn't say –'

Both men were like this. If she raised a topic that in any way connected with her other life – either her gender or her money – then both men instantly backed away. But she wasn't having it.

'Great,' she said, scraping her seat back, 'it'll be great to learn.'

She dragged Arnie up. He was a strong man, but came over a babe-in-arms when asked to lead Pen through the dance. But she persevered. She gave him the confidence to lead her correctly. He was a slightly literal dancer: too keen on getting the steps just right, not happy just to let the music flow. But all the same, she was pleased. She enjoyed her dance.

The record finished. Pen didn't put another one on. She wanted Abe to ask her to dance, but he didn't, he just sat at the table drinking coffee and flicking playing cards through his hands. It was rude, she thought. Even if he didn't want to, he should have asked anyway. But he didn't. He didn't ask her. She didn't ask him.

She was about to say her goodbyes and go, when she noticed something new.

The workbench ran along the back wall of the hangar, then turned at right angles and ran halfway up one of the side walls. For a long time, Abe's collection of castings had sat on a shelf above the workbench on the back wall. The shelf had finished right there at the corner. But not any more. Someone, either Abe or Arnie, had fixed a shelf along the other wall too. The collection of castings was already crowding along the new shelf towards the end. At a rough guess, Abe's thirty or forty castings had suddenly become fifty or sixty.

Pen's brain, a little drunk, a little tired, suddenly sobered up. Going to the shelf, she reached one of the new castings down. The size of a loaf, the casting was metal and very heavy. The model was of an aircraft fuselage, but had no wings, no undercarriage, no tail fin.

'What's this?' she asked.

Abe came over. 'It's the Dayton-Wright O-W fuselage, as near as we can get it.'

She looked between the two men and saw closed faces, a secret shared away from her. Abe took the casting from her and began stroking it unconsciously, always in the direction of air movement, nose to tail, nose to tail.

'It's a kind of hobby of ours. The accuracy is better than one part in twenty.'

'You do it just for fun?' Pen's voice rose in disbelief.

'Well, there's a serious purpose, I guess. I've long had a feeling that airplane design has been too much about engine development, not enough about aerodynamics. These castings are a way to look at some of the aerodynamic issues.'

'And how do you do that?'

'Oh, you know, we'll figure something out.'

Abe's statement hardly marked a natural end to the

conversation. Mostly, you'd think a pilot would want to go on from there, talk about his passion to somebody who could understand. But he didn't. He put the casting on the shelf, went back to the table, drank another cup of coffee, yawned.

We'll figure something out. That was a meaningless statement. Or rather: it had plenty of meaning, but not the one contained in the actual words. Abe's answer meant: I'm sorry, I'm not going to tell you, you don't belong.

Pen heard his answer: not the words, but the real message. She felt his physical presence very close to her, like a second shadow. But the closeness was an illusion. This was a race-car driver who didn't own a car; a combat pilot who hated war; a friend who wouldn't dance; an airman who wouldn't share.

She felt isolated. She felt unwanted. She felt betrayed.

59

From the cockpit, the runway looked long, but from the cockpit runways always do. Beyond the end of the grass strip, there was a litter of grey rocks funnelling down to a stream bed. Beyond the stream, there were pines, forty feet tall and more, climbing a steep slope up the hillside.

Willard felt bad.

A sense of danger hid in his stomach, like a wild beast curled in its burrow. He couldn't make it out. He'd done a careful pre-flight inspection and run the engine for twenty minutes at half revs to check out any irregularity. He wasn't familiar with the type of plane, a Martin C-1, and in any event, Willard had been a pilot, not a grease-monkey. Nevertheless, Willard knew enough to know that the basics seemed completely fine. He was even surprised by the apparent competence of the two card players, who turned out to be responsible for servicing the plane.

Weather was an issue of course. There were no phones in Ruxion, and no telegraph closer than the station telegraph fifty bone-crunching minutes away. But even if Willard had had a phone, he wouldn't have known who to call. All he could do was gaze up at the sky, which was cloudless and still.

'It don't get better than this,' Ben the Pilot had commented. 'In summer, you get the dry spells, only the air's so busy, it's like driving over rocks.'

Willard knew what he meant. Warm weather could create

violent turbulence which made for rougher flying than fine, cold weather. If the weather held, it should be good to fly in.

The route, of course, was an unknown, but the two pilots had bent down over Ben's route maps in the smoky room. The older pilot (who didn't seem to be vastly unwell, in Willard's cynical opinion) talked through the route in detail, marking hazards on the map as well as possible emergency landing sites. 'Get clear over the border and you shouldn't have too much trouble taking her down if you have to. 'Course, you've always got the 'chute.'

Willard had never used a parachute, though in some of his films a stuntman pretending to be Willard had made jumps.

'It's up there? In the cockpit, is it?'

Ben the Pilot nodded slowly. 'Yah! You used one before?'

Willard hesitated. He never liked revealing the extent to which stuntmen had carried him through his movie career. Besides, a parachute was just a knapsack with a bit of string to pull.

'Yeah, sure. In the movies. Used 'em plenty.'

Ben wrinkled his mouth as if to spit. 'Yah. Well, try not to use it today, willya?'

The only real awkwardness had been over fuel. When Willard had fired the engine up, he'd noticed the fuel tank was only a quarter full. He slid angrily down the stepladder to demand a full load.

Mr Chatty said, 'You got a quarter tank there. Plenty to take you over the border.'

'Right. And you've got the rest of it right there.' Willard pointed down to the row of fuel cans, painted in the bright Standard Oil red. 'It belongs in the plane.'

'Ben never likes to take that much on board.'

'Ben isn't flying this crate.'

'He generally takes more fuel on just over the border. Enough to take him on to Shakeston.'

274

'I said I want more fuel.'

There was a moment of eye-to-eye confrontation. Willard refused to back down. A full fuel load meant safety. It meant more time to find a landing site if he were forced down early.

Mr Chatty dropped his eyes. 'OK. It'll take a while.'

They'd fuelled the plane. Willard had rooted around in the stove room and found enough bread and ham to serve as lunch and dinner. Then he'd taxied the plane out of the hangar. She was an ugly brute, but both engines (a pair of 400-horse Liberties) and instruments all looked and sounded fine. The runway was long and clear, the weather still good. But for all that, Willard felt the anxiety curling and breathing in his stomach.

He looked down. The four Ruxion men stood by the plane, arms folded, muttering to each other – talking about Willard, he had no doubt. He turned back to his instrument panel. Ignition on this monster was automatic: the propellers stood too high to be swung by hand, in any event. He put his hand to the throttle, which already trembled with the interior life of the airplane. Down below, he could almost hear Ben the Pilot crowing 'Willard T. Thornton, America's favourite flying ace!' through his brown and stinking teeth.

He was about to push down, ready to begin his forward roll, when his fear suddenly sprang up, the way a gasoline fire can flare up from nothing. All of a sudden, Willard was trembling violently, desperately eager to be out of the cockpit, on the ground, holed up in Ruxion for the entire Canadian winter, if need be. If he hadn't been so far down the line, if he hadn't actually been in the cockpit, engines on, hand on the throttle, he would have done just that.

Vanity doesn't sound like a major-league emotion. It sounds like it belongs down there with the tiddlers, like boredom, irritation or curiosity. But not always. Not all the time. On this occasion, vanity fought with fear and vanity won.

Willard eased the throttle forward, adding power slowly to both engines. It was the right way to handle machinery: firmly but steadily, without haste.

That was his error.

He knew it within seconds, by the time the runway was sliding by, by the time the plane had picked up speed, by the time the dark-shadowed pine trees at the end of the runway were starting to show their real height, by the time the grey rocks began to gather shape, size and mass.

He should have stopped. He should have aborted the take-off. He should have snatched power from the engines, done everything he could to slide to a halt.

Because, although the plane was on maximum throttle, although the engines were screaming at maximum power, although everything was just as it should be for a normal take-off, the tail was heavy. The wings weren't buoyant.

The plane wasn't taking off.

60

Sam Young, a farmer from just outside Independence, came in to Hennessey's store to pick up a new axe handle for himself, a bolt of printed calico for his wife.

'What d'you know,' he said, as he leaned up against the counter, a wad of chewing tobacco plugging his cheek. 'I was clearing some land yesterday, brought down some of them old oak trees down there in the creek bottom. The oaks got kinda tangled with the phone wire, must have pulled down maybe one, two hunnert feet of the stuff.'

'Easily done,' said another local farmer. 'Them phone people oughta think about things like that when they put up the poles.'

'But that ain't the strange thing. The strange thing came this morning. When I got back down to the creek bottom to fix things up again, the phone line was gone. All two hunnert feet, mebbe more. Doggone thieves.'

'That so? Folks these days . . .'

An acute observer might have noticed a look pass from Sam Young to Hennessey. A look that said 'job done', an answering flash of acknowledgement. Only maybe not. It was dim in Hennessey's store, and it was hard to read such things.

❧

If Independence was cut off, then so was Marion.

Abe found out when he landed back from a long reconnaissance flight, checking out the Coastguard stations north of Brunswick, not just those on the Georgia coast but right up all the way to Wilmington in North Carolina. It had been a long, exacting day, but one that had revealed a lot of valuable information.

Abe landed in a steep side-slip, levelling out only just before the ground. The coastal winds, the mangrove forests, and the short runway made landings in Marion a connoisseur's art and one that both Abe and Pen had brought to a high pitch of perfection.

Mason was on the gound waiting with undisguised impatience.

'Hey, buddy! Good day?'

'Yep. A long one.'

'Not too long, I hope.'

Abe shrugged.

'You know what them loused-up neighbours of ours have gone and done? They've brought down the phone lines, would ya believe it?'

Abe shrugged again.

'Listen pal, I know you've had a long day an' all, but I got business to communicate kind of urgently, business that's just a little private for the public telegraph.'

Mason had letters in his hand.

Abe shook his head. 'I've flown a lot today, so has Sue. She needs a clean and an oil-change before she's taking off again.'

'Anything I can do to help, you just let me know. I'll have a hot meal brought out to you here.'

'Hell . . . Where do your letters need to go?'

'Jacksonville. Miami.'

Abe sighed, letting his genuine tiredness show through, and keeping his delight at Mason's eagerness to hand over his secret correspondence strictly under cover. He noticed too, not for the first time, how he and Pen had a special status with Mason. Anybody else, even the freighter captains, Mason would just have told to do something. It would have been an order, that no one would have dared to disobey. Abe wiped his eyes, feeling the rim of dust, sweat and oil left by his flying goggles.

'OK. We'll be off again in thirty minutes. Some hot food would be good. Also cold beer.'

Mason grinned like he'd been given the gift of a lifetime. He put his little clutch of letters on Sue's lower port wing with a flourish.

'Cold beer. You got it, pal. And thanks. I appreciate it.'

In thirty minutes, Abe was off again, but not straight to Jacksonville. On the way, he made a small detour to a north Florida farmstead, and a cornfield still stubbled and spiked with the stumps of the harvest. The corn spikes were rough on Sue's wheels, but OK. At the end of the field, a man in a dark suit advanced on Abe.

'Haggerty McBride,' he said, introducing himself. 'Colleague of Jim Bosse.'

'Abe Rockwell.'

The two men shook hands, but lost not a moment in getting down to business. In the cockpit, Abe had already steamed open Mason's letters. He'd clipped the orginals to his map boards, top and bottom to avoid them ripping apart in the wind, then made copies. McBride first verified each copy against the orginal, then initialled each page and signed the final one, 'Authenticated against the orginal, Haggerty McBride, Nov 12, '26'. The letters themselves were, in effect, routine business letters, but Mason's business was never exactly routine. There was a letter to a railroad official notifying him of dates when the coastal freight train would need to stop at the Marion spur line and how many railcars it would need to add to its line. There was a letter to Mason's Jacksonville bank, dealing with money transfers to Cuba. There was a letter to an individual in

Miami dealing with the 'product import' schedule for the coming month. There was a letter to the most senior cop in Jacksonville, arranging a date to negotiate new 'sponsorship arrangements for the Police Support Fund'.

Haggerty McBride didn't say much, but when he saw the last letter, he snorted and said, 'This is good.'

'You know how long the lines will stay down?' asked Abe.

'No. We don't want to contact the phone company direct. Too risky. But we've pulled line down in two dozen other spots, all of them higher priority than Okinochee County. We reckon on weeks, not days.'

'Good.'

McBride then took from a wrapped wooden box a flat-iron, with hot coals smoking inside. Without wasting time, the two men gummed Mason's letters closed again, then used the iron to eliminate any creasing or other signs that the letters had been opened.

That was it. The two men nodded goodbye, then Abe climbed back into the cockpit, taxied until he had his nose in the wind and made a swift take-off.

He'd liked McBride and trusted him instantly. It was a good mark for Bosse's commitment to doing things right. Abe felt reassured.

And down in Miami, the same thing.

Pen carried the air mail from Miami to Cuba. Most of it she didn't read. Some of it she did. They knew now which bank conducted Marion's business in Havana. She looked out for letters to that bank; to Frank Lambaugh or any of his cronies; to any of the booze suppliers who crowded the island. Sometimes she found nothing. Other times she did. When she did, she opened the letters, copied them, had them authenticated by one of Bosse's men down on a beach east of Havana, before continuing her flight to her usual airfield.

Bit by bit they were accumulating information. And still Abe took his photos. And still Pen gleaned all she could from the repellent Frank Lambaugh. Jim Bosse's list of information requests began to seem less daunting by the day.

No matter which way they looked at it, they were getting closer.

61

Clocks are stupid.

Clocks think that every second is like the next, every minute like any other. But, fortunately for the world, fortunately for Willard, nothing could be further from the truth. If every second were like any other, Willard would have died in Ruxion.

Here was the situation.

He was flying a Martin C-1 biplane. Its theoretical take-off speed was approximately fifty-three or fifty-four miles an hour. Willard was travelling at fifty-six miles an hour down the runway and the plane was refusing to lift. If he'd had enough clearance to stop, he would have stopped. But the clearance wasn't there. By the time Willard was certain that he had a problem, the end of the runway was too close to let him. Willard guessed the grey rocks at the runway's end to be a little over three hundred yards distant. That gave him twelve seconds – plus or minus – to figure out how to get his plane to fly. If he failed, he'd be running into that rock-strewn gully at more than fifty miles an hour, in a five-ton airplane, brimming with hundreds of gallons of highly flammable gasoline.

And that was when time changed.

What did Willard normally get done in twelve seconds? It took him longer than that to add sugar to his coffee. It could take longer than that to light a cigarette. It took Willard more than ten times that long to comb his hair in the morning.

But time changed. Willard's brain came alive in a way only danger makes possible. Perhaps only pilots and racing-car drivers truly understand the transformation. Willard's brain raced, but more than that: his hands were ahead of his conscious mind. By the time he'd understood something, his hands were already doing whatever it was that needed to be done.

And the first thing was this.

Willard mustn't try to make the aircraft fly. It sounded illogical. It sounded so illogical that many pilots would have killed themselves attempting to haul the plane into the air. But although Willard could adjust his elevators to increase lift, every increase in lift also caused an increase in drag. Willard's attempts to lower the tail and tweak the nose into the sky had been slowing the aircraft, and if anything could save him now it would be speed. He kept his hand clamped down hard on the throttle, to make sure that every last ounce of power was getting to the engines. Apart from that, he did nothing to try and nudge the plane upwards. Nothing except pray.

The runway raced away beneath the Martin's wheels. The grey rocks in the gully sped ever closer. Beyond the gully, there was a broken slope and a scattering of pines. Already, Willard's mind noted the trees. Lifting the plane into the air wouldn't do much for his life expectancy if he were only able to run it into the trees. But he put that problem out of his mind. His twelve seconds were running away.

The needle of his airspeed indicator was lifting. It hit fifty-seven miles an hour, then fifty-eight. The feel of the plane definitely changed. It had an aliveness that it had lacked before.

Willard knew now the plane would fly if he asked it to, but there was the problem of the trees to be considered. The runway angled away from the worst of the trees, but there was a solitary clump lying dead ahead of Willard's course. The clump lay a hundred yards from the gully bottom, or perhaps two hundred and fifty from the end of the runway. With the plane as heavy and unresponsive as it was, it would be impossible to climb fast enough to avoid them. Once in the air, Willard could bank to right or left – but any turn produces a loss of airspeed, and Willard had far too little to afford anything of the sort. If he stalled the plane close to the ground, disaster was all but inevitable.

The end of the runway sped closer.

Eighty yards, sixty, forty, thirty . . . The first grey rock was a big one, a low-lying humpbacked beast, looking like a wild boar at sleep. If the aircraft wheel so much as nicked the rock, the plane's motion would be violently interrupted.

The needle read fifty-nine miles an hour. The plane was begging to fly, and at last Willard let it go. He touched the stick so that the nose followed the tail into the air. The ground flew clear beneath his wheels. The humpbacked rock disappeared beneath the plane.

The trees. He couldn't turn. He couldn't climb. The way things stood at present, Willard was flying straight for the upper branches of an all-too-solid Canadian pine.

If he couldn't turn and couldn't climb, there was only one thing left to do.

Dodge.

Hunched over his controls, he waited for the trees to get closer. If he acted a moment too soon, he'd fail. If he acted a moment too late, he'd fail just as surely. Then, just as it seemed the trees were about to smack him in the face, he jerked back on the stick. The airplane, which had reached sixty-two miles an hour of airspeed, jerked upwards with surprise.

One of the things Willard had learned as a pilot was that height can be exchanged for speed, speed can be exchanged for height. He made the exchange. With the little bit of airspeed he'd built up, Willard flung the plane uphill. The aircraft lifted sharply, but it was running far too slowly to put up with that type of manoeuvre. The trees slipped beneath the aircraft, but the airspeed indicator was plunging rapidly downwards through the scale.

Willard knew what was coming and was ready.

The airplane lost speed and stalled. The wings were no longer delivering enough lift to fly the airplane. The airplane was no longer flying, it was falling.

But clear of the trees, and with the engines still screaming at full power, Willard was able to jam the nose back down again. Like a cyclist running out of power at the top of a hill, the plane began to curve back down again – and as it curved it built up speed.

Speed was everything.

Willard kept the plane headed downwards in a low dive. The ground rose to meet the plane, but the plane recovered speed. The wings spoke again. Breathlessly, Willard nudged the plane ever so gently leftwards to where the ground fell away to the lake.

The plane steadied. The ground fell. The plane lifted.

Knowing he was clear, Willard levelled his course up over the lake, scanned the horizon ahead for its lowest point and guided the plane slowly upwards and away from danger. The plane ran smoothly over the lake and into the sky. In theory, the plane was capable of climbing four or five hundred feet a minute. No matter how he set the controls, Willard wasn't able to find more than about a quarter of that power. But he was OK now. No need to worry. He felt the breath of survival – the very feeling of life itself – spread slowly through him. He felt joyful; in control; like he'd conquered something inside himself. It was the opposite of the feeling that had dogged him all these months. He checked the map, set his course, began the thousand other routine checks and adjustments that would keep him busy for the rest of the journey.

Busy, but not too busy.

Positioned all alone between earth and heaven, a pilot

is in the perfect place to think things through. To think out riddles such as: Why did a plane designed to leave the ground at fifty-three miles an hour refuse to leave it until fifty-seven or fifty-eight? Why did a plane with a notional climbing speed of four hundred and fifty feet per minute seem to manage only one-fifty at best? Why did a simple smuggling operation go to all the trouble of buying planes and building runways in such remote spots as Ruxion, Alberta? And what in hell's name was Powell Lambert doing smack-dab in the midst of all of this?

A cockpit is the perfect place to think things through and Willard was ready to think. Before he'd even crossed the invisible line which took him from Canadian airspace into American airspace, he had figured out the entire thing.

62

It couldn't last long and didn't.

Mason tried getting the phone company to fix their lines; failed; then got the job done himself with phone engineers paid to make the trip down from Atlanta.

The intermission had lasted just ten days, but ten productive ones. On the last day, when Abe touched down on his cornfield, a softer landing now that the spikes of corn had been ploughed under, he greeted Haggerty McBride with a short nod.

'McBride. This is the last lot of letters we'll get for a while.' He explained that Mason would have the phone lines up by the following day.

'OK. We've done well, any case.'

Abe nodded and the two men went through the routine of checking Abe's copies against the orginals, then signing them off. They sealed Mason's originals up again, and ironed them flat. The entire procedure took less than ten minutes. Abe liked McBride's brevity and directness. He liked the way McBride was scrupulous about re-gumming Mason's envelopes so there was no trace at all of them having been opened; so there was not even a tiny blob of gum left anywhere except the flap where it was meant to be.

Abe got ready to leave again. He kept his stop-offs as short as possible, to ensure that if Mason had a guy watching out for his landing in Jacksonville, there would be no time discrepancy to account for.

But before he climbed into the cockpit, McBride stopped him.

'I've been speaking with Bosse.'

'Yes?'

'We reckon we're just about there.'

'So soon?'

'We've done very well. You have. We've accumulated more than we thought, faster than we thought.'

But McBride's voice wasn't congratulatory. It was reserved. A 'but' waited just out of sight. Abe prompted.

'Right. Only?'

'Only there's one last thing we need.'

'Uh-huh.'

'We've got good material. Proof of alcohol importation. Proof of transport connections, finance connections, police connections. We know a lot of names. We can tie a lot of them into the business.'

'Right.'

'Only we don't yet have the one thing we really need. If we really look hard at the evidence we've got, we can hit Mason for handling booze. We can hit the guys who physically load and unload the stuff. But the rest of them? How do we prove that the finance guys know they're financing booze? That the railroad guys know they're transporting it? They do, of course, we both know that. But we need to prove this thing in a court of law.'

'What are you telling me?'

'It was your idea to hit these guys for tax evasion. That's why we got involved. It's still the best route in. That way, anyone who draws a salary high enough to be declared for tax purposes is guilty. That way we pick up everyone we need.' McBride paused to allow Abe to respond, but Abe said nothing, so the taxman continued. 'We need the Marion payroll. Everyone on it, how much they earn. Plus the accounts, if you can possibly get them. Two or three years, ideally, but one year minimum.'

'Accounts? You think they . . .?' Abe tailed off. He didn't have to ask. Marion was a heck of an efficient organisation. It didn't run itself that way by accident. 'You're right. They'll keep accounts. And payroll. I don't know where. I don't know how to get them.'

'One other thing. It's going to be helpful to us if you can get us the materials for us to copy and authenticate, and then return the orginals, so they don't even know they've been gone. However fast we work, it'll take days and maybe weeks to get all the arrest warrants we need. We don't want to alert them beforehand. I know that's a tough brief.'

There was a pause, a long one. There wasn't much breeze out there on the cornfield, but what there was sighed through Sue's wings and wing struts like a blues song.

McBride said, 'You'll need to think about it. We understand that.'

'OK.'

'Either way, just let us know.'

The taxman held his hand out and they shook hands: the first time they'd done so since their first meeting. Abe felt, more strongly than before, that McBride was a good man; intelligent and safe. He respected Bosse all the more for picking subordinates like this. And Abe understood the taxman's request. It made sense. If he'd been in Bosse's position, he'd have wanted the same thing.

But it was a hell of a lot to ask. So far, all they'd done was to snipe at Marion from a distance. He and Pen had managed things so that they had run almost no risk of being caught. He'd had rising hopes of ending this whole escapade soon; of escaping the network of ties and obligations that he hated with all his heart.

And now this. An invitation to enter into the very heart of Marion. To snatch its most secret possessions. To take them, copy them and return them, all without anyone knowing. It seemed impossible. But Abe knew himself by now. However reluctant he might be feeling, he'd always take the next step.

Little as he liked it, he knew that the only way out was forwards.

63

Up on the Canadian border, a November day doesn't provide a whole lot of daylight in which to fly. But Willard wasn't worried. Though he'd taken off later than he'd liked – engine checks and the extra fuel had delayed him – the extra gasoline had allowed him to skip Ben the Pilot's re-fuelling stop just inside the US border. The rivers, railroads, towns and mountains disappeared under the airplane's nose just the way the map predicted. And just as the sun was balling itself for one last shriek of rosy fury in the west, the little grass airfield at Shakeston came duly into view. Willard lost height and flew at low speed over the field to check it out.

The grass airstrip wasn't long, but it looked very tidy: short grass, clean approaches, plenty of room to line up the approach against the wind. There was a new-looking hangar, a couple of tin-roofed office buildings, a windsock. There should have been a field identification number clearly painted in the north-west corner of the field, but there wasn't. Willard snorted softly through his nose. At this stage, it would have been more of a surprise if there had been. On a short concrete strip alongside the two office buildings, there were three cars parked and a cluster of men.

Willard glanced at the men, then stared. One of the men was in uniform. Willard was still high enough that he couldn't be sure, but it certainly looked as though the man was a police officer. He continued his flight path for a few seconds longer than he'd intended. *A police officer?* It would be the irony of ironies if Willard had finally bottomed out the mysteries of Powell Lambert, only to be jailed for the privilege.

He flew on uncertainly, glancing at the map for alternative landing sites.

Glanced at it, then tossed it aside.

He was being a fool. He brought the big-bellied aircraft around in a long swoop, lined up against the wind. He reduced power, dropped the aircraft and landed her – not a great landing, but good enough. He taxied up to the hangar and cut the power, first on the port engine, then the starboard. The noise died away. Willard felt the ringing in his ears which denoted the arrival of silence. His legs were cramped, his arms tired, his whole body frozen and sore.

He kicked at the cockpit door and it opened with a dull clang. Christ, he was cold! His woollen Brooks Brothers coat, gloves and felt hat had been nowhere near enough clothing to keep him warm eight thousand feet over the Canadian Rockies. The only time he'd ever been that cold before was on dawn patrols with Abe Rockwell, when they'd coaxed their little Nieuports to twenty-one thousand feet in search of German prey.

A ladder thumped up against the aircraft. Willard looked down. The cop was standing at the bottom. Willard felt a surge of anger. It felt like he was angry at the one last little joke being played on him, but in a way it was a burst of anger at everything that he'd been through since being given the boot by his studio and the whole fiasco of *Heaven's Beloved*. He came down the ladder so fast, his hands burned and his descending feet almost kicked the cop in the face.

'Hey pal, easy.'

Willard ignored the cop and strode over to the trio of parked cars. Anger gave him energy, but the cold made his movements jerky and stiff. A man detached himself from the group by the wooden office buildings and came over to Willard. The light was coming from behind the man's head, and it was hard to make out the face. But Willard had got it all figured out, hadn't he? He'd stirred things up enough. He'd more or less let Larry Ronson know what he was up to before he left. And Ronson was in on the whole game, wasn't he?

The man ahead was visible only as a well-wrapped silhouette and a cloud of cigar smoke, but Willard knew who he was.

'Hey, Powell,' he said, when he was still some forty feet away. 'I brought you your beaver skins. I might even have a bottle of Scotch or two in the back there, you never know.'

The silhouette revealed a set of white teeth, pulled back in a grin. 'Nice work, Thornton. The guys tell me that isn't an easy baby to fly. Reckon you've earned a bottle or two yourself.'

A bottle of Scotch.

The final confirmation of Willard's suspicions had been his near-death experience by Ruxion lake. With one hundred per cent power to both engines, there was only one reason why a plane couldn't fly and that was weight. The plane was overloaded.

Willard had checked the freight manifest, and the boxes that were meant to be full of beaver skins had been full of beaver skins. But he hadn't counted the boxes. Still less had he plunged around in the darkness of the hold checking the contents of every box. At a rough guess, the plane was carrying three-quarters of a ton more than her supposed maximum load – and a full two tons more than her declared cargo.

Of that two tons, a fair portion was the extra fuel Willard had had put on board. But most of it had to be something else. Something that not even smugglers wanted to put in writing.

Booze.

It had to be. Everything about Powell Lambert had fallen into place. *Trade Finance*? You bet. The importation and distribution of alcohol was America's most booming industry. A prosperous industry needed effective modern financing. That was Powell Lambert's job. For almost six months, that had also been Willard's job. That wasn't to say that everything touched by Powell Lambert had to do with booze. It didn't. No doubt Powell Lambert did plenty of regular trade finance transactions. Real buyers and real sellers all over America.

But the regular work was the perfect place to conceal the fake stuff. Willard had been working his ass off in order to make sure that the criminal distribution of alcohol was as well organised as any legitimate industry. And the stuff coming in from abroad was only a part of it. Willard had financed plenty of deals made by tanneries, paint factories, chemical plants, porcelain makers. All those businesses stank. Not figuratively, literally. To make whiskey you need to pulp grain into mash, then leave it to ferment. The mash smells. Where better to hide the stuff than in places that already stank? And there was a further advantage. All these places, the tanneries, the chemical plants, already handled liquids on an industrial scale. Tankers, vats and barrels were a part of their business. Why not use some of them to store and transport whiskey?

Looking back, Willard could even admire the little games which must have passed for jokes. The Association of Orthodox Synagogues? What horseshit! The nonexistent, never-existed invention of an alcoholic Irishman. But here was the joke. The Volstead Act had a few exemption clauses. Medicinal alcohol was one (and Willard remembered a few strangely large pharmaceutical deals he'd financed). Sacramental wine was another. Importing seventy thousand dollars' worth of sacramental wine wasn't just good business, it was technically legal.

Willard caught up with Powell's warmly-wrapped figure and stopped.

He wasn't sure how he felt. On the one hand, the pretence was over. It was pretty darn clear that Powell didn't intend to kill Willard for his new-found knowledge. As a matter of fact, it was pretty clear that Powell had somehow expected or wanted Willard to find out. So, in amongst Willard's emotional swirl, there was certainly relief.

But also anger.

The fear Willard had felt! The shock of being watched. The horror of finding out about Arthur Martin's murder, of seeing Charlie Hughes in jail. And Willard remembered his punishing workload, his debt to Powell, his fear that he'd be a slave to that debt for the rest of his life. Willard was a strong man. He was angry. Part of him wanted to draw back his fist and smash Powell full force in the face.

But he didn't. Instead, misjudging his pace as he strode up to Powell, Willard found himself going too fast and put up one hand to Powell's coat collar to steady himself. But the gesture was ambiguous. It was almost as though Willard himself didn't know if he was leaning on Powell for support or getting ready to punch him.

'You almost killed me, you bastard,' he panted. 'The plane. It was ridiculously overloaded. It almost wouldn't fly.'

Powell, who seemed oddly ready either to be leaned on for support or to be hit in the face, looked genuinely concerned. 'The plane? We've never had a problem before.'

'I put more fuel on board her. At that stage, I knew about the untaxed beaver skins. I didn't know there was booze as well.'

'The fuel was the problem?'

'The booze was the problem, Powell. A plane's meant to have fuel.'

There was a short pause; a pause in which Powell neither grinned nor smoked.

'I'm sorry, Willard. We never meant to put you in danger. I don't understand about planes. They shouldn't have let you take on fuel.'

We.

We never meant to put you in danger. Powell's comment triggered a connection in Willard's brain. He'd thought he had it all figured out, but maybe there was some further part he hadn't yet seen . . .

The men by the office buildings had mostly either disappeared inside or come out to the plane to begin unloading. One of the men, well dressed against the cold, had climbed back inside the dark sedan and sat there only just visible in the dying light. Powell was fumbling in his pocket. He brought out a sheaf of documents and held them out.

'Here.'

'What's that? You want a customs stamp, you better ask your goddamn flunkey.'

Willard indicated the uniformed cop, who was helping the others unload the cargo. Willard hadn't expected to see a cop on the ground, but when he'd thought about it, it hadn't been a surprise. What was the point in paying them, if you didn't get some service? The cop was working as fast as anyone in bringing crates out of the airplane.

'I don't want a customs stamp.'

Powell continued to hold the documents out. Willard took them. He held them up to the light in the western sky. The documents comprised the original loan contract, signed between the two men, together with every other piece of paperwork related to the loan. The topmost document was a single-page letter, acknowledging receipt of the loan amount in full. The letter was signed in Powell's unmistakable hand.

'What's this? I haven't paid you.'

Powell jerked his cigar towards the plane. 'Sure you have, Willard. Sure you have.'

'You think because I flew that plane out of Ruxion that

I'm joining your shitty little racket? I flew that plane out of Ruxion because I didn't fancy hunkering down there for the winter.'

Willard held out the documents to Powell, nevertheless hoping that he wouldn't take them.

'I didn't say anything about you joining, Will. That's up to you. One hundred per cent up to you.'

'Then what about these papers?'

'They're yours whatever you decide. Don't want to force you. It's the sort of thing a man has to decide for himself.'

He patted Willard on the arm.

'Arthur Martin? Did he get to decide for himself?'

'Nah!' Powell virtually spat. 'The guy should have been a priest.'

Willard, as so often before, was taken aback by Powell's bluntness. Willard shook away his distaste. At least he was free of debt. He folded the papers roughly and shoved them into an inside pocket.

'Thanks for this.'

'Don't mention it. Jesus, it's cold enough, isn't it? How you kids go flying in this kinda temperature, I'll never understand.'

Powell began walking back towards the cars. Willard followed him. His anger had subsided once again. *The loan*. He was free of it at last. He could rejoin the world, unfearful and free. The freedom felt good. Felt wonderful, in fact. The hopeful world symbolised by Thornton Ordnance burned ever brighter in his mind. And he knew now that, awful as it had been, his experience with Powell Lambert had made a man of him. He was ready for work now. Ready to follow where his father and grandfather and great-grandfather had gone before.

But Powell, a pace or two ahead, was speaking once again.

'. . . got someone here who wants to congratulate you. Thought we'd pretty near freeze waiting.'

Powell strode ahead. Frost nipped in the air and before too long, the ground would be sparkling white beneath a diamond sky.

But Willard didn't follow Powell. Not to begin with. He thought he'd had it all figured out, but there were more wheels turning in his head: click, click, click. And with every turn of every wheel, something new fell into place. Powell was over by the car now, leaning to speak through an open window. The light was going and Willard could see nothing of the car's interior, aside from a white face gleaming palely in the darkness. It all made sense now. It was like the moment that comes to a pilot, when he suddenly realises that he's master of his plane, that he can order it about the sky the way a showjumper orders his horse around the field.

Willard strode quickly up to the car. Ted Powell stepped back. Willard put his gloved hands on the roof of the car and bent down to the window.

'Good evening, Father,' he said.

64

Hennessey's business was general goods in an age when general meant what it said. He sold nails and roofing tin, seed and scythe blades, linens and soaps, sugar and wheat flour, children's toys and ladies' hats. But the business didn't stock itself. Hennessey did.

And so, on the third Tuesday in November, Hennessey was down in Jacksonville meeting his dry goods supplier and his linen merchant. His meetings over, Hennessey rewarded himself, as he always did, with a visit to the Southern Glory SodaBar for a fix of vividly-coloured carbonated milk fats. Already present, in one of the yellow pine booths, was a young woman, sitting on her own. Her clothes were unremarkable: lemony-yellow day-dress, flat shoes, a hat ridiculous enough to be fashionable. She had a paperback crime mystery in front of her. Her arms were tanned, her blonde hair short and mussed up. Her eyes were turned away from Hennessey, but he already knew they were blue and startlingly clear.

He didn't give her a second look. She gave no sign of looking at him. A few minutes later, she left.

An hour later, his soda and his newspaper both finished, Hennessey left the soda bar, then twisted his way through backstreets to shake any possible pursuit. Once he was sure he was clear, he entered the general freight warehouse down by the rail depot. Up above, a voice called, 'Up here. It's cooler.'

The storekeeper climbed a wooden ladder to the top of a mound of cotton bales. Pen greeted him with a smile. A window behind her let in a draught of cool air. When the three conspirators had met Bosse, they'd arranged a number of different ways to meet up. The Jacksonville soda bar was one of them and this was the agreed rendezvous. Hennessey had a chocolate bar in his pocket. He offered some to Pen, who took a piece.

'What's up?' said the storekeeper.

'Jim Bosse. That's what's up.'

Pen told Hennessey briefly about their successes so far, about their success in reading the mail, about Jim Bosse's latest request as relayed by Haggerty McBride.

'Phew!' The storekeeper whistled. 'They sure want plenty.'

'Yep.'

'What does Abe think?'

'He wants to know what you think.'

'And that's why you dropped in on me today?'

'I guess.'

That wasn't quite a full answer. Their usual way of getting in touch with Hennessey was to drop a note into his backyard from the air. If they needed to speak to him, they'd arrange a time for him to call them drug-store to drug-store, so the phone line would be clear. All the same, Pen had brought a freighter all the way up to Marion and she needed more fuel before heading back south, so it had made sense enough to drop in on Hennessey now. The storekeeper took another piece of chocolate and chewed it slowly.

'You mean, do I think we should place somebody on the inside? I mean, right on the inside? Further in than you or Abe?'

'Yes.'

The storekeeper took his time with his chocolate, not chewing too hard, not in a race to swallow. At last he was done.

'OK. Then yes. Yes, I do.'

'Abe thought you might have some ideas.'

'He's right. He knows that there's a kid . . . Heck, I didn't want to do this. I've got obligations. Obligations to a friend of mine, dead now, the boy's father. I know Abe felt much the same . . . Any case, this man left a son, who's desperate to help. The boy's sixteen now, old enough to choose. I'll talk to him.'

'Gosh, I'd hate bringing a kid right into the middle of this.'

'Yes, me too, but like I say, he's old enough to make his own decisions. And if we need him . . .'

There was a long pause. Down below them, there was the quick, sharp movement of mice across the floorboards, brown on brown. Hennessey had his hat in his hands, ready to put it on his head to go. On the one hand, they were in a safe place to chat and Hennessey had taken a liking to the young woman flier. On the other hand, the unseen power and threat of Mason's organisation loomed over them. They knew they were watched. They didn't always know how intensely or by whom. Every minute they were here was a minute unaccounted for. It wasn't a good idea to stop for long. But somehow, and for the first time, a peculiar thought had taken hold of him and he couldn't quite shake himself free of it.

'Listen,' he said, 'this isn't really my place, but might I ask you a mighty personal question?' The storekeeper had his hat in his hands and stared down at it like he'd never seen a hat before.

'Sure. Go ahead.'

'Is it possible – please don't take this wrong – is it possible that you have feelings for our mutual friend, Captain Rockwell?'

Pen was taken aback. She wasn't offended by the question, but had no idea why Hennessey had taken it into his head to ask it. But she tried her best to be honest, staring hard into her feelings. When she answered, she spoke slowly and with careful thought.

'No. I don't think so. When we first met, that first time . . . well, I guess I thought about it. I mean, I'm different from most girls. He's different from most men. Some of those differences seemed like they were leading in the same direction. So, yes, I thought about it. But now? No. The more I've got to know him, the less I find myself knowing him. Sometimes I feel I'm working with a stranger.'

Hennessey quit looking at his hat and stared straight at her. He was old enough to be her father and there was a kindliness and intelligence in his face that Pen had trusted from the outset.

'Maybe that's the real problem you wanted to talk about. Maybe that's why you dropped in on an old storekeeper today.'

Pen swallowed twice. Perhaps he was right. If so, he'd seen something that she'd managed to keep hidden from herself.

'Maybe you're right.'

'Things aren't . . . he's not making life difficult for you, is he? I guess he's not much used to working alongside women.'

'I don't think he's used to working with anyone very much. Sometimes he doesn't really seem to want to include me at all. If it weren't that I've made a commitment to you and to Jim Bosse and all, then I'd think about going home. I really would.'

Hennessey scowled down at his hat, as though he'd suddenly become fiercely critical of every detail of its construction.

'He's a good guy. But there you have it. He's a guy. I don't figure he's hung around with girls too much. Maybe he's shy. Or worse.'

'You think he's scared?'

'I don't know. But you'll never know unless you go find

302

out now, will you? And if you don't – well, heck, it ain't my place to say – but I wouldn't want either of you to miss out on something that might be the right thing for you both.'

'No,' said Pen. 'No.'

It wasn't quite clear what she meant – if anything – by her answer. She looked a little dazed, unfocused. Hennessey suddenly gripped his hat hard and jammed it on his head.

'Well, then. It's been good seeing you. You take care now.'

Crawling to the edge of the cotton bale mound, he let himself slide to the ground. He took one sharp look outside, then left, walking fast.

65

The Shakeston Hotel was a two-storey wooden affair that had probably looked swell when the Montana hills still swarmed with Indians, but was looking old and beat up now that history had moved on. All the same, the place did its best and its menu, based only on food that was grown, shot or hooked within thirty miles, was excellent.

'Try the duck,' said Willard's father. 'You won't get better.'

'Or the trout,' said Powell. 'I've got an outstanding Muscadet here. Give yourself an excuse.'

Willard compromised and ordered trout to start with, duck to follow. The other two did likewise. Both courses were excellent, and the wines, provided by Powell, were simply exceptional. Willard's stress, cold and fatigue began to melt away.

'Did I tell you?' said Junius Thornton. 'I just got a call from Ben Krakus, the pilot who normally does the Ruxion run. He said the way you handled that plane of yours over some bunch of trees at the end of the runway was some of the best flying he'd ever seen.'

Willard shrugged modestly, as though he'd be happy to fly like that every day of his life. He emptied his glass and closed his eyes.

The idea was so simple. So beautiful and so simple.

Ever since the introduction of Prohibition, America had begun to seethe with illegal alcohol-related activity. Rum-runners brought in booze from the Caribbean. The Mexican border was an open invitation. Canada, astonished at her big sister's fit of madness, was only too happy to stuff her pockets with as much money as she could. And the foreign imports weren't the half of it. There was home-brewed moonshine, industrially-brewed moonshine, wine cooked up out of Californian raisin-cakes, whiskey stocks spirited out of the now-silent distilleries. And there were the loopholes: the sacramental wine, the medicinal alcohol, the half-degree proof 'near-beer' which was easy enough to convert into the real thing with a little time, sugar and yeast.

But any new industry needs organisation. The mobsters and hoodlums who operated the rackets at street level were hardly competent to manage a vast and complex business, organised on a continental scale.

'Think about it,' said Powell. 'Early 1920, Prohibition had just come in but already booze was coming back too. In small amounts to start with, of course, but more all the time. Your father and I saw the opportunity. Your father brought his experience, his contacts, his flair for industrial organisation. Meantime, I was running Powell Finance on Wall Street – a nice little business then, but nothing compared with what it is today. We put our heads and our money together. We came up with what we've got now. Powell Lambert, the most profitable bank on Wall Street.'

'Why Lambert?' asked Willard. 'Why not Powell Thornton?'

Junius Thornton shrugged. 'We didn't want the attention. *I* didn't want the attention. I chose Lambert after a racehorse I owned.'

The Firm was an idea of genius. Its agents bought alcohol in Bimini and Havana, Tijuana and Ontario. Its men arranged transportation. Not just the trains, trucks, boats and airplanes, but the payments. The police. The border guards. The federal enforcement agents. Its deliveries were as precisely timed as they were in any other modern industrial organisation. The Firm was happy to smuggle virtually anything, but its core business, its main money-spinner by a mile was booze, just booze.

'Quality and reliability,' said Powell. 'We don't water our stuff down. We don't substitute cheap for expensive. We don't play games with the labels. And we get our goods there. We have a better than ninety-eight per cent delivery record. Quality and reliability.'

'And when the goods arrive, do you sell them on yourselves?'

'You mean do we operate speakeasies? The answer is no we do not. The operation of speakeasies –' Powell spoke with distaste '– is in the hands of mobsters. Racketeers and mobsters. The speakeasies are kept open through payments to cops on the one hand and through gangland killings on the other. It is not a business segment which attracts our interest.'

Willard's father raised a finger. 'Now, Ted, that's not quite fair. There is one speakeasy we're happy to operate.'

'That isn't a speakeasy.'

Junius Thornton nodded. 'True.' His gaze turned to his son. 'It's the best club in America. We operate the best served, the best stocked, and the most exclusive club in America.'

Willard waited to be told more, but neither of the older men chose to add anything further. Willard changed the subject to something that had been bothering him.

'How about the distilleries? All those things hidden away in tanneries and paint factories? Are they yours, or do you just arrange the transport?'

'Some of them are ours. Some of them belong to friends,' said Powell. 'As you know, there are legitimate businesses in every location. Sometimes we own the legitimate business too, mostly not. We rent space, we keep it private. Not many people even know we're there. Not even the people that work all around.'

'And insurance?' Willard asked. 'On some of the deals

306

we financed, the Firm insured its shipments. What does that mean? Why would a gangster want to insure something? And is it possible that our insurance folk are based on the part of the twentieth floor that's closed off?'

Powell exchanged glances with Willard's father. Willard intercepted the glance. There was amusement in the look, but also something he didn't understand. Junius Thornton cleared his throat.

'Perhaps insurance isn't quite an accurate term, Willard.'

'Oh?'

'Our problem isn't federal enforcement. In this fine country of ours, our lawmakers decided to pass a law without allocating any real funds to enforcement. Enforcement officers are paid so little, it's pretty much of an invitation to graft; an invitation that not many officers refuse. As a consequence, the feds get less than five per cent of all liquor moved in America, and in our case the percentage is far, far less than that.'

'So?'

'It's hijackers. Bandits. Whatever you want to call them. They don't want to operate in a proper professional way. They'd sooner steal our products instead of purchasing the goods themselves. So one of the services we offer is insurance. Not paper insurance, where you can get your money back. What we offer is real, effective, get-your-goods-there insurance.'

'I'm not sure I follow.'

Junius Thornton sank back in his seat and Ted Powell took up the conversation. 'Your father sells armaments, Willard. The best in the world. And we've hired men. Former soldiers. Good men. American men. No Italian trash. No Jews. No Irish. No Negroes. No Catholics. Just good, disciplined American men. Very well armed. Very well trained. Insurance that counts.'

Junius Thornton nodded slowly. 'We don't lose much to hijack either.'

'Gosh!'

Willard was shocked, despite himself. He lived in a world where most of the people he knew were in favour of Prohibition, at the same time as they broke the rules. It was hypocrisy, of course, but it was hypocrisy that Willard could live with. But his father and Powell were talking about something in a league of its own. A private army. Soldiers armed and trained to kill. Willard was stunned by the sheer scale of the Firm's lawbreaking.

'If people didn't try to steal our goods, we wouldn't need to protect them,' said Powell. 'And we're building a reputation. It's not often now that hijackers try to bust in on our consignments. They try it once, they're not likely to try a second time.'

'The twentieth floor,' said Willard. 'The part that's closed off. You told me it was lift machinery. I knew it wasn't.'

Powell nodded. 'Our insurance arm is headquartered there. It likes its secrecy.'

'The men that followed me? They were insurance agents?'

'Yes. We needed to keep an eye on you, Willard. We didn't want you doing anything stupid, and if you got into trouble, we wanted someone there to go and fish you out.'

'The way you fished out Arthur Martin?'

'Arthur Martin was on his way to an appointment with a federal enforcement officer when we intercepted him. We only learned about it at the last possible moment. We had little choice in the way we handled that matter. Our instinct is to avoid violence.'

'Right. Little Charlie Hughes just wound up with a bootlegging felony charge. What's a year in jail to a guy like him?'

'Mr Hughes was a friend of Martin's. Not as brave and not as stupid. But all the same, he began saying things he shouldn't have said to people he shouldn't have said them to. Our men spoke to him, came to an arrangement. He won't be a problem.'

Willard's brain was working all the time these days, click-click-click, making connections, figuring things out. 'You threatened him, didn't you? Not just him. His sisters. You told him if he blabbed to anyone, it would be his sisters who ended up wrapped around a tree.'

Powell shrugged. 'I'm not aware of the details.'

Willard shook his head with amazement. 'You know, I thought Leo McVeigh was one of the guys I had to be careful of. I thought he was threatening me. He wasn't. He was trying to warn me. It was Larry Ronson who –'

'Larry Ronson is a very good man,' said Powell. 'He kept an eye on you for us. He was very helpful. McVeigh is an idiot, but at least he has the sense not to speak to anyone about his idiocy. He understands what the consequences would be. We allow him to work only on legitimate transactions. He is a good worker, I understand.'

Willard rubbed his face with his hands. That day, he had busted a smuggling operation in a shithole called Ruxion, he had almost killed himself hauling an over-loaded aircraft into the sky, and now he was being let into the most valuable secret in America. He felt a wave of tiredness so strong, he was almost ready to fall asleep at table.

'We won't keep you long, son,' said his father with rare gentleness. 'But first, if I may, a question.'

'Yes?'

'When you leaned down to the car, you said "Good evening, Father". It was too dark for you to see me. Nobody told you about my involvement. How did you know?'

'Oh, lots of things.'

'How?'

'Powell said *we* when he should have said *I*. But that wasn't it. It was *Heaven's Beloved*. The more I learned about Powell, the more I knew he would never have financed a deal like that. The deal wasn't . . . the movie wasn't . . . Hell, it was a turkey. Everyone knew it except me. It was you who suggested I approach Powell. It was you who wanted me to quit the movies and get involved in something serious. It had to be you in that car. Had to be.'

Junius Thornton smiled. He said nothing, but there was pleasure and satisfaction in his face.

'Which brings me to my question for you, Father.'

'Yes?'

'Why didn't you just tell me? Instead of scaring me halfway to hell, you could have just come and said, "We have a business proposition for you". What would have been so hard about that?'

'You'd have said yes.'

'So? Isn't that what you wanted?'

'Yes. Yes and no. Mostly no.' Junius Thornton leaned across the table. 'Occasionally, son, you've had things a little easy. Maybe my fault, or maybe just the way the world is nowadays. You flunked Princeton. OK, maybe you could have turned things around, but it wasn't going the way it should have done. Then you did well in the war, certainly. But afterwards, you strolled into a job in the movies and flunked it. You tried making a movie of your own. That flopped. You've never known hard work, not what I'd call hard work, anyway.'

Powell nodded. 'Don't blame me, Will. I'd have done things the regular way. Your father said we needed to push you. He wanted to see how you'd react. Would you fight? Would you work hard? Would you figure things out? Would you persist?'

'And that's why I ended up with the lousiest files? The one with the biggest workload?'

'But that's not the point now, son,' interrupted Junius Thornton. 'The point is that you succeeded. You did as well as I'd hoped. Better. We were proud of you. Son, *I* was proud of you. I hope that one day, you will lead Powell Lambert to even greater things.'

The old man's eyes misted. Willard felt an answering lump in his own throat, a glow of pride.

Powell stayed quiet for a moment, letting father and son regain their composure. Then, in a soft voice, he added, 'And one other thing. This business of ours can get a little rough. Every now and then, we find we've hired a precious little altar-boy like Arthur Martin. That doesn't help us. We need to keep the Firm secure. We didn't know how you'd feel about the rough stuff and we decided it was better you knew about it first, so you could make your decision in full knowledge of the facts.'

'Like how Arthur Martin was murdered? How Charlie Hughes was framed? How you protect your booze with a small army of mercenaries?'

'Yes, precisely.' Powell was totally unmoved by Willard's sharpness. 'You needed to know all that. This is a dirty industry, Willard. What it needs is organisation.'

Junius Thornton nodded heavily. He took the Muscadet from its bucket of ice and poured more into his glass, then Willard's. Like any rich man, Junius Thornton bought only the best of anything. The best clothes. The best wines. The best furnishings. The best properties. He bought them, then acted as though he'd forgotten them. He swigged his wine like spring water. He bought two-thousand-dollar suits, then had a way of wearing them so they looked like twenty-dollar ones on the shoulders of a speakeasy bouncer. He drained his glass and shoved it away.

'That's it, that's it in a nutshell. This is a dirty industry, my boy, and it needs organisation. It needs good men to do it. Clever men. Strong men. Men like you.'

He finished speaking. The room was suddenly very quiet. Willard felt as though a million eyes were watching him.

'Well?' said his father. 'It's time to decide. Are you in? Or are you out?'

66

The door opened sharply and caught little Brad Lundmark on the behind. He fell sprawling onto the tangle of wires he'd been on his hands and knees trying to sort out.

'Whoops!' Mamie, a pale-faced, straggle-haired, enner-vated twenty-three-year-old, looked at the sprawling boy and giggled. 'Sorry.'

Brad Lundmark straightened up and dusted off. 'That's OK.'

His answer wasn't entirely accurate. As he'd fallen forward, he'd caught his palm on a thumb tack and blood was spurting from the wound.

'Oh, you're bleeding,' said the girl, in a rising voice, halfway towards accusation.

'Sorry.'

'Come on. If I knock you over, I guess I ought to patch you up,' said Mamie, still with a giggle trembling at the back of her throat.

She led the way. Brad followed. In the Brunswick garage, he'd picked up plenty of mechanical knowledge, mechan-ical and electrical. Marion was always short of handymen. Brad's services were cheap and he had eagerly, albeit at Hennessey's instigation, insinuated himself into Marion with surprising ease.

The boy recognised Mamie as one of two girls who handled most of the paperwork in Marion. Both girls lived in Marion, either married to one of Mason's goons or at least living with one. But though there were plenty of couples in Marion, there were almost no kids. Babies, yes, but once the youngsters were old enough to run around, Mason moved the families on and out. Aside from the handful of babes in diapers, Brad Lundmark was either the youngest, or certainly the youngest-looking, human in Marion. Even in girls like Mamie, there was something about his big eyes and freckled cheeks that brought out the maternal.

She took him into her office where the second girl, Suky, sat behind a huge iron typewriter swatting feebly at a bug.

'Hey, Sukes. Look what I managed to do,' said Mamie, taking Brad's still-spouting hand and holding it up.

'Ooh!' Suky made a face.

'He was fixing something and I knocked him over,' said Mamie, speaking as though he weren't there, or was deaf, or Chinese, or very stupid.

'Ooh,' said Suky again, grimacing at the blood. 'And he's . . .? You have a name?'

'Brad.'

'Brad?'

'Uh-huh.'

'Oh. And you live in town, Brad? I haven't seen you around.'

'Kind of. I sort of came to fix things. There's been a lot to do so I ended up staying around.'

'I'll get some tissues.'

Suky dug around in her bag and handed him some tissues, then cut him a slice from an iced lemon cake by her desk. Brad pressed a tissue to his hand and began to eat.

And, though he didn't show it, his heart had begun to race. *He was in Mamie and Suky's office.* There were papers strewn around. A metal filing cabinet had one drawer flopped open like a pregnant heifer. On the table in front of Suky, a sheet of paper was covered with figures ruled into two neat columns down the right-hand margin. If these weren't accounts, they sure as hell looked a lot like 'em. If this wasn't the place to find the company payroll, then it sure as hell looked like a good place to start.

Brad ate slow, thought furious.

Mamie and Suky watched him for a while, as though he were a trick animal. The fly that had been annoying Suky before buzzed around her again. She swatted at it feebly, as though actually connecting with it would have been unladylike. Brad's gaze travelled to the screen window.

'You want me to fix that for you?'

'Huh?'

'The screen there. It's torn. If I patched it, you wouldn't get the bugs, ma'am.'

'Ma'am! You hear that?' Suky and Mamie tittered at each other, before Suky turned back to the kid. 'You think you can mend it?'

'Sure.'

'Now?'

'If you want.'

The two girls looked at each other. 'That'd be great, Brad. Like payment for the cake, huh?'

'It's good cake, ma'am, thanks.'

He fetched his tools and dropped his bag with a crash.

'Ooh, Brad! Did you have to do that?'

'Sorry, ma'am, it's going to get worse than that. I'm going to need to hammer some.'

'Oh.'

The two girls looked at each other. It was a strict rule, strictly enforced, that they weren't allowed to leave the room empty unless papers had been cleared away and the office locked. On the other hand, Mamie was prone to headaches and Suky didn't want to sit right next to the hammering. Besides, how much of a threat could a little wide-eyed kid be, a little chap hardly old enough to be out of school? Suky bent down and spoke slowly.

'Brad?'

'Yes, ma'am?'

'How long do you think you'll be?'

'Not long. Maybe five minutes.'

'And you have to hammer, do you? Mamie here gets the headache terrible bad.'

'I can't fix it without hammering. Sorry.'

The two girls looked at each other again. Then Mamie said, 'How old did you say you were?'

Brad hadn't said anything about his age but, silently deducting two years from his real age, said, 'Fourteen.'

'Fourteen!'

'Uh-huh.'

'And listen Brad, now this is very important, do you have any idea of what goes on in Marion?'

'What goes on?'

'Right. What all this is about?'

'I guess . . . Some kind of business, is it? I don't see no farming, ma'am.'

It was a perfect answer. The two girls simpered, nodded and twitched finely-plucked eyebrows at each other.

'We'll be just down the hall, Brad. Mind you come get us as soon as you're done.'

'Sure thing. You got it.'

The girls left.

The bunch of keys to the filing cabinet, door and window all swung from a clumsy hoop pegged up by Mamie's desk. Brad hammered a bit, then went to the cake. He lifted the strip of icing from the top and pressed the keys, one by one, into the soft sugar. Each key made a clear impression and came away only a little sticky. Brad licked the keys clean, then dropped the precious curl of sugar in his pocket. He hammered a little more for effect, then wired the hole in the screen window tight shut. The whole job had lasted just six and a half minutes.

67

The train was an express – in theory.

In fact, miles from any scheduled stop, it let out a long screech of black steam and clattered slowly to a halt. A grey sea beat dirtily against an empty shoreline. Away from the thin dune grasses, the land was swallowed by a thick growth of trees. The sun was low in the west, making ready for bed. Willard was a man who liked civilisation. He liked big cities. He liked the noise and the lights, the people and the rush. The conductor opened the door of his compartment.

'It's here, sir.'

Willard only had one bag with him and not a heavy one even, but the conductor grabbed it before Willard could reach it and made a big show of carrying it to the end of the carriage and the open door. Three steel steps descended to the cinder track. Aside from the train and the railroad itself, there wasn't a hint of civilisation as far as Willard could see.

'You're sure?'

'Huh?'

'You're sure? This is the right place, I mean? I don't want to get out here and . . . Jesus!'

'Yeah. This is right. We stop here plenty.'

Willard climbed down after the conductor, who handed the bag over, like he'd just done the twelfth labour of Hercules. Willard gave the man a buck. The conductor climbed back on board and raised a grimy hand to the driver. The train moaned once, then heaved into motion.

Willard felt all alone at the end of the world.

A sea breeze drifted through the dunes then lost itself in the trees. A quarter of a mile on down the line, a branch line joined the main track. In the meantime, with the train gone, Willard was able to see a dirt track through the woods. He found a thin path down from the cinder embankment and half-climbed, half-slid to the track beneath. A wooden plank stretched across two posts formed a kind of bench, perhaps the only indication that this place had ever been used as a rail-stop. Willard sat down and waited.

Ten minutes went by. Long minutes. Then the sound of a car. Then a car. It drove up, then stopped. The man inside was bald and smooth-shaven, but strongly hairy on his bare arms and in the cleft of his open shirt. He had an open, leering look which Willard instinctively disliked.

'Thornton?'

'Yes.'

The man swept the front passenger seat free of some clutter and indicated that Willard should get in. Willard watched the clutter fall to the floor in front of the seat and raised his chin in a mark of disapproval. He threw his bag into the open rear seat and followed it.

'OK,' he said.

The man in front raised his eyebrows and half-shook his head. He didn't say anything out loud, but his look said, 'Swell-headed son-of-a-New-York-bitch.' He started the car with a clash of gears, then swung the car around in a dusty circle. On a shelf in front of the driver, a handgun bumped around with a packet of cigarettes and some matches. The journey was a short one – not even twenty minutes – but it felt longer. Once the man said, 'Ride down OK?'

Willard said, 'Yes.'

Two minutes later, the man wiped his bare head with his hairy arm and said, 'Warm enough for you?'

Willard said, 'Yes.'

The drive approached its end. The trees gave way. A town opened up amongst the swampy, overgrown land. Despite the back-of-beyond setting, the town was new and glossy: white, modern houses, cars not buggies, telephones and electricity. The car rolled up to a suite of office buildings. A long low warehouse squatted down behind them, like a giant beast at rest. Beyond a Tarmac parking lot, Willard saw a long grassy strip cut out of the scrubby trees. The driver indicated a door.

'In there,' he said.

'Thanks.'

Willard picked up his bag and entered, to find a man advancing in greeting. The man was dressed in shirtsleeves and pale fawn pants. He was middle-aged. He had a face that had taken some punches but given some back, a face with humour, intelligence and bite. He smiled.

'Thornton? Hi, I'm Bob Mason. Welcome to Marion.'

68

From the moment of Abe's last meeting with Haggerty McBride, he had entered into a kind of daze. He ate, flew, washed and slept just as though things were normal, but they weren't. It was as though something inside had been cut off, as though his own connection to himself had been severed.

The feeling wasn't unfamiliar. Years back, in France, as a junior lieutenant pilot under another man's command, he'd had the exact same feeling. A day might be sunny and warm. The men might be loafing around the airfield, bare-chested, goofing around with a baseball. And then everyone would be called together to be briefed on their next mission. The briefing would be short, clear, unemotional. And it would quite likely kill one of the young men who stood to listen. Then the lecture would finish. The men would go back to whatever they'd been doing before, throwing a ball or fussing over an engine problem. And Abe could never do that. The upcoming mission filled his thoughts. He unrolled every mile of the ground he was about to cover, envisaging it as it would drop away beneath his nose cone. He foresaw and played out every scenario of attack, defence, weather, mechanical complication and wind. And meantime, he felt numb, as though his feelings were hidden away in some locked compartment in a far-off place.

And it was like that now.

If he could, Abe would have wished away the chain of decisions that had brought him to this moment. But he wasn't much given over to thinking about the past and he didn't spend a lot of time regretting things that were done and irrecoverable. And as he saw it the future was becoming ever clearer.

He'd committed himself, like it or not, to a project. He couldn't now quit until that project was done. Jim Bosse had asked for some of Marion's most secret documents. Brad Lundmark's enterprise had brought those documents within reach. But Abe knew that he could never ask Brad himself to take them. Nor Pen. Nor Hennessey. Nor Arnie. Abe knew with a kind of dark foreboding that taking the documents was his job and his alone.

So he got ready.

He called Bosse in Washington, explained what he needed and why he needed it. On one of the days when it was his turn to carry the mail, he walked into Havana and bought himself a Colt revolver, with plenty of ammunition. Sending Arnie away for a couple of days on a pretext, he used the workshop to make castings from Brad Lundmark's lemon icing. Because the icing wasn't an exact guide to size, he made several copies of each key, filing each one differently so he had plenty to choose from.

And that was it. He waited for the day, then acted. During a pre-flight check, he sabotaged one of his cylinders, so that it burst during flight. The accident wasn't instantly dangerous, but it forced an immediate landing and repair. Abe had a spare cylinder in Marion, but only a defective one. He told Mason, truthfully, that it would take him hours to fix it. Mason told him to get on with it as fast as possible, as there would be a freighter due early the following day.

And that was that.

Abe was committed to a course of action that might

leave him victorious or might leave him dead. But the strangest thing was still this: that he felt nothing. He felt almost nothing at all.

69

He'd done it. Why not? He'd taken the deal, taken the money, taken the good things that were on offer. '*Are you in or are you out?*' What a question! Willard had been genuinely surprised they'd felt the need to ask.

'In or out? Gosh! In, of course, in.'

His father had been powerfully moved.

'Good boy, Willard! Good boy!'

He'd leaped from his seat and gripped Willard's hand so tightly that the two locked hands went completely white, with spots of red burning at the knuckles. Willard had seen his father's face as he'd never seen it before: tears swimming in his eyes, emotion trembling in his lips.

'By God, son, I'm proud of you. The old Firm will be in good hands for a while yet.' He struck Ted Powell on the shoulder. 'This old dog never had any kids.' He punched himself on the chest. 'And this old dog tried hard enough, but only managed one son from five attempts. There have been times when I've doubted you, but I shouldn't have done. I made things tougher for you than Ted would have done if it had been just down to him. I don't think I could have stood it, if you'd flunked. But you didn't. Brains and guts and persistence. You've done the family proud.'

And when he looked back on his decision, Willard realised that it hadn't been the money that had swayed him. Not the money, not the yachts, not the houses, not the job. It had been simply this: his father. For the first time in his life, Willard had felt the full rush of his father's approval. The feeling was intoxicating. It was better than wine, better than money, better than Rosalind.

Powell too had been generous with his congratulations. 'Take a holiday. You've earned it. What's the name of that girl of yours? Rosalind? Take her somewhere nice. Instead of freezing your ass off up here, why not head down to the sun? Go to Florida, fish a little, swim a little, eat plenty, get some sun, hit the casinos down there. I can give you some names.'

'Don't hit the casinos too hard, though.' Willard's father spoke like the protective parent, then immediately regretted it. 'Hell, Will, hit 'em hard as you like. If you lose money, come to me. I don't want you to feel short. The Firm will be happy to stand you a good time. What's that place you stay at, Ted? The Royal Poinciana? That's all right, is it? Comfortable? Take yourself a suite there, Willard. A nice one. Just let me know what it costs. I'll take care of it.'

It was only after a while (and two more bottles of the Muscadet), that Willard realised he still had a problem.

'Gosh, though,' he admitted, 'I don't know what I'm going to say to Ros. She's awfully hot on this whole Arthur Martin business. I don't know what she'd say if she thought I'd just turned chicken at the last moment.'

Powell had a cigar in his hands and began the whole business of lighting up. 'Girl trouble, huh? How many times have I heard that?'

Junius Thornton raised a finger in warning. 'You understand that under no circumstances do you tell anybody what you know about the Firm. Womenfolk most certainly included.'

'Yes, of course.'

Powell got the cigar going and spent a few seconds imitating a Detroit factory chimney. 'We'll fix things, don't worry.'

'Yes, but how? What shall I tell her?'

Powell shrugged. 'Tell her you found out the bad guys. Say there were some folks at the bank who were up to no good. Taking money from the mob. Involved in the rackets. Something like that. We'd prefer it if you didn't mention alcohol as such, but if you must, you must. Let her ask a few questions, give her a few answers. Then clam up. Say there's a police investigation. You've been told not to talk. The details will emerge in due course.'

'It'll be a bit difficult if there's nothing at all to show for it. I mean, wouldn't the cops want to make a few arrests, that sort of thing?'

'Good point. We'll fire a couple of people, have the police pick 'em up for something. That man McVeigh is a pain in the ass. We could lose him, no problem. I can think of some others we could toss out, at that. And we pay the City cops plenty. They'll be happy to help. We'll make sure it makes the papers. Nothing too big, of course, but a few column inches in the *Times*. That should keep her thinking you're the big hero.'

Willard gulped. The briskness with which Powell dealt with wrongful arrest, police corruption and the sundry details of running a large criminal organisation still came as a shock.

'Good idea. OK. I'll tell her. She'll be pleased, really.'

Pleased? She had been ecstatic, adoring. Before he'd left for Canada, Rosalind had loved Willard but – as they'd both secretly known – she'd always held something back. Something in their relationship had always been slightly reserved, provisional. That changed.

Willard had played his part to perfection. From Montana he sent Rosalind a telegram stating simply, 'GREAT NEWS AM SAFE TELL ALL ON RETURN'. He hadn't hurried back. The two founders of Powell Lambert wanted to use their time in the north to meet some of their major clients, Chicago-based mostly, but others from Detroit, Cleveland and Pittsburgh as well. Willard tagged along, keen to learn the business from the men who had built it. Five days later, he was back in New York.

'Oh, Willard!'

Rosalind had pressed herself into his arms like one of Willard's movie heroines after Willard had snatched her from the clocktower, untied her from the railway track, or used his plane to fight off twelve carloads of highly armed bad guys. She'd swallowed the story. Why wouldn't she? Willard could point to the men that had been fired, the arrests that had been made, the letters of thanks from the Chief of Police, from Ted Powell himself. And the thing that had only ever been provisional between them vanished.

Rosalind was – not in a crude way, but definitely never-theless – waiting for Willard to ask her to marry him. If he had done, she'd have said yes. Not just yes, but yes definitely, yes blissfully.

70

The heat of the day was decaying into long green and brown shadows. Up on the roof of the world, the sun was ribboning the sky with twenty-mile streamers of rose and white. It wasn't hot, but Abe felt stifled. The air in his lungs felt as thick and unrefreshing as boiled seawater. But that was a physical feeling, not a feeling-feeling. He still felt cut off from himself, still determined to do what he was about to do. He worked slowly, clearing the wreckage of the damaged cylinder from his engine, checking carefully for any lodged shards of metal which could come loose and cause havoc.

Then he heard it: an aero engine's beat, when the sky should have been clear. He heard it, then saw it: the DH-4 shouldering up against the wind, ducking through the belt of turbulence at the end of the airstrip, then that awkward-beautiful side-slip landing. The big plane shook its speed off into the coarse-bladed grass, then fish-tailed over to Abe. He watched it come, grim-faced and unwelcoming. Pen cut the engine, then swung herself out of the cockpit, smiling.

'Hey there, Cap'n,' she said, offering a mock-salute.
'Hey.'
'Mason called. Said you had an engine problem.'
'Right.'
'A cylinder? Is that right? Something about a cylinder?' Pen's voice floated off uncertainly, not quite sure whether planes had cylinders or not.

'Yep. One busted over the ocean. Had to come in.'

'You told him you had a spare, only there was some kind of problem with it.'

'Right. Inside of the cylinder wasn't milled right. Problems with the piston-head.'

'The piston-head, huh?' Pen backed quickly away from the technicalities. 'Anyway, he was anxious to get things moving. Arnie thought it might save time if I brought you up a spare.'

She pulled a cylinder from her jacket, shining dull gold in the dying light. Abe felt a spasm of annoyance. Little as he liked what he had committed himself to doing, he'd sooner go ahead on his timetable and without interference.

'Let's see,' he said rudely.

Pen gave him the cylinder. Abe stumbled slightly as he took it, then stood up. During his stumble, he switched the two cylinders, substituting the bad one for the good, keeping the good one concealed in the fold of his jacket. He pretended to examine Pen's cylinder, then said with annoyance, 'Tsk . . . now that's not like Arnie.'

'There's a problem?'

'This cylinder has the same problem. Here, feel.'

He passed her the metal tube and she felt silently for the flaw. She couldn't find it at first, then could.

'Gosh! Yes, I see.'

'Doesn't matter. We can file it. It takes time, but it's not hard. If you like, I'll show you how. You can do it.'

He didn't wait for an answer, just turned on his heel and entered the tool shed, where he switched on the single fly-speckled bulb. He looked around, expecting Pen to follow, but found her hanging just outside the doorway, staring in. Her face, usually so composed, had become complex, like a puzzle that was beyond Abe to decipher.

'Pen?'

'You want me to file it? Me?'

'Sure. Why not?'

327

'And Arnie gave me a dud cylinder? One with, I don't know, a bad piston-mill, or whatever you said.'

'A milling problem on the inside surface. It does happen, you know.'

'Right. One cylinder bursts in flight. You've got a spare, but it's dud. Arnie gives me one to bring up to you, only it's busted too. That's some bad cylinders we've got.'

Abe shrugged. There was something rough and ragged in Pen's face and voice; he wasn't sure what. His own emotions had turned into a swirl. He tried to look inside himself to see what was going on, but everything seemed opaque, tobacco-coloured, hidden.

Pen stepped suddenly into the hut and reached down to Abe's jacket. She felt the hard smooth bulge of metal. Abe's stumble – a misdirection – one card trick too many. There was a moment's strained and unbearable silence. Then she said, 'How about we use the perfectly good cylinder you've got right there?'

Abe stuttered for a second. He didn't like being out of control of things, but didn't seem in control of anything just at the moment, not even himself.

'Just a moment,' he said hoarsely.

He walked out, twenty or thirty feet away, and took a leak. He came back around the hut the other way. Then he went to Pen's plane and started the motor at low revs. The beat of the engine blotted out all other sounds. He came back. 'I don't see anyone, but we'll still talk low.'

She nodded.

'How did you know?' he asked.

'Everything. Too many bad cylinders. Working after dark. Everything.'

'I didn't want you to know.'

'Know what?'

The muscles in Abe's jaw knotted and unknotted. He wanted to say and didn't want to. He didn't know what he wanted. But he put his hand beneath the worktop and,

328

from some unseen compartment, drew out a handful of dark metal shapes. The shapes were keys.

'Brad got a hold of some keys to an office. He thinks the office is the one where the papers we need are kept. These are copies of the keys.' He put his hand into the tray of keys and let them run, chinking dully, through his fingers. The warm metal and the noise of the keys as they fell was the most real thing in Abe's world right now.

Pen stared at the keys, her face puckering in something close to dislike.

'So that's it,' she said bitterly. 'We try to work together up until this point, then that's it. Brad gets you the keys and you don't even tell me you've got them. I guess you've got some dumb-ass plan to break in and get the documents. How are you going to get them copied, authenticated and returned tonight?'

'Bosse. He's up the creek in a rubber boat. He'll come down at one a.m. We'll go upriver until we're far enough from Marion, then copy the documents, sign off on 'em, then he'll bring me back.'

'And if you're caught?'

Abe shrugged. If he were caught, he would be killed. He had a gun in his pocket, but he'd been an airman, not an infantryman. He wasn't a skilled shot and he'd be heavily outgunned on ground that wasn't his own. If he were killed, he hoped that Mason would do it quickly and cleanly, but worried that the Marion way might involve a good measure more brutality. Aside from that, he wasn't sure he felt anything much apart from the dull heaviness that had been filling him.

'I meant what about me? What about Arnie?'

'Bosse has sent McBride to fetch you both away tonight. Obviously now you'll have to go with Bosse by boat. Sorry about that.'

'I beg your pardon?' Pen's mouth fell open with contempt

and disbelief. 'You're still going to go ahead? You're unbelievable! Jesus Christ, if I'd only known . . .'

Pen's extremely uncharacteristic blasphemy took Abe aback. Even in his dullness, the shock of the expression woke him up.

'Why wouldn't I go ahead? I don't . . .'

Pen came fully into the light now, her voice scathing and her face disgusted. 'Listen. You know how I knew what you were up to? The real answer? It wasn't the light or Arnie screwing up. It was you. That you wanted me to file the cylinder. That you gave me a job to do.'

'I don't understand.'

Pen was hissing her words now, quietly but with a furious intensity. 'You know why I joined this venture? To be a part of something. I didn't want to be just a girl with a hobby, I wanted to be an aviator with a job. This job seemed like a good one. But I was wrong. You haven't included me since I started. You think you have but you haven't.'

Abe's face was grey in the dim yellow light. The corners of his mouth had a downward slant, a grim tightness. He felt assaulted by Pen's anger, but there were other feelings too, lost in the dark-brown swirl of his mind. He said, 'You wanted to help with the mail route and you fly it almost on your own. You fly the ocean. You watch the freighters. You collect information like the rest of us. That's including you, isn't it?'

'Right. That's what you tell yourself. That's why you think you've done what you need to do.'

'Yes. I think I have.' His voice abbreviated and tightened. He sounded like a military officer handing out orders. Perhaps it was that which prompted Pen to switch tack abruptly – or appear to switch tack, anyway.

'I'm *not* in the army. You are *not* my commander. This is *not* the war,' she said.

'It *is* a kind of war.' Abe leaped up from his stool, found the shed too small to go anywhere and sat back down again.

'It isn't! In the war, your men weren't free to choose.

330

They were there to fight or be shot for desertion. I'm here because I choose to be. I know the risks.'

'Do you? Do you?' Abe had caught Pen's fever. His eyes were burning. 'Mathematically, perhaps. In terms of flying, then certainly. But do you really know what it's like? Because I *do*. I *do*.'

'This isn't the war.'

'It isn't? Pen, you don't know death until you've lived with it. Lived and lived and lived with it. I became squadron commander on May 18th, 1918. In less than six months, the war was over. In that time, I lost three quarters of my men. Killed, wounded, captured, missing or too shattered and exhausted to fly another mission. Three quarters! And each man lost meant a new face in the cockpit. A boy. A novice. A child who could turn a plane and thought he knew how to fly. A child whom I sent out to face the enemy because he had no choice and I had no choice and the poor goddamn enemy had no choice.'

'So that's it. I'm right. You think you'll keep me safe. You'll keep me out of it. You'll take the risks yourself, get killed yourself, sacrifice yourself because you still feel guilty for staying alive.'

'That's not it.'

'Horseshit. That's horseshit. I'm just so right you can't admit it.'

Then suddenly, and for no obvious reason, something changed. The heat had gone out of Pen's anger. She had surrendered not an inch of ground, but her manner changed. She put her hands to the back of her head and scrunched up her sandy bob. It was a gesture she used little. Her hair was hardly even long enough to be scrunched. But the unconscious action, just for one short moment, made her look positively short-haired, *boyish*. Abe remembered his very first sight of her, sliding out of her cockpit, half-expecting a male hand to help her, pulling her helmet off and shaking her hair free of the grimy sheepskin. She had

331

looked boyish then. Boyish, in the same way that Abe's eighteen-year-old recruits had been boyish.

Abe gaped at the sight. He almost literally didn't know if he was looking at Pen Hamilton in peacetime America or a pursuit pilot in wartime France. The two times and places began to merge in his mind. The commotion in his mind subsided – or clarified. A huge sadness rolled over him. He nodded, suddenly tired.

'You're right. You're totally right.'

'Oh!' Pen was taken aback by the speed and completeness of her victory. She floundered for a moment, then simply put her hand to his shoulder and said, 'I'm sorry.'

'I did the best I could. I have never reproached myself for not doing more. But all the same. I was their commander and they died. I felt like the overseer, the factory foreman, tending a conveyor belt of death. And you remind me. I hadn't realised that you did, but you do. From the first time we met. I never knew.'

Pen was profoundly moved, her eyes full of the tears that Abe was too much of a man to shed. Outside, the airplane engine continued to beat. Inside, Abe remained seated, Pen standing close, her face damp with the tears that were really his. Time passed.

After a long while, Abe covered her hand with his and pressed it. 'Thank you.' She shook her head, brushing aside thanks or apologies, content to remain in the silence. Eventually, they pulled away. Abe grinned at her: a ghostly, hollow grin.

'It was a pretty lousy plan, any case.'

Pen nodded. 'The worst.'

'All action, no preparation. The way to kill people.'

'Right. What happened to "Prepare, Observe, Manoeuvre, Destroy"?'

'Oh, I don't know. In the war, most of my fellow squadron commanders preferred, "Rush In, Be Brave, Shoot Like Hell, Then Die".'

They smiled.

'Listen,' said Abe, 'Maybe we can do something smarter. Suppose we make tonight just a reconnaissance trip? I won't go further than is safe. You can watch out for me all the time. I won't aim to take any documents, just find out if I can get to them. I'll call Bosse from the airfield and tell him to back off.'

'You can do that?'

Abe nodded 'Pre-agreed code. I've got a number where I can reach him.'

Pen fixed Abe with her gaze. Like Abe's, the silence and steadiness of her stare could be disconcerting. Abe guessed she was trying to evaluate if he was fit to do anything dangerous tonight.

'I'll be careful,' he said. 'If I smell any trouble, I'll back off.'

'OK. In that case, OK.'

Abe looked at her again. The woman-flier and the boy-soldier merged once more. He still felt the sadness that had come over him, but beyond the sadness there was something else, like sunlight glimmering on the edge of cloud.

'They were only kids,' he said. 'Just kids.'

'I know.'

'You're sure you want to do this?'

'I'm sure.'

Abe took a deep, shuddering breath. Outside, it was dark, but in another couple of hours it would be inkier still. He picked up the bad cylinder from the worktop.

'OK. Well, we've got an engine to fix, then an office to burglarize.'

Pen grinned, wide and white in the gloom. *We*, he'd said, *we*. Said it and meant it.

71

Mason escorted Willard through the office building to a big white stucco villa compound at the back, to a big easy room, nice rugs over tiled floors, cute reed furniture dotted with sage green cushions, big windows screened by venetian blinds, heavy air conditioning, and a smell of cigar smoke and whisky.

'Trip down OK?'

'Yes, thank you. I must say, I wondered about the train stop. I could see myself waiting on the track-side for ever.'

'Privacy. We like it.'

'I can see.' Ted Powell's office had taken care of all the arrangements for the Florida trip, but had booked tickets which brought Rosalind and Willard south from Charleston by different routes. Willard had given her some excuse to do with meeting up with old acquaintances – but Powell's real purpose, he now saw, was to maintain the near perfect cloak of secrecy which covered Marion. When he met up with Rosalind in Palm Springs first thing the following morning, she'd have no idea that her lover had had any business in a place so far from anywhere that most deserts were better connected.

'Drink?'

Mason pulled down the lid of a folding bar affair at the side of the room. Every possible sort of alcohol was on offer, from Italian grappa to Southern sour mash whiskeys. Willard chose a white Jamaican rum with a splash of soda and helped himself to a thick Cuban cigar. Mason took a shot of whiskey, no ice, no water, and sat down.

'So,' said Mason, 'you get the pleasure of looking after us?'

'Yes. Just promoted.'

'You're kind of young-looking, if you don't mind me saying. You been with the Firm long?'

'Long enough,' Willard said, thinking that really he'd been part of the Firm all his life. But it was true about the promotion. He was now an Associate Banker in the Investment Bureau. 'The Bureau houses everything important in the Firm,' Powell had told him. 'It's the only area where there are no secrets, where everyone's in the know.' And though Willard had joined the Bureau as its most junior citizen, he was also the boss's son, a possible leader of the Firm.

But Willard had done a lot of growing up since Hollywood. Willard knew that though he was a possible leader of the Firm, he had only passed the first test of many. He had to prove himself and was aching to do so. And Powell Lambert being what it was, its two leaders hadn't wasted much time in getting Willard started. When Powell had suggested bringing Rosalind down to Florida for a vacation, he'd had an ulterior motive. And his motive had been to bring him here.

Every large import channel (or cluster of smaller ones) was looked after by an individual officer in the Investment Bureau. Willard was to be given this: the Marion import route. He would be responsible for supervising Mason, for liaising with clients, for arranging transportation, for co-ordinating the whole complex network of alcohol, finance, transport, and bribery on which the Firm depended. How well Willard discharged his new responsibility would do a lot to determine whether he'd ever be trusted to lead the Firm. There couldn't possibly be a bigger reward for success. There couldn't possibly be a bigger penalty for failure.

'And by the way,' Willard added, 'I should say that New York is very happy with the way things are run here.'

'They oughta be.'

'As a matter of fact, there's a notion going around that we need to pick our import channels, then build them. At the moment, we've got alcohol coming from all over. It's not efficient.'

'You're saying more business is going to be coming our way?'

'At the moment, we have twenty-two import routes active on the east coast. Fifteen more coming in from Canada. More in the west. More in the south. More than fifty active routes all told.' Willard recited the figures as though they were the most familiar facts in the world.

'That don't sound too efficient.' Mason's voice went still and careful, as though not wanting to interrupt Willard's stream of thought.

'No. We built things that way in the beginning for safety reasons. If we lost a route or two, if we lost a consignment or two, then we had plenty of others to cover the loss. That made a lot of sense while we still had a big problem with hijack. It made sense before our relationships with the law enforcement services were put on a proper professional basis.' Willard continued to speak, almost exactly as his father had put it to him.

'Right,' said Mason in a whisper. 'But now there ain't a cop in the country that doesn't want our money. There ain't too many hijackers who want a crack at our booze.'

'Exactly.'

'So?'

'So the idea in New York is that we should eliminate most of our import routes. We should concentrate on the best.'

'Including this one?'

'I'm here to tell you that Marion is the most important route we have. Mr Powell himself asked me to come down here. He wants me to verify that everything is being run in the proper way. A security check, if you like. A double check on all your excellent work. But assuming that I'm happy – and I expect to be – then we'll expand.'

'Expand? Any idea of . . . Any clue at all as to . . .?'

'We'd aim to treble the quantities you handle within a year. After that, maybe the same again. After that, who knows? Powell wants this route to be the largest entry point for alcohol anywhere in the United States.'

Mason had held his breath as Willard spoke, then went on holding it for a second or two more. Then he breathed out, and his face broke into a smile, bigger and bigger, until his whole face seemed consumed by that one huge, sunny, criminal smile.

'And you're gonna be the guy in New York helping us do it, right?'

'Right.'

'You have sole responsibility, or are you reporting to someone else on this?'

'Sole responsibility. I report directly to Mr Powell.'

'Powell? Shit, pal, someone likes you a lot.'

'I guess.'

Mason rolled his whiskey glass around in his hand. His face was twinkling with a rising pleasure and excitement. He punched Willard softly on the shoulder and said, 'If we do things right here, I figure there are gonna be a few bonuses flying around. Some for you, some for me.'

'Mr Powell told me to tell you that there is virtually no limit to the rewards available.'

Mason smiled and raised his glass. 'No limit. I like that. No limit.'

They got down to business.

Willard knew the way things worked at Powell Lambert in general terms. He knew about the import, transport and distribution of alcohol. He knew about the extra smuggling which made a further profit on the side. He knew about the bank's careful financing and organisation of the trade. He knew something, not much, of the close relationship between the bank and its clients, the way the Firm had almost overnight become sole banker to the elite criminal fraternity of America. He knew, again in general terms only, about the way the Firm set out to bribe anyone who mattered, from federal law enforcement down. But he knew nothing about the specifics of Mason's operation. Ted Powell had been careful on that point.

'No reason for you to know, Will. I want you to go down there with an open mind. Come back. Tell me what you like, what you don't. If I brief you too hard in advance, I'm gonna make it harder for you to see things fresh.'

And that, almost, had been that. But Willard had noticed something. That '*I*' which Powell always used. And it wasn't just the way he spoke. It was Powell who came into work on Wall Street every day. It was Powell who was there when daily operating decisions were made. It was Powell who oversaw the insurance department. It was Powell who, as far as Willard could see, ran the Firm. Willard had asked his father about it.

'Oh, you know, it took two men when we were getting things set up. These days, I spend most of my time with the armaments business. Thornton Ordnance is still a dependable profit-maker, but it needs attention. Too much damn peace-making.'

Willard had found it odd, but no more. In the meantime, he had plenty else to worry about. Mason began talking about the operation under his command. He talked about the Havana purchasing agent, the principal suppliers, the current state of prices. Outside, a humid Georgian evening rolled over into a humid Georgian night. Over the air conditioning and the burr of conversation, Willard once fancied that he could hear the sound of an airplane engine. Not in the air, but on the ground. But the thought was an idiotic one, and he shook clear of it. The sound was probably just an electric generator or a car engine idling. The conversation ran on, until they reached the topic of transportation.

'We used to run these little launches up and down. They were cheap to run, only we lost some to the Coastguard, some to hijack. There's plenty of activity off the coast these days. Fishing boats, rum-runners, you name it. Everyone's carrying rods. Tense. Things happened. We lost boats and men. Costs kept riding up. So we changed things around. We got a coupla freighters, barge-type things, enough cargo space to take three thousand cases of drink. They're heavily armed and there's not many fishermen fancy the look of 'em.'

'Freighters, though?' said Willard.

'Too slow, you mean?'

'Well, aren't they?'

'They didn't tell you?'

'Didn't tell me what?'

'Mr Powell and Mr Lambert have operations all over this great country of ours. You honestly don't know why they picked you to look after this one?'

Willard shook his head, feeling irritated.

'You're going to like this. They picked you, 'cause you're a birdman. America's favourite ace and all.'

'I don't get you.'

'Airplanes. That's our secret. We got airplanes looking out for us. They check out the coast, tell us if it's clear. We only go in if we get the OK.'

Willard gaped. 'You have observation planes?'

'Two of 'em. DH-4s, if that means anything to you. It's just a box with wings to me.'

Willard got control of his astonishment. The airplane engine, the grass strip, the whole improbable set-up seemed to get both stranger and more explicable in an instant.

In the meantime, Mason was running on to other subjects. There was the railroad, for starters, and Mason wanted to be able to load up ten or twenty railcars at a time. That meant complex negotiations with railroad officials – negotiations that Willard would need to handle from New York. Everyone needed their bribe. The thing was getting the payments right. Not too little. Not too much.

'And the police, presumably? These freight trains have to move through a lot of states.'

Mason shrugged. 'We take care of county officials. You guys take care of the state and federal side of things. Don't seem like any of us have a lot of problems these days. That's who's making the real money. You wanna make a little dough, be a bootlegger. You wanna get rich, be a cop. Ain't that the way?'

'County law enforcement? Down here I guess . . .?'

'Yeah, you guess right. We ain't on no road. Our railroad line's a dead end. We ain't in anybody's faces. Sometimes I've been with operations where the cops are friendly, only they think every now and then they've got to make a bust 'cause otherwise folks think they ain't behaving like cops no more. That's not like that here. There's only one regular cop in the whole of Okinochee County. We make sure that cop is very, very happy with us. A couple of times a year, he gives us a call, says he's gonna come and bust us. He gives us plenty of notice. We clean things up, invite him in. He goes away saying he ain't found nothing aside from a load of bananas. After that's happened a coupla times, it kinda takes the pressure off.'

'I'll bet.'

'And aside from that, there ain't too many folks in the state that even know we're here.'

Willard looked out of the window. Up on a low hill, not more than a mile away, stood a cluster of low wooden-built houses, poor-looking, suffering.

'Your neighbours there?'

'Independence.'

'Huh?'

340

'Independence, name of the town.'

'You have any trouble with them?'

Mason grimaced. 'No, not really, only that's a way of saying, yeah, a little bit. It's a funny kinda town, Independence. It's one of those real old-fashioned places. A slice of old-time America. Independence was dry way before Volstead. Most likely they'll be dry a century after. And some of the folks there are mighty keen on their principles. Caused us trouble. Called the cops. That didn't do a lot for them, but then they shook things up with the county newspaper men. Wrote letters to State Congress in Atlanta. Got a meeting with the state governor. We sorted everything out, of course, but those kind of things don't come cheap. And you're always worried that one of these days, something's gonna spring a major leak.'

'So? How do you manage things now?'

Mason shrugged. 'Some of 'em we buy. The farmland round here is poor as hell. You don't see a lot of autos on the roads here. Shouldn't think most of the houses up there even have an indoor tub. But we've got money. Jobs. We're generous. Mostly people are on our side because our dough talks louder than their principles.'

'And the exceptions?'

'Some of them have taken their precious principles straight up into heaven.'

'Yes.' Willard gulped, still not entirely used to Powell Lambert's approach to business.

'And some of them we're working on. We can't just go into town with a couple of Tommy guns, like we could in Chicago. There's not a lot of homicide round here. People get kind of upset about it. But we apply pressure. A broken leg here. A fire there. I wouldn't say we got 'em licked, but we got 'em hemmed in, defensive. The town's dying to be quite honest with you. Another few years and there'll be nothing much there, 'cept for poor folks on our payroll. Meantime, we keep an eye on the main troublemakers. If they start to kick up stink, we'll go do what we gotta do.'

They continued talking. Detail. Detail. Detail. Modern industrial organisation and fanatical attention to detail was what kept Powell Lambert fifteen miles out ahead of the chasing pack. Willard was searching in his questions. Mason was efficient and thorough in his answers. Eventually, Willard reached out for his glass of rum, found it empty, and stood up.

'It's a fantastic business unit you have here. I'm impressed.'

Mason grinned. 'You haven't even heard the best of it. This bit'll really crack you up.'

'Yes?'

'You wanna guess who I've got flying observation for me?'

'Who?'

'Go on. Guess.'

'How should I know? Charlie Chaplin. Shoeless Joe. Jack Dempsey. Mary Pickford.'

'He's here now. Out there. Fixing up his engine. A pal of yours.'

'A pal of mine?'

'Uh-huh.'

Willard shook his head. A friend of his? He doubted it.

'Rockwell.'

'Rockwell? Captain Rockwell? The guy who . . .?'

'Yeah. The guy you flew with. The guy who shot down around two million Krautheads.'

Mason grinned like he was training to wrap a smile right around the back of his head. Willard knew he was expected to respond with something similar. But he didn't.

'Out there?'

'Right there, out on the landing field, unless he's done already. You wanna go along, say hi?'

Willard was about to let out an appalled 'No!' when he

realised that Mason had been joking. The precise connection between Marion and New York was unknown to anyone except Mason, and possibly also Frank Lambaugh in Cuba.

But Willard's feelings were still in tumult. Having been standing, he sat back down. His hands gripped the side of the cane armchair so tightly it began to creak. He had one of those episodes, where the world suddenly goes buzzy and distant, where it feels like you're seeing things from down the end of a long, dark tube. Leaning forwards and with deliberate emphasis on every word, he said, 'You cannot use Captain Rockwell to fly for you.'

Mason laughed. Sure this kid had theoretical responsibility in New York, but he, Mason, was the man who ran things. 'He's a good guy. You oughta know that.'

'Captain Rockwell is one of the best men in the world. That's why you can't use him.'

Willard wasn't even quite sure why he was saying what he was saying. Was it that he didn't trust Rockwell's motives? Or was it that he didn't want one of the few true heroes of the last war to be sullied by contact with a grubby reality? He didn't know, he didn't care. He just knew he didn't want Rockwell within a hundred miles of Marion. The buzzy feeling had gone, but he still felt hot discs glowing high up on each cheek.

'He's OK,' Mason persisted.

'So you say.'

'He never even wanted to join us. I practically had to go on my knees.'

'Maybe he just wanted to see you on your knees.'

'And we tested him. He came through two hundred per cent.'

'Tested him?'

'We gave him an opportunity to blab to the cops. Encouraged him. Did everything we could to make him.'

'What is that supposed to mean?'

'We offered a little bit of carrot, then a little bit of stick. I'm sorry. I know you like the guy.'

Willard jerked his mind away from Mason's 'little bit of stick'.

'And?'

'He didn't say nothing. Not a word. He's probably the best value guy on our payroll.'

'You said you had two planes. Who flies the other one?'

'Aw, now this bit I don't like so much. We got a girl, would you believe it? Rockwell insisted on her. She can fly some, so it seems. Our freighter captains think the world of her.'

'I don't like it.' Willard's watch ticked loudly on his wrist. He thought of Rosalind. He needed to catch the next train down the coast if he were to arrive at Palm Springs first thing tomorrow. He moved restlessly in his chair. 'It stinks.'

'It's working a million dollars.'

'Can't you get some other fliers?'

'Why? Why would I? Besides, you'll know more about this than me, but it ain't so easy flying out over the ocean, is it? One of these days, one of those airplanes is gonna fall out of the sky and make a big splash. Not to mention the storms we get down here.'

'Well, they aren't going to fly in bad weather, are they?'

'They do.'

'They do?'

'Yeah. All except the worst.'

'Even the girl?'

'Yeah, her too.'

Willard fidgeted some more. 'D'you watch them?'

'Yeah. Some.'

'That's not good enough. Jesus Christ! This is Captain Rockwell you're dealing with.' Rockwell had shot down nineteen German machines. He'd been able to do that by being invisible when he wanted to be, lethal when he didn't. 'I don't care what it costs, we need to watch him.

344

Twenty-four hours a day. See where he goes, who he sees, what he does. Everything.'

'You wanna do that, you'd better get your insurance department involved. We normally only handle the little stuff ourselves.'

'No!' Willard's answer was explosive.

'No?'

'No.' Willard repeated the word more quietly this time, surprised by the force of his own reactions. 'I want to keep this as quiet as we can. If we get the insurance men involved, we may find it hard to get them uninvolved.'

Mason nodded. It was a reason he could sympathise with. 'OK.'

'And you've got guards on the office buildings now? I mean, if he's here at night . . .'

'Sure. Least, I send a guy around every hour or so. We've never had a problem . . .'

'Every hour? That's nowhere near enough. I want two men around the perimeter all night. I want another man inside. And a fourth guy to prowl around and check that those three are doing their job. This is Rockwell you've got outside.'

'This isn't the first night he's been here, not by a long stretch.'

'Then you'd better hope he hasn't taken advantage before now.'

'The doors are all locked. We're strict about who gets keys.'

Willard puffed scornfully at the idea that his old commander might be stopped by a set of locks. He wouldn't budge until Mason had picked up the phone and given the necessary orders.

Willard nodded. 'And his phone? His home telephone? You can listen in on it, I assume?'

'Sure . . .' Mason's tone was uncertain.

'Sure? What does that mean? Yes or no?'

'He don't exactly have a home phone. He lives in a shack behind the airplane hangar. There's a phone in there, though, and we listen to that . . . He lives kind of rough for a guy on his income.'

'Oh, and that gives you a lot of reassurance about his motives, does it?'

'He's bought his parents their farm back from the bank. Every month it's a new tractor, or a harvester, or whatever. I guess maybe the guy plans to make his bundle then retire there.'

'Sure. I can just see Captain Rockwell planting string beans and going to bed happy.'

The two men stared each other out. Willard was, in theory, the boss. Mason was twenty years older and a million times more experienced. At last, Mason grunted.

'OK. You want us to track him, I guess we can sort something out.'

'Good.' Willard relaxed. 'And don't trust him. No matter what. Don't trust him. He's a pursuit pilot, remember. One of the very, very best. If you let him get close, close enough so you can see him, then it's too late. By that point, you're already dead.'

72

They hadn't done it, hadn't got close.

Abe had got inside the office building, but he hadn't taken two paces inside before there was a repeated owl call behind him – the agreed warning signal from Pen – and Abe himself heard the tread of a guard further on down the block. He'd left the building ultra-cautiously, blessing the dark night that surrounded them. He found Pen and the pair of them waited outside for two hours, watching the block, waiting for an opportunity to enter safely. But the building was always guarded. Tightly, seriously guarded. The weird thing was that, inexplicably, it seemed as though security had just been radically tightened; literally that night, that hour almost. There seemed an extra tension, an extra sharpness in the movement of the guards.

Eventually they gave up and crept away into the shelter of some thick scrub.

'Sorry to ask,' said Abe, 'but I think it might be a good idea if you lay down and kind of messed yourself up a little.'

'You want me to . . .?' Pen began to ask, then she realised what he meant. 'Oh.'

She lay on her back in the dirt and rolled around until her hair and clothes were muddied up with dirt and leaves. Abe knelt down and got dirt on his elbows and knees. They both undid some buttons. The darkness hid Pen's face, which was blushing hotly.

'Sorry to ask,' said Abe, 'only if they wonder where we've been, then –'

'Right. You're right. Don't worry.'

Embarrassed, they made their way to the boarding house which Mason operated for themselves and the freighter crews and anyone else who passed through Marion without staying long. As the booze volumes had increased, Mason had increasingly avoided bringing any gambling business into the town, but a couple of villas still housed gaming rooms, and there was a beat of loud gramophone music and alcohol-fuelled laughter from some of the doors they passed. When they reached the boarding house, they stood outside and brushed some of the dirt away, as any furtive couple would have done. As Abe swept the dust from Pen's back, bottom and hair, he realised that, having almost never touched her before today, he had now touched her twice in one evening: the first time in the tool shed when she'd put her hand on his shoulder out of sympathy for his feelings and kept it there, with tears damp in her eyes; and now this. Her body felt shockingly slender, shockingly warm. It felt like the most intimate thing he'd ever done.

Ten days later, they hadn't bottomed out the mystery of the sudden acceleration in security. Brad Lundmark heard from someone that there had been a visitor in town that night, an out-of-towner but not a gambler, an important person, apparently. But Mason had visitors often enough. Whoever the vistor had been, he'd gone again almost straight away and the heightened security remained. Brad had made a couple more visits to Mamie and Suky, begging iced tea and cake off them and allowing them, in exchange, to treat him as some kind of exotic pet. Brad said he was sure the two girls looked after all Marion's key paperwork. He said if the accounts and the payroll existed anywhere, they'd be in that office. Brad himself had offered more than once to investigate further, but Abe, Pen and Hennessey were all unanimous about refusing to let the kid place himself in any further danger. The boy still did odd jobs for Mason, but most of the time now he was back in Brunswick, looking after the tin Lizzies and battered De Sotos that crept through the door of the garage with steaming radiators or tattered brake pads.

But meantime, a piece of much brighter news.

That night in the tool shed had changed something for Abe. When before he had been reluctant to share, he now seemed, not eager exactly, but willing to try. He and Arnie had some big demonstration planned. It involved Abe's collection of castings, and, though Pen knew Arnie knew more than she did, they both knew that Abe had kept the biggest secret from them both.

They stood now in the cool green shade of the water tank.

Arnie had rigged up some complex arrangement of hoses, tanks and pumps which Pen didn't understand. At the bottom of the big tank, there was a chute leading down to a secondary tank beneath. A dozen of Abe's precious models sat on the grass, like a combat squadron in miniature. Arnie smacked a thick coil of rubber hose into an outlet valve then stood back.

Abe looked at Pen. 'Ready?'

'Ready.'

'OK, now this is a water tunnel. A poor man's wind tunnel. See this?' He picked up one of his castings and handed it to Pen. 'Recognise it?'

After a hard day battling headwinds the day before, Pen's arms were tired and the little model felt heavy. But the shape of the plane was unmistakable.

'Of course. This is my Curtiss racer.'

'Right. And what you've got there is a scale model, exact to one part in twenty. Now watch.'

Abe took the model and fixed it on two steel pins in the empty water chute. The plane's nose faced uphill as though attempting to fly up the chute. Then Arnie released the sluice gate. Water ran down the chute in an even, unbroken stream, completely submerging the little model plane. Abe produced a surgical needle filled with red ink.

'Watch.'

As he spoke he held the tip of the needle down into the water and injected a stream of ink into the water flowing around the nose. The line of ink flowed completely straight and unbroken, then caught just a little around the nose, before evening out and moving on down the airplane fuselage.

'That's probably the nicest nose shape out of the planes we've been looking at. No turbulence. Minimal drag. Glenn Curtiss always was a genius. But now look at this. The wing-struts.'

He moved the needle and now injected the ink so that it flowed down towards one of the struts connecting the upper wing to the lower one. Once again, the ink moved in a dead straight line until it hit the plane. And then something strange happened. The ink fluttered, eddied and swirled around the wing-strut. Twists and curls became visible in the water. Behind the little airplane, the water became filled with murky pink.

'Ain't that horrible?' said Hueffer, who was crouching over the chute like an anxious hen. 'The poor old engine's gotta fight all that turbulence. It's the same with every strut. And this plane's a good 'un, mind you. The best biplane we've looked at.'

'Yes. You can feel that,' said Pen slowly. 'Flying her for real, I mean. There's a . . .' she didn't know how to phrase it. The knowledge was in the tips of her fingers, the tremble of the fuselage as the plane banked into a curve. 'I don't know how to say it, but that turbulence there, that drag, you can feel it when you fly her. Probably just as well. It's the only thing that slows her down.'

'Right,' said Abe, 'only what if you wanted to build for distance?'

'Distance? She's not really that type of plane. She's . . .'

She stopped. Of course her little racer wasn't built for range. In order to get range you needed big fuel tanks. But big fuel tanks needed big wings. Big wings needed big engines. And big engines meant the whole plane had to be scaled up. Her clean lines would be lost. And half the extra fuel capacity would be wasted in battling the drag which the need for greater fuel capacity had itself created.

'I don't get it.' Then, pointing to the water chute, which was now closed off with the little model airplane already steaming dry, she added, 'Now this I get. Water tunnels, wind tunnels. They're telling you something which in a way you already know from flying it. I mean, it tells you in a more useful way. But where it takes you, what the purpose is . . .'

She shook her head a second time. Abe lifted the little racer off its stand and cradled it, stroked it, running his hand always in the direction of air flow, nose to tail, leading edge to trailing edge. She realised that whenever he handled his models, he always touched them like that, feeling their shape the way the wind felt it.

'You want to know where it takes us?'

'Uh-huh.'

Arnie stopped and stared too. He, after all, had known the mechanical point of Abe's castings, but not the real point: not the point that had absorbed Abe's energies for so long.

'Orteig,' said Abe. 'Orteig is where it takes us.'

Pen stared. She stared at Abe, at Arnie, at the model plane, at the water chute. And then she got it. She really got it.

73

On 14 June 1919, two British aviators, Captain John Alcock and Lieutenant Arthur Whitten Brown, climbed into the cockpit of their modified Vickers Vimy biplane. The Vickers was a monster. It was a monster in terms of size, but also in terms of ugliness. The giant fuel load required a huge two-tier wingspan supported by a whole cat's cradle of struts and wires. The big ugly beast was powered by a pair of 360 horsepower Rolls Royce Eagle VIII engines.

The two men took off.

Flying east from Newfoundland, over the Atlantic, bound for the Irish coast.

In good conditions, the venture would have been crazy. Little more than a fortnight earlier, a trio of US navy airplanes, backed by radio, air-sea rescue, refuelling stops, and more than a hundred ships, had attempted to fly from Newfoundland to Portugal. Of the three planes, only one had made it. Alcock and Brown would attempt the flight, non-stop, without radio, without air-sea rescue, without naval support.

And the conditions weren't good, they were awful.

The majority of the flight was spent flying blind, in a murderous combination of darkness, foul weather and fog. At one point, a build-up of ice on the wings was so bad that one of the two men had to climb out onto the wing in the full rip of a hundred-mile-an-hour gale and hack the potentially lethal ice away from the plane. To add to everything else, halfway across the ocean, the airspeed indicator failed, seriously increasing the risk of a dangerous stall.

After nineteen hours of appalling flying, the two men found the Irish coast beneath them. They found a broad and level field and brought their aircraft in to land.

Only the field wasn't a field. It was a swamp. The first genuine transatlantic flight wound up axle deep in sucking Irish mud.

And that's where Orteig came into it.

The date was now 17 December 1926. Seven and a half years had passed since Alcock and Brown had led the way. In the history of a technology just twenty-three years old, those seven years were a lifetime. And still the Atlantic hadn't been properly crossed, except by zeppelins, those over-stuffed overflammable bags of gas.

And so, aware of all this, a French millionaire, Raymond Orteig, had offered a $25,000 prize to the first aviator to cross the Atlantic non-stop from New York to Paris, or vice versa. The prize would require a new distance record to be set. It would require an unprecedented degree of confidence in pilot, engine and machine. And it defined, in advance, the points to be connected. The prize – and the ambition which lay behind it – was unquestionably the most important goal in world aviation.

And Abe had a plan. The problem, as he saw it, was that airplane designers had concentrated for too long on engine strength over drag reduction. The plane which won the Orteig Prize would be big enough to carry plenty of fuel, of course, but it would be built slim and light. It would meet the wind, not with a shrieking mass of piano wire and wing supports, but gracefully, cleanly, like a dolphin meeting waves or a hawk angling into its dive.

'We'll use this water chute here to explore anything and everything,' he explained. 'Like how should a wing join onto the fuselage? Not too square, of course. Rounded, presumably. But how? Rounded in a pointy way or rounded in a more curvy way? And what about the nose shape? What about the tail fin? Now, of course, our water chute isn't going to give us exact results. Water isn't air. Small scale isn't full scale. But we can sort out the shapes which definitely don't work from ones which maybe do. We'll try to work out the shape of the plane approximately, then hand over to some real engineers to sort out the detail.'

'And then?'

'And then, I'll commission a plane, with Mason's money . . .'

'And then. . . do you . . .? Will it . . .?'

'Huh?'

Pen got a grip. 'Nothing, really. Nothing. Only, you'll have a copilot, I assume. I was wondering if you'd already thought of who . . .'

Abe's voice gentled suddenly, and his eyes looked away. 'A tank of fuel. For something like this, the best safety isn't a second flier, it's plenty of fuel.'

'You'll fly solo?' Pen found herself absurdly disappointed, as though she'd already booked the seat next to his.

'It's the only way to do it,' said Abe. 'I'm sorry.'

74

Captain Rockwell!

Willard couldn't get over it. America had come home from war with plenty of heroes, but Captain Rockwell belonged to the very highest rank. It hadn't just been his individual record – more victories than anyone except Rickenbacker. It hadn't just been his collective record – his squadron narrowly beating Rickenbacker's for total victories. The point was, it hadn't just been his war record. Rockwell remained unsullied by peace. No newspaper man ever succeeded in digging out anything to tarnish him. No seedy affairs. No greedy desire to turn fame into banknotes. No grasping after honours. No grubby self-promotion.

And America had understood. Amidst all the ballyhoo of victory and demobilisation and red scares, America had somehow managed to separate its enduring heroes from its temporary ones. Rockwell hadn't just been awarded the ticker-tape parades, the civic receptions, the Presidential photo sessions. He'd been awarded the Congressional Medal of Honour, one of the few men in history to have been so honoured.

And now this.

Captain Rockwell was flying observation for a bunch of booze-smugglers. Willard didn't know what to think. Logically, only two things were possible. First, Rockwell was behaving like everyone else in America had behaved. War had been a time for commitment and sacrifice. But peace was peace. Perhaps Rockwell had figured the angles the way everyone else had. Being a hero bought him nothing. Not much fame, certainly no money. So he'd quit. He'd resigned the position, handed in his notice, packed up and gone. Instead, he'd entered a more lucrative line of work. And why not? He was only human. A human doing what humans do.

But there was a second explanation. Rockwell hadn't resigned. Others had. He hadn't. He was still the man that Willard had once admired more than any other on earth. And if Captain Rockwell, hero, was flying observation for Bob Mason, then something didn't add up. He had some agenda of his own. Willard couldn't guess what it was. But whatever Rockwell's precise motivation, if he had come to Marion as the war hero he'd once been, his presence there spelled red danger to the Firm.

That was the logical way to think about it, but Willard was hardly able to stay logical. *Captain Rockwell*! The man, almost literally, had brought Willard from boyhood into manhood. He had, quite literally, saved Willard's life. During those intense and terrifying months of war, Rockwell had been a second father to him. A first father, even, because a distant parent on the far side of the Atlantic scarcely counted for much.

And Willard could hardly fail to be aware of something else. *If Rockwell were attempting to engineer the downfall of Marion, then Powell Lambert would have to take action*. If the insurance department became involved, that action would result in Rockwell's sudden and violent death. If Willard could manage it so that he dealt with the issue himself, then maybe he could write a different ending to that story. Maybe. Rockwell had been a persistent and danger- ous pursuit pilot. He would be a persistent and dangerous adversary in any other form of warfare too. Willard was unable to imagine how he could neutralise Rockwell without murdering him. He was equally unable to imagine giving the instructions which would end up with Rockwell dead.

But if Rockwell had been the man he had once been, then one of those two things needed to happen.

For the two weeks of his sun-drenched holiday with Rosalind, Willard thought things over. Rosalind, seeing him distracted, silently assumed that his adventures in Canada had taken more out of him than he'd ever let on. She saw his behaviour as confirming his curious but genuine bravery. He was a vain man, a spoiled one, sometimes a boastful and petulant one – she knew all that. But more and more, she was coming to see his better side: courageous, committed, resourceful, solid. In the baking Florida sun, Willard was at his charming, delightful best. Little by little, Rosalind felt herself slipping further into love with him. In bed, she gave herself to him. Awake, she gave him the adoration she knew he craved.

For two weeks, Willard thought things through and came to a conclusion. On arrival back in New York, he took up his new place in that hallowed space, the Investment Bureau. He arranged his desk, fussed over his furniture, began to order new lamps, new deskstands, new fountain pens, all now without any regard at all for cost.

And he placed a call. The call was to Bob Mason. Willard issued an order and gave it immediate effect.

75

The effect of Willard's instructions was immediate and over-whelming.

Security, which had been tight before, just got a whole lot tighter. Armed men, with weapons loose and eyes watchful, paired up on the road, the rail line, and the river, both upstream and down. And Mason, at Willard's specific request, did another thing too. He told Abe that he wanted the flying team to relocate to Marion. 'Keeps it in-house. Things'll be safer that way.'

'We've never had a problem down in Miami,' said Abe.

'Right, and I don't want to wait around for that to change.'

'Why should it? Have you heard something to make you worry?'

Mason shook away the question with a punch on the shoulder and an affable, roguish grin. 'Nothing, pal. Only I got worry as a kind of medical condition.'

'We can't relocate. Pen needs to keep in touch with your freighters in Havana, plus that mail route is still perfect cover for us. How else are you gonna explain having planes into Cuba and over the ocean every single day of the week?'

'So she stays. And that mechanic of yours can stay.'

'Me? That's what you mean? You're relocating me?'

Mason grinned and punched Abe again. 'We're pleased to have you, kid.'

76

It was the blue light of first dawn. Stars still twinkled in the west, where the night was thickest. It was early to leave, but Pen hadn't been able to sleep and loved nothing better than watching dawn break from high overhead. She took off alone, unwatched. She made her take-off so fast, she had a hundred feet of air clear beneath her by the time the low scrub of the airfield boundary flashed under her wing. She soon hit the rumble of coastal turbulence, but the big plane rode the bumps uncaring. The throttle was open and the plane climbed fast.

Beneath her nose, the ocean spread out, like finally it had room to stretch. In contrast to the whitening east, the land below was dark blues and browns, spangled here and there with the glow of electric lights. She climbed higher and higher, far above her normal altitude. The altimeter reeled around, grimly committed to its single truth-telling task.

Pen was not flying like her usual self. There were no difficult winds, no bands of weather to avoid. She could have made a long, slow, steady climb to her normal cruising height of three thousand feet, and flown direct to Havana, with no need to do anything but check her course and keep an eye on her instruments. But not today.

You'll have a copilot, I assume. It hadn't been a dumb thing to say. Alcock and Brown had flown as a pair. Most of the fliers who'd tried to follow had done the same. And

Abe hadn't been unkind. Far from it. His voice had gone soft and sympathetic. But his sympathy had only made it worse.

A copilot. Pen realised she had already written herself into that role. For the Orteig Prize for certain, but also for life. The simple truth was that she was in love with him. Catastrophically so. Head over heels. Spinning like a plane without a pilot.

Her brain muzzy with the oxygen-poor air and the abruptness of her ascent, Pen forced herself to think things through logically. Perhaps, this was just the first rush of feeling. In a way, on meeting Rockwell, she'd been prepared to fall in love. She'd got herself ready for it, more than half-expecting it. After all, what else should have happened? They were two of the leading fliers of their generation, both committed to their pursuit, both single, both with a passionate love for the soaring freedoms of the air. So she'd been ready to love him. What else should have happened?

But then there had been the chain of disappointments, her mounting anger at Abe's aloofness, his stonewall ability to keep her away from anything which threatened his masculine isolation. But their conversation in the tool shed had broken all that. She could even now hear his unadorned admission. 'You're right. You're completely right.' She could feel his head on her shoulder, the tears that were really his sparkling in her eyes. She could sense the presence of all the men whom Abe had once commanded to their deaths. And she had understood. From that point on, her tumble into love had been headlong, unstoppable.

But his answer had been remorseless. *I fly solo.* Over the Atlantic and in life.

And perhaps he was right. Perhaps Abe was made differently from other folk. Perhaps he felt nothing at all of the tumult in Pen's own heart. Never had, never would. Forcing herself to think things over in a light as cold and empty as the air she was flying through, Pen was compelled to admit that there was nothing at all to give her hope.

The air continued to brighten. It had become bright enough to read by. Pen picked up the US Post Office mailbag down by her feet. It was stuffed with mail, five or six pounds of it, a big load by their paltry standards. Pen began to riffle through the letters, looking for mail it might be valuable to open and read.

As luck would have it, she found it almost straight away.

The fifth letter in the pile, postmarked Jacksonville, was addressed to Marion's bank in Cuba. Pen steamed the envelope open. Extracting the letter with care, Pen clipped it to her mapboard and began to read. The letter was signed by Bob Mason himself and it contained just five lines: an instruction to alter the signatory arrangements on Marion's principal Cuban bank account. Instead of Frank Lambaugh's signature alone being sufficient for funds to be paid out of the account, any such disbursements would in future require both Lambaugh's signature and Mason's personal authorisation by telephone. That was all.

But the more Pen thought about it, the more she was certain that there was more to the change than met the eye. Lambaugh was a cocky, aggressive, domineering man. He liked to show off his big American cars, his gold jewellery, his big villa, his latest imports. He hated her, she'd realised, not just because she was a woman, but because she saw his ostentatious displays of money and was deeply, utterly unimpressed.

She turned back to the letter. Just for a moment, Pen's love for Abe and the impossibility of it ever leading anywhere dwindled into the background. Perhaps, just perhaps, this letter held a solution to their problems.

77

Abe stared at his new bedroom.

Twenty feet by twenty, it was somewhat larger than the house he'd been born in. The bed was an enormous affair, all polished wood, sprung mattress, fancy counterpanes, and matching nightstands. The bathroom opened right off his bedroom and contained a huge tub, a shower, two basins, and (to his impressed astonishment) a bidet. The house had central heating, air conditioning, a fridge, a freezer, marble tiling in the front hall, a two-car garage, telephones in three different rooms and – of course, because this was Marion – a built-in bar in the living room with enough booze to light up a city.

'OK?' said Mason, grinning at Abe's dumbstruck reaction. 'It's a little small, but we figured there was only one of you.'

'You've got places bigger than this?'

'Oh sure. This one's just two bedrooms, plus it don't have no pool, things like that. But don't worry, pal, we think highly of you. You've got one of the nicer pads all right.'

Abe led Mason into the gigantic living room, where a huge fire threw its unnecessary heat straight up the towering chimney.

'Drink?' said Abe, playing host.

Mason didn't just nod, he went behind the bar and poured himself a glass of Jamaican rum, taken on the rocks, and poured a smaller glass of whiskey for Abe. The airman couldn't guess if Mason's action was deliberate, but it made the point all right. Though Abe might get to live in the house, he did so because Mason let him. This was Mason's house, Mason's booze, Mason's town.

'How come you brought me here?' asked Abe, once they were settled across two vast white couches that faced off across the fireside.

'You bring the boats in here, it makes sense for you to base yourself here.'

'Only I start watching the boats fifty or a hundred miles south of Jacksonville. Miami made every bit as much sense, and that way I could cover more easily for Pen and vice versa.'

'Yeah, well, we've made the decision, ain't we? Oh, and I meant to say, an extra hundred bucks a week, for you and Hamilton, kind of a thank you.'

'Thanks.'

Mason held his drink up, so the glass obscured everything of Abe except his head. To Mason's eye, Abe was just a head atop a whiskey glass.

'I've been figuring it all up,' he said at last.

'Huh?'

'How much we've paid you since you started with us.'

'Must be a lot by now.'

'Ten thousand bucks. More than. More than ten thousand bucks.'

'That's a lot.'

'Yeah, only you haven't exactly gone crazy with it have you? How many suits you got?'

'Suits? Two. My normal one and my —'

'Yeah and your one for best. Jeez. Ten thousand bucks in six months and you still have a suit for best. A car? You used to race 'em. You even own one?'

'I've been thinking about it.'

Mason shook his head in disapproval and raised his glass so that Abe's head dunked below the drink.

'Why d'you work for us? Most people, I don't have to ask. They work for money. I give 'em money. They go spend it. Most of the guys gripe about not getting as much money as they think they deserve. Not you. Not Hamilton.'

'The farm. You know I've been –'

'– digging your folks out of debt. Yeah, yeah, I know, only how many more tractors can your pa use? He's gotta leave some room for cows.'

Abe held Mason's gaze for a while. He was being interrogated, he knew. The fireside drink and the big house and the show of warmth didn't cancel out the fact that Mason was a hoodlum checking out one of his employees. Abe's tone grew a little more serious.

'You're right. It's not just the farm.'

'Oh?'

'I've got a project. An aviation project. It's gonna need money. All you can give me and more.'

'What's the deal?'

'It's none of your business.'

'Buddy, you are my business.'

Abe tensed before answering. Telling Pen had been one thing, telling Mason was quite another. He'd cherished the idea of the Orteig Prize for so long and in such privacy, he had to unclench something inside before he could release it.

'The Atlantic. It's never been crossed. Not properly. Not the way it ought to be done.'

Mason goggled a second. 'You want to fly across the ocean?'

'Uh-huh.'

'In an airplane? . . . I mean, that's possible, is it?'

'I think so.'

'And if it ain't? You gonna have a boat underneath to catch you?'

'Uh-huh, if I can find one that does a hundred-twenty miles an hour.'

'Shit. That's why you're here?'

Abe didn't give an answer, but Mason didn't need one. He began chuckling into his drink, swallowed it, then threw the ice cubes fizzing and spitting into the fire. He poured himself another drink, but smaller this time, no ice. He didn't sit back down.

'Hamilton. Why does she fly? The dame's loaded.'

'No, of course, not for the money . . .' Abe thought he knew what he was going to say. He was going to talk about flying, about Pen's commitment to aviation, about the difficulty of a rich girl finding something serious to commit to. But he stopped dead before he'd even started. *She loved him.* In the sudden emptiness following Mason's question, in the huge emptiness of that cavernous room, the fact seemed so obvious it was astonishing to Abe that he hadn't seen it before. She loved him. How could she not? What else could possibly motivate a woman, no matter how remarkable, to do what she was doing, to run the risks that she was running?

He couldn't reply. His mouth moved, but nothing came out. He felt dazed by his sudden knowledge. Mason was about to repeat his question, but stopped. His face was intent for a moment, then broke into a wide and friendly grin.

'OK, buddy, I get it,' he chortled. 'I shouldn't have asked. Least, I *should* have asked, but I don't necessarily need you to answer. Dames, huh? Ain't it always the way?' He held his drink up, then swallowed the lot in a single draught. He belched. 'Yeah, and maybe you're a straight guy too. I wouldn't know. I've forgotten what they look like.'

He made ready to go. Abe – still dazed, but somehow still alert – stopped him.

'If I'm gonna live here, I'm going to need someplace to work.'

'Huh?'

'So far I've been running the paperwork side of things

from Miami. Maintenance schedules, fuel supplies, equipment needs, flight timetables, all that kind of thing. Plus Arnie and I have our little project to work at. There's a fair bit of paper involved there too.'

Mason swept his arm around the room. The thing about huge houses is they need filling. But once you've bought yourself a couple of sofas, a bed, a kitchen table, pretty much everything you need is already taken care of. So big houses fill up with stuff which is darn near pointless. Fancy little tables with polished tops and bendy legs. Dainty little chairs. Desks so gleamingly polished it would be pretty much an insult if anyone used them.

'You want space?'

'It's not space I need, it's . . . Heck, Mason, this place don't look or smell or feel like a place to work. Don't you have a room somewhere with a desk and a chair and a lightbulb and a window and maybe a file cabinet and nothing much else at all?'

Mason went still.

He wasn't normally the still-going kind of a guy. His face liked to move. Even when he wasn't talking, his lips and eyes were signing encouragement, disbelief, enthusiasm, surprise – whatever kept the conversation rolling forward. But now he went still. Abe could see the calculations unfolding behind his eyes; could see the distrust and the promise of violence which lay only inches behind. But, as Abe saw it, the mobster had only one way to decide. If Abe was OK, then he could have his office. If Abe wasn't OK, then he should be given it anyway, to encourage him into doing something which would end up damning him.

Mason reached the same conclusion and nodded, 'Yeah, I see your point, now. It ain't what you'd call businesslike this place, now is it?'

And the very next day, a room was found for Abe. It met his requirements exactly. It had whitewashed walls and a royal blue linoleum floor. Aside from that, it boasted a cheap metal desk, a folding wooden chair, an unshaded lightbulb, a good-sized window with a view of the airstrip, and a two-drawer filing cabinet that rattled emptily when he opened it. And that wasn't all. Just four doors on down the corridor lay Mamie and Suky's little office.

Abe was so close to his goal he could almost smell it. But no matter how close he got to doing what he had set out to do, Abe was still not free of the feelings which had gripped him all those long months ago, when Hennessey had first asked him to help save Independence. Would he stay and help or would he up and go? There was an inexorable current of events which was dragging him ever closer to the final decisive combat. Abe could feel the current dragging at his feet, his ankles, his knees. But he still hadn't committed. In his heart, he hadn't committed. A large part of him, perhaps most of him, still wanted to run, take wing, escape.

78

The yacht shone out like an advert for a better life. Crisp white paintwork contrasted with polished brass and wood so dark it had almost the colour of gingerbread. A flag, which maybe meant something, maybe didn't, fluttered from a short wooden flagpole behind the bridge.

'Like it?' asked Junius Thornton, squinting against the sun.

Since Willard, dressed in tennis whites and slapping a racket against his calf, hadn't yet set foot on the newly-purchased boat, his answer wasn't based on anything much except the distant view and the knowledge of how many millions she had cost.

'She's glorious, Father.'

'Hmm.'

Junius Thornton examined the yacht once more, then began to crunch up the seashell and pebble Connecticut beach. He had bought the boat with the same brute decisiveness that marked most big steps in his life. Willard wondered whether his father actually enjoyed anything about the nautical life, or whether he simply felt that a man of his income needed a yacht to keep pace.

'How did you get on?'

'I'm sorry?'

Junius Thornton stopped dead and examined his son, before repeating the question using the same words and the same tone of voice.

'How did I get on? Eh? Oh, you mean in Florida. I guess you mean with Bob Mason – at least I hope you do since the roulette tables weren't kind to me in Palm Beach.'

Willard left a little gap in his answer, in case his father felt like filling it with a chuckle or a smile of encouragement. But the gap went unfilled.

'He seems like a good guy, Mason. It's quite an operation he has there –'

'*We* have.'

'We?'

'Mason doesn't own a cent of it.'

'Of course, yes, *we* have, *we* have. Anyhow. He runs these freighters, huge things really, big river barges if you like, only obviously seaworthy enough . . .' Willard left another gap for a response, got none, and ploughed on anyway. 'Loaded with booze. I mean, absolutely loaded. And – of course, you know this, but it's quite something – there's an airplane overhead the entire time, just keeping an eye on the Coastguard, ready to give warning.'

Willard stopped again, leaving a longer gap this time. Since arriving at that icy airfield south of the Canadian border, Willard had got to know the Firm very much better – but the more he saw of it, the less he saw of his father. Powell was the man in charge and in control. Junius Thornton didn't even possess a desk in the New York office. Junius Thornton spent his time down in the Washington office of Thornton Ordnance, lobbying the Federal government for bigger arms deals. Even now he was theoretically a member of the Firm's inner circle, Willard didn't know how much his father knew – if anything – about the day-to-day operations of the Firm.

But the older man just nodded. The nod could have meant: 'I know everything about the airplanes. You don't need to tell me.' Or it could have meant: 'This is the first I've heard about the use of aerial reconnaissance in booze-smuggling. What a very enterprising innovation.'

The rare burst of warmth that Willard had felt from his father back in Shakeston had long since dissipated. His father's manner had reverted to his normal stern, almost Victorian stiffness. But though Willard continued to be unnerved, things had shifted. He *had* his father's approval. He would need to continue to earn it, of course – Willard was under no illusions there – but at least he now knew it was there to be earned. So for all that he continued to be unnerved in his father's presence, things had changed, things were better.

Willard waited for a further response, got none, and decided to rattle on anyway. The wind off the ocean had a chilly edge, and the horizon was plated with steel-grey rain clouds moving in. Willard was cold after his tennis game, but his father kept crunching up the beach as though there were something important to be had there. Willard's account rambled and jolted, describing the strong points and weak points in Marion's defences.

After a long while, the older man interrupted.

'You've got doubts.'

'I beg your pardon?'

'Doubts. Powell tells me you've reassigned the pilot.'

Willard gaped for a second. He hadn't told Powell about Rockwell's relocation. He'd carefully avoided doing so, not wanting the trigger-happy men in the insurance department involved. But Powell knew. His father knew. Presumably Mason spoke to other people in New York than just Willard. Or perhaps New York kept a spy down in Marion to keep Mason honest. But, though taken aback, Willard kept his cool with his answer.

'Not doubts exactly. The pilot looks after freighters coming into Marion. It seemed to make more sense to base him there.'

'You know him?'

'Yes, of course. It's Captain Rockwell, Father.'

'Oh?'

'Captain Rockwell? My old commander? Lord, Papa, you must remember. The man had a ticker-tape parade in his honour.'

'Ah . . . And he's a good man?'

'The best.'

Willard replied too fast and the older man stopped abruptly. One foot had come to rest, its toes bathed in a small rockpool. Salt water began to seep into the shoe. Willard stood back, to let his father take the quarter-pace needed to rescue his foot, but the older man did no such thing. He continued to stand with his left foot half underwater, gazing with belligerent frankness into his son's face.

'The best? Do you mean the best for the Firm or the best in some other sense?'

'Well both, I suppose. I mean in the war, he was magnificent, of course . . .'

Willard spoke quickly, covering up for his first too-speedy answer, then covering a second time for any obviousness in his own cover-up. He spoke too much, too fast, too confusedly. He stuttered to a close – a habit his father detested. Junius Thornton said nothing, then turned abruptly and marched back down the beach towards the house. Willard followed, tennis racket swiping at the air.

'Your girl.'

'Rosalind? Yes?'

'There is gossip.' The businessman spoke the last word the way a Puritan might have spoken the word 'nakedness'.

'Gossip? Well, Pa, you know, Rosalind is a terribly good-looking girl, and the Sherstons have always been a good family. Not on a par with . . : but good. And then, these journalist folks have to write about something. And ever since the war and Hollywood, you know, they seem to have a thing about me. It's always photographs or something. I don't encourage them.'

'You are not clear about your intentions?'

There was a path along the shingle which the older man

occupied. Willard was left with the choice of dancing along amongst the rougher stones to either side, or trailing his father like a spaniel puppy. He went for the dancing option.

'My intentions? You mean, do I mean to ask her to . . .? Gosh! We do get on awfully well, though.'

'You know your own mind, I take it?'

'Yes, Father.' Willard sprang over a barnacle-clotted boulder, checked his footing and straightened to find his father staring at him. The younger man felt a moment of sudden clarity and confidence. 'I shall ask her to marry me, of course.'

Junius nodded. 'Good. You will tell me what you would like as a wedding gift.'

'Yes, Papa.'

The rain clouds which had threatened began to dot and speckle the beach. Willard fell in behind his father, walking single file. Conversation halted. And Willard realised his father was right. Why wait? What was there to wait for? Rosalind looked wonderful on his arm. They got on terrifically well. They would be one of the most splendid couples in New York, their wedding one of the most talked about weddings of the year. Why hadn't he thought of it before?

Marriage was definitely the way to go.

79

Abe looked down at the deck of cards.

He let his attention flow into his fingertips. He waited until the rough edges of the cards spoke to his fingers. Then he began to move. He made cards flick in and out of existence. He retrieved cards from his jacket pocket, from the seat of the couch, from underneath the leg of the table in front of him. Since picking up his cards again around the time he had moved into the Miami airfield, he had become quicker, defter, more accurate than he'd ever been.

But he wasn't interested in cards. He only played because there was too much in the current situation which disturbed him.

For one thing, he was watched all the time now; a thing he hated. As a pursuit pilot, he equated safety with invisibility. He liked to watch, not be watched. What was more, up here in Marion, Mason had far too many men for Abe to be able to keep track of his watchers. There were too many of them, they changed too frequently, there were always too many reasons for them to be hanging around somewhere close. The only time they didn't seem to watch him at all was when he was in his little office, down the hall from Mamie and Suky. At those times, nobody entered to disturb him, nobody lingered beneath the window or in the corridor outside. It was a freedom which Abe found even more troubling than the watching.

And they searched him.

Not him personally, but everything else. His new house, his office, the tool shed, even the plane. And these guys were thorough. Once Abe discovered that they'd even prised off the heel of his flying boots to check if Abe had secreted anything there. The only way Abe knew was that they hadn't been able to use the original nails to resecure the heel and had had to use shiny new tacks, their nail-heads not yet ground down and dirtied.

So Abe kept his head down. He made friends with Mamie and Suky, got into the habit of sharing cake and coffee with them, but did nothing to confirm Mason's suspicions. And Brad had been right. The two girls handled everything: payroll, accounts, expenses, petty cash, product inventories – everything. It was a trove of information which Jim Bosse would have given his left arm to obtain.

And in one way Abe liked his new isolation. It gave him space to figure things out. That night in the tool shed with Pen, he had felt something clear from his heart, like some heavy weight he'd never even known was there. Afterwards, he'd expected the world to feel brighter, cleaner, easier. And so it had – briefly. Certainly, he had found it easier to bring Pen and Arnie inside his plans. Certainly, he was relieved not to have had to go it alone that night when the office buildings seemed suddenly alive with guards. But there was still something missing. An open cockpit is a lonely place, and flying is a lonely game. For all his flying life, Abe had loved the solitude. If being alone had sometimes had a melancholy tinge, he'd accepted the fact, just as he accepted bad weather, low cloud, headwinds and engine failure.

And now? Now he was unsettled. When he was on the ground, he wanted to be in the air. When he was in the air, he wanted to be on the ground. He got jumpy in Marion and fidgety in Miami. He was very conscious of Pen's feelings for him. Much as he tried to keep relations between them normal, they both found it hard and Abe's absence up in Marion was almost a relief.

But meantime, nothing held him for long – nothing except dreams of the Orteig Prize and the grey Atlantic. It was just as well, in a way, that he now had something else to worry about.

It wasn't just Mason's sudden intensification of his surveillance. It wasn't just the watchers and the searches. It was something in the air, a sixth sense that Abe trusted with his life. And he knew that the endgame was approaching and *at somebody else's pace*. Somewhere, somehow, the organisation had grown suspicious. It was getting tired of Abe and friends. It was as though his little attack formation had been spotted, as though the ambushers were about to be ambushed.

He looked down at his deck of cards and riffled it. Clouds of loneliness seemed to fill him. He got up abruptly, spilling the cards. Then, moving quietly through his empty villa, he went to the fuseboard in the understairs cupboard. He checked the wiring for a second, then put his hand to one of the cables. He tugged it free and exposed the live wire. He touched the wire against a couple of others where there was a flash of naked copper. He produced a bang, a blue flash, a tang of smoke. Throughout the house, the lights failed with a sigh.

In the darkness, Abe groped his way to the phone and dialled Mason.

'Yeah?'

'Mason, it's me, Rockwell.'

'What's up?'

Abe explained. Complete power failure. Did Mason have anyone to get it fixed?

Mason's voice, heavy with drink, swatted the problem aside. 'Yeah, there's a kid around here who fixes these things. I'll get him to you first thing in the morning. Lundquist, his name is. Lundberg. Something like that. Any case. Tomorrow. OK?'

Abe nodded, said thanks, and hung up. He had just taken

one more small step towards a destination he wasn't even sure he wanted to reach. The grey Atlantic clouds, the endless ocean, the savage weather all pressed themselves into the forefront of his mind. Before going to sleep that night, Abe drank a pint bottle of whiskey and fell asleep, fully clothed and snoring.

80

The steel-plated prison door thudded heavily home.

Willard and Larry Ronson both felt the thud, but neither spoke while the heavy bulk of the prison continued to loom behind them. Parking was prohibited within fifty yards of the gates and a pair of armed prison officials watched the two Wall Streeters as they walked to Willard's car. Only once they had made it to the band of sunlight across the street and the reassuringly expensive comfort of Willard's Packard, did either man speak.

'Poor little fellow,' said Ronson. 'He's lost weight.'

'Yes, he was always pale, but he looks shocking now, really.'

Ronson's mouth twitched and he shot a glance over at Willard, who was contemplating his feet. A hint of devilry flashed in Ronson's mouth, but his voice was steady as he said, 'I shan't be recommending it.'

'Eh? Shan't recommend what?'

'That hotel. I mean, the place was a positive prison!'

Willard looked at his friend. Ronson kept a straight face – then Willard cracked a smile – then Ronson chuckled – then, before they knew it, the two men were doubled up laughing, thumping the dashboard and rocking the heavy car on its tyres. It was their fourth joint visit to Charlie Hughes. Neither man liked going, but by keeping the visit short and by going together and taking a stiff drink before and after, the whole ordeal didn't seem too bad.

'Appalling service. Those waiters acted more like guards!'

'And the guests! Really, they looked like a bunch of jail-birds.'

Willard tried something which involved a pun on bars – prison bars and hotel bars – but the joke escaped before he was halfway through. Ronson laughed anyway. They shared a drink from the flask in the Packard's glove compartment. Willard put his key in the ignition and began to nudge the big car home to Manhattan.

'How's the lovely Rosalind?' said Ronson.

'Oh, very well. Yes, very well indeed.'

Ronson leaned across the car and punched Willard on the arm. 'Lucky dog.'

'Yes. As a matter of fact . . .'

'Yes?'

Oh, nothing. Say, did Charlie Hughes say something about Annie?'

'Oh yes, she comes out every week. Stays as long as she can.'

'Really? Gosh, it's hard to imagine little Annie going there. The place gives me the chills.'

'And so inconvenient, when you have the Plaza midtown, the Ritz . . .'

They chuckled again, but not for long. Willard turned the conversation back to Annie.

'She isn't . . . I mean, she can't be sweet on Hughes can she? That isn't why . . .?'

'Oh God, no!' said Ronson emphatically. 'No if you ask me, there's another former employee of the Trade Finance team who has her heart . . .'

Ronson leered at Willard, who pretended he was too busy driving to notice. He changed tack.

'You know, I was about to say . . . do you ever think of settling down?'

'Me?' asked Ronson. 'I guess . . . one day . . . if Clara Bow ever answers one of my love letters. Why?' Willard didn't answer right away, and Ronson leaned across the car again, thumping Willard's arm, but softly this time. 'I would if I had a girl like yours.'

'Yes, I've been thinking . . . I mean I'm still only twenty-six, but all the same, if a girl is right, she's right, isn't she?'

A bolt of pale winter sunlight fell across Ronson's face and he held an arm up against the glare. Willard was about to make a left turn across the traffic to the Brooklyn Bridge, when a shop front caught his eye. Ebner's Flowers – Retail – Wholesale – Export – Trade. Willard made a violent course change, pulling right over to the curb. A frenzy of horns blared in outrage. A truck driver hung out of his cab window in order to roar abuse as he gunned past in a flare of petrol fumes. Willard stopped the Packard and yanked the handbrake on.

'Stay here just a moment, would you?'

He entered the shop. A Jewish-German shopkeeper approached from a back room smelling of cut green stems and flower pollen.

'Listen,' said Willard, 'I'm interested in buying some flowers. Roses, I suppose. Red.'

'*Ja*. Roses. How many you need?'

'Um . . . Gosh, I should say about a thousand. No. More. Two or three thousand. How much would that be?'

The florist managed to control his expression well as he began naming sums. Willard fenced briefly over price, before admitting to himself he didn't really care. He wanted the thing to be done in style. The cost wasn't important. They talked dates and quantities and prices and delivery arrangements. Willard surprised himself by his conviction and decisiveness.

Because Rosalind was the right girl, wasn't she? Willard felt sure, as sure as he'd ever been. He added another five hundred roses to his order and finalised details with a flourish. Should he tip off one of the magazines, he wondered? Get a photographer to take a 'surprise' snap of

380

the happy moment? Perhaps that would be crude. On the other hand, it seemed a shame to go to all the trouble and have no one know about it . . . He'd think about it, maybe consult Larry.

'*Gut*,' said the florist, his carefully managed expression finally breaking out into a widening smile of commercial satisfaction. 'Hey, you want a sample to take home? No charge.'

He went into the back of the shop and came out with a cardboard carton, slightly damp, containing a dozen rose stems. The rose heads were perfect: velvety, intense, inviting, fragile. Willard put one to his nose, not for any particular reason, but because that was what people did. The rose smelled of nothing at all. Or rather, it smelled of its surroundings: damp cardboard, greenery, crushed leaves.

'Oh, it doesn't smell!'

'Ah, no, sir. It is January, remember. These are hothouse roses of course. They don't smell.'

'They don't? But they have to!'

Willard stayed standing in the little florist's shop, the rose stem still held to his nose, the sunlight bleaching the sidewalk and Packard outside.

81

Three days later, Mrs Gibson Hennessey was bringing in her washing when her foot kicked against a small cloth-wrapped parcel, about eight inches by five. The parcel was just lying on the ground and certainly hadn't been there earlier that morning. It looked for all the world as though it had just dropped from the sky.

She didn't like touching these gifts from the heavens. She knew where they came from and why. But though she didn't like to get involved, she put the parcel under her arm and brought it in with the wash. When Gibson Hennessey opened the package later that evening, he found a short paperback book entitled *The Rudiments of Morse Code* and a one-word note from Abe: 'Enjoy!'

82

Arnie Hueffer, airplane mechanic and detester of heights, slipped on climbing spikes and swore softly.

It was twelve minutes past nine in the evening. Ahead of him, forty yards down the dark Havana street, Frank Lambaugh's villa was lit up. Jazz music from a gramophone sidled out through the shuttered windows. The music was interrupted from time to time by bursts of laughter, mostly female. There was a dark shape on the porch, which could be a guard dog or a human being, but could equally well just be a dark shape.

Arnie took a broad leather belt from his bag and wrapped it around the telephone pole, through a buckle, then around his waist. He looked up at the metal junction box fifteen feet above his head and swore again. Then he kicked his spikes into the soft wood of the pole and leaned back on the belt. He began to climb.

He was in Havana because Pen's engine wouldn't start. The reason why Pen's engine wouldn't start was because she had sabotaged it. And the reason why she had sabotaged it (following Arnie's own patient instructions on engine sabotage) was because she needed Arnie to be out here, in Havana, climbing a telephone pole.

He swore and blasphemed his way up. It was nine fifteen.

At the top of the pole, horizontal pegs driven into the wood gave him a chance to get a proper foothold. He did what he could to secure himself, but continued to swear gently all the same. The grey metal junction box was locked, but was easily forced. The little door swung open to reveal a terminal board containing some seventy or eighty terminals. There was nothing to indicate which terminal belonged to which home.

Arnie glanced back at the villa. On the front porch where the dark shape was lurking, the tip of a cigarette glowed orange in the darkness. *Hell*! Arnie winced and glanced up at the sky. He was OK, maybe. The moon had run behind a scrap of cloud. Without the help of moonlight, Arnie doubted if a dozy guard would notice a man forty yards away up a telephone pole.

There was no time to lose. He gathered his breath, then pulled out a pair of headphones from his bag. The headphones were connected to a wire ending in a crocodile clip. Arnie settled the headphones over his ears and, one by one, touched his crocodile clip to the terminals on the board. He listened to each for a second or two, then moved on. Most of the terminals were silent, only a few seemed live. When Arnie picked up voices, they were men's voices, speaking Spanish, none of them Lambaugh, and certainly not Pen.

The plan contained no room for error. Pen had promised to ring Lambaugh at nine fifteen on the dot. Though Arnie had never heard Lambaugh's voice, the pair of them would be speaking in English, a sure-fire sign that he'd found the right line.

But, after working right through the board, he'd hit nothing. He went back to the first terminal, gripped it with his clip and listened again. Nothing. He moved on to the next and the next.

With one eye on his work, Arnie watched the man on Lambaugh's porch throw away his cigarette and get up from his sitting position. Arnie let his fingers fly from terminal to terminal. He connected all of them. Still nothing. He tried again. He covered sixty of the terminals and could feel a rising certainty that the plan had failed. Then he hit it. He clipped the next terminal in line and instantly Pen's voice rang out loud and clear in the headphones.

'A winch,' she was saying. 'Apparently Hueffer can't fix the engine unless he can lift it.'

A man's voice answered, thick with drink and irritation. 'Christ! Didn't you know you'd need a winch before? How did you think you were gonna lift the engine?'

Pen began to answer. Her answer was circuitous, talkative, uninformative, bogus.

'Good girl!' said Arnie in a low whisper. 'You tell him.'

Working at top speed, he wrapped a wire around the Lambaugh terminal, then let the rest of the coil drop to the ground. He closed the junction box and half-skidded, halffell down the pole.

He took the loose wire, ran it along to a neighbouring alleyway, where a row of former stables had been colonised by the poor of Havana. There was a smell of sewage, spicy food, the sweet tropical blend of richness and decay. The entrance to the alley was marked by a broad stone arch, half-covered in a crumbling render. Arnie clipped his wire to the top of the arch and let the wire down the other side.

The difficult part had just been done.

83

Rosalind smelled them even before she reached the lake.

Even though the evening was mild by New York standards, the park was still locked in winter. But something magical had happened. As she came around the corner towards the ornamental lake at the southern end of Central Park, she saw them: roses, thousands of them, at the peak of their bloom; so many that the little rowboat seemed to glow. Roses twined along the sides of the boat, they sprouted from the stern, they arched up from the bow like a figurehead. She stopped dead in her tracks, her hand over her mouth, her pulse accelerating to a racing beat.

Beside the little boat stood an elderly boatman, almost comically dressed in the English fashion: pale trousers, striped blazer, straw boater.

'Miss Rosalind,' he said, in an accent straight from Brooklyn. He held out a hand.

She wanted to stop. She wanted to drink in the sight. She wanted to smell the roses, to absorb the picture, to bathe in the dwindling January light that crept between the Manhattan skyscrapers. But the fairy tale's hold was too strong. There was the magical boat, the comical boatman, the roses. Rosalind allowed herself to be wafted on board. She was dressed as Willard had asked, ready for an evening at the opera. She wore a sage-green dress under a pale fur coat, silk stockings, pearls, and a fringed silk shawl. She looked – felt – almost like an accessory to somebody else's outfit.

She sat down. Closer to the flowers, the smell and colour was almost overwhelming. The floor and seat of the boat were carpeted with rose petals. There were so many of them that wherever Rosalind put her hand, she felt, not wood, but the softness of flowers. In her dreamy state, it felt as though the boat itself were made of flowers. Only the judder of woodwork and the creak of rowlocks was there to prove otherwise.

The oars splashed through the water. Unlike its big sister further north, the lake was purely ornamental and though the boatman rowed slowly, even a slow rower couldn't take long to cross.

Facing forward, Rosalind craned her head to see what she knew had to be on the other side. To begin with she saw only the dull browns and greens of January. Then she caught a glimpse of a strong black and a clear white behind the shrubs. Then there was a further movement and Willard, in a dinner jacket, stepped out from his hiding place in the bushes. Rosalind was vaguely aware of a handful of evening strollers gawping at the spectacle. Away to the side somewhere, a camera bulb popped and flashed. The boatman eased the boat gently into the bank. At the spot where Rosalind was to step out, the damp earth had been sprinkled with white sand, then showered with rose petals.

She got out. In the bushes, a gramophone played a Mozart string quartet, her favourite. The boatman had shipped his oars and sat with his face totally impassive, like that rare type of family servant who sees everything and never gossips. Up on the bank, Willard took Rosalind's gloved hand and sank onto one knee.

'Dearest Rosalind . . .'

She'd known what was coming. She'd known from the moment that Willard had asked to meet her here. As soon as she'd seen and smelled the roses, she hadn't just known, she'd felt overwhelmed by her knowledge. She felt like an actress playing out a script.

And she said 'yes'.

Of course she did. She loved Willard. Loved and admired him. He was a man any woman in the world would be proud to have as a husband. Who else could have arranged something like this? The roses. The evening sun. The lake rippled in gold and crimson.

And it was only afterwards – after she'd said yes, and they'd kissed, and Willard himself had rowed back across the lake, and after they'd drunk champagne, and eaten oysters and lobster, and phoned their families, and made love not once but twice – that Rosalind even became aware of a tiny drip-drip-drip of disappointment.

'Will?' she said, addressing her three-quarters asleep fiancé.

'Mmm?'

'Those roses, they smelled so wonderful.'

'Mmm.'

'How did you manage it? Hothouse roses, they hardly ever smell.'

'They didn't smell. Not a whiff.'

'Not a whiff? But . . .'

'Had to use perfume. Buckets of the stuff.'

'You used perfume? That was perfume?'

'Mmm.'

But Willard's 'mmm' didn't mean anything at all. He'd been mostly asleep to begin with. He was fast asleep now. And Rosalind wasn't. She was wide awake. Feeling her new diamond ring colossal on her finger. Feeling desolate in the knowledge that she'd been wooed with three thousand perfect roses, not one of which had smelled.

84

'Gee, it's hot, isn't it?' Mamie plucked at the neckline of her dress where it hung damply over her breasts.

'Eighty-seven in the shade, barometer high, humidity high, wind six knots from the sou-south-east.'

'You must get kind of lonesome in that little office of yours. You OK in there?'

'Fine.'

'You always say that. "Fine." You ever not fine?'

'Sometimes I guess.'

Abe reached for the cup of coffee Suky had made for him earlier. Suky believed that coffee grounds were reusable for as long as they continued to colour the water at all. Abe's cup of coffee was a thin grey, with an oily sheen floating on the top. Neither Mamie nor Suky were the sort of company that Abe enjoyed most, but he liked the break, and the girls too enjoyed their chats with the famous airman. The two girls exchanged glances. After a little nudging and winking, Suky cleared her throat and began.

'Do you ever . . . I mean . . . No, sorry, I shouldn't ask.' Suky blushed hard and giggled furiously.

'What? It's OK to ask.'

'Me and Mamie were wondering if you ever had a girl. I mean . . . I don't mean . . . You know . . . We were just wondering. That's all.'

'If you mean, have I ever, then yes. If you mean right now, then no.'

Something rose and fell in Suky's throat at that information. It was a fairly simple bet that there was a lot of speculation over Abe's relationship with Pen Hamilton. But Suky's blush was pressing even harder now.

'And Miss Hamilton. Is she . . .? Does she . . .? I guess . . . I've never heard of a lady wanting to fly airplanes before.'

'There are a few ladies who do fly airplanes these days. Miss Hamilton happens to be exceptionally good at it.'

Suky was bursting to ask whether Pen had a boyfriend – or better still, a succession of super handsome, fabulously daring, millionaire aviator boyfriends – but Abe's jaw was clamped shut. It wasn't something he liked talking about. Heck, these days even the thought of it all made him uncomfortable. He kept silent and the girl went stuttering on until eventually she bottled the question. He finished his coffee and stood up.

Mamie and Suky were responsible for typing up and filing most of the paperwork that came into Marion. When a freighter unloaded its wares, a scribbled cargo note was hastily initialled and sent up to their office. Their part of things was to type up the note, making two carbons for each original. The original was filed, the two carbons passed on to Mason. Everything was like that. Somewhere down the hall, a book-keeper processed all Marion's financial transactions into a standard set of accounts. Each week he passed up his most recent book-keeping sheets to Mamie and Suky for typing up. Payroll: the same thing. A clerk somewhere else came up with the weekly who-gets-what list. Mamie and Suky typed and filed.

And the two girls had a system. Incoming paperwork went straight into a wire basket that sat on the filing cabinet closest to the door. When they were ready – and they weren't girls who liked to rush – they unloaded the basket and went to work. And Abe got into a system too. When he entered the room, he put whatever he was carrying down on top of the basket. When he left again he picked it up and took it away.

'I'd best get on,' he said.

'Sure.'

'Thanks for the coffee.'

'You're welcome.'

'Well then . . .'

Abe reached down and picked up his papers. Not just his, but those below as well. He didn't do it with any secrecy, he just did it.

He walked back to his office, leaving his door wide open, so anyone at all could just walk in. He began work on his flight logs. The papers he'd taken from Mamie and Suky lay on the table in front of him. It was the weekly payroll charts, written out in neat black ink. The papers lay close enough that Abe could see them, but he wasn't copying them. If anyone had happened to enter his office at that moment, he'd have looked the picture of innocence: a man bent over his work, a man who'd accidently picked up some tedious little papers that didn't belong to him.

And that was all they'd see. Even if they ransacked the office, examined every shred of paper, if they'd strip-searched Abe and ripped his plane, his possessions, and everything else into minuscule fragments, they wouldn't come across so much as a comma that belonged to the incriminating accounts.

Because the chances are they'd be looking in the wrong places for the wrong things. They wouldn't even know to keep their eyes out for the only things they should have been looking for. Things, such as:

– A cotton thread about five feet long running from Abe's hand, casually tapping against the side of his chair, to the window outside.

– A bent paperclip, tied to the end of the thread, but only loosely tied, so that one short, sharp tug from Abe would dislodge the clip and send it tumbling to the ground.

- A couple of loose wires, each showing about a quarter inch of bare copper, part of a bundle of cables that ran down from the roof. The paperclip was hooked around one of the wires, so that every time Abe's hand tapped on the thread, the wire touched the other one, completing an electrical circuit.
- A length of drainpipe on the roof, invisible from the ground, aimed like an artillery piece up the hill towards Independence.
- And finally this: an electric light bulb, concealed inside the drainpipe, that came on only when the circuit was closed. Because of the length of pipe shielding it, the bulb's glow was completely invisible to anyone closer at hand.

Plus, of course, if the people looking had been almost super-humanly smart, they'd have guessed the final part of the jigsaw: a lanky storekeeper up in Independence, sitting at his bedroom window with a telescope, steadily pointed at the winking light down on a Marion rooftop. And Hennessey's good at this game by now. *The Rudiments of Morse Code* is no longer needed. The storekeeper's right hand copies Abe's message as fluently as if he were copying from a sheet of newsprint.

But this isn't newsprint that he's copying. He's copying Marion's most secret financial documents. These are the documents which may one day clinch the case for the prosecution. The documents will prove that Marion is a business; that the business is vastly profitable; that the people who draw salary or profit from the business are earning easily enough to be liable for federal income tax. All the other information that Abe and Pen have so far collected hasn't been worth as much as this. And it's being steadily copied.

Letter by letter. Line by line. Incriminating page by incriminating page.

85

It was late afternoon. Willard had drunk half a bottle of wine over lunch and was feeling sleepy. But sleep would have to wait. He had wedding plans to sort out, endless Firm-related business to sort out, a marital home to buy and get ready.

And then there was Rockwell.

Mason was watching the man constantly now. He had put his best men on it. And so far they'd found nothing. Not a string bean. Mason's latest report covered everything: movements, conversations, timings, dates, items searched. As ever, the man looked clean. Willard studied the report, then phoned Mason for their daily briefing. They went through various items of business, before the conversation turned, as ever, to Rockwell.

'The guy's clean, Thornton,' Mason complained with a sigh. 'He's actually a nice guy. I reckon it's about time we laid off him. I'm getting kinda sick of it.'

'Yes, yes.' Willard wanted to believe Mason, but he also felt the pressure of his father's scrutiny, his own burning desire to prove his capability. 'As soon as we're sure.'

'We *are* sure. He's sitting three doors away from the most secret papers we've got. He's not made any attempt to copy them, leastways not unless he's writing in invisible ink on invisible paper. The guy doesn't even keep his door closed.'

'But he asked for an office, right? When he had a whole house to work in?'

'Right. Only he's not the luxury villa type of guy. You know that.'

'Right. So why does he work for us? When he doesn't give a damn?'

It was a well-worn dispute. The two men batted familiar arguments at each other, both only half-convinced by their own assertions. Only this time, Mason came up with something new. He brought it up with a chuckle swelling in his throat.

'Ha! Only he does.'

'Does what? Give a damn?'

'Right. He wants money pretty bad. You want to guess why?'

'His parents have a farm, you said.'

'Yeah, only it ain't that.'

'There's something else?'

'What else would get him? What would the guy want more than anything in the world?'

Willard rubbed his hand across his forehead and was suddenly struck by a quite unexpected picture: a picture from wartime, from the simple French aerodrome where Captain Rockwell had briefed his pilots. There was a sadness in the man's face which Willard had never noticed at the time, but which he was quite sure he hadn't invented. What would Captain Rockwell most want? That was easy: he wanted his pilots to come back alive.

Willard didn't say so. Instead he answered, 'I don't know. What?'

'An airplane, of course. He wants an airplane which can fly to Paris.'

'The Orteig Prize?' Willard gripped the phone more tightly. He felt a glow of happy relief begin to spread outwards from his chest.

'The Ortik? Yeah, something like that. Jeez, Thornton, maybe you understand that kinda thing. Me, I think the guy's nuts. He says he doesn't even like Paris.'

But it made sense. The thing that had always bothered Willard most was this: what possible motive could drag his old commander into a life of crime? If the answer were in order to win the Orteig Prize, then maybe the whole thing began to make sense. But Willard had become too much the perfect Investment Bureau professional to relax too quickly.

'That accounts for Rockwell, maybe. It doesn't account for the Hamilton girl.'

'Right. Only like you say, she's a girl.'

'So? I don't –'

'She's got a thing for him. I didn't know it for sure before, but now I do.'

'They're together? He and she, they're –?'

'No. Leastways, I'm pretty sure they're not. Only she's hot for him. He came pretty close to telling me as much, but I figured the rest. Why else would a dame do something like this?'

The happy glow spread further still. Rockwell was nuts about planes, the girl was nuts about Rockwell. It all began to make sense. And if so, then Willard could relax. He needn't take action. His old commander would be allowed to live, not die.

'So we can lay off?' said Mason.

'Gosh, well it's certainly nice to know . . .'

'I sent some guys down to check what this mechanic Hueffer is up to. And everything Rockwell says seems to be true. They're testing out a whole lot of airplane designs, they've already been speaking to a couple of airplane makers . . . It all checks out, buddy.'

Willard hardened. It wasn't Mason's place to call him 'buddy'. Willard felt a mean-spirited desire to remind Mason who was boss. He leafed through the most recent batch of documents Mason had sent up and found a list entitled 'Marion newcomers: last four months'. Mason had compiled the list at Willard's request. There were fifteen names on the list and Willard began to question Mason on each one, with a needless combination of sharpness and pomposity.

But Willard's attention was only half taken up with Mason's answers. *What had Captain Rockwell wanted most? He had wanted his pilots to come back alive. He had wanted Willard to come back alive.* The realisation prompted a curious mixture of feelings: happiness, pride, nostalgia, longing, grief. His attention was only half on the conversation as he and Mason worked their way down the list. They reached the last name: '(Lundmark, Bradley ??)'

'Why the question marks? Why the brackets?'

'Not sure about his first name. It's only a kid. A young-ster from Brunswick that does jobs for us. He ain't strictly a resident, only we keep him kinda busy, so he hangs out with us plenty.'

Willard shifted in his seat, annoyed. 'Why? Why do that? That's a security risk. We should only keep people in town who . . .'

Willard lectured Mason, until even he grew bored with the sound of his voice.

'Yeah, sure, you're right. We'll send him back. He's only a kid though. I wouldn't worry.'

Somewhere a thought jabbed in the back of Willard's brain.

'A kid? How old?'

'Don't know. Fifteen, maybe.'

'The surname? It's not so common. Wasn't one of your neighbours up the hill called that?'

'What? Lundmark?' Mason's voice suddenly tightened. Willard spotted the tightening with glee. He'd caught Mason out and would relish pressing home his advantage.

'That's the name we're discussing,' he said primly.

'Shit, yeah, let me think . . . it was a while back . . . only, yeah, we did have to waste a couple of guys. Think one of them could have been a Lundmark, yes.'

'Could have been?'

'Was. Was a Lundmark.'

'And old enough to have a fifteen-year-old boy?'

'I guess so. Yes. Shit.'

'You killed the father and you've hired his son to run errands for you?'

Willard's voice was icy. Mason's voice was unnaturally hushed and submissive as he replied. Something on the phone line between them suddenly took on a deathly edge. Not figuratively, literally. Both men knew what had to be done.

PART FOUR

Control

The thing about riding bikes is that it's fun in the summer, but a pain in winter.

So, as autumn came around, two Ohio bicycle manufacturers, Wilbur and Orville Wright, found themselves bored. Aviation caught their attention. They got hold of the available literature and read it with care. And the more they read, the more they realised that the whole problem now lay with control: how to manoeuvre an aircraft in flight.

Most people before them had thought about using a movable tailplane, rather like the rudder of a ship. But the Wright brothers knew about bicycles, and bikes depend on a different action: the action of banking into a turn. Perhaps aircraft would need to do the same? And perhaps that could be achieved the way birds did it: by turning the tips of one wing up and the tips of the opposite wing down . . .

It was a good idea. But just having one smart idea didn't make an airplane. Though the Wright brothers got a start from the literature which George Cayley had first stimulated, they still had to solve every single problem as it came along. How to make the plane light enough? How to make it strong enough? How to design the propeller? How to generate the thrust.

But they were brilliant mechanics – visionary and practical; creative and persistent. One by one, the problems were solved. On 17 December 1903, the Wright brothers made the world's first true flight: manned, powered and controlled. Over the next two years, they made a series of improvements, culminating in a non-stop flight of no less than twenty-four miles.

And how did the world react to this conquest of the skies? The answer is simple: it didn't. On the day the Wrights invited the press to witness their accomplishment, the engine had a problem and the Flyer No. 2 didn't fly. The following day, the press witnessed a sputtering twenty-yard glide. And after that, they just plain weren't interested. Three years after the Wrights had conquered flight, the number of working airplanes in the world numbered just one.

So, inevitably, the airplane was invented all over again. In France this time, by a dapper little Brazilian, Santos-Dumont. The Brazilian's plane was less well-designed than the Wrights', but it conquered the fourth and final challenge of flight: to get into the air in a place where there were pressmen and cameras. In 1906, the age of aviation had truly begun. The world went aviation-crazy, led by the French. Many of the words that describe the airplane come to us from the French, for that reason: fuselage, aileron, aerodrome.

And the Wright brothers' most lasting achievement? To realise that a plane needed to bank like a bicycle, not steer like a boat. The Wrights' wing-warping technology itself didn't last long. Ailerons did the job better and safer. But there it was. Cayley's magic trio was complete. Lift, thrust, control.

Now it only remained to find people willing to risk their necks and fly.

86

The hotel was a crummy little dump on the Gulf coast, a few miles up from Naples. Once upon a time, the place had been painted pale green, the colour of seasickness on a girl's face. But that had been long ago. Since then, sun and rain had amused themselves picking scabs of paint from the flaking wood, splintering and cracking the sagging veranda. A few tough weeds had found footholds in the corners of the red-tiled roof. The sun tried to burn the weeds. The weeds tried to outlast the sun. As a hotel, the place was worse than awful. As a hide-out it was better than excellent.

Jim Bosse and Haggerty McBride looked like – well, they looked like what they were: Washington bureaucrats. Serious men. Dark suits, white shirts, navy ties. Briefcases. Something weighty in their faces, something unsmiling, businesslike and tough. The farmboy look in Bosse's face was still there, only further back this time, maybe too far to reach.

The two men sat in a private room off the hotel lobby. They rose from their seats as Abe, Pen and Hennessey entered. On the table in front of them, a plate of cookies and a jug of tepid water grew bored together. Everyone sat.

Bosse spoke first. 'Miss Hamilton, Mr Hennessey, you haven't met my colleague, Haggerty McBride. He's been working with me on this case. He's the only one in the IRS who knows as much as I do about it. 'Most everyone else knows 'most nothing at all.'

McBride shook hands – strong handshakes, but not warm – then sat back down, flicking a couple of crisp white business cards across the table. Nobody looked at them.

Meantime, Bosse opened his briefcase. Photos and documents spilled out. It was everything that the team had accumulated over the last three months. Freighters loading and unloading, bringing the booze that flowed out across America, releasing a whole tide of money in its wake, money and violence, money and blood.

'Well boys – ma'am – you fellers have done good. No. It's beyond good. You got everything we wanted. Everything and more.'

'You got the accounts? The payroll?'

Abe licked his lips. He'd obtained less than Bosse had asked for, more than he himself had hoped for. They had eight weeks' continuous payroll data. They had a set of management accounts covering the last six months.

'Yes. Copies. Which I know you're happy to swear to.'

'Right.'

'Of course, it's a question of whether the courts will acknowledge them. The mob will try to have them struck out as fabrications. But still, Captain, you're an excellent witness. It ain't every witness who's got a drawer full of medals and a citation direct from Congress.'

'Suppose we produce a witness to authenticate them?' It was Pen who spoke. Bosse and McBride swivelled to look at her.

'A witness? Who? It all depends. A court would need to find the person credible.'

'How about the chief buying agent for the organisation? I'd say he was credible. And a louse, by the way. I hope you stomp on him.'

She pushed a fat manila envelope over the table. The envelope bulged with paper. Bosse opened it and began to read, handing the papers to his partner as he read. 'Jesus,' he said after a moment. 'Jesus.' The way he said it, it sounded less like a blasphemy, more like an acknowledgement of prayers answered.

He put the package down.

'You put a wire tap on his phone?'

'Uh-huh. Hired a bilingual secretary in Havana to transcribe it.'

'And these conversations . . . Lambaugh's taking kickbacks direct from his booze suppliers. He must be making six, maybe seven thousand dollars a month.'

'At least. A lot of the time he does business face to face and we didn't pick up anything from the phone.'

Bosse's grin spread slowly, like a sunflower opening. 'How the heck did you know? What made you think it'd be a good idea to stick a wire tap on his phone?'

Pen shrugged. 'Various things. The way he lived . . . I know it is Havana and all, and his regular salary must be sweet enough. All the same . . . the cars, the gold watches, the girls. I couldn't figure it.'

'And?'

'And I found a letter changing the security arrangements on Marion's purchasing account in Havana. That seemed like Bob Mason had some of the same suspicions I did. It seemed worth a try.'

Bosse put his hand on the documents, proprietorially. 'Does Lambaugh know about this material yet?'

Pen shook her head. 'No. We figured you might want to tell him.'

'Sure . . . I go along there, offer him a choice. He gets to cooperate with us or we hand all this material over to Uncle Bob Mason and your buddy Lambaugh gets to try and explain this to him . . . Uh-huh, he'll cooperate, I figure he'll cooperate.'

He glanced across at McBride, who nodded too. Now it was Bosse's turn to produce some documents. He doled them out in three piles and pushed them over the table.

Abe looked down at his. The documents were all stamped with the crest of the IRS.

'What the . . .?'

Bosse chuckled. 'Sorry, folks. Only looking over our records, it seems like none of you fellers have filled out a tax declaration. We wouldn't want to go arrest everyone in Marion and then have some smartass lawyer start pointing out that we hadn't made all the arrests we should've.'

Abe and Pen looked at each other, incredulous but smiling. Hennessey said nothing, just put his fingertips to the tax documents and pushed them away. With Mason's money, Abe and Pen had earned plenty that year, easily enough to make a declaration. But the shine on the storekeeper's suit told its own story, and Bosse took back the third pile in silence. For the next fifteen minutes, Abe and Pen sat side by side, their pens scratching away over the black and white forms. They completed their forms and passed them back to Jim Bosse, who grinned. 'Ain't taxmen awful?' He began folding away the forms. The room was silent.

Abe felt Pen's love tugging at him from three feet away. He felt strange. If Bosse concluded – as he should do – that their task was complete, then there was no reason for the team to stay together any longer. Abe had his plane to build and fly. But because his mind was far away, it took him a moment or two to realise that Bosse hadn't yet said what he needed to say. He hadn't said: 'Good job, well done, we've got everything we need, now there's nothing more for you folks to do.' Abe looked over at the two taxmen with sudden concern.

'Well?'

'Well, good,' said McBride, speaking for almost the first time.

'Meaning?'

'Meaning that if we choose to go ahead at this stage, we've got absolutely everything we need. Thank you.'

And there it was. *If*. A little word with a big voice. An *if* with no place in that room, not then, not ever.

'If?' said Abe a second time, his voice cracking with sudden dryness, 'What the heck are you talking about *If*?'

87

Brad Lundmark was eating a sandwich down by the river. The Okefenokee ran dirty green, the colour of pond water mixed with old tea. Brad sat on the dirty concrete quay, leaning up against one of the steel mooring bollards, feeling its warmth against his back. His sandwich was a favourite: smoked ham and dill pickle. That was one of the good things about Marion. Unlike its poor cousin up the hill, Marion had money. Easy money, lots of money. The boarding house where Lundmark stayed had things on its menu which he'd never even heard of in Independence. So he experimented with new things. Smoked ham and dill pickle; new types of soda; candy like he'd never known it.

There was a movement down the quay. Bob Mason was there, hat in his hands, shading his eyes against the sun. He saw Lundmark and approached.

'Hey there.'

'Hey.'

'You're Lundmark, right?'

'Right.'

'Getting on OK?'

'Yep.'

'Good. You ain't had no problems with anyone?'

'No. Folks have been real nice, sir.'

Brad knew who Mason was – everyone in Marion did – but he didn't understand why the man had sought him out or what these questions were all about. He shifted position on the quayside, still keeping his back against the bollard, but shifted around so he could see Mason more easily.

'Good, that's good.'

Lundmark nodded. He didn't know what to say, so he said, 'Thanks.'

There was a pause.

Mason stuck his hands in his pockets and said, 'Hey, you want gum?'

'I got some.'

'You want more? What have I got here? Peppermint. I hate peppermint. You like it?'

'Sure.' Lundmark took the gum. He still had half a sandwich to finish, so he laid the gum beside him on the hot concrete. 'I'll have it after. Thanks.'

'You're welcome.' Mason wiped his head and put his hat back on. 'You take care, right? Any problems, you come tell me.'

'Sure. Thank you, sir.'

Mason nodded. Lundmark twizzled around again, his back to Mason, staring out over the dirty green water. He was a strange guy Mason, Brad thought. He was a murderer, of course, but a nice guy too. In the world where Brad had grown up, morality had tended to come in simpler colours. He'd never imagined that a hoodlum like Mason could also be a pleasant individual, one to one. He bit into his sandwich, reflectively.

It was at that moment that Mason squeezed the trigger.

The shot cracked out, but the kid never heard it. The bullet, speeding ahead of its own detonation, entered the back of his head dead centre, just above the furthest outward bulge of the skull. The bullet did what it had to do and moved on, exiting Brad's forehead in a bloody mess. The boy – or rather the corpse which had so recently been a boy, still holding its sandwich – toppled face forwards into the greasy water. The water made a brief glooping sound, then closed over the site.

The only sign that there had ever been anyone sitting on the quayside was the packet of gum lying by the bollard in the sweltering sun. Mason didn't have the heart to pick it up.

88

It had been Haggerty McBride who had used the word *if*,
but it was still Jim Bosse who answered, albeit indirectly.
He tapped the pile of documents.

'These documents. They detail a business enterprise on
a major scale. Revenues are vastly in excess of costs. The
payroll alone provides grounds for prosecution. We have
no records of anyone in Marion filing a tax return. The
documents you have collected are, in our opinion, sufficient evidence of systematic tax evasion – not to mention
numerous other counts if we can get them to stick. On the
basis of this evidence, I have no doubt we would obtain a
large number of convictions.'

'Good. That's what we wanted to achieve. That's all we
ever wanted to achieve.'

'Really, Captain. You're sure?'

'Damn right, I'm sure.'

Bosse nodded and sat back as though satisfied by
Abe's answer. Only McBride continued to sit forwards. Abe
suddenly realised that he'd been wrong to assume that Bosse
was in charge. The power-chemistry suddenly flipped, and
Abe realised that all along it hadn't been Bosse, but the
younger-looking McBride who was running this show. If he'd
bothered to look at it earlier, McBride's business card would
have told him as much: Haggerty N. McBride, Director,
Special Investigations Unit. The sudden shift of authority in
the room was unsettling, as was that as-yet-undetonated *if*.

McBride took a cookie from the plate, crumbled it in his hands, but didn't put it anywhere near his mouth. Outside, a gull screamed with sudden loudness beyond the window.

'Captain, let me ask you a question,' said McBride. 'In your opinion, is Robert Mason the head of an entire organisation or merely the head of one of its important subsections?'

Abe went still. The room went still. Strange though it seemed to admit, it was a question Abe and the others had never really considered before. Hennessey had asked Abe to destroy Marion. Abe and the others had pretty much fulfilled that brief. What lay on beyond Marion was a question to which Abe didn't attach a lot of importance. But his answer, when it came, was unhesitating.

'The volume of alcohol we shift. It's vast. It's enough to supply entire cities. Large ones. If Mason acts independently, then he's got some pretty good buddies in the business . . . but no, on balance no, I don't think he's independent. I guess he takes his orders from someplace else.'

McBride nodded.

'We think so too.'

Abe shot a glance sideways at Pen and Hennessey. Their faces were carefully impassive, but he guessed their feelings must be in as much tumult as his.

'I'm afraid that's not my business, McBride. Hennessey here asked for help freeing up Independence from an unpleasant neighbour. We set out to do that. And only that.'

McBride made a courteous gesture with his hands that didn't mean a whole lot. 'Like I say, that's fine. If you want us to go ahead with what we've got, we'll get things moving right away.'

That *if* again. The word didn't improve with repetition.

'And why wouldn't I want you to go ahead?'

McBride sat back, appeared to notice the cookie crumbled half to powder in his hand and dusted it off onto the plate.

'In our view, you have broken into one of the most important criminal organisations in the country. Perhaps the largest and the most important. You've busted one of their major import routes right open. But these documents suggest to us that there's a whole lot more to do. Suppose we smash Marion? Hit it so hard it never grows back? Mr Hennessey, you'd get your town back. Captain, Miss Hamilton, you'd be able to get on and live your lives knowing you'd done a great and courageous thing. But you'd know, all of you, that someplace else, unknown to you and unknown to us, another Marion was being built. An organisation like this isn't just gonna throw in its hand. It'll rebuild. There'll be more mobsters. More guns. More booze. More violence. In the end, we'll have shifted the problem, not eliminated it. That's why I say *if*. But it's up to you. Few people could have accomplished as much. Perhaps nobody would choose to do more.'

Outside the room, waves beat up on the white Naples shoreline. Gulls pulled stunts in the air. The old wood of the hotel creaked and settled.

McBride spoke again. 'I haven't been specific. I ought to be. What we are asking is for you to deliver the entire organisation to us. Not just the right hand, but the head and the heart as well. We want to smash not a sub-unit of the organisation, but the organisation itself. To do that, we'll need to connect Marion to the headquarters. We'll need enough evidence to obtain search and arrest warrants. Those warrants will give us enough further evidence to do the rest.'

'You say you want to connect Marion to the centre . . .?'

'Money. There's only one way to do that meaningfully and that's by tracing the flows of money. Bank transfers between business units. And we would need the documents themselves. We can make witnessed copies ourselves and return the originals to you, but no Morse code, no light bulbs, no handwritten copies, no witnesses making a confession under duress.'

Abe thought about his little team. Gibson Hennessey, Pen Hamilton, Arnie Hueffer, Brad Lundmark. Hennessey had only ever asked for help in claiming Independence back from the mob. He wanted peace and quiet to return to town, maybe a little prosperity too. He hadn't wanted to clean up America. He hadn't asked for Abe to do that.

And meantime, Abe's Atlantic dream sprang up at him with renewed force. He could almost feel the shudder of a metal wing ripping through a North Atlantic gale. He could see the dirty weather battering the windscreen, hear the howl of an engine out-screaming the winds. He couldn't wait any longer to devote himself to that dream. He couldn't bear any longer to devote himself to an objective which wasn't really his.

He shook his head, just once but with absolute decision.

'I'm sorry, McBride. I've done what I was asked to do. And that's it. That's where I stop. I've reached my limit.'

Pen heard those words through a fog.

He was giving up. He was moving on. Having done something brilliantly, he was abandoning it unfinished. With the vital exception of his wartime career, he was doing what he'd always done: running away. And it was in that moment then Pen knew something else as well: that it was useless for her to love him. He'd never give her what she wanted. The greatest man she'd ever met was also, strange to say it, a coward.

Her eyes dazzled with tears. He would never love her, she realised now, not because she wasn't the right girl for him, but because he was too much of a coward to commit himself. It seemed like the worst reason in the world, but also the most final. Her grief was so strong, she was hardly able to speak.

89

The port decanter shone dully in the candlelight.

It was late in the evening. The women, including Rosalind, had already retired to the drawing room, in the English style. There were a few house guests staying for the weekend, but one or two had gone to bed, another trio had headed off to the billiard room. There were only four men left at table: Willard, his father, and two young men who were here as guests of Willard's middle two sisters. Junius Thornton didn't drink much and never got drunk. Willard had drunk plenty but was practised enough to hold it. The other two men had drunk excessively and were slumped staring at the candlesticks on the long mahogany table, trying to keep the two dozen candle flames from blurring into four or even six dozen.

Junius Thornton glanced contemptuously at the two youngsters, then got up heavily to take a couple of cigars from the sideboard. He handed one to Willard, and the two men, father and son, shared the ritual of preparing then lighting the tobacco. They inhaled, let their dinner jackets fall open, sat back, stretched out.

'The war,' said Junius.

'Yes, Father?'

'That conversation at dinner. I didn't ask what you thought.'

'No.'

The conversation had been a rare one. In these days of

peace, it had almost become as though the war had happened in a previous century or to a different country. Mentions of it were rare; discussions still rarer.

All the same, it had happened. Abby, a girlfriend of Willard's youngest sister, had been speaking about the negotiated Armistice of November 1918, which many in the American army had been fiercely opposed to. 'How could anyone have wanted that terrible war to have lasted a second longer?' she'd cried. 'Every day young men were being killed. Think of them! Think of their poor families!'

Her speech had been followed by a half-second of silence. Then Junius had spoken, his tone of voice ended the conversation as firmly as his words.

'The consequences of aggression must always be brought home to the aggressor. Germany needed to feel the pain of invasion and defeat on her own soil. Though the English and the French lacked the stomach to continue, they may yet regret their timidity.'

Willard nodded to indicate that he remembered the conversation. His father said, 'Well? What is your opinion of the question?'

'Well, I mean I can see what Abby meant. After all, it was one thing in the Army Air Corps. It was dangerous enough, but at least it was quite civilised. It was quite different for the poor soldiers on the ground. They lived underground, little better than rats, really, not to speak of the danger and the bloodshed, the endless mud, the guns going off around them all the time . . . But then again, Papa, I think you're right. If a person starts a thing, he needs to finish it. Properly finish it. I'm not sure we ever really did,' he concluded, pleased with himself.

Since joining Powell Lambert – and especially since being elevated to the heights of the Investment Bureau – Willard had become more decisive, more single-minded. Although he could still become tongue-tied or excessively talkative with his father, the problem now was nothing like as bad as it had been. His father seemed to agree with him, nodding his head sharply twice in a gesture of assent.

'The Firm – Thornton Ordnance, that is; Powell Lambert didn't exist back then – the Firm spent five and a half million dollars seeking to persuade people that an unconditional surrender by the Germans was the only acceptable outcome. Five and a half million dollars. If we could have spent more to any effect, we would certainly have done so.'

'Gosh, Father! Five and a half million dollars!'

Willard spent a moment trying to imagine how that vast sum of money had been spent – who had taken it? And in exchange for what promises? – but he failed entirely.

'It wasn't much. At that time, the Firm was earning eighteen million dollars a month in net profit. Each further day of combat was worth approximately half a million dollars. The arithmetic was not difficult to perform.'

Willard tried to get his head around his father's way of thinking and failed – then tried again, and succeeded; or almost succeeded; or achieved something that felt like succeeding. Willard thought of his father's utter commitment to success, his blunt attitude to violence. *And perhaps he's right,* he thought. *Perhaps Europe and America would now be more secure if the victory had been clearer. Perhaps Powell Lambert's ruthlessness does mean a cleaner, better organised, less anarchic industry.*

In any case, something had suddenly become clear. He had been firm in Marion, but not yet firm enough. It was no use waiting to see if Rockwell was a danger or not. The man had to be pushed. He had to be provoked into revealing his intentions. And Willard realised he knew how to do it. He stood up abruptly.

'I'm sorry, Father. I've just realised I've got a call to make. Right now. Business.'

The older man nodded. The ghost of a smile hung on his heavy features, looking as permanent and appropriate as a lace handkerchief on a lump of granite. 'Good boy. I'll see you tomorrow.'

Willard made his call, waking Mason but not caring. Willard said what he had to say. Mason understood the first part of it, not the second, but agreed to get both parts done in any case. Willard hung up and walked slowly back to the drawing room, looking forward to seeing Rosalind's slim grey-gold beauty again after the black-and-white sombreness of the exclusively male company.

For another two hours that evening, he was dazzling, lively, the centre of an adoring family's attention. And it was only when he went upstairs to get ready for bed that night, that a thought struck him.

His father had spent five and a half million dollars trying to procure the extension of the war. If he could have spent more usefully, then he would have done. But his son, Willard, had been in a front-line combat unit, flying as a pursuit pilot. And of all the bloody and dangerous occupations in a bloody and dangerous war, then perhaps the pursuit pilots had the most bloody and dangerous job of all. To put it bluntly, each day of war increased not insignificantly the chance that Willard wouldn't survive it. His father had presumably considered the matter, then made his decision.

And as he'd said, the arithmetic had hardly been difficult to perform.

90

Sam Skeddings was quite a guy.

He wore silk shirts in bright colours. He had a rack of neckties to match. He was six foot two and had a handspan that could curl all the way round a fat man's neck. He wore a gun in a shoulder holster and carried three hundred bucks cash in his hip pocket. If he wanted a girl, he got her. If he opened a bottle of whiskey at the start of an evening, he threw it away empty at the end. If he fired a gun, somebody dropped back dead. That was Sam Skeddings. He was quite a guy and both he and his employer, Robert Mason, knew it.

The first part of his assignment was the regular type of thing. Take a big car up the hill to Independence. Shoot the place up a little, but the storekeeper's house in particular. The instructions were quite specific. Nobody was to be killed, but the storekeeper had to be badly frightened. So Skeddings did as he was told. He picked a small group of men, then went straight up the hill and shot the place up. They shot out windows, damaged woodwork, entered the store itself and wrecked the place. Then they ended by aiming their Tommy guns high through the shattered windows and blazing away non-stop until their firing pins came clicking down on empty air.

But that wasn't the strange part of the assignment. The strange part was this.

After the shooting, he had been instructed to go back

into town. Not in a big black car with Tommy guns poking out of the windows. But quietly. At noon. On foot. And he'd been asked to find out – figure this – to find out what kind of laundry the storekeeper's wife had been doing.

'You want me to look at her smalls?' he'd asked Mason, outraged.

'Buster, I need you to count the frills on 'em.'

Skeddings didn't like that kind of thing. Shooting a guy was man-to-man stuff. It wasn't always pretty, but what the hell, the way the world had gotten, it was the kind of thing that now and again had to happen. But poking around amidst another guy's laundry! And a married guy! With daughters! It wasn't right. It wasn't right at all. But still, orders were orders, and Skeddings was a guy to do as he was told.

91

Abe had meant what he'd said.

A cold, clear, calm resolution had come over him. He knew precisely what he needed to do and could see instantly the exact sequence of steps required to do it.

He gave his instructions to Pen and Arnie. For the time being, they would need to adhere exactly to their existing routines. They would give Bob Mason no reason for suspicion. Meanwhile, in Washington, Bosse and McBride would be working to get the legal machinery in place for a series of sweeping arrests across Marion. As soon as the taxmen had what they needed, they'd call the Miami airfield with an enquiry about chartering an aircraft. That call would be the signal for the three conspirators – and Hennessey up in Independence – to vanish away. None of them would return home, but hide out somewhere in the country. After four weeks, they would rendezvous with Haggerty McBride and Jim Bosse in Washington.

In the meantime, Abe would carry on working on his plane. He had a friend up in Ohio with a field big enough for airplanes and a well-equipped workshop. He'd go up there with Arnie, push their airplane design as far as they could themselves, then bring in the pros. Within a few months, he hoped he'd have his plane. He'd test it briefly, then he'd make his flight. The Orteig Prize was the brightest treasure in world aviation at the moment. In America,

Britain and France, rival teams were already tracing designs and commissioning planes. That the prize would be won within a year or two, Abe had no doubts. The only question was who would win it.

Until then, following his own instructions to the letter, he returned to Marion on flying duty. The volume of booze seemed to be increasing by the week. A freighter-load of booze was entering the river every day or two. Coastguard activity was becoming more intense and persistent. But it wasn't the workload that bothered him.

The first thing was a grisly scene laid on especially for his benefit down by the quayside. Having landed his plane, it was his normal practice to seek out Mason to check on the latest schedule of freighter arrivals. Enquiring at Mason's office, he was directed down to the concrete loading quay down behind the warehouse.

He found Mason all right, with four of his men. Two of the men were in a flat-bottomed rowboat hauling something out of the river in a net. The other two men stood on the quay, holding their noses at the stench of rotting river mud. In the net was Brad Lundmark, bloated, drowned and dead. The front of his skull was smashed to a pulp: a bullet wound almost certainly.

'Hey there, Captain,' said Mason. 'You OK? Shame this. Boy fell in the river and drowned. Pity.'

His voice said there was no pity at all. Abe could feel Mason's eyes hard on his face, scrutinising him for any reaction. Abe looked at the dead boy. Something in the green water had done something to the kid's hair. Instead of dulling in the filth, the submersion had actually clarified it. The boy's red hair shone out bright red, like burnished copper. Abe looked at the boy and saw himself. Abe knew now that he wouldn't abandon his mission until he'd destroyed every single element – head, hand and heart – of the organisation that had done this.

But he showed nothing in his face. His voice was steady

as he replied, 'Really, Mason? Looks to me like somebody shot the kid first. You fellers ought to be more careful with your firearms.'

He shrugged and turned away. Rage refined down to a cold, dark point inside his heart. He felt enclosed in darkness, but this was a darkness that he understood; that satisfied him; that he would follow to the very end.

But that scene by the quayside was only the first of his surprises that day. The second was this. Going out on patrol that afternoon, he took off from the Marion airstrip and curved up and around over Independence, as he always did. He looked down, as he always did. And saw them.

Red sheets.

Blazing in the sunshine like a spillage of blood. Blazing in the sunshine like a second corpse. Abe saw the sheets from high overhead and his face, already grim, turned a shade or two harder still. Lundmark was dead. And now this: Hennessey's red sheets, the emergency signal agreed long ago in an Atlanta restaurant.

Once again, and stronger than ever before, Abe had the sense of the endgame approaching at somebody else's pace. In the air, in combat, he'd have been reviewing the air above and behind him. He'd have been checking the blind spots under his nose, beyond his wings. He'd have twisted and turned to check that there was no predator lurking in the eye of the sun. But this wasn't combat. There was no sky to check, and try as he might, Abe couldn't guess what was going wrong and why.

But meantime, there was Hennessey's distress beacon to attend to. Beneath Abe's instrument panel was a black-handled lever. The lever was out of sight, unmarked, hard to find. Only two planes in the world possessed such a lever. Abe flew one of them, Pen flew the other. Abe reached for the handle and pulled it. Eight feet forwards of where Abe sat, a sheet of black rubber slid gently over the hottest part of the engine. For twenty seconds nothing happened, then a thin thread of smoke needled sideways from the engine cowling.

First a thread. Then a stream. Then a torrent.

92

Pen stood naked in her apartment, looking out over the beating surf. It was a fine day, but hazy. The ocean never really ended, it just dissolved into the sky. She was just back from Havana; had showered, put a comb through her hair, drunk some water.

Later that day, she had an engagement with friends, but she had no appetite for it. She ought to phone and cancel, only she didn't feel like speaking to anyone. She examined her body in the long wardrobe mirror. She had always been slim, but the experience of daily flying in the DH-4, an emphatically masculine plane, had toughened her, given her more strength in the arms, more squareness in the shoulders. And more wrinkles. She was smooth-skinned, but high altitude flying wears the skin like nothing else. Tiny crows' feet danced outwards from her eyes. She didn't mind. She liked them.

She put on some underclothes, thought vaguely about putting on a dress, but couldn't be bothered. She lay on her bed, kicking her feet in the air and picking from the fruit bowl.

This was the end. McBride and Bosse would use what they had to launch an all-out assault on Marion. The town would be destroyed. Independence could begin to rebuild. The organisation that had run Marion would be annoyed, but would start up all over, someplace else. It would kill more people, burn more property, ruin more livelihoods, smash more lives.

And it was the end in other ways too.

It was the end of Pen's one and only excursion into a world of discipline, where people got up every morning because they had a job to do, where they saw the same group of workmates each day, where flying was not only a pleasure but a task. Pen supposed that she'd go back to the life she'd had before. She'd know to appreciate the good things it offered. She'd miss some of the things it could never provide. She'd settle down.

Because things had ended in one final way.

She'd given up on Abe. She'd love him, always and for ever, but she knew now that the men she could most easily love were precisely those least likely to tie themselves down. Abe was a flier, an adventurer, a man who had made a lifetime's habit of leaving things behind, of committing to nothing, of moving on. Loving Abe was as beautiful and foolish as loving the wind. Right now, though Pen felt desolate at the thought of giving up, her head told her that it was time to move on.

But that was for the future. Right now, she felt like doing, saying and feeling nothing. Her eyes slid out to the smoky haze in the far horizon. She lost herself in the blur.

Her trance was interrupted.

Pen's apartment was a top-floor penthouse, serviced by an elevator whose doors opened directly into the living room. To ride the elevator to the top, you needed a key. Pen had her own key, of course, as did the concierge downstairs. If anyone called for her, the concierge called Pen on the house phone and only let them ride up if she okayed it. Right now, the elevator began to whine. It went past the lower floors. It was coming all the way up.

And Pen still had her key.

And the concierge hadn't called.

She froze. Her first thought was the obvious one. McBride and Bosse had screwed up. They had promised not to hit Marion until she, Abe and Arnie had made their excuses and melted away. But they must have acted too soon or allowed their information to leak. Inside the elevator would be a couple of Mason's men, armed, deadly, and looking for her . . .

Pen stood at her bedroom door, still in her underwear, breathing fast. She had only two thoughts, both of them useless. The first was she wished she were dressed. The second was that Abe would have known what to do. The elevator stopped. There was a thin hiss of hydraulics, then silence. The doors opened automatically, but there was a moment's delay first. Pen snatched up a patterned Japanese-style housecoat, but hadn't time to put it on.

The doors clanked open.

From where Pen was standing, she couldn't see directly into the elevator car, only the doors. For an instant, there was silence. Pen thought, *it's all a mistake, they haven't sent anybody, I'm going to be OK.* Then there was a sound. A man moved, then stepped out. Her throat caught. The man turned.

It was Abe.

But not Abe as she'd seen him before. This was a man so different, he seemed almost a stranger. His face was empty but also murderous, calm but also remorseless. It was a face, she guessed, that only men were capable of – and perhaps only those rare men who, in some part of their being, had always been shaped for combat. Men for whom the kill-or-be-killed nature of warfare came naturally, like a talent for cards, or a perfect singing voice.

His eyes found her straight away, as though he'd always known that she'd be standing half-naked at the bedroom door.

'They've killed Brad,' he said. 'They murdered Brad.'

93

Pen felt too many things too quickly to have any hope of sorting them into logical order. But from the jumble, here were some snippets.

One: she wasn't about to be killed, or not imminently, at any rate.

Two: how come Abe had a key to her elevator?

Three: Brad Lundmark dead! And it was all her fault!

Four: she was pleased to see Abe. For all her confused feelings, he was the man she wanted to be with more than anyone else in the world.

Five: he could see her in her underclothes. She felt naked.

Six: his face was terrifying.

Seven: all right, the kid's death wasn't entirely her fault, but she was implicated.

Eight: something must have gone horribly wrong for Abe to be here.

Nine: in a way she was pleased he could see her in her underthings.

Ten: it was good to be alive.

She must have made some kind of sound. She certainly stumbled forwards, half in greeting, half in shock. Abe's face changed. It became solicitous, worried. Pen found herself being helped into her robe. She sat down. Abe rooted around in the kitchen and came out with a glass of ginger ale from the icebox. She drank it.

'I'm sorry,' he said, 'I shocked you by coming up like that. You must have been worried.'

'You don't even have a key.'

'Arnie copied it once. We should have told you.'

'Yes, you should.'

'Are you OK?'

'I thought . . .'

'You thought Bob Mason was going to step out of there with a Tommy gun. Yes, I'd probably have thought the same. Sorry. It was dumb of me.'

'You were meant to be up in Marion. I thought you'd be there for the next couple of days.'

'I was. I used our emergency lever, faked an engine fire and made a kind of crash-landing in Marion. I pretended to patch up the airplane, but told Mason I'd need to come down here for proper repairs. He believed me, I think.'

She half-smiled. 'Faking the engine fire. Did it work OK?'

'Yes. It was fun, actually.'

'Brad Lundmark. You said . . .'

'They killed him. Mason gave me some horseshit story, but he meant me to know it was horseshit. And that's not all of it.' Abe went on to tell her about Hennessey's distress signal. 'I've spoken to him by phone – drugstore to drugstore, of course. He's fine, his family is fine. They just shot his house to pieces. He thinks it was a warning. I've told him to get out. He's going up to Atlanta with his family.'

'And what are you going to do?'

Abe smiled. Or at least, he widened the corners of his mouth and showed his teeth. But it wasn't a smile. A smile is about warmth and friendly feelings. This smile was nothing like that. It was a glimpse of the face that Pen had seen to begin with: the warrior's face, implacable and dangerous.

'I'm going to continue,' he said. 'McBride was right. I should have known. There's no use striking down one part of the organisation. It's all or nothing.'

427

'Is that safe?'

'Pen, I owed that kid. For reasons I can't even tell you, I owed him and his mother. The truth is, I don't really care too much if it's safe. I just want to smash the bastards. Sorry.'

'Yes, but . . .' Pen was about to tell him that she personally cared very much about her safety, when she suddenly realised that Abe was having another one of his flying solo moments. It wasn't just the face of a warrior she'd seen before, it was the face of a man who actually preferred to fight solitary and die solitary. She shook her head, stunned at him.

'You're unbelievable. You know that? You're unbelievable.'

'What? What are you talking about?'

'Now, even now, your first impulse is to fight alone. Are you even aware you have friends?'

'Of course. It's not that. I know you and Arnie –'

'Did you know that Arnie and I thought you were wrong? That you should have said yes to McBride in the first place? That we shouldn't run from a job we haven't finished?'

Now it was Abe's turn to look shocked. It was obvious from his face that he had no idea. But Pen wasn't done. She was sitting down, leaning forwards, crying. But her tears were strange. They fell without effort or pause, more like dry sand than salt water.

'And you know something else? You're wrong. About everything you think you are. You've spent all your life running and the person you run from, finally, is yourself. You know why you never talk about the war? Why you hardly even keep your medals, let alone remember them or honour them? It's because those medals tell you something true about yourself and you're too pig-headed to hear it.'

She looked up at him. Her voice, though quiet, had been perfectly composed. It hadn't sobbed or choked or halted even once. And yet still those tears fell, falling like sand.

'You're not a war hero, you're simply a hero who came to prominence in wartime. I don't know why you can't see that, why you don't know that. It's like you spend your whole life with your face turned away from the mirror. You have something remarkable. Hennessey saw that within days of getting to know you. And yet you bury it. You always have. You do now. And I guess you always will. And I'm only sorry because, I saw that thing too. I wanted to see it shine.'

There was a long silence. There seemed nothing to say in the aftermath of such a speech. Abe found a towel in the kitchen and handed it to Pen, who dried her eyes with a couple of dabs. Her face didn't seem altered by the crying in any way. Her eyes were red, they weren't puffy, her cheeks weren't tight and scrunched up.

After a long time, Abe said, 'And you say you're happy to continue? To fight the mob until they're destroyed?'

'I told you, didn't I?'

'And Arnie too?'

'Of course Arnie. He hates those bastards.'

Abe nodded, but said nothing. The room was silent, except that because every window was filled with the wide blue ocean, the silence was filled with the rhythm of the sea. Eventually he seemed to emerge from his trance.

'OK,' he nodded: half-question, half-statement.

'OK.'

'I'd best go see Arnie. Let him know plans have changed.'

'Sure.'

'I'll call McBride from a drugstore as well. Tell him.'

'Yes. You need to do that.'

'We'll carry on. I've got some ideas.'

'I'll bet you do.'

'Ideas which maybe involve you making a little career change.'

'If you like.'

'OK then.'

'OK.'

Abe left the room, so quietly he could have been a ghost.

94

'On fire?'

'Yeah, on fire. I just told you.'

'Bad?'

'Jeez, Thornton, the plane looked like it was going to come down as a lump of charcoal.'

'But he took off again?'

'Sure. He had to fix it up though.'

'How long did that take?'

'I don't know. An hour. Maybe an hour and a half.'

'What did he say was wrong?' Willard pursued Mason relentlessly.

'Don't know. Something to do with the oil.'

'What to do with the oil?'

'How the hell should I know?'

'How far out was he when the fire started?'

'A few miles. Maybe eight, maybe ten.'

'How high?'

'High?'

'Yes, how high was he?'

'No idea. He was just a teeny little speck.'

'If you'd been underneath and he'd waved at you, would you have seen him wave?'

'No. Don't think so.'

'If he'd waved something large, a bath towel say, would you have seen him then?'

'I guess, maybe. Don't reckon he was going to spend

a lot of time waving bath towels though.'

Willard ignored Mason's deflection. At a rough guess, he'd say Abe must have been higher than two thousand feet, lower than eight thousand. Five thousand seemed like a fair estimate.

'OK. I want to know how he came in. Everything you remember.'

'Burning. On fire. Like a hog on a spitroast.'

'But his flight. Describe his flight. Was it steady or unsteady?'

'Unsteady. He was diving down, then looping up. One time it looked like he was gonna come down on the warehouse roof.'

'Was he side-slipping? Is that what he was doing?'

'That like the foxtrot?'

'Side-slipping . . . it's kind of when you slip sideways through the air, nose into the wind and the leading wing slightly down. It's a technique you can use to keep any flames from blowing back from the engine into the cockpit.'

'I didn't see no flames.'

'Did you see any side-slipping?'

'Not sure. Don't think so.'

'How about the landing? You see that?'

'Not me, no, but I heard about it. He pretty near rammed a gasoline truck.'

'Apart from that, how did he land? Apart from the fire, that is. Did he come in straight and steady? Was it a good landing?'

There was a short pause. Willard could hear Mason swigging something – whiskey, most likely – and setting the glass back down. When he spoke again, Mason's voice had an edge of irritation.

'Listen, Thornton, I don't know what your kick is here, but the way that guy brought the plane in was unbelievable. He bounced. He swerved. He virtually skidded off the end of the runway. But he came down in one piece and all he seemed to care about was getting the plane fixed up and back in the air. I got a phone call from him just now, telling me he'll be back in time to bring in the freighter tomorrow mid-morning. That's not just devotion to duty. He's way beyond that. I'm sick of mistrusting the guy. He's the best guy I've got, bar none. I say we let up on the poor sap.'

'Anything strange in the engine noise?'

'No. The engine was just fine. It was a real picnic up there. Oh, wait up, I was forgetting. *It was on fire*, I'm telling ya.'

'I was asking about the sound.'

'Jeez . . . It was up and down, just like the airplane.'

'And he said the problem was the lubrication? He didn't have a problem with the controls?'

'Sure he had a problem with the controls. Must have done. The way that thing came down.'

'But he told you it was the oil?'

'You want me to tell you again?'

'OK. Thanks. You've been helpful.'

'You wanna tell me what's going on?'

'Yes, of course, as soon as I know.'

'This got anything to do with that guy Hennessey's laundry habits?'

'Maybe.'

'You think he's up to something?'

Willard's lips went dry. Not just his lips. His tongue, his mouth, his throat went gluey and cramped. It was the question he'd been dreading. And this time he evaded, knowing he wouldn't be able to evade for long.

'Keep up the surveillance. Don't let him out of your sight.'

They signed off and hung up.

And Willard hadn't been honest. Because he was an airman, trained by Rockwell himself. Willard knew that a real engine fire would have destroyed the plane, that Rockwell would have been lucky to get out alive. And

Willard knew that Rockwell hadn't even been afraid of fire, because if he had, he'd have side-slipped like crazy to keep the flames at bay. And as for all that stunting around – the up-down flight, the crazy landing – Willard knew that for the bullshit that it was. The plane had been just eight miles out and five thousand feet up. It had had at least partial engine power and intact controls. If Rockwell had been in real trouble, there'd have been nothing stopping him from just gliding gracefully home.

And one last thing. The day he'd been shot up, Hennessey had hung red sheets out to dry in his garden. Who did that? Who had red sheets in that part of the world? No one. No one at all. No one, who didn't want to send a signal to a pilot flying overhead.

Willard had set his test and Rockwell had failed.

95

Abe left the apartment, his head still filled with the boom of Pen's words. They roared in his brain like the ocean waves, which were genuinely audible now, pounding the white sand as though the stuff needed to be punished forever. Abe walked out on the beach, almost unaware of where he was, or why. The air was quiet, but what breeze there was drove the little breakers in long diagonals up the shelving beach. The rolling curl of the waves was like a long sneer, endlessly repeated. A sneer at Abe. At his self-delusions. At his long history of running.

After an hour of aimless pacing, a new thought struck him. He stopped dead, as though physically struck. For two seconds he stood there, then went racing back, up to Pen's tall pink-fronted building, through the marble lobby, into the elevator, crunching sand into its carpet. He jammed the key into the lock and hit the button for the top floor. He couldn't get there fast enough. The elevator car reached the top floor. The doors paused, then staggered open. Abe almost tumbled out, he was so eager.

Pen was standing eight feet away from him, in evening dress, pearls and heels, a slightly incredulous smile on her face.

'Again?' she said.

'Again. I –' His words gave up before even properly starting.

'Yes?'

'I –'

Pen smiled again. In heels she was the same height as him or even a little taller. They had the same strangely blue eyes, the same very tanned skin. They even had something less common than that: the same way of moving, the same quiet watchfulness. At times it could almost seem as though they were like mirror images of each other, male and female versions of the same human being. It was like that now. Something peculiar in the atmosphere made Pen look away momentarily.

When she looked back, she found Abe with a pack of cards in his hand, spread fan-wise and face-down. His eyes silently invited her to pick one. Feeling strange, not understanding why Abe had come rushing back to her apartment to play stupid tricks that she'd seen before, she was about to pick a card, when Abe's finger, pushing from beneath the deck, slid one card out in front of the others, making it look as though the card had slid out of its own accord. As though in a trance, she took the card: the jack of spades, the black knave, a one-eyed, unlucky card.

Abe took the card and began to play with it. Pen followed the card – or not the card, but Abe's fingers and not always even his fingers, but the places she knew she wasn't meant to look. She followed the knave's progress as he was palmed, switched, concealed and dropped. When Abe finished a routine, he caught her eyes. She either pointed or glanced at the location where she knew the card to be. She was right each time. She felt a mounting sense of disappointment. What did this second visit mean? Abe's tricks looked like foolishness now, foolishness of a feeble, see-through kind.

Abe stopped again. Sadly now, Pen indicated his jacket sleeve. Abe smiled – a tiny half-smile – and shook his head. He opened his sleeve and shook it: nothing. He removed his jacket: nothing. Pen was puzzled. She'd been sure that the card had gone into the sleeve, but had she missed its coming out again? Or had she not seen what she thought she'd seen? Abe's trickery suddenly seemed more purposeful, more pointed.

With a small nod, Abe indicated the wastebasket beneath the side-table. She stepped over and looked inside. The knave was there, face-up. It couldn't have been there, but it was. She straightened again. She didn't know why words had all of a sudden become forbidden, but it made sense somehow. The silence rang with significance.

The two fliers now stood facing one another. Abe had put the deck of cards down. His hands were by his sides, not moving. His face gave Pen no indication of what she was meant to do or see next. She queried him with a tiny movement of her shoulders. Abe's mouth flickered with a smile of encouragement. Still puzzled, Pen began to shrug again, but more attentively this time. She was wearing a pearl-grey evening dress to just below the knee. The dress was rayon, but with two folds of chiffon that came down from the shoulder and met over her breasts.

And as she shrugged, the dress moved, but not quite evenly. There was a stiffness on the left-hand side, over her heart. Her mouth slightly open, and her breaths coming slow and deep, she put her hand to the area of stiffness. There was a playing card there, held in the fold of the chiffon. She couldn't even remember him stepping close enough to reach her, let alone to slide a card inside her dress. Perhaps when she'd bent to look in the wastebin . . . ? But she'd only made a half-step, she hadn't bent far, she hadn't taken her eyes off Abe for more than a second . . .

She removed the playing card from her dress and held it, not looking at it.

The pilot opened his hands once, stretching the fabric of his shirt over his chest. Pen saw the outline of a card in his shirt pocket, a pocket that had been empty before. He drew it out and turned it over. It was the king of hearts.

Pen's heart was suddenly doing a hundred beats to the

minute. Slowly, she turned over the card in her hand. It was the queen of hearts.

Her eyes crept up from the card to the man opposite her. His mouth and eyes were full of enquiry; full of hope; full of love. Still without words, he was asking her if she loved him still.

She nodded.

He breathed out. Relief and joy swept through him.

They came together and kissed, and the kiss was endless.

96

'Do you have a date yet?'

The man in McBride's office was nearing sixty, a heavy build that had run to fat, aggressive eyes locked behind thick glasses, balding. The man was McBride's direct boss, Jim Carpenter, the Commissioner of the IRS.

'No. No date.'

'Aren't you going to push?'

'I'd push if I needed to. I don't need to.'

'Christ, you know, action, we need action. We've got a special budgetary allocation for you. We've given you a big title, nice office. Now, talking frankly, we gotta have scalps. Congress will want scalps. The Treasury. The press. Jesus, I want scalps.'

'You'll get them.'

Outside the window, Washington had become locked under a rain cloud. Grey skies were hammered down low over the city, bolted down to the horizon in every direction by drifts of rain and rags of mist. Carpenter gazed out, as though the rain was a sour joke played on him personally.

'Yes, and I was asking when.'

'Mr Carpenter, sir, I have a source inside probably the largest criminal organisation in America. In scale, reach, effectiveness and financial muscle, this organisation will dwarf any group ever brought to justice in the courts of this country. My principal source is a man of exceptional resource and total integrity. We'll get the documents.'

'What documents? What do we need?'

McBride paused before answering. From the outset, this investigation had been need-to-know only. That had included McBride and Bosse. It had not included Carpenter.

'At present, sir, we have enough evidence to move against one unit of the organisation, but only one. If we do things right, I think we could smash it completely.'

'Yes, yes, I know. You already told me that part.'

'What we're currently seeking are financial documents linking the operating unit to the organisational headquarters.'

'Financial documents? You think the Mafia runs accounts?'

'These aren't the Mafia, sir. And you bet they run accounts.'

'So that's what you're after? Internal accounts?'

'No sir. I don't believe those will be available. But money transfers must be. I have asked my source to obtain them. Money transfers between the headquarters and the operating unit. If we get our hands on those, then I'm confident we would obtain a warrant to raid the headquarters.'

'And if you got your warrant?'

'I believe we'd hook every single member of the conspiracy.'

'Hah!'

Carpenter made a noise which could have meant anything, everything or nothing at all. He stared gloomily out at the rain.

'Tennis is gone to hell.'

'Sir?'

'Tennis. I was going to be playing tennis with Senator Paulet this afternoon. Won't now.'

'No sir.'

There was silence. The building was a modern one and the trouble with modern buildings with their air-conditioning systems and ducted air was that you couldn't just

throw open the window and listen to the rain. McBride
didn't like that. He was a country boy by origin. Knoxtown,
Ohio. Population, 863. He liked knowing that the rain
would be good for farmers and he liked just plain listening
to the rain. Jim Carpenter didn't.

'OK.'

Carpenter shifted his bulk, making it clear he was about
to leave.

'So you don't have a date?'

'No sir.'

'These bank records will either just show up or not.
There's not a lot we can do about it, right?'

'That's correct.'

'You've got a strange way of running things, McBride.'

'This investigation is a little different from most, sir.'

'Hah! . . . This operating unit. Where did you say it was
based?'

'I didn't.'

'What?'

'I've kept every detail of this investigation strictly need-
to-know, sir. I haven't told you where the operating unit is
based.'

'Well, I'm your boss and I need to know. So where is
it?'

'May I ask why you require the information, sir?'

'Fuck you, McBride.'

Carpenter's swearword spread out on the silence like a
stain. McBride held his face carefully impassive.

'Of course, you're welcome to know, sir. I apologise for
not filling you in sooner.'

'Well?'

'The unit is based in Illinois, sir. Our source lives and
works in Chicago.'

'Chicago, huh?' Carpenter nodded, scowled, stared out
at the rain and glowered at it, as though promising to get
his own back some time. 'Chicago.' He left the room.

McBride had plenty of work to do. It sat in piles all around him. He had a list of reminders from his secretary and a schedule of meetings as thick as the rain cloud outside. But he didn't touch his work or his phone or go to any meeting. He just sat at his desk, wondering why in hell's name he'd just lied to his boss. That and the rain.

He missed listening to the rain.

97

Willard did what he had to do. He gave instructions for the immediate tightening of security.

Lookouts were doubled, on the road, on the rail line, on the river.

All non-essential documents were burned. Barrow-loads of paper were carted outside, doused in gasoline, burned in braziers, and then the ashes were mashed into powder with a rake.

The warehouse was surrounded with bales of straw and tins of gasoline. In the event of a raid, the straw would be drenched with the fuel, then set on fire. Mason reckoned his lookouts would give him at least ten or fifteen minutes of warning. In less than half that time, the entire warehouse could be set ablaze, leaving nothing for the feds to find except burning timber and molten glass.

And as for the essential documents, the ones that Marion absolutely required for its daily business, Mason built a safe cemented into the wall of his very own villa. The safe was a large one and only Mason and Willard knew the codes. And there was one extra ingredient. At the bottom of the safe there was a can of gasoline and a stick of dynamite. A tiny fuse hung out of the safe door and stuck out into the room like a length of cord. In the event of a raid, Mason himself would go to his safe, put a match to the fuse and walk away.

But on one crucial point, Willard hesitated.

That point was Rockwell. Willard knew that he should have his old commander killed. The Independence store-keeper, the focal point of the town's resistance, had sent a distress signal to the airman. The airman had responded by faking an engine fire and getting out of Marion. Presumably he'd used his time away to make contact with Hennessey. That and what more besides? The truth was, that in the world Willard now moved in, the facts he knew were easily sufficient for him to issue the necessary orders.

But he hesitated.

He tried to persuade himself that he was concerned about the security of goods coming into Marion. If he had Rockwell killed, he'd have to kill the girl and the mechanic too. That would leave the Marion import route hopelessly exposed to a determined effort by the Coastguard. And on top of that, Willard could argue that it was important to find out precisely what Rockwell had been up to; that there was no proof, after all, that Rockwell had got anywhere at all, or that, if he had, any problem was remotely imminent. But in the end, all those arguments amounted to excuses, not reasons. In his heart, Willard knew he could hardly bear to have Rockwell murdered.

But he didn't hesitate for long. Just as he was seeking to persuade himself to issue the necessary order, he got a phone call from Marion. It was Bob Mason calling to say that the Hamilton girl had just quit.

'She quit? Just like that?'

'Uh-huh. I guess she figured she wasn't getting anywhere with Rockwell. The guy always seemed kind of stony towards her.'

'You know where she's gone?'

'Off home, I guess. She said something about wanting to take a holiday in Europe, but I guess she'll want to go visit her folks first.'

Willard got off the phone, with his hand shaking. The Lundmark kid was dead. The storekeeper had fled to

Atlanta. And now the Hamilton girl had quit. Did that mean that Rockwell's plans were beginning to fall apart? Or beginning to come to fruition? He didn't know and couldn't guess. But he realised this much: that there was no way he could have Rockwell murdered if the flier had already been beaten into surrender. And if the flier hadn't yet given up, then presumably somewhere amongst the federal enforcement agencies there were people who knew what Rockwell was hoping to achieve . . .

Willard thought things through, then strolled along to Powell's office and requested a meeting. He got it at once. He began by telling Powell what he'd done to improve the security at Marion. The banker listened, goggle-eyed.

'You did what?'

'It was time we tightened up. Marion's gotten to be too important to us.'

'There something we ought to be scared of?'

'No, at least nothing specific,' said Willard, lying easily. 'We discovered that there was a kid in town doing maintenance work for us, whose father we'd killed a little while back. We dealt with that issue, but it seemed like a good opportunity to get more serious all round.'

Powell laughed softly.

'What's funny?'

'What's funny? You are, Will, you are. You've grown up, you know. The guy who made that movie – what was the title?'

'*Heaven's Beloved.*'

'Right. That was one hell of a lousy movie. It stunk like a coffin full of dead cats. But you ain't that guy any more. You know who you've become?'

'No.'

'Your father's son. And that's a compliment. Shit, your own safe full of gasoline and dynamite. Ha! Any case, I guess you weren't calling round just to cheer me up. What can I do for you?'

'It's just . . . I don't know. It's just in case there has been any leak out of Marion, we ought to know about it. I don't know if we have any way of checking what the feds might be thinking, but if we did, then I reckon it'd be worth finding out.'

Powell chuckled. 'Maybe. Maybe we do.'

'You'll take care of it?'

'Sure.'

'Good . . . good.' Willard breathed out in relief. His moral problem seemed suddenly simpler. If Rockwell hadn't spoken to the feds, then Willard could simply replace him with a clear conscience. If Rockwell was transmitting sensitive information to places he shouldn't, then he'd have to take his chances. Willard stood up to go. 'Thanks, Powell.'

Willard was about to leave, when the banker raised a hand.

'Just a minute, Will. We got a rule round here. Any breach of security, any hint of a breach, we get our insurance guys involved. Just to look things over, a sort of double check.'

Willard went cold.

'I don't think . . .' he began, but Powell wasn't listening.

'Like I say, it's a rule. Have you even met Roeder yet? You'll like him. Everyone does. How does tomorrow look?'

Tomorrow looked rotten. Willard's day was filled with meetings, appointments, phone calls, work. But Powell didn't really mean his question. His question was a nice way of giving an order.

'Tomorrow,' said Willard, feeling a rim of ice gathering at the pit of his belly, 'tomorrow looks fine.'

98

The new girl seemed OK.

She wore her brown hair very short but, unlike some of the other girls, she didn't use any kind of make-up, and her clothes – flat brown shoes, dark skirt, dark jacket, white blouse, no jewellery – were not of the husband-catching variety. Her skin, which was very tanned, suggested some kind of farm girl, but her small hands and slim figure suggested the exact opposite. But Mr Rogers, the Deputy Manager at the Savings Bank of Northern Florida in Jacksonville, didn't, in the end, mind about the girl's origins. All that mattered was that she was reliable, competent, hard-working and settled.

'Goodnight, Mr Rogers,' she said, reaching for her hat.

'Goodnight, Sarah,' he told her, rocking back on his heels with his thumbs tucked into the side buckles on his waistcoat. 'Same time, same place tomorrow. Huh? Ha, ha, ha!'

The girl settled her hat on her head, gave her boss a shy half-smile and walked out into the night. She turned down the block and walked for two hundred paces without stopping or looking back. Then she stopped, put her foot on a fire hydrant, and began to retie a shoelace. Not tie, but retie. The shoelace hadn't come undone. It hadn't been loose. She retied it anyway.

And as she did so, she swept her gaze back the way she'd come. There were a handful of people out, but nobody gave her a second look. After finishing with her shoe, she remained watching for a moment, then retraced her steps. Nobody paid her any special attention. Nobody altered their course. Nobody looked at her too long or too little.

She walked another half-mile, then entered a café, bought a cup of coffee, spun it out. When she emerged, there were only a couple of people outside, neither of them ones who'd been there fifteen minutes before. She ducked down a side alley, ran hard to the end, ducked behind some garbage cans and waited. Nobody followed. She was in the clear.

Less cautiously now, Pen moved through the gathering darkness to the waterfront. The beach shone with the new white hotels which the Florida land-boom had thrown up in their scores. Bright lights and big cars gleamed between palm trees and hibiscus bushes.

Pen ignored the hotels and headed down the beach, out of town, towards the sprawling encampment known as Tin Can Field. The tin-canners were northerners who came south for winter, cars loaded with a full winter's worth of canned goods. Now, in towards the end of February, the place was beginning to empty as people began to head off to their northern spring. A few tin huts, that housed latrines and water pipes, rattled in the thin sea breeze. Those people choosing to stay on into March hung around battered jalopies and threadbare canvas tents.

And Abe. There was Abe.

The airman uncurled himself from the ground underneath a knobbly old palm tree, stubbed out a cigarette, and came smiling over to Pen. They reached each other in the twilight, put their arms around each other and kissed long and passionately. Abe didn't need to be in the air again until daybreak. Pen – in her capacity as Sarah Torrance the bank teller – didn't need to be at work until eight forty-five. They had all night together.

'I brought a tent,' said Abe, when his mouth eventually became free. 'I don't know why, it seemed safer than a hotel.'

'I agree.'

'Should be OK for one night's sleep, anyhow.'

'Who said anything about sleeping?'

It was dark enough now, that the sea was one big mass of dark grey. The sky was violet at the edges, deepening to midnight blue above. Holding hands, they walked to Abe's encampment. He had brought a rudimentary canvas tent, a couple of sleeping rolls and blankets, a Primus stove, a paraffin lamp, food and water. He also had a bottle of French red wine, a *grand cru*, one of the best of the pre-war vintages. Abe indicated it with a smile.

'Present from Mason.'

'Does he know he's given it?'

'Not exactly,' admitted Abe, who'd stolen it, 'but he'd have been glad to, that's the point.'

But they ignored the wine and everything else. They crept inside the tent, closed the flap, and faced each other beneath the cramped canvas walls. They held each other, kissed, then began to undress. He began with her jacket, then the buttons of her shirt. She did the same with his. But it was too slow. They began to tear their own clothes off, then before they were done, they simply fell upon each other. Pen's tongue burned like something on fire. Abe's hands were simultaneously strong and soft, urgent and understanding.

They made love.

It wasn't their first time, but it somehow felt like it. Abe was inside her for around twenty minutes. He climaxed once. She climaxed again and again, softening her cries until the final minutes, when she moaned like an airplane wing locked into a full-throttle dive. When they finished, they didn't pull apart. They just held each other, listening to the wind.

After forty minutes, something changed. She felt it in the muscles of his body and the curve of his back, and she prompted him.

'Don't you want to know how Sarah Torrance is getting on with her new job?'

'Yes. Yes, I do.'

'Very well, I think. They handle all Marion's business. All bank transfers come in by telegraph. I've got myself a desk close to the telegraph machine itself. None of the other girls like it. They think it leaks electricity.'

'Excellent.'

'It doesn't leak electricity, does it?'

'No.'

'I don't want to move too fast, but I'm sure I'll be able to take copies of the bank transfers as they come in.'

'Excellent.'

'And they've got records. Every transfer of money that's ever passed through the bank. Domestic and foreign. Going back years.'

'Excellent. Excellent.'

'And I know where the records are kept. They're in a locked cupboard in the office of Mr Rogers, the deputy manager. As far as I know, he's the only one with a key.'

'Does he ever put his keys down?'

'Not that I've seen.'

'Is there any way to force the lock?'

'Maybe, but I'm not the best lock-forcer in the world.'

Abe thought of Pen's near-total mechanical incompetence and was forced to agree with a grin. All Pen could see of his response was the white glow of his teeth. She kissed him softly.

'Don't worry. I'll find something.'

99

'You've met Roeder, of course,' said Powell, knowing that Willard had done no such thing.

Except that in a way, Willard had.

Dorcan Roeder was a short man, with the heavily muscled upper body of a man who worked hard in the gym. His face was ugly but powerful; the face of a man with no doubts as to his own importance. It had been Roeder outside Powell's office on the afternoon when Powell had given Willard the forty archive files; Roeder who had positioned himself there just to see him.

'Dorcan heads our insurance arm,' added Powell, blandly.

The two men shook hands. Willard found himself wondering how many men had been killed by the hand he'd just shaken; how many men in their last seconds on earth had seen that very hand striking down, gathered to punch, squeezing a trigger. It was a loathsome thought, one that made Willard want to wipe his palm. They sat down.

From the start, the meeting ran away from Willard. He could tell from the first moment. The way Powell sat beside Roeder. The way the two men hardly looked at each other. The way the air seemed to be thick with an understanding that had nothing to do with Willard.

'You've cleaned Marion,' said Roeder.

'Yes.' Willard explained briefly and clearly what he'd done.

'Why?'

'Two reasons. First, a general one. Marion started out as just another supply route. It made a little money through booze. A little through smuggling. A little through gambling. The situation has changed completely. We needed to update security arrangements. That's what I've done.'

'And the specific reason?'

'The specific reason is very minor.' Willard had rehearsed this conversation a thousand times in his head. He fought to hold his voice steady, his body relaxed. He spoke about Lundmark, about finding out they'd already killed the boy's father. He said nothing about scaring Hennessey, nothing about the red sheets, nothing about his certainty that Rockwell was out to destroy them.

'You shot up somebody else too. A local guy. Ran a store.'

'Gibson Hennessey, the storekeeper from the town just up the hill from Marion. He was the ringleader of the town's resistance. We've been wanting to lose the guy for a long time now. He's gone to Atlanta with his family. Mason's delighted.'

Willard was angry with himself. He'd spoken the last part too quickly. How the hell had Roeder known that they'd shot up Hennessey's place? Had Mason told him? If so, what else had Mason revealed? Willard flicked a glance at the insurance man, but Roeder's eyes were empty. Or to be more exact, they were the exact opposite, they were too full. Roeder had pale hazel eyes, but his left-hand iris was clotted with dark purplish-black blots. The clots made him hard to read, made it hard to hold his gaze. Willard looked away.

'Good,' said Powell. 'Sounds like you've done well. Always nice to clean things up without making a mess. That's the trouble with corpses. You just can't get the cops to stay away.'

That's what Powell said, but Willard had learned not to listen too much to what he said. Instead, he had a sense, stronger than ever, that the two men had already choreographed this conversation. Powell would come across as the nice guy. He'd get to smile, as his executioner put the boot in.

'Your fliers,' said Roeder.

'Yes?'

'Who are they?'

'Captain Abraham Rockwell and, until just recently, a Miss Penelope Hamilton.'

'Miss Hamilton?'

'Yes.'

'*Miss*?'

'Yes.'

'Maintenance personnel?'

'Just one man. A local mechanic, Arnold Hueffer.'

'Who's in charge?'

'Captain Rockwell.'

'What are his qualifications?'

'As a pilot, he's the best there is. Bar none. As a lookout man, the best. As a leader, also the best. On the maintenance side, the same. He's an exceptional hire.'

'Who has been responsible for hiring Hamilton and Hueffer? Rockwell or yourself?'

'Captain Rockwell.'

'So the integrity of the operation depends on the integrity of Captain Rockwell?'

'I guess so. Yes.'

'Please identify any doubts you may have regarding his suitability.'

'My only reservation concerns his motivation. I knew Captain Rockwell during the war. He is a man of exceptional calibre. Mason came across him when he was running small amounts of booze over the ocean from Havana. Mason wanted to recruit him then and there. Rockwell resisted. He had to be pushed. When Mason tested his loyalty, he passed the test, no problem.'

Roeder looked at Willard for a long time, but there was so little of anything in his eyes that it was like being scrutinised by a corpse.

'I asked you for your doubts. You spent most of your answer telling me why you don't have any.'

'I don't, not many. Any problem I have is to do with his reasons for working for us. Does he really want the money? That's my issue. He says he wants to build some kind of airplane. With Rockwell that's probably credible.'

'You think money isn't his motivation?'

'I didn't say that. I said I wasn't sure.'

'If not money, what then? Give me the worst possible case.'

Willard swallowed. The honest answer to Roeder's question was: *I know for a fact that Captain Rockwell is out to destroy us.* But he couldn't say it. Something in him simply refused to come out with it.

'I don't have a clear answer to that. I have no reason to distrust him.'

'You just told me you did. You said his reason for working for us was probably credible. Only probably. That means you suspect his motives. You think maybe he's working for some other reason. What?'

'We've got men watching him. We've got a tap on his phone. We open his mail.'

'You're watching him?'

'Right.'

'How many men?'

'As many as necessary. I've told Mason to make it a priority.'

'So you don't trust him. That's obvious. Tell me about your other flier. Ex-flier. Hamilton. You said she was a dame?'

'Yes.'

'That's usual in the flying world, is it?'

'No.'

'But she needed the money, right?'

Willard swallowed uncomfortably. 'I believe she was fairly well-off.'

Roeder threw a photo across the desk: a picture of the Hamilton mansion in Charleston. It lay in front of Willard like an accusation fired at point-blank range

'Fairly well-off?'

'I believe her parents are very well off. But in any case, she's not working for us any more. It's just down to Rockwell now.'

Roeder snorted, but appeared to change the subject. 'Please describe your personal relationship with Rockwell.'

'He commanded my squadron during the war. I respected him. I believe he thought well of me.'

'You flew together?'

'Sometimes, yes.'

'In situations of danger?'

'Of course, yes.'

'And he was a good commander?'

'No.'

Powell's eyes, which had been elsewhere, jumped instantly to Willard's face.

'No?'

'No. Not good. He was the best. I owe him my life.'

'Hah!' Roeder grinned and leaned back in his chair. 'So you're not in a position to assess his risk to the organisation.'

Willard opened his mouth to protest, but Roeder hadn't made it a question and Powell showed no sign of wanting to hear what Willard had to say. Powell grabbed the ashtray, and shook a quarter-inch tube of grey ash into the bowl. He didn't replace the ashtray, but held on to it, like a two-year-old with a bag of cookies.

'Well?' he said, speaking to Roeder.

'I think Thornton's right to clean Marion. I like the way he's gone about it. I've got a couple of ideas for improving things, but nothing major. We need to keep a close ear on anything state or federal enforcement might be up to, but that's routine. Over all, Thornton's done a good job.'

'Hey, Will, you hear that? Roeder telling someone they've done a good job. Not often I hear that. Huh, Roeder?'

Roeder showed no sign of wanting to join in Powell's play-acting. Willard's sense of gathering disaster grew stronger and stronger. He knew now that he could never have had Rockwell killed. The thought of Roeder doing it was nauseating.

'Anything else?' continued Powell. 'Or maybe I shouldn't spoil things. I just oughta pick up the phone to old man Thornton down in DC and tell him that his boy's done good.'

'Only one thing,' said Roeder. 'The pilot. I don't like him. I don't trust him. I don't want him.'

Willard sat bolt upright. 'The operation depends on him. It's unworkable without him.'

'That's exactly what I don't like. I want to hire some new guys. Our guys.'

'You don't understand. It's not like driving an auto. This is difficult flying. And dangerous. It takes skill.'

'Spotting a Coastguard boat on the open sea? Sounds like it just takes a pair of eyes.'

'And what if they hide on the coast? There are a million inlets there. A million places to hide.'

'So? Fly up the coast and look.'

'It's not that easy.'

'It's not that hard.'

'Flying low? With coastal winds? Turbulence? In all weathers? In single-engined planes? Where one cough on the fuel-line means you're going to smack into the forest at a hundred miles an hour?'

Roeder smiled. 'Like I said, you're not in a position to assess the threat.'

There was a pause. A nasty one: short but ugly.

Roeder turned to Powell, saying, 'This guy Rockwell. I want permission to replace him.'

Willard's ears had grown more sensitive since starting to work for Powell Lambert. Because he heard it: the thing that wasn't even there. Roeder had inserted a tiny pause before the word 'replace'. A meaningful glance had accompanied the pause. And Willard knew what they meant. They weren't planning to replace Rockwell, they were planning to kill him.

'And I object.' Willard surprised even himself with his forcefulness. 'The operation depends on Rockwell.'

'Which it shouldn't,' said Roeder.

Powell put down his ashtray. 'I'm sorry, Willard, I know you like the guy, but –'

Willard had one second to say the right thing. One second to save Rockwell's life.

'If Rockwell goes, then I cannot be responsible for the security of goods coming into Marion. I'll have to reduce the flow of supplies coming in. We'll have to turn down customers.'

For the first time, Powell hesitated. Willard realised he'd hit the right note. *Customers*: a golden word. Powell turned to Roeder.

'You don't actually know anything against the guy.'

'I don't want to wait until I do.'

Powell's hesitation lasted another second, then ended.

'I'm sorry, Will, in cases of doubt, I always have to go with Roeder. I want you to find some new fliers. Guys we can trust. Roeder will help. Maybe they won't work out as good as Rockwell. That's OK. If we lose a couple of planes, a boatload or two, we'll just have to swallow the losses. But they'll learn. In time, they'll learn. And if Roeder's not happy, then nor am I. OK?'

'OK.' Willard agreed because he had no other option.

'In the meantime, Roeder, I want you to take over surveillance duties from Marion. Use as many men as you need to. Keep track of Rockwell. Don't miss anything. If he is up to something, let's make sure we know about it.'

There was nothing else to say. Willard felt sickened.

'And Roeder. Give Thornton time to hire his pilots and get 'em trained. We're pulling too much booze through Marion just to foul things up for the sake of a hunch. OK?'

Roeder nodded.

'And I mean it. I don't want this guy showing up in some auto wreck the day after tomorrow and you pretending like you never heard anything so sad. No replacing Rockwell until we're ready.' He turned back to Willard. Unusually for him, his voice dropped. It became quiet, even sensitive. 'I'm real sorry, Will. The Firm asks sacrifices from us all.'

Willard nodded. He pretended he was a businessman doing his job. He pretended he didn't care. But he did. Captain Rockwell might not know it yet, but his death warrant was already signed.

100

Mr Rogers, the deputy manager of the Savings Bank of Northern Florida, was forty-four years old. He enjoyed grilled beef, French-fried potatoes and anything involving cream and sugar. His complexion was an explosive combination of scarlet and chalk. He was losing hair from the front and top of his head. His belly looked as though he'd swallowed a watermelon whole.

Yet, the odd fact was, that Mr Rogers was careful of his appearance and even a little vain. He combed his hair three times a day. He flossed his teeth. He was fussy about the way his shirts were starched and ironed. He kept a spare shirt and necktie in the drawer of his desk.

And Pen noticed.

She noticed because she made a point of noticing everything. She noticed the ring of dandruff that shone like a middle-aged halo on his jacket. She noticed the fact that, regular as clockwork, he went to the toilet after his morning coffee, after lunch, and after his cup of afternoon tea.

And, as she noticed these things, a plan began to germinate. She already had, from Arnie, a small rectangular tin containing a flat pad of modelling putty, kept damp under a strip of gauze. To this, she added two other items. First, a sweet pastry with custardy goo in the base and lashings of white icing sugar on top. Secondly, she bought, from an advert in one of the women's magazines, one of 'Sally Simpson's *patented* MAGICAL Clothes Genies – three rubs is all it takes to turn *old* into *new*!!!' The Clothes Genie was basically a small wooden pad with a fine-bristled brush set into it. The brush had a kind of waxy adhesive coating, which Pen guessed would gum up completely after a couple of uses.

She began to keep watch. From her desk in the open area of the bank, she could see Mr Rogers' glass-paned office door. The tea came around at four o'clock. As the bank's second most senior officer, Mr Rogers was the second person to receive his tea. It took him six minutes to drink the tea, finish his biscuit and get up to go to the loo.

One Tuesday afternoon, she watched Mr Rogers' door as the girl went inside with his tray of tea things. Using the big black-numbered clock on the wall, Pen counted the minutes. As she did so, she took her pastry from its bag and began to eat. She ate untidily. A piece of the pastry fell off, making a big white floury blotch on her skirt. She appeared not to notice and kept her eye on the clock. Five minutes.

She stood up. She had a file in her hand and a pointless question ready to ask. She walked over to her boss's office, knocked and entered. He hadn't yet finished his tea, and a quarter of his biscuit remained unnibbled.

'Oh, Mr Rogers, sir!' said Pen, in her demure Sarah Torrance voice. 'I'm so sorry. You're in the middle of tea.' She stood, visibly hesitant.

Rogers frowned. He didn't like being interrupted during his tea break. On the other hand, he liked any opportunity to display what a glorious thing it was to be a deputy manager of the second biggest bank in north-eastern Florida. He adopted a magnanimous expression and waved his quarter-biscuit in a lordly, commanding way.

'That's all right, Sarah. Just so long as you remember to think first next time.'

'Yes, Mr Rogers.'

He finished his biscuit and drained his tea. 'Now what was it?'

She opened the file. 'It's these checking accounts. Some customers have got fifty-cent credits against their names, while others . . .'

Hers was a long, confused, rambling question – not one that could be answered in a minute.

'I don't have time right now,' Rogers began. Then his eye fell on Pen's skirt. It wasn't the first time that he'd looked there, but it was the first time Pen acknowledged his glance.

'Oh!'

She looked flurried and embarrassed. She couldn't quite manage a blush, but did her best anyway. She patted her skirt ineffectually, then pulled out her Clothes Genie.

'My Clothes Genie,' she explained apologetically. 'It really works.' She dabbed at the icing sugar, which duly began to disappear. Pen looked at the dandruff on his suit jacket, which was so thick it looked like someone had been dusting for prints. 'If you want, I could . . .' she began, then tailed off. She let her eyes slide away again, as though guilty of impertinence.

Mr Rogers was caught between a rock – his desire to take a leak – and a hard place: his desire to get rid of his dandruff. He shuffled awkwardly. His ring of keys sagged heavily in his right-hand jacket pocket. He could take them with him to the toilet, of course, but it would look a little odd. Mr Rogers was not a man who enjoyed being laughed at. Pen decided to give him a nudge.

'It would only take a moment. I'd be all done by the time you were back.'

That decided it. He shrugged off his jacket and handed it to Pen, as though she were his personal maid. 'Thank you, Sarah. We can talk about those checking accounts in a moment.'

'Yes, Mr Rogers.'

He left. Pen now had two and a quarter minutes. She knew how long, because she'd timed his toilet visits in the

461

past. With one brisk shake, she shook most of the dandruff off the jacket and laid it out on the desk. She reached for the keys.

There were fourteen keys on the ring and she needed prints of just two: the key to the office and the key to the cupboard where the ledgers were kept. The office key was easy. It was a five-cylinder mortice lock and there was only one key which looked remotely right. She took the key and pressed its cold metal head softly into the bed of putty. One done, one to go.

The key to the cupboard was harder. It was a smaller, simpler key, and Rogers had four possible versions on his keyring. Working fast, Pen took three prints cleanly and accurately, but she'd left herself too little room to take a fourth print. All she had was the quarter-inch edge of the putty, which might be too little for Arnie to work with.

She pressed the tip of the fourth key into the edge of the putty. It didn't seem to come out right the first time, so she did it a second time, then a third time to make sure. Down the hall, the door to the toilet clicked open, then shut. There were footsteps in the corridor. Pen jammed the bunch of keys back into the jacket, put the tin of putty into her pocket, and bent over the dandruff with her Clothes Genie. Rogers came in.

'Ah, Sarah! Still working away?'

'Done, Mr Rogers.'

Pen held his jacket up, the keys sagging in the pocket. The dandruff ring had almost completely gone. Mr Rogers put his jacket on, patting the collar and twitching the front to conceal his belly. With a sudden wash of relief, Pen realised she was in the clear.

'Now what was it you wanted to see me about?'

'That's OK, Mr Rogers, I'll figure it out.'

101

Willard was sick of Manhattan.

Money! The town was obsessed by it. From Wall Street banker to Bowery bum, everyone was clawing their way over the next guy to make a nickel, a buck, a million dollars. It wasn't that Willard didn't like money. Far from it. He loved the stuff. But his boyhood had taught him some wrong lessons. He'd thought money was a thing you grew into, like a pair of shoes or a family yacht. The reality of hustling for it had come as a shock, an unpleasant one.

And so, though he made a living, got on, did well, from time to time he grew sick of it all. Times like now. Times when a tired afternoon was collapsing into an exhausted neon-lit evening. Times when the last shreds of conscience set up a wail in his head that never quite left. Then a shadow fell across his desk. He looked up.

'Hello, Larry!'

'Speaking as your doctor, I have to tell you that you're imbibing too much work and too little alcohol.'

'Don't tell me, tell Powell.'

'What do you say to going out and seeing if we can drink until we see quadruple?'

'I'd say you were drinking too much.'

Which was true: Willard had begun to realise that Ronson was a drunk, a capable one admittedly, but still a drunk and getting worse each month.

'All right, we'll compromise. Triple. Or triple and a half.'

'I –'

Willard stared down at his desk. He'd hired eight pilots and had sent them to an army airfield in West Virginia to train in low-level flying and aerial observation. The pilots were the sort of men that Roeder liked. Most of them had served jail terms. All of them had either no wives and no kids or several wives and too many kids. They all liked booze, or girls, or gaming, or fist fights, or all four pastimes combined. The eight men would train for a month. At the end of the period Willard would keep the four best and send them to Marion. Some time in between now and then, Dorcan Roeder would have Rockwell killed.

'God, Larry, don't you ever get sick of it all?'

'Why should I? The first signs of civilisation are always the same: proof that man had learned to ferment and distill. The grape, the grain, even, my dear sermoniser, the humble potato.'

'I didn't mean the booze, Larry, I meant –'

He paused. The air in the building began to seem not just stale but actually suffocating. He had a clear picture of his old commander, being cold-bloodedly killed by one of Roeder's stooges.

'I –'

'Do you know that's the third time you've started a sentence without finishing it?'

'Listen, Larry, I'm not feeling well. I need to get out. Sorry.'

He grabbed coat and hat and strode out to catch the elevator. It jerked its way down, collecting departing clerks and secretaries as it went. Willard stood aside to let a couple of people get in. A mousy little woman in a blue felt hat. A clerk in a thin grey suit. More people got on. No one got off. The elevator hit the ground floor and began to clear. Willard was at the back and waited. But the woman in the blue hat didn't leave. Willard looked at her properly for the first time and recognised her: Annie Hooper.

'Gosh, Annie, sorry! Hello! I didn't recognise you under that hat.'

Annie pulled her hat backwards a little, as though apologising for wearing it. 'They're working you too hard, I expect. Too busy.'

Willard, always quick and subtle in reading the signs of feminine attraction, saw that Annie was thrilled and slightly nervous to be talking to him again. Her cheeks pinked a little and her hand moved twice to her blouse collar. He also heard a tiny hint of disappointment, as though her last words had been code for 'too important to see your old friends any more'.

'Busy? Well, you know the Firm, Annie. They sweat us hard enough, don't they?'

While talking, they walked outside. A miserable east wind brought in air cold and wet from the ocean. The streets were heavy and damp. Annie tucked her coat collar up and pulled out a delicate woman's umbrella.

'No, no, no,' exclaimed Willard, and whipped out his own much larger brolly, which he made a great show of unfolding and holding over Annie's head.

'Thanks.' Because of having to stand under the umbrella, Annie was brought right up close to Willard. She blushed again, harder this time.

'Where to?' he asked.

'Well that depends . . .'

'On . . .?'

'Well I'm going home, but I don't want to drag you out of your way.'

'No, not at all.'

'I usually take the subway.'

For no reason except habit, Willard had already begun to steer Annie towards his usual cab rank, although, if he'd bothered to think about it, he'd have known that Annie wouldn't think of taking an expensive taxi ride. It made sense to turn around and walk her back up to the subway, only that would have meant admitting a mistake with his first choice of direction.

'Gee, no, can't have you taking the subway – not in weather like this,' he said illogically. 'Let me run you home in a cab.'

A moment later, they were in a cab splashing its way uptown. Annie smiled at him. He smiled back.

'Where are you off to?' she asked.

'Hmm? Me?'

'Business, I suppose? Larry says you're terribly important these days.'

'Lord, no! I mean, I'm busy enough, but I had to get out today, Annie. I couldn't take another minute.'

There was a short pause.

'Congratulations, by the way.'

'Sorry?'

'On your engagement, I mean. I haven't seen you since then.'

'Oh, yes. Rosalind.' Willard nodded.

'She's a lucky girl.'

'Yes, isn't she? I mean, she's a super girl. I thought that's what you said. Super.'

The conversation remained idiotic and halting as the cab clattered through traffic. It reached Annie's apartment building, then stopped. Willard got out, paid off the cab, and saw Annie to her door. The two of them watched the cab grind away in a spray of puddle water.

'You're getting out here?' she asked, in surprise. 'Aren't you . . .?'

Willard grinned brightly. 'Thought I might ask an old friend for some coffee. If that's all right.'

'Of course, yes.'

Annie pushed through the front door to her apartment building and led the way up. Before long, Willard found himself, as had happened once before, sitting on Annie's little sofa, drinking coffee, watching the rain fall outside.

Since he was last there, there'd been one addition to Annie's apartment. It was a movie poster, from *When We Were Heroes*. Willard's magnificently resolute frown dominated the little room. Noticing the pinkness hiding up in Annie's freckled cheeks, he didn't mention the poster. Nor did she. They drank coffee, finished, then made more. He didn't get up to go. He felt like he'd dropped out of his own life. Not for long, just for an hour or two. But crazily, and just for that hour, Willard felt something he should never have felt. Not there. Not with Annie. He felt this: he felt relaxed. He felt at home.

102

Pen had told everyone she was going to Europe. She'd packed bags, made arrangements, booked tickets, gone to New York – and never got on the boat. Admittedly, there was somebody on the boat, name of Penelope Hamilton, but it wasn't her. Wrong height. Wrong build. Wrong everything. Roeder took the call from his man at the docks, then called Powell.

'The Hamilton girl. She's given us the slip. She hasn't gone to Europe at all.'

'You telling me this because you want a crack at Rockwell early? I said to wait.'

'No. Not that. Least not until we got the girl. Once we got the girl, I want to take her, Rockwell, the mechanic, and anyone else I feel like, all at the same time.'

'All of them together? This ain't Chicago, you know.'

'We'll do it nice. Nothing that even looks like homicide.'

'You asked young Thornton? He should have a say in this.'

'He's split on this. One way, he's doing a good job. Another way, he looks up to Rockwell. Wants to save him. Best thing is if we take care of things without involving him. Thornton can be mad at me for a while. Then he'll see we helped him out.'

'Hmm . . . You're still watching Rockwell, of course?'

'Yeah.'

'He up to anything he shouldn't be?'

'Not that we know. But as soon as he gets into his plane we can't follow him.'

'How you going to find the girl?'

'That's my business.'

'And when you find her . . .? Shit, Roeder, first find her. It'll probably turn out she's busy necking with some rich lover-boy in a beach house someplace private. We'll find her first, then figure out what to do. I'm sure we'll sort something out.'

There was a tiny pause. Roeder's pale lips opened into a smile.

'Sure, we'll sort something out.'

They hung up, but Roeder's grin persisted. Powell hadn't ordered him not to do what he wanted to do. He'd left his instructions deliberately vague. He did it that way, so he could come over all sympathetic when young Willie Thornton woke up to find his favourite airman had been swatted into oblivion. Roeder liked that. Typical Powell: always neat, but always businesslike.

All he needed now was to find the girl.

103

The ball rose high into the eye of the sun, then began to curve back down again.

The lob made for an easy smash and Senator Paulet stood underneath, waiting. The ball came down. The Senator smashed it. The ball, from no distance, slammed into the wire of the net, fizzed along it for a second, then dropped uselessly to the ground on the wrong side.

'Fuck it.' The Senator, a photogenic forty-six, hoofed the ball up with his racket, then banged it against the mesh fence surrounding the tennis court. 'Lousy balls aren't running for me today.'

The Senator threw his racket down and grabbed a pullover from the seat. Jim Carpenter muttered silently to himself. Paulet finished the match when he was winning it. He always bailed when he wasn't.

'Let's get a drink,' said Paulet, making it a statement not a question.

The two men walked over to a group of white metal tables under sun umbrellas. On each table, there was a card indicating the drinks available: ice-cream sodas, regular sodas, sparkling waters, juices, teas, coffee. One of the tennis club waiters, seeing the two men take their seats, went silently away and returned a minute later with two martini glasses and a jug clinking with ice. The waiter, saying nothing, poured the drinks and moved away.

Paulet, one of the two senators from Wisconsin, had

been elected with the strong endorsement of the Anti-Saloon League. The ASL, the country's leading anti-alcohol group, knew that Paulet was a confirmed drinker but it didn't care. Paulet had promised to vote the way the ASL wanted and that was enough. In the United States Senate, the votes of hypocrites counted equally with the votes of non-hypocrites.

The two men chatted for a while: about tennis, about the weather, about the latest adventures of Paulet's wild daughter. Jim Carpenter was the Commissioner of the IRS, in effect the chief tax collector in the United States. Senator Paulet, as Chairman of the Senate Finance Committee, was, in a way, Carpenter's boss. They finished their first martini and moved on to a second. Paulet finished his second and poured another.

'So, Jim, how are you and your crook-busters doing?'

'Crook-busters? Our Intelligence Unit?'

Paulet nodded.

Carpenter shrugged. 'OK. We nail a few tax avoiders every month. We just sent down a California realtor. He gave us a return showing a few thousand bucks of income. It turned out he had nearer half a million.'

'Quit handing out the crap,' said Paulet, softly. 'I meant the bootleggers. You had some kind of idea you could nail bootleggers for tax evasion.'

'Yeah. We're working on it.'

'Right. And that was my question. How you doing?'

'OK. We're still digging for evidence. We're looking to build a case that'll hold.'

'Shit, I'd never have thought of that. You're a goddamn genius.'

Paulet's eyelids tended to sink with liquor. What with the martinis, or the sun, or his anger, his eyes looked hooded, half-drunk, half-malevolent. His jibe caused a little pool of silence to form in its aftermath.

'What do you want to know?' Carpenter asked.

'Who are you investigating?'

'I'm sorry, Senator, I'm not able to say.' That was a truthful answer, thought Carpenter ruefully. McBride still wasn't being candid with him, even though Carpenter, under pressure from Paulet, had been on at McBride to open up.

'Don't screw around with me. We're having a committee meeting in a few days. Management of the IRS is on the agenda. Management and salary issues.'

'Oh?' Carpenter was nervous.

'The committee's divided. It's arguing things out. Don't know which way it'll jump.'

'And the issue exactly . . .?'

'Well, the first bunch of people says, we oughta pay our top guys more. A lot more. Hire the best, then retain them. The secret of success.'

'Uh-huh.'

'The second bunch agrees with the first.'

Paulet stopped. Carpenter knew he was being prompted to ask the obvious question. Knowing he was about to walk into a sucker punch, he went ahead and did it anyway.

'Two groups of people, you said. What's the difference?'

'Half the committee is happy with existing management. The other half isn't.'

'Right.' Carpenter knew he was being jerked around by Paulet, but he couldn't help being jerked. 'I don't suppose . . . I mean, there isn't anything, is there . . .?'

In a sudden burst of energy, Paulet swivelled around in his seat, yanking the table with him.

'I'm a straight-shooter. You want me to tell you straight?'

Carpenter nodded dumbly.

'OK. Here it is. I think you're OK. Sometimes you're a dumb bastard, but the way I figure it, most likely anyone else we hire will be a dumb bastard too. But we need successes. We're spending voters' money here. We need something to boast about. Your shitty little California realtor isn't it. You keep telling me you've got some big project going, but you feed me chicken-shit. I don't live on chicken-shit, Carpenter. I won't accept it.'

Carpenter swallowed. 'It's a big project, honestly. My investigator's a good man. He thinks we've got a good chance of blowing one of the country's biggest rackets into pieces. That's straight, too, Senator.'

'Where? The racket is based where?'

'It's a national thing. It's got reach all over.'

'And if you didn't give me the bullshit answer . . .?'

'Our source is based in Chicago. We've been getting great results.'

'Chicago? You're sure?'

Carpenter nodded. He was angry with McBride and McBride's obsessive secrecy. Shit, the man had put him in a position where he couldn't even pass sensible information to a United States senator.

'Chicago. Right. Goddamn gangsters.'

Paulet had looked surprised, but the look passed. 'And what are you waiting for?'

Carpenter swallowed. His feelings about McBride were moving from anger into fury. Maybe he should take over the investigation himself. He'd do that, except he knew how good an investigator McBride could be.

'OK, Senator, I'll tell you what I know. But remember I've been very tough on confidentiality all the way through this. I don't even ask my investigations team to tell me stuff I don't literally have to know.'

'That's no way to manage things. That's just being yellow.'

'Yes, yes, well, I've been thinking of getting more involved, for sure. Now things are coming to a head.' Carpenter was speaking too fast and his mouth was running dry. The only liquid on the table was in the martini jug. Carpenter drank more to ease the gluiness in his mouth, then immediately regretted it as the alcohol, its effect doubled by sunshine and stress, took instant hold.

'And the answer to my question?'

'We've got the local operation pretty much busted. Now we just have to link it to the centre, the headquarters.'

'How d'you plan to do that?'

'Money. This outfit is pretty slick in most ways, but they can't hide the money going to and fro. We're picking up the bank transfers. That'll give us enough evidence to put before a judge. We'll get search warrants. Then we'll go in, all buns glazing – I mean, bums lazing. Blazing. Guns blazing.'

'And the headquarters is based in?'

Carpenter swallowed. He didn't know. He took a guess. 'Chicago.'

'Chicago?'

'Right.'

'You're sure?'

'Sure. Sure I'm sure. Ha! That sounds dumb, doesn't it? Sure-I'm-sure, sure-I'm-sure.'

Paulet stood up. He picked up his pullover and his tennis bag. The waiter approached with the check, but Paulet showed no interest in paying his share.

'You're a dumb bastard, Jim. Just remember. I need information. Facts not bullshit. And I need it soon. You got that?'

'Sure. Sorry, Tom. It's the sun. Yeah, I've got that. Facts. Not bullshit. Of course.'

'It's your future we'll be discussing, remember. Me, I don't really give a shit.'

Paulet looked down at his tennis companion, shook his head, and walked away.

104

Tin Can Field and another windy night beneath the stars.

Down the beach, a woman walks alone, quickly, carrying a slim leather briefcase held against her belly. As she approaches the field, another shape suddenly becomes visible. It's a man's figure, purposeful and decisive. The two people see each other, begin to run, then quickly find themselves in each other's arms.

'My love!'

The two lovers said the same thing, in the same way, at the same time. They caught each other's eyes in the feeble light and smiled.

Back at camp, Abe's fondness for domestic simplicity was still highly in evidence. There was the same threadbare canvas tent, the same pair of folding chairs, the same paraffin lamp, the same Primus stove. All the same, Abe had upgraded in a couple of respects. An air-filled mattress now supplemented the two sheepskin sleeping rolls and a white enamel water jug stood just inside the flap of the tent, with a dozen yellow roses standing bolt upright in the lamplight.

'Gee whizz!' said Pen. 'No need to go crazy.'

Abe smiled. In many years of sleeping wherever his plane happened to be, he had never once thought of buying himself an inflatable mattress. But he was beginning to see his past life through the eyes of a woman. Though it was hard for him to admit, he knew much of his old way of life was incompatible with his new life with Pen.

'I got lobster too.'

'You cooked lobster?'

Now Pen was really surprised.

'No, no, I got some from a place up the road. If I'd have cooked it, I don't think you'd have wanted to eat it. I got some of that sauce they use a lot in France . . .'

'Mayonnaise?'

'That's the one. And – uh –' Abe was about to list the rest of the meal, when he realised that a loaf of bread, some hard-boiled eggs, a hunk of cheese and a bag of tomatoes probably wouldn't strike Pen as a great feast. 'There's some other stuff,' he added lamely, 'a bottle of wine and mangoes for pudding.'

'I love mangoes.' After the first giddiness of love had begun to calm down, Pen had started to understand how Abe was disconcerted by his own feelings. She'd seen him reassessing the assumptions on which he'd built his life. She'd even realised that her own background – a woman who could afford her very own Curtiss racing plane without even troubling to think where the money would come from – made the process of adjustment harder. She pulled him close, kissed him, and ran her hands over the fine prickles of his scalp. 'And I love you.'

He knew what she was saying and why she was saying it. He kissed her. His fingers dropped to her waist, to the join of her skirt and blouse. But his fingers stopped there, hesitating, asking a question. She put her own hands to his waist and slid a finger around inside his waistband.

'It's been hot, hasn't it? You want to swim?'

'Sure.'

Abe didn't usually think of swimming as a pleasurable activity, but he did now. They went down to the shore, stripped naked and swam out into the whispering surf. Pen was the better swimmer and her lithe body slipped through the water like a creamy-skinned mermaid. Abe had to swim hard to keep up. They swam for a while, then came back to shore, headed back to the tent and made love.

Abe had turned out to be a terrific lover. There was nothing show-off in his technique. As a matter of fact, he hardly had any technique, no fancy positions, no athletic heaving around and grunting. But he was simple and to the point. Gentle. And exquisitely sensitive to Pen's tiniest sensation. She realised – and amazingly enough she felt flattered by the realisation, not insulted – that for Abe, making love was a little like flying an aircraft. He listened with his fingertips and the muscles of his belly. He reacted to a change even before his brain had consciously registered that there was a change. Pen let herself float off, feeling herself like a glider on the wind, teased and nudged and coaxed into an ever higher heaven of sensation.

They made love long and slow, then lay together, salty from the sea and sweaty from the exertion. But at their feet, there was a briefcase full of papers. Though they wanted to forget where they were, why they were there, and everything else except the other's body naked against theirs, they couldn't do it.

They got up.

Abe pumped the paraffin lamp to maximum brightness. Pen took papers and her tin of putty from the case. He quit fiddling with the lamp and looked at her. She passed him the tin. He opened it and held the putty carefully to the light, checking the impressions Pen had taken.

'It's OK, is it?' asked Pen anxiously. 'I didn't press too deep?'

'Nope. It looks fine.'

'I ran out of room. I had to use the edge as well.' Pen explained about the fourth key, about the indentations down the edge of the putty strip, about her worry that she'd made a mess of things.

'It's fine. Arnie can make casts of these tomorrow. He

can send the keys on to you in the mail. No one has your name, after all, or address.'

She smiled with relief. 'Phew,' she commented, softly. In her hands, she had a bundle of papers, held in a slim roll. Abe looked at them questioningly.

She held them up. 'Money transfers. Only the last couple of weeks. I know McBride wants records going back months or years, but in the meantime I thought it might help to see these first.'

Abe nodded. 'Of course.' He reached out excitedly, then saw her face. It wasn't happy. It was worried.

'That's what we wanted, isn't it?' he asked.

'Yes . . . Maybe . . .'

She passed the papers over. Abe held them under the arc of the paraffin lamp, where the light was strongest. Pen had copied them exactly as she'd found them, without altering either layout or punctuation.

DATE, ACTUAL	27 FEB, 1926
DATE, EFFECTIVE	27 FEB, 1926
RECEIVING BANK	FIRST NATL N FLORIDA, JACKS, FL
ATTN:	MRROGERS
CLIENT ACCOUNT	COSIMO REALTY (FLORIDA) INC
ACC NUMBER	44500745
SENDING BANK	GT LAKES GUARANTY, CHICAGO, IL
RESP	MRPHELPS
CLIENT ACCOUNT	MRGKBARROW
ACC NUMBER	67701011
AMOUNT	DOLLARS 1320 CENTS 00
AMOUNT WORDS	DOLLARS ONE THOUSAND THREE HUNDRED TWENTY CENTS NIL
TRANSACTION REF	BARROW
CLIENT REF	NONE
CONFIRMATION	PHELPS TGR IMD

'Confirmation?' queried Abe.

'We need to confirm the money transfers once we've executed it. That one means we need to contact Phelps by telegraph, on an immediate basis. They're all immediate.'

'And these references at the bottom?'

'Most transactions are just referenced by the name of the person sending the money. If the client wants to add any reference of their own they can. Most don't.'

Abe flipped through the next two or three sheets, all of which contained the same kind of information in the same layout.

'This is perfect.'

'I hope so.'

'Why? You sound unsure.' He gazed up at her sharply. Dark shadows threw a jagged patchwork across her face.

'I . . . It's . . .'

Abe stared back at the sheets. Haggerty McBride had told them that he wanted documentary evidence of substantial bank transfers between Marion and its headquarters.

'This is it, Pen. This is exactly what McBride asked for.'

'I know. But the amounts. The amounts don't make sense.'

Abe frowned and looked back at the sheets. Most of the transactions were small – a thousand bucks or less – but of course most of the transfers coming into the bank would have nothing to do with Marion. He flipped through the sheets. There were some larger transactions – five, seven, even ten thousand bucks – but nothing huge. He reached the end and looked up.

'Correct me if I'm wrong,' said Pen softly, 'but you're bringing in at least three shiploads of booze a week. Each shipload – what? – thirty or forty thousand bucks.'

'Yes. At least that.'

'And according to Mason, the money is transferred to Cuba the moment the cargo is checked.'

'Sure. He makes a point of it.'

'And there's nothing. Nothing like that. We've handled one single transfer for twenty thousand bucks. Aside from that, nothing over ten. Hardly anything over five.'

Abe said nothing, but his eyes connected with Pen's. They both understood the same thing, both felt the same way. Over the last few months, they'd burrowed deeper and deeper into the heart of the enemy defences. And now they were in the inner sanctum. The holy of holies. The place that McBride himself had named as the key to a successful prosecution. And it looked as though McBride had been wrong. It looked as though they'd dug their way through to an empty vault, a strongroom with nothing inside.

'Someone has to be paying for that booze.'

'I know.'

'And the money arrives in Cuba. It arrives from this bank, this branch. It has to come from somewhere.'

'I know.'

'You're sure you see all the transfers? If we were missing some, then . . .'

'I see them all. I'm certain. There's only one telegraph terminal inside the bank. I sit next to it, for God's sake.'

'The mail?'

'That comes to me too. I'd know if there was anything else, I swear it.'

'Then it has to be here. It has to be.'

Pen didn't say anything, didn't even shrug. Abe turned back to the papers, the flimsy little stack that riffled slightly in the sea breeze. Abe had a sudden strong sense that the answer was in his hands right now. He read each sheet, one by one, searching for the clue that would give them what they needed.

But Pen was right, or seemed to be. Although, in total, there was plenty of money being transferred into Jacksonville, the individual amounts were too small to account for the quantity of alcohol which Abe knew was coming in. He checked the client names and locations. They were all different. The banks responsible for making the transfers seemed to come from all over the place too. Only one name cropped up more than once. 'Powell Lambert, NY, NY' came up again and again, on transaction after transaction. Abe pointed it out to Pen, who said she'd raised the same thing with her boss. 'According to Rogers, Powell Lambert is a big Wall Street outfit. It does a lot of trade finance, apparently. We're the Powell Lambert correspondent for the south-east.'

Abe nodded. He was no money man. He'd long worried he might run into a problem he simply didn't have the expertise to understand. But he looked back at the sheets and then he saw it.

He saw it and, without for the moment being able to explain anything, he knew that he had what they'd been searching for. On one of the Powell Lambert transactions, Abe read:

SENDING BANK   POWELL LAMBERT, NY, NY
RESP   MRWTTHORNTON

Was that Mr W. T. Thornton as in Willard T. Thornton? Willard Thornton, whom Abe had nursed through his flying infancy? The same man, whom Abe had seen develop into one of the better pilots in America's finest aviation unit? The odds seemed stacked against it, Thornton was a common enough name after all . . . and yet Abe remembered the note that Willard had sent via Brad Lundmark. He remembered Willard's words. 'I've decided to chuck the film business – a dumb game really – and make a new start on Wall Street. Trade Finance, would you believe it!'

Trade Finance.

Willard Thornton on Wall Street.

An ocean of alcohol pouring through Marion from Cuba – and a torrent of money which had to be flowing the other way. *Had to be*. And what was trade finance, after all? It was being the middleman. Perhaps the point wasn't that each ship brought in thirty or forty thousand bucks' worth of booze. Perhaps the point was that on each ship there were consignments for five, ten, maybe twenty different customers across the US. If each customer-consignment was paid for separately, then Pen's tear sheets were accurately capturing exactly how the business operated. In a flash Abe saw the business, the way the business actually operated. Booze pouring in from all over. Customers buying from all over. And money, torrents of money, pouring through the system, controlled and manipulated from Powell Lambert's Wall Street base.

Abe looked up and caught Pen's eye.

'You look shocked,' she said. 'Have you . . .?'

'Yes.' He nodded. 'I think I have.'

105

Paulet went home and made a local phone call to a Washington number. The person he spoke to listened, asked a couple of questions, then thanked Paulet and replaced the receiver. That person then went ahead and placed a long-distance phone call direct to Ted Powell. Ted Powell listened too, asked a couple of questions, then hung up. Although it was getting late, Powell dialled Dorcan Roeder's extension, and told him to come straight up.

Less than a minute later, the insurance man stood in Powell's office.

'Chicago,' Powell said without introduction. 'Not Marion at all.'

'Chicago?'

'Right.'

'Says who?'

'Paulet. Who had it direct from Carpenter.'

'When?'

'Today. Just now. An hour ago.'

Roeder frowned. His fingernails were pretty much chewed down to the bone, but that didn't stop him gnawing at them anyway. He thought for a moment, chewed his nails. Powell watched.

'That make sense to you? How's things up there?'

Roeder looked up. 'Chicago? Good. It's not one of our weak spots.'

'You think.'

'I think, yeah.'

'Maybe this whole Marion thing is a red herring.'

Roeder shook his head. 'No. It doesn't smell right. Any case, we've got new pilots hired. Training's going fine. We're almost ready to make the change.'

'You've got the girl?'

Roeder shook his head. 'No. Soon.'

'Maybe we ought to move some men to Chicago. Tighten up.'

Roeder thought some more. His fingernails took a battering. Then he decided something.

'No.'

'No? What no?'

'It's not Chicago.'

'You're saying Paulet is lying?' Powell's voice rose with incredulity.

'No.'

'Carpenter?'

'Maybe. No, I doubt it. But maybe he's being lied to. Or he's looking at the wrong thing.'

'Why would you think that? Chicago's a big enough racket for us, after all.'

'That's why it's wrong. Chicago is big for the bootleggers there. We've got great customers in Chicago. They buy a lot of our stuff. But we don't bring booze over the border there. We don't even run a distillery in town. All we do is sell it.'

Powell shrugged. 'That's still a big operation.'

But Roeder's mind was made up. In moods like this, he wasn't easily shifted. 'What else did he say? Paulet, I mean.'

'Not a lot. The IRS thing is serious, though. Prosecutions for tax evasion! Jesus! You'd think they could find something else.'

'Not a lot? But something? He must have said something else. We pay him enough.'

'They're digging around bank transfers. They want to

484

connect the local operation to the centre. That means here on Wall Street – assuming it's us they're talking about, and we don't know that.'

'Bank transfers?' Roeder jumped on the information greedily. 'Bank transfers?'

'Yeah, which is another point in our favour. Young Will Thornton has cleaned Marion more thoroughly than we've ever cleaned any place ever. The only papers that matter are sitting inside a safe on top of a stick of explosive and a can of gasoline. I don't see how Carpenter's guys are going to dig it out from there.'

But Roeder didn't answer directly. He didn't always. Ted Powell was his boss, only it didn't always seem that way. He grinned nastily, yellow teeth in pale gums. 'Two things. One, get Thornton out of here. Send him on vacation. Just lose him for a week or two.'

Powell nodded. 'OK.'

'And the second thing is, I take back what I told you a minute ago.'

'What? You haven't told me a goddamn thing.'

'The girl,' said Roeder. 'I got the girl.'

106

The ribbon on Pen's typewriter was exhausted.

She'd never used a typewriter before coming to work at the bank, and she still had to stop and search when she needed one of the less useful letters: x, z, j, or v. What's more, she'd never yet changed a ribbon. Which was why, with fingers inky from the carbon, and the ribbon already tangled around the typewriter's carriage return, she got up from her desk to wash her hands. On her way to the wash-basin, she passed Mr Rogers' office. As she passed, he looked at her.

There was nothing unusual in that, except for the *way* he looked at her. He was on the phone and he didn't just glance, he stared. At her. Through her. And he was still on the phone. Still listening, still talking.

Pen held his gaze for a full three seconds. Eyeball to eyeball for three full seconds. A man she hardly knew. Three seconds. Pen let her gaze break away and she walked down the corridor to the toilet, where she carefully washed her hands.

Rogers had been talking about her. That was the fact which raced through her body like a wash of ice. And whatever it was he'd been speaking about, had changed him. Rogers had been alert, not bored. He'd been – what was it she'd seen? – something unusual, something new. Then she got it. He'd been *thrilled*. Scared, but most of all thrilled. Into Mr Rogers' tedious little life, something dangerous had suddenly walked.

Pen dried off her hands and walked back to Rogers' office.

'Was there anything you wanted to see me about, Mr Rogers?'

He was taken aback. His mouth was dry, but he was working hard to appear normal. 'No, Sarah. No, no. Nothing like that.'

'It was just that you were looking at me very hard.'

'Was I? Probably thinking about something else. No, no, Sarah, if I want you I only need to ring.'

He gestured at his phone and the gesture woke him up. His self-importance returned like a favourite coat. Whatever it was that Pen had hoped to discover had slipped away again.

But she'd seen enough. There's no better way to train your instincts than to fly. In her days of pylon racing, Pen had flown at full speed around a course marked out by thirty-foot steel pylons. She'd had to fly close to the ground, turning the plane up to two hundred and seventy degrees, and doing it all at more than two hundred miles an hour. The turns had been so hard that the blood had literally drained from her head. A couple of times she'd momentarily lost vision as the plane came around, regaining sight only as the plane levelled. What had kept her on course, above ground, still flying, still racing?

Instinct, only instinct.

And it was Pen's instinct that told her what had happened. Somehow – she couldn't even begin to guess how – the Marion mob had uncovered her new identity. Or to be precise: it suspected it. Someone had phoned the bank for confirmation. Had they hired anyone recently? A new girl, name unknown, short hair, probably blonde but maybe dyed, slim, taller than average, tanned?

Easy questions to ask, easy questions to answer. Rogers would have identified Pen within a few sentences. And then what? What had they told him? What had they asked of him? It was something that had shocked him, thrilled him, made him lie.

107

The movie theatre was advertising a Buster Keaton picture, but some dimwitted projectionist had leaned the reels up against a heating pipe and the celluloid had begun to crumple and melt. The management searched around for something else they could play instead and all they could come up with was an old flying picture: Willard T. Thornton in *When We Were Heroes*.

Susan grabbed her sister's arm. 'Oh, Ros, look! It's one of Willard's.'

Rosalind stopped uncomfortably. She'd seen a couple of Willard's movies and hadn't liked them. She didn't want to see another, but couldn't very well say so. Meantime, Susan was putting her hand in her purse to find the admission money and asking Rosalind if she wanted her popcorn sweet or salted.

They watched the picture. Willard played a war hero. Eve Moroney, 'the Prairie Flame', played his girl. There was no plot. The girl kept on being kidnapped. Willard kept rescuing her, being captured, risking his life, escaping, then doing the whole lot again. The movie finished. The lights came up. The theatre, not full to start with, emptied.

'Ros! No wonder you're in love,' said Susan. 'Didn't he look wonderful? Those stunts. Did he fly them himself? I hadn't realised how –'

She broke off. Rosalind wasn't crying, but she was close to it. She sat forwards in her seat, eyes fixed on the empty screen.

'Ros? Ros? Are you OK?'

Rosalind nodded.

'Was it seeing him with Eve Moroney? It's only a picture.'

'It wasn't only a picture. He got her pregnant.'

'Really? Wow! But, you know, that's all over now.'

'It's not her. I don't care about her.'

She spoke the truth. She didn't care about whatever had once happened between her fiancé and the famously beautiful Prairie Flame. A black kid in a uniform two sizes too big for him finished sweeping out the trash from the other seats in the theatre and stood leaning on his broom, waiting for the two women to leave. He had big sad eyes and seemed ready to wait for ever.

'Let's go.'

Out on the street, they walked for a block in silence, before Rosalind spoke her mind.

'You know, Suze, I once said to him that I loved a man who couldn't act.'

'Oh, Ros! That was a bit hard of you.'

'Well, it's not his strong point, is it? But the point is, what I saw in that picture was what I see . . .' She was going to say in the bedroom, but the truth was she saw it everywhere else as well. 'It's what I see all the time. The same gestures. The same expressions. It's like he's always in front of a camera.'

'Well, I suppose a thing like that gets into the blood. There are worse things in a man.'

'Yes.'

Rosalind knew she was expected to say something stronger, but somehow couldn't. When they were with friends, they seemed like the most brilliant couple in New York. But when they were alone, not dancing, not eating out, not getting drunk, just together alone, their relationship seemed to dwindle until Rosalind sometimes wondered whether she could see it at all.

'He is brave, isn't he?'

'Yes. Very, I think.'

'Clever? Handsome? Charming?'

'Oh, I'm probably being an idiot. It's probably just wedding nerves.'

'It probably is, you know.'

'So that's all right then.'

Rosalind spoke bitterly, and it was half an hour before she seemed herself again. But though her mood improved, there was one image from *When We Were Heroes* that she couldn't get rid of.

When Willard had finally thwarted the bad guys, rescued the girl, landed his plane, he had looked for a long moment direct into camera. Susan had been right, of course. Willard's face wasn't just good-looking, it was exceptional, a face made for the movies. But his expression! Bold – determined – triumphant – resolute – loving – masculine. There was nothing wrong with the expression. It was just right for the movie, Willard's best scene of the film.

But it wasn't the first time she'd seen it. She'd seen the exact same expression the time he'd come back from Canada, having, so he said, exposed and defeated the racketeers inside Powell Lambert. There was no reason why he shouldn't have worn such an expression. He'd been through a time of uncertainty and danger. He'd used his guts and his brains. He'd avenged a good man's death and brought justice to a criminal conspiracy. But it was so like the movies!

Rosalind played the moment over and over in her head. And the more she played it, the more she saw something different in it. Willard's expression had been careful, controlled, deliberate.

Fake.

108

Willard had travelled plenty in his life. Manhattan was 'his' town, the East Coast his back yard. He had skied in Colorado, sunned himself in the south, visited relations in Canada, spent Augusts in England and Scotland, travelled west to Hollywood and the blue Pacific. But oddly enough, he'd never once been to Washington, his nation's capital.

And now he was on his way. Not because he'd chosen to go, but because Powell had made him.

'A vacation, Will. You've earned it. Think of it as a gift from the Firm. And when did you last see your old man? I swear to you, your pa spends too much time thinking about his guns and bombs. You go tell him how business is done in the rest of America.'

'But, listen Powell, I'm busy.'

'No, you're not. You're not if I say you're not. I'll get people to cover for you.'

'Well, there's Rosalind too. I'm about to get married, Powell. I've got –'

But Powell had his hand up. 'Send her a postcard.' The banker had a grin pasted across his face like an advert for toothpaste, but with Powell, Willard knew, you should always look at the eyes and the eyes weren't smiling. And this wasn't a vacation. He was being sent away so Roeder and Powell could do whatever the hell they wanted in Marion without interference. He felt powerless, stupid and angry.

But what could he do? Nothing. If he didn't agree to go to Washington, Powell would make him go anyway. So he agreed. He agreed, but he did one extra thing. He booked a ticket on a liner leaving Los Angeles for Sydney, Australia in sixteen days' time. He booked the ticket in the name John Jackson and arranged with one of the Firm's clients, a drinks peddler with a profitable sideline in counterfeit documents, for a passport to be prepared in the same name. He put the ticket and passport in an envelope along with two thousand dollars in cash. He kept the envelope in his inside jacket pocket, close to his skin.

Because Willard had finally made a decision. He would do everything he could to get the package to Rockwell. He'd do what he could to make Rockwell see sense and get the hell out. He'd do what he could, and if he failed then he failed. Captain Rockwell had voluntarily entered a dangerous game.

Unltimately the consequences would be down to him.

109

Out on the airfield in Miami, the air was deathly still.

The hangar had its doors open, but not a single draught penetrated its gloomy walls. Hueffer's shirt stuck to him as though glued. Any movement brought on a prickle of sweat. Two hundred yards away, down on the beach, the sea was an odd combination of sluggish and turbulent. On the surface, the waves looked dead. Greasy waves rolled over with hardly a ripple. But all the time, an uneasy swell grew in size. Bigger waves, not high but very broad, rolled steadily in.

The humid lifelessness of the air could mean only one thing, and that thing was confirmed by a glance to the south-east. Out to sea, a line of clouds, like some vast fortification, crept slowly forward as though on giant rollers. Hueffer had already been out to check that Poll was snug outside under her canvas cover. She was settled down as tight as could be, but even so Hueffer went out with extra ropes, a couple more steel pegs. He did what he could, then thought about checking the hangar roof. It was no good securing Poll if the hangar went and blew itself to bits. But before he could act, the phone rang. He snatched it up.

'Yes? Hello?'

'Hello?' The voice was a woman's, its pitch and intonation unfamiliar yet also reminiscent of something or someone.

'May I help you?'

'My name is Miss Torrance calling from the Savings Bank of Northern Florida. Who am I speaking with please?' The familiar-unfamiliar voice suddenly made sense. It was Pen's voice shifted and distorted, but still hers. She was speaking strangely in order to fool any listeners on the line. Hueffer gripped the phone harder and answered carefully.

'This is Arnie Hueffer. I'm afraid Captain Rockwell is away on business. I can reach him by telephone if you wish.'

'No, I'd like to speak with Mr Anderson, if possible.'

She spoke very clearly and deliberately. A wrong number call for Mr Anderson was the agreed code calling for instant help, for Abe to launch an airborne rescue mission.

'There's no Mr Anderson here. You maybe need to check your number.'

There was a pause. The code had been used and acknowledged. By rights they ought to hang up, only neither of them wanted to. Hueffer wanted to ask what the problem was, but knew he couldn't.

'I guess so. I'll check it,' said Pen. She too was hanging on to the call: a friendly voice, a trusted one. Oceans of unspoken friendship and concern washed around in the silences.

'Listen, if you've got a call to make, you should make it soon. There's a bad storm coming in. Real bad. I'd say there ain't gonna be many phone lines standing after it's passed through.'

He wanted to say: *There's no way on God's earth Abe can fly in this weather.* He wanted to say: *'Get the hell out. We'll come find you later, soon as we can.*

'Right . . . It's Mr Anderson I need,' said Pen stupidly. 'Mr Anderson.'

She was saying: *I have to have Abe. With an airplane. Storm or no storm, I have to have them.*

'Right . . . Well, like I say, no Mr Anderson here.

Code acknowledged once again. He'd do what he could. He wanted to say. *Look after yourself, Pen. For Christ's sake. Whatever happens. Look after yourself.*

495

'OK. Sure. I'll check the number.'

Maybe it was the line, but Pen's voice sounded a million miles away, small and lost.

'You do that.'

'Sure.'

Hueffer hung up. It was no use checking the hangar now. Loose sheets of tin, cracked roof joints, who cared any more? That phone call meant the endgame was in its last desperate stage. The three of them had already agreed that if Pen made her emergency call, they'd all assume their cover had been finally compromised. Arnie could no longer risk remaining where he was. He'd have to run for it, try to escape into the vastness of America.

But first he made the call he had to make. He called Abe in Marion.

'Just had a call. Some dame wanting a Mr Anderson. You don't know an Anderson, do you?'

'Not me,' said Abe. The same unspoken sentences washed between the two men. Then Abe changed the subject, or appeared to. His voice mostly sounded like its normal self: unhurried, decisive, quiet. But beneath the confidence there was something else. Anxiety not just for Pen, but for the conditions in which he was being asked to fly. 'I don't quite like the weather up here. There's a bank of cloud a long way out still, but maybe you can see more your end.'

Hueffer glanced out of the gaping hangar door. The storm was unmistakable now. The sky south and east of Miami was dominated by the vast black wall of thundercloud. A greyish-yellow lightning flickered evilly between the parapets of clouds.

'It's bad,' he said simply. 'As bad as we've had. Not flying weather. It'll hit here soon.'

'I guess . . .' Abe started, then let his voice fade. But Hueffer knew what he'd wanted to ask.

'I told the dame there was a storm coming in. I told her if she wanted to reach this Anderson guy, she'd better do it before the phone lines are blown to hell. She was sure anxious about it.'

'Uh-huh. OK . . . No, Arnie, I don't know anyone of that name. Sorry I can't help.'

'OK. Don't worry.'

A pause.

'Take care, buddy.'

'Yeah, you too. Take care.'

Just before they hung up, Abe said, 'Oh, Arnie. I guess . . . I mean it isn't worth worrying about or anything, I wouldn't want you to . . .'

'You're worried about Poll?'

'Not worried, I just wanted to know . . . well, OK, yes, darn it, I am worried.'

'I've been out to check her out. I put a couple of extra turns around her. She's as snug as I can make her. But this is a bad one, buddy. I don't know if the hangar will be here in the morning.'

'OK Arnie, thanks anyway. Any case, I'd prefer her to smash up in a storm than just rot away.'

'Yeah.'

'But still . . .'

'I know.'

'OK, anyway, you've got stuff to do. So long.'

'Yeah, so long.'

Hueffer hung up.

The hangar filled with silence and the unstirring air. Up in Jacksonville, Pen was in danger, running for her life. In Marion, Abe was about to take to the skies, hoping to snatch her up and away. And here in Miami, Arnie Hueffer's work was done. He moved along the silent workbenches, straightening things out, replacing tools, his cherished friends. Quietly, not seeming to rush, but quickly all the same, he found his hat and coat, went to the door of the hangar and slipped quietly away.

110

The train pulled into Washington at four o'clock on that bright March afternoon, with the sun still heaping gold on the buildings and monuments. Willard felt what every patriotic American ought to feel. A glow. An expectation. A sense of an all-American promise being abundantly fulfilled. In the rush and bustle of Manhattan, it was possible to forget all that was best about America. But not here. Not in Washington.

Willard was met off the train by a suave executive from Thornton Ordnance. The man, Henry Geddes, was only a year or two older than Willard, but the man's demeanour – something between an international diplomat and a senior civil servant – gave him the air of a man two decades older again.

'A good journey, I hope?'

'Fine, thanks.'

'It all depends on whom one is obliged to travel with. I always seem to get the nervous old ladies. Either that or the pot-bellied snorers.'

'It was OK. It wasn't like that.'

'Excellent.' Geddes' tone of voice somehow implied it was Willard's fault that he'd ended his journey with nothing to complain about. 'I have a car waiting. You'll want to freshen up before meeting your father.'

'Yes. Where are we . . . am I . . .?'

Geddes ignored Willard's question as he eased through

a crowd to a silver-grey Buick with a uniformed chauffeur sitting at the wheel. Geddes waved Willard into the car then got in on the other side. *Velvety*. Geddes was velvety and everything he did was velvety too. That was OK if you liked velvet. Willard didn't.

He tried again. 'You mentioned a meeting with Father. He's coming to the hotel is he, or . . .?'

Geddes had produced a white envelope from his pocket and held it up. 'The details you need are here. This car is yours for the duration of your stay, as is Gregory here –' The chauffeur caught Willard's eye in the mirror and nodded slightly, but was otherwise completely impassive. 'We've found a suite for you at the Jefferson. It wasn't our first choice, but its suites are first-class. Please call the Firm's offices if we can help in any way. Opera tickets, excursions, dinner reservations, anything. The Firm has a fine tradition of hospitality, so please try us out.'

Willard nodded, suddenly unsure of which Firm Geddes was talking about. Thornton Ordnance or Powell Lambert? Willard had assumed that Geddes belonged to Thornton Ordnance's discreet lobbying organisation, but he was suddenly unsure. There was something in the way he spoke about 'the Firm' that was somehow reminiscent of Powell Lambert. Perhaps the two organisations crossed over from time to time. Willard was about to ask, when he saw that Geddes had put the envelope away again, sat back in his seat and had turned to look out of the window. Willard closed his mouth and did the same.

Washington!

The city's spell descended. Fragments of history learned as a schoolboy came rushing back. '*We hold these truths to be self-evident: that all men are created equal . . .*' Here in Washington the words from the Declaration of Independence took on a new and deeper resonance. Willard's lips actually moved as he continued the recitation in his head. '*That they are endowed by their Creator with certain unalienable rights, that among these are life, liberty and the pursuit of happiness . . .'*

The driver took them up Constitution Avenue towards the Lincoln Memorial, now glowing orange-pink in the late afternoon sun. Willard craned forward to look.

'You've been in Washington before, of course,' said Geddes.

'No. Never.'

'Really?' Geddes' answer was theoretically polite, but his tone somehow implied that Willard had just admitted to something shameful – like being Jewish or having an uncle living in a tin shack in Alabama. Willard wondered how Geddes would sound if he punched him full force in the mouth. Mushy? Soggy? Not so goddamned velvety.

They drew level with the Lincoln Memorial. *'Fourscore and seven years ago, our fathers brought forth on this continent a new nation, conceived in liberty, and dedicated to the proposition that all men are created equal . . .'* Lincoln's Gettysburg address boomed through Willard's mind like half-remembered gunfire.

'The statue's such a pity, don't you think?'

'I'm sorry?'

'You were looking at the Memorial,' said Geddes. 'I think Lincoln must have been one of the ugliest men ever born. Personally, I'd have dispensed with the statue.'

The conversation sputtered out. The Buick rolled forwards through city traffic until they arrived at the Jefferson. Geddes saw Willard out of the car, then wished him a good stay and handed over the white envelope. It was typical of Geddes that he could hold a largish envelope in his jacket pocket throughout a longish car journey, then produce it utterly uncreased, unmarked, and gleaming new. Geddes left. Gregory, the chauffeur, let Willard know how to reach him, then the Buick slid away too.

Up in his suite, Willard sat on his bed and opened the envelope. Inside was a single sheet of paper, Thornton

Ordnance stationery, with a handwritten note from his father.

'Dear son, I'm delighted to catch you in town. I shall be in the Senate Library from seven. I'll let the people there know to expect you. Your father, Junius.'

The Senate Library! The private sanctum of the country's most senior lawmakers. The holy heart of the holy city.

111

Pen stood by the window, sipping slowly from a cup of coffee.

From her vantage point she was able to survey the street outside, including a parked car – a Ford sedan, with a single man inside. At this distance, she couldn't make out much, but the man had been there for an hour already and hadn't moved once. People didn't do that. No one just goes to a place to sit doing nothing. They have a reason. Maybe they're waiting for someone. Waiting to pick them up, to give them a kiss, to give them a ride. Or to kill them.

Pen felt nauseous and giddy. As a pilot, she had accepted a high degree of risk. She was a stand-out participant in a pastime which killed a significant proportion of its adherents. But they were risks she knew and understood. The threat represented by the assassin outside was of a totally different nature. What if he had a sadistic streak? What if, where women were concerned, he liked to violate them before murdering them? The thought of dying was bad. The thought of a strange man's fingers touching her with lust and violence was utterly repugnant. She reeled back from the window.

She needed to get out.

That was certain. There were two exits from the bank. One at the front, which gave onto the street outside and the fat assassin. There was a second one at the back, which might also be watched. But there was a third option. A flight of stairs led up to a couple of offices and a stationery room on the first floor. From the window at the head of the stairs, Pen had seen a flat roof and the possibility of escape.

But first: a dilemma.

If she ran, she'd save her skin but lose everything that she and Abe and Arnie and poor Brad Lundmark had worked to achieve. Nobody would blame her, but her failure would still be total. Or she could do this. She could try to snatch the bank documents that Haggerty McBride had asked for. She knew where they were. She had the keys. She was literally just a matter of yards away from the documents that would link Marion to New York, Cuban booze to Powell Lambert.

It was dangerous, foolish, but she knew she had to try.

On the street outside, the light glittered with unhealthy intensity. Pen felt sweaty and warm, but also calm. Suddenly calm. She went up to Rogers' door, knocked and entered.

'Ah, Miss Torrance, Sarah! Yes?

'Sorry to bother you, sir, only it's this Southern Fruit Growers account.'

'Yes?'

The Southern Fruit Growers was one of the bank's major accounts, and the client had been kicking up a fuss recently over a string of interest charges.

'I've just had them on the phone,' Pen lied. 'They seemed very upset about their latest statement.' She began a confusing and hard-to-follow explanation of the customer's complaint.

'Yes, yes, Sarah, you need to try to get things in order. What exactly were they asking us for?'

'I don't exactly know, sir. They just seemed quite upset. I wonder if this is the kind of thing you need to talk over with Mr Ashley . . .?' Mr Ashley was the head of the bank and Mr Rogers' boss.

'Yes . . . yes, this has gone on long enough. Lord's sakes!

If it's not one thing after another!' Rogers stared at Pen, looked suddenly uncomfortable, then spoke with excessive sharpness. 'Thank you. That will be all. You've work to do.'

'Yes sir.'

Pen turned and went, but only down the corridor to the water fountain. Rogers left soon after her. He knocked at Mr Ashley's door, then went inside. Instantly Pen turned.

She was still calm, but calm in the way that she was when racing planes. She only had a minute or two but – to a pilot used to making a racing turn in an open cockpit at two hundred miles an hour – a minute or two can seem like all eternity, run slow.

She let herself into Rogers' office, duplicate keys in hand, not knowing which of the keys was the right one. She tried the first key. Her hand was steady. The key didn't jitter or shake, it just slid steadily in. Pen turned. She could feel the tumblers inside catch and begin to turn. And stop.

She didn't get rattled, knowing that if Abe had been there he wouldn't have been rattled either. She felt his presence. A smell of leather and sunshine, oil and soap; something quiet, strong, and reassuring. But the thought didn't slow her down. She tried a second key, which didn't even enter the lock, then a third which entered easily, turned the tumblers without difficulty. The steel drawer slid open with a hollow metallic boom.

The drawer was precisely ordered, precisely labelled. Thank God for Mr Rogers! Thank God for his fussy vanity, his prissy orderliness. The ledgers that Pen needed were in the second drawer down, marked 'Money transfers in'. Pen took them, all four of them. She opened one at random and checked to make sure that the data she needed was there. And it was. Money coming in from Powell Lambert. The name cropped up again, then again, then three more times on the same page.

Booze flowing from Havana to Marion, from Marion to

every last corner of the United States. And now here was the money, flowing the other way, the trail that would lead the whole rotten business to the courthouse and the prison.

She left quickly, holding the ledgers. Crazily, she had an impulse to go back to her desk, to gather up her things, as she always did at the end of a day. She thrust the impulse away and ran up to the first floor. The window at the top of the stairs was stiff. Pen put her hands to it and heaved. The heavy frame shot up with a bang. Pen bundled herself out onto the tarred roof, lugging her ledgers after her.

The afternoon heat squatted like a dumb animal. The air vibrated with it. The lemon-yellow light had a dangerous intensity. Pen couldn't, from where she was, see the storm clouds coming in, but she hadn't forgotten Arnie's warning. In any case, as a pilot, she could feel weather. Her skin was a barometer, her brain a map of the sky above.

She ran across the roof, keeping her body low. She was wearing her Sarah Torrance kit: neat white secretarial blouse, long blue skirt, stockings, flat shoes. It had been OK as a means of disguise. The long skirt and slippery shoes were worse than lousy as an outfit with which to run from armed and purposeful killers. She came to the parapet at the roof's edge and looked down. There was a drop of ten feet down to a heap of builder's rubble. She threw her ledgers down, then slid down after them. She landed safely, but scraped her belly on the wall and pinpricks of blood dotted her blouse. She didn't care. She picked up her books, lost a shoe between two blocks of concrete, fished for it, found it. She ran across the lot, trying to look like a busy secretary, not a desperate fugitive.

And in a second she was free: out on the streets of Jacksonville, in the dense light of the gathering storm.

112

Willard was showered, changed, combed, shaved. He looked a million dollars. He looked like a flying ace turned movie star turned banker. He was head-turningly handsome and he knew it. But he didn't know how to get to the Senate Library. As casually as possible, he called his chauffeur.

'Gregory, I'm going to need to run along to the Senate Library this evening. Around seven o'clock, that sort of thing. I was just wondering the best way to –'

'I'll take you to the north entrance, sir. Mr Thornton will have a man waiting there to take you through. I'd suggest you come down about a quarter of.'

Willard was relieved at Gregory's competence, but tried not to show it. He had fifty minutes to kill. He wanted a drink, but didn't know how to get one. He called room service and asked for soda water. When the boy came, Willard took the drink and sipped crossly.

'Jesus, this doesn't taste right,' he exclaimed, using a well-worn Prohibition gambit.

'The hotel doesn't allow liquor on the premises, sir,' said the boy impassively – and, in theory, unnecessarily given that liquor was permitted nowhere in the United States of America.

'Of course not.'

Willard and the boy sized each other up.

'Look, I wouldn't usually ask, but –'

'What d'you want? I got everything.'

'Can you mix a martini?'

The boy grinned, five years too old for his skinny frame. 'Two bucks a glass. A ten buys enough to pickle your head.'

Willard handed over ten bucks. 'And fast, OK? I'm leaving soon. Appointment at the Senate, as a matter of fact.'

The kid took the money and vanished. He was back inside five minutes with a clear glass bottle and a scrap of paper. He waved the paper.

'This is your prescription. Medicinal alcohol. All part of the service. When you're done, empty the bottle and rinse it. The number of sick people in this hotel, you wouldn't believe.'

The boy went. Willard drank. He imagined himself in a new career. Public service of some sort. Defence department. Responsibility for the Army Air Corps. He imagined himself at the White House. 'Mr President, the future of warfare is in the air. Can any army resist aerial attack? No, sir. Can any navy? No, sir. This country must look to the sky for its security, to the sky for its greatness.' He rephrased the speech a couple of times until it sounded right. He drank more, then went into the bathroom to comb his hair again. He leaned in to the mirror. 'Listen, Mr President,' he murmured. 'If I were you, sir . . .'

It was time to go. He hurried downstairs, where Gregory had the Buick running. Willard climbed in and the big car slipped away. Willard felt the slow fire of patriotic excitement and pride. His father lived and worked in these surroundings, among the great men of his nation. It was an honour: an honour and a privilege. Willard sat forwards, watching the great white dome of the Capitol creep closer.

'A beautiful sight, huh?' said Gregory, quietly dropping the 'sir'.

'Wonderful.'

'Even better by day.'

'I'll bet.'

'Just a shame about the skunks inside, right?'

Gregory's comment spoiled Willard's mood. He knew what most people thought of their politicians. He knew, if it came to that, what *he* had said about politicians most of his life. But he'd been wrong. The great white dome faintly gleaming against the night seemed proof of that.

'They've got a tough job to do,' he said, shortly.

That was the last thing Willard remembered in detail. The car arrived at the West Door. Gregory escorted him to a desk inside the entrance. Willard gave his name to the clerk and a man appeared to waft him down corridors of marble. Willard had an impression of white pillars, classical busts, oil paintings, dark panelling. The building had an atmosphere half-businesslike, half-reverent. Willard walked along half a pace behind the man, feeling like a peasant in a cathedral. At last, the man stopped outside a pair of wooden doors.

'The library, sir.'

The man led him on inside. Willard was breathless with excitement. The library was furnished like the best sort of gentleman's club. There were rows of leather-bound books, tables with that day's newspapers neatly folded, a couple of generous log fires crackling away inside marble hearths. And everywhere there was the subdued murmur of great men directing the affairs of the greatest nation on earth.

Willard followed his guide down the length of the room. At the end, part of the library was partitioned off by a heavy red velvet curtain. The man went to the edge, drew a flap aside and motioned Willard forward. Willard stepped through alone.

And saw this: his father, jowled and craggy, too coarse for these refined surroundings, but also at home in them. Very much at home.

And this: around his father a small group of men, senators of the United States, some of the most important men in the country.

And this: a long mahogany bar, crowded with bottles, bottles of *alcohol*, every sort you could imagine. Beer, champagne, whiskies from Scotland and Ireland, American bourbons, white rum, brown rum, London gin, French brandy, port, madeira, sherry, tequila, vermouth, vodka, schnapps, liqueurs of every colour and description, wines red and white from the very best European vineyards, Californian wines with labels proclaiming the best pre-war vintages, glasses of every kind and size, cocktail shakers, ice buckets, lemons cut in cutesy little slices, bowls of nuts, olives, dumb little parasols for making dumb little drinks. Everything.

Willard experienced a rushing in his head. He wasn't sure what he was seeing. He saw, or felt, his father coming towards him. His father with a glass in his hand. His father's face with a crooked smile of welcome. His father saying something, repeating it, saying it over and over.

'Willard, my boy, welcome to the Senate of the United States.'

113

Sometimes the air that lies just ahead of a big storm is absolutely still. So still, it can feel like flying through a churchyard: solemn, quiet, and in the looming presence of something vast. Other times, the air is troubled. It has bands of stillness, then sudden bursts of turbulence, like long fingers eddying out from the wall of destruction in the sky. This storm was of the second sort. It was harder to fly, but also more exhilarating. It needs to be *flown* not simply crossed. Abe liked the way his DH-4 hit the winds and sailed them, he liked the strength of his wings, the roar of his engine.

The miles rolled past. The grey, white and red of Jacksonville came into view and then, north of town, Samana Field. The field was a stretch of dune grass and beaten mud, once part of some developer's scam, now derelict. It was large enough, flat enough to take a plane. Abe and Pen had designated it their emergency field, their secret, their rendezvous.

And although Abe flew clearly, handled the controls, the regular minor course adjustments with perfect accuracy and authority, he felt as he had never felt in his life before. Pen mattered to him like nothing else in his life before.

He remembered how urgently he had felt the loss each time one of his young pilots in France had been killed or captured. He remembered how deeply he had wanted his kids to come back alive. But those feelings had been negative ones. He hadn't been especially attached to the individual kids, he just hadn't been able to bear the constant useless deaths. The experience had seared him. He'd run from commitment, run from feeling.

All that had changed. With Pen, the whole of Abe was liberated. He could be an adventurer *and* a lover, a loner in the cockpit *and* a romantic on the ground. Abe had so many plans for them both. He imagined them flying together, making a home together – good grief, he even thought of them having kids together. He loved her talk, and he loved her silences. He liked her face when she was unaware of him. He loved her body when it was close to him.

He flew as he had always flown, but his heart raced as it had never raced before.

He flew over the field. He could see nothing beneath, no sign of Pen. That in itself meant nothing. She'd be keeping out of sight until the last possible minute. There were a couple of low, dark metallic shapes concealed in a thicket of maritime oak. Abe tried to see them better, but couldn't. It didn't matter. The developers had begun a little construction before going bust and they'd left some rubbish behind. The shapes were probably just tin huts left over from the build.

He came in to land.

The storm was out of reach. The air was still. Abe could pick his approach, give himself the maximum length of clear runway. It was a simple landing.

He touched down.

The front wheels hit the ground cleanly, the tail skid began to kick up a trail of dust. Abe kept his hand on the throttle, closing it down but not off. He kept his eyes on the little clump of trees.

The mystery of the metallic shapes resolved itself. Cars, two of them, full of men. Men with guns. Rifles already jabbing out of the windows and shooting. The plane was rolling towards them. Abe couldn't veer, brake or turn.

The plane still raced forwards. The cars approached, firing wildly. Abe's hand was still on the throttle. He was still running fast. He'd never intended to land this time anyway. The touchdown had been a feint to draw out anything that might be lurking.

He pushed forward on the throttle, gathered speed, felt the wings complain at him for keeping them down, then touched back on the stick and leaped into the air. He passed the two cars seventy feet over their heads. Any bullets passed harmlessly behind. Keeping close to the ground, Abe tore away, out of range, out of sight.

And all he could think was, *What has happened to Pen?*

114

Willard actually staggered back.

He caught his foot in the curtain that divided the Senate library and had to reach for a white marble pillar to steady himself. His father smiled indulgently.

'Quite an impressive sight, huh? I think you once asked if the Firm operated any speakeasies, and I said we did. Just one.' He waved his hand. 'This is it. The most exclusive, the best-served, the most fully stocked, the best-run club in the entire world.'

'But . . .'

'But what?' His father carried on grinning, as though unable to guess Willard's objection.

'But, Father, *here*? Of all places, *here*? How do you . . . ? I mean, don't you . . .?'

Junius Thornton put his hand to his son's back and steered him through to the bar.

'What'll you have?'

'Anything, Father – or no, nothing, water. I had a drink before I came out. I hadn't thought . . .'

His father's grin was beginning to look wrong. Some men have faces made for smiles. Others don't. Junius Thornton didn't. Willard wished his father would stop smiling.

'Water, really?'

Willard nodded. A barman was hovering close by ready to take any order. Junius Thornton said nothing, just nodded. The barman vanished. Thornton stopped smiling. He turned back to his son.

'How do we operate a fully-stocked bar in the heart of the United States Senate?'

Willard nodded.

'Depends what you mean. If you mean, how do we keep the bar supplied with liquor, then the answer is that we have a procurement office downstairs. We take stock every night. Any requirements are logged right away and phoned through to Wall Street. We aim to supply any liquor in the world from stock within twenty-four hours. The gentlemen here –' Thornton waved his arm around the room, including about a dozen senators in his wave '– they enjoy testing us. "Neapolitan grappa, splash of blue curaçao, served on the rocks, twist of lime." If we can't do it then and there, we pretty much guarantee to have it ready for them same time, next day. These days, there's not a lot we can't supply on the spot.'

'That wasn't what I meant.'

'What did you mean?'

That was a fair question. What *did* Willard mean? He chose his words carefully.

'These men are the nation's most senior lawmakers. They're here to . . . Hell, you know what I'm saying. These guys here make the law. Make it and uphold it. And this bar isn't some minor violation. This bar violates the Constitution . . . Father, isn't this wrong?'

Junius Thornton had a way of showing nothing in his face. He could hold his face that way in the midst of conversation. His brown eyes never stopped assessing the situation, gathering and analysing information, but neither his eyes nor his mouth gave anything away. In those moments he looked like some highly efficient predator, coolly judging the coming kill.

The moment passed.

'Wrong? What's right and wrong these days, Will? Do

you know? Damn me if I do. When I married your mother, she'd never kissed a man before. Hardly looked at one. These things girls put on their faces nowadays – your sisters, no less – lipsticks, powders, colours – if your mother had worn anything of the sort, she'd have been considered no better than a chorus girl, and quite likely a good bit worse. Your girl – what's her name, again?'

'Hmm?'

'Your girl?'

'Oh.' Willard had to pause for a second to find the name himself. He got it straight away, of course, 'Rosalind,' but the strange thing was that it was little Annie Hooper's dimpled, freckled face that came to mind.

'Rosalind, right. Now I'm not saying a word against her, times have moved on, but those dresses she wears, your mother would have died rather than worn. Or take your jaunt into Hollywood. I was wrong about that. I thought it was a business that no gentleman should undertake. But I was thinking about the way things used to be, not the way things are today. Maybe it was the war that changed things. Maybe progress. Maybe money. But things change, you can't judge things in the old-fashioned way.'

'But the law? There's no law about what a girl can wear. There's no law against motion pictures.'

'No, no.'

Junius's answer implied a tone of total agreement, as though he hadn't understood Willard's objection. Willard pushed his case.

'If we can't trust the lawmakers, Father, then what's left? Even now, aren't there things too sacred to touch?'

'Sacred?' The older man lifted his massive eyebrows for a moment, as though questioning Willard's entitlement to use the word. 'Hmm! Tell me, in your view, Prohibition, is it a good thing or a bad thing?'

The question put Willard on the spot. He'd never thought about it much.

'Well, you know, Pa, the American working man needs protection. He comes home at the end of a day, wants a drink, takes too many, then what have you got? Illness, accidents. Businesses can't run themselves. And the wives and kids, what are they meant to do? I mean, I don't know, but I'd say, on the whole, a good thing.'

Junius Thornton's massive head began slowly nodding. 'I'm with you, my boy. I agree.'

'You do?'

'And look around.' Willard looked at the senators talking and laughing over their drinks. The curtained-off area only occupied about one third of the total library floor space, but it held at least two thirds of the library's occupants. 'What do you see? Do you see any illness? Accidents? Unhappy wives or fatherless kids?'

'No. Of course not. No.'

'Anyone here not up to the job?'

'No, no, of course. I didn't mean . . .'

'Well that's it, my boy. The entire story. Judgement and discretion. Some men have it, other men don't. If you make a law, you can't try to separate between the two. You have to make a law that applies to everyone, no exceptions. But that's the law. The practice is different. These men are some of the best in the country. Patriotic. Committed. Thoughtful. Honourable. And now and again, some of them want a drink. Can you think of any reason on earth why not?'

Willard shook his head. He was dizzy and lucid at the same time. No wonder his father was always down here in Washington. 'Mr Lambert' of Powell Lambert was every bit as busy as his Wall Street partner. Powell's job was to keep the supply lines ticking like clockwork. Willard's father's job was to make absolutely sure that the Firm had paid off everyone who mattered.

'The Firm, Father, how far does it reach?'

'It?'

'Yes, how far?'

'It, Willard, it? That's no way to speak of a family concern.'

'Huh? . . . Oh, right, *we*. How far do we reach? The United States Senate, obviously.'

Junius nodded.

'Congress?'

Another nod.

'Law enforcement? I guess the federal enforcement agencies . . .?'

'Know us and love us. We do things properly, in a businesslike way. They like that.'

'Customs?'

The older man shrugged. 'We've spoken to them. They pitch their demands a little high. It's a business we run, not a federal hand-out program. So, no. The answer to your question is no.'

'And what else?'

'For instance?' His father was impassive.

'What else, Father? The Department of Justice? The Attorney General? The White House?'

Junius Thornton smiled. He took a small leather notebook from his pocket and tore out a sheet. He wrote some names down on the sheet of paper using a slim pencil in a silver case. He showed the paper to Willard, who read the names.

'Jesus Christ!'

'Amongst others, I should say. Amongst others.'

Willard read the list again. 'Jesus Christ.'

His father turned away. A cardboard packet of matches lay in a silver tray on the bartop. Junius Thornton struck a match, lit the paper, and let it burn. He stopped watching even before the last spark of flame had vanished into ash. A barman with a white cloth wordlessly swept the ash out of sight. Aside from the lingering smoke, it was as though the sheet of paper with its handful of names had never existed.

517

Down by his right hand, Willard found the glass of water that he'd ordered what seemed like half a century ago. He stared at it dully, then raised it to his mouth. The water tasted flat, cold and insipid. It was a stupid drink for stupid people. He put it down. He found his father watching him, but not in a hostile way, in a kind way, a loving way even.

'Jesus, Father, I hadn't even imagined!'

'Not your fault, my boy. It's not something we shout about.'

Willard gestured down at his glass of water. He smiled. His father smiled back.

'Say, Pa, you know anywhere I can get a drink around here?'

115

On the edge of the field there was a movement in the sharp salt spines of dune grass. A girl, mid-twenties, conservatively dressed, but spattered with dust and dotted with blood, shifted position as she followed the plane's flight away to the south. She'd seen the cars, seen and heard the bursts of gunfire, known Abe had done the only thing he could do.

Pen watched Abe go in a storm of feeling. She felt intense and furious joy at his escape. At the same time, she saw the cars begin to creep around the field's perimeter, looking for her. And it wasn't just Marion's men in the cars, it was whoever else Powell Lambert could provide – that, plus the entire city police force which seemed to have been purchased lock, stock and barrel. She was horribly afraid.

First things first: her feet. Her slim leather-soled office shoes had already chafed her feet bare. Blood was bubbling up between her toes. The pain she didn't mind, but any time she tried to move fast her shoes flew off. On sand and grass that didn't matter. On gravel, rock, or the stony unmade roads of the area, bare feet would be cut to ribbons. She pulled off her shoes and stockings, then put the shoes back on and tied them to her feet with the thin silk. She pulled the knot tight and already felt more comfortable.

Then: think. *Abe*. What would he do next? He wouldn't just abandon her, she was certain. There was no chance of him simply giving up. But what would he do? He couldn't come back to Samana Field. The risk of capture was far too high. But he'd do something. *What?*

Meantime, she needed to hurry. One of the cars continued to tour the field, but the other one had stopped and had discharged its men. Six men, three of them cops, all six of them armed. For a second, she watched them come. Then, in a single golden moment, she realised she knew what Abe would do. She knew where to go and what to do.

She slid quietly down a sand dune, keeping out of sight. Forty yards away, a scatter of low bushes hunkered down against the fierce light and impending storm. She held her ledgers tightly against her chest. She was filthy now, no longer the neat bank girl who'd come into work that morning. But she didn't care about any of that. Right now, all she needed was shelter.

She caught her breath, gathered her strength, then ran, bending double, staying low.

116

Roeder lifted the phone. A man on the other end spoke for half a minute. Roeder asked one or two questions and listened in silence to the answers. Then, 'Keep going,' he said and hung up. The room was silent for a few seconds, but not empty. There was a concentrated fury in Roeder's pale face. His hands opened and closed, as though ready to mangle something.

But Roeder hadn't got where he'd got by failing to think. His anger wasn't vengeful, it was thoughtful. And suddenly, after a few seconds, it disappeared, or seemed to. He pushed back his leather-sprung chair and went to the hat stand. His hat was pearl-grey, soft felt, comfortable. From the drawer of his desk he took a gun. The gun was a .38 calibre Colt Army Special, dull black, cold metal, lethal.

Down in Jacksonville, his men and the city cops would either catch Rockwell and Hamilton or they would not. If the worst came to the worst, the last hand of this game would be played out somewhere else altogether and Roeder was a man who hated to miss a finale. He put his hat on his head, his gun in his pocket. He stepped out of his office and told his secretary he was taking a trip.

'Yes, sir. Should I tell people where they can reach you?'

He nodded. Smiled and nodded.

'Washington. I'm going to Washington.'

117

The storm wall was close now, less than a mile distant.

It was vast. The size of it was beyond words, beyond description. Storm clouds reached up thirty thousand feet. The length of the weather front was easily forty miles, and probably more. Abe had seen bad storms, but never one worse than this. He'd certainly never flown in anything like it, didn't know if a plane could even stay aloft in those conditions.

Down on the beach, the long dangerous rollers from the Atlantic were changing their tune. The rollers were still there, still bigger if anything, but they'd begun to break up. Waves curled in long lines of white up and down the coast. The white had a nasty edge to it. This was no pleasant, frothy, ice-cream white. This was the savage green-white of a violent ocean, growing more violent with every wave.

And down below: Tin Can Field.

There was no reason to go there, except for one. Abe and Pen had no back-up plan. Or rather: Samana Field had been their back-up plan. So where should Abe go? He should go wherever he'd be most likely to find Pen. She'd go wherever she'd be most likely to find him. They hadn't spoken about it, hadn't thought about it. But there was only one choice. The site of their best and longest love-making. The place where they hadn't come together as war hero and rich girl, just as man and woman. Their nights alone on Tin Can Field had been like something dropped from heaven, like nights snipped from the rest of their lives. It was here, if anywhere, he'd find Pen.

Abe hugged the ground. He was flying so low that nobody on the ground would be able to locate his direction unless he passed more or less directly overhead. But it was hellishly dangerous. The wind was getting stronger and gustier. Twice a sudden bolt and drop of air thrust him downwards. Only lightning reactions saved him from smashing up. The second time, he actually felt the thwack of a tree-top against his undercarriage, the plane's sudden hesitation in flight.

He came to Tin Can Field. On a still day, he'd have come down on the beach. The sand slanted a little down to the sea, but it was hard and even, and there was plenty of space.

But today was no still day. Landing in a strong and gusting crosswind was an all but certain route to destruction. An imbalance in wind pressure between one pair of wings and the other would tilt the aircraft. In the air, that meant nothing. Close to the ground, if one wingtip snatched the ground on landing, then a tilted aircraft was probably a wrecked one.

Abe surveyed the approach. He would have to land in the path of the wind. That gave him a maximum distance of two hundred feet, far less than he usually needed. On the other hand, the wind, blowing directly in his face, would help slow the aircraft. He flew over the landing field checking for obstructions. Infuriatingly there was a drainage ditch running clean across the field, two thirds of the way down his proposed landing strip. The ditch cut his landing distance to just a hundred and forty feet, an all but impossible distance.

He was in a quandary.

He'd be of no help to Pen if he smashed up his plane and himself with it. On the other hand, he was of no help to her in the air either. He hesitated for a second, then knew he had to attempt the landing. He brought the plane around and lined her up with the little strip of sand and earth. Ahead, the sky was a mountain of black. Below, the sea was whipping itself into a frenzy. Abe watched a squall come spitting across the water towards him: a scurry of rain, white foam lashing off the tops of waves. In a flash, Abe realised that squall was his chance. The greater the windspeed in his face, the shorter his stopping distance. But the squall was a small one. He could already see past it to a lull in the water beyond. He moved as quickly as he could.

He dropped the plane faster than he wanted, spent a second or two racing full throttle towards the squall. A burst of rain crashed into him. Light vanished. His goggles streamed with sudden water. It was hard to make out anything below. But Abe couldn't postpone movement. His hands and feet raced ahead of his eyesight. He throttled back, lost height, felt the plane snag on the buffeting wind. Desperately trying to judge his position in the swelling chaos, Abe caught a glimpse of his landing site. He moved the stick down, kept the rudder steady, throttled back to nothing. A lurch of wind slammed him down hard on the earth. The aircraft rocked once – whether from wind or something under his wheels was hard to tell – then corrected itself before Abe could react. He already had his elevator up. He felt the ground racing too fast beneath him. He could see the edge of the landing strip horribly close.

He was slowing. The violence of the squall did what he needed. He was losing speed fast. He thought he'd done it.

Then the squall lifted. The rain stopped. There was a second of bright sunshine and absolute calm. Slowly, at no more than five miles an hour, but unstoppably all the same, the DH-4 rolled forwards another couple of dozen yards and sighed a little as the wheels eased gently into the drainage ditch. The plane stopped, angled gently down, stuck fast.

118

Pen was losing the race.

To begin with, she'd done well. She made her escape from Samana Field without being noticed and, her bloody feet thankful for the newly secured shoes, she'd made good progress south. But, passing town, she'd been forced to compromise every rule of safety. It was broad daylight still – if that was the right term when half the sky was as black as a five-day bruise. She would need either to walk through town or try to sidle past it, down the waterfront. Either way was bad, but town was worse. As Sarah Torrance, Pen had been inconspicuous. She'd been the sort of person you could sit opposite in a bar for half an hour, then be hard pushed to remember one solitary detail about her after-wards. But that had been this morning. She was Sarah Torrance no longer, just Pen Hamilton the fugitive. Blood continued to leak from her shoes. Her silk stockings were ragged. Her skirt was torn. Her blouse was damp and filthy. Her hair had made the short but familiar step from well-combed and demure, to unkempt and ragged.

She chose the waterfront, trusting not to subtlety, but to speed.

She almost made it.

With the weather turning so foul, sightseers and tourists had abandoned the beach. Hoteliers were closing shutters, bringing tables inside, bringing down awnings, securing whatever could be secured. At the top end of the beach,

Pen had seen a pair of uniformed cops lurking in the shade of a hotel veranda. Beyond them, there was a parked sedan car with a man inside, watching the beach and doing nothing. Pen cut inland, crossed a patch of rough ground to a hotel service road, then made her way behind the cops and the parked car. Then, pushing her way through the lush beach-side garden attached to a white-pillared casino, she cut back to the beach, sticking to the broken ground and spiky dune grasses.

Isolated and obvious, her best refuge was speed. She tore her shoes off, and ran. The four bank ledgers were heavy and had made a damp rectangular print against her belly. But she made good progress. Every hundred yards left in her wake was a hundred yards closer to Tin Can Field.

But, on reaching a small headland that marked the edge of the built-up area, Pen almost ran slap into a Marion goon, lying face down in the low grass. Pen came running within a dozen yards of him. The first she knew of his presence was when a shot cracked into the sand ahead of her.

She was so surprised she almost stopped running. When she turned, she saw the man – a fat guy, thank God, two hundred and twenty pounds at least – belting down the beach after her. She heard another couple of shots, but didn't spot the fall of the bullets. Lungs and limbs burning with pain, Pen stretched the distance between them to thirty yards, forty, fifty, sixty. The fat man gave up, clutching his gasping side. Pen stopped for a second, gasping herself, and the two of them grimaced, before the fat man turned lumbering back to a nearby restaurant. From there he'd make a call for help. If the organisation was smart – and it was – it would have enough information to join the dots. Pen was on the run. Abe was there to get her out. They'd abandoned one pick-up point. They were going hell-for-leather to the next. A city plan would be enough for them to guess the rest.

So Pen ran.

She had always been fit, but today had been a challenge beyond anything she'd ever known. Feet, legs, arms, lungs all burned with the effort. But she did it.

She made it to Tin Can Field. She saw the plane while she was still four hundred yards away. A kind of tearful relief began to well up in her. And there was Abe, running towards her. She saw the steadiness in his face, the strength in his arms. The woman in her melted at the sight.

But then the pilot in her went dizzy with shock.

The plane stood at the wrong angle. Not badly wrong, but wrong enough. It was a tiny thing, but aviation is all about the tiny things. The way things stood at present, the plane would never take off.

119

Willard bent over the map.

The United States it portrayed was a colourless affair: all sandy yellows, dry pinks, stony whites, sombre blues – a true picture of Junius Thornton's America. Next to the map was a book. It was leather-bound and unique. Only one copy of it existed and only one copy would ever exist. The book was three-quarters full, and each completed page was filled with the same handwriting: Junius Thornton's close-set, over-inked, hard-to-read scrawl.

Willard knew now why he had been sent to Washington. It was the last part of his initiation. The drink in the Senate Library had been a carefully designed piece of theatre. This small black book was the final stage. Not theatre any longer, just business.

And what a business!

The book recorded the money and gifts handed by Powell Lambert to state and federal officials nationwide. The list was stupefying. On each page, there was the name of a state, then a date, then a list of names, job titles and amounts paid. Junius Thornton's list-making was scrupulous. If a mink coat had been given to the wife of a particular official, then the gift was recorded along with a short description ('floor-length, silver, gd quality') as well as the dollar value. Names, dates, places, bribes began to blur in Willard's head. He shifted in his seat, feeling dazed. His father saw the motion and came over. He tapped the map then traced

528

a line that included the entire United States, excepting only Alaska and Hawaii.

'There are forty-eight states here. Each state boasts a Prohibition Director charged with the implementation of Prohibition in their territory. Forty-eight states. Forty-eight Directors.'

Willard nodded. He knew that. Everybody did.

'How many of those officers do you think have accepted money from us?'

'How many?'

The older man didn't even bother to nod, just held his son's gaze remorselessly. Something in the intensity of the gaze confused Willard, making it hard for him to concentrate.

'I don't know, Pa. Those places where we looked like getting into trouble perhaps. Twelve, maybe? Fifteen? Twenty.' He changed his answer a couple of times in an attempt to get a signal back from his father's eyes, but there was no signal to be found. 'Twenty. I'll guess twenty.'

Junius Thornton spun the silence out a moment or two more, then looked away.

'Forty-six. Every state of the union outside Indiana and Kentucky. The Directors in those two states earn $4,600 a year from their current positions. We offered them each 150,000 to step aside into a regular job. They rejected our offer. We are now working to get the two gentlemen replaced.' The way he spoke was odd. He sounded contemptuous, weary. It didn't sound like he was triumphant about the Firm's success. It sounded like the only guys he had respect for were the two hold-outs in Indiana and Kentucky.

'No, Pa, you're kidding! No? You're not? Really? Shee shucks!' Willard changed his expression from 'sheez', which his father detested, to 'shucks' which he only disliked. 'Forty-six?'

His father closed the book and put it away. Silence filled the room. From the corner of the K Street office, it was just about possible to see the dome of the Capitol. It was a beautiful place, but a rotten one. Willard felt nothing but disgust. Disgust and disappointment.

Junius Thornton broke the silence.

'Do you understand now, Willard?'

'Huh?'

'Do you understand?'

Willard paused before answering. He felt like he did understand. No wonder Powell Lambert drove everyone else off the streets. No wonder Ted Powell was happy to sit in New York and work his butt off – knowing full well that his partner was here in Washington doing the same.

'Only one thing, Pa. Thornton Ordnance. I guess . . .'

Junius Thornton generally hated it when his son trailed off without completing a sentence, but on this occasion he nodded before Willard had finished.

'Quite right, my boy. The arms business has always required intensive lobbying. Much of the success of any weapons company is related to the strength of its contacts.'

'And that's why . . .?'

'Yes. Ted Powell had the finance organisation, but that wasn't sufficient. He needed my network. And let's be blunt. The purpose of lobbying is to make friends, but this is Washington, not the schoolyard. Money buys friends here. Nothing else. We buy our friends. We insist on loyalty. We expect it. We obtain it. The Firm succeeds because we do.'

'And the Firm. I used to think that there were two separate outfits, Thornton Ordnance and Powell Lambert. I guess I was wrong there too.'

Junius Thornton shrugged abruptly. He was getting to the end of his desire for communication. 'Legally, the two companies remain separate. But this is peacetime. With our nation in the mood it's in, I can't see us engaged in any war of consequence. Defence spending is low. If you want to know where the family's profits come from, then it's alcohol. Ninety-eight per cent.'

'Yes, Father, then I understand.'

Willard nodded.

He should have felt good. This had been the final baptism. How many people in Powell Lambert knew about the black book he'd just seen? Ted Powell, of course. Dorcan Roeder, most likely. Quite likely no one else. Willard, the son of his father, had just been taken into the last bastion of trust, the innermost sanctum of the family Firm. But he didn't feel good. Something sour lived in the room. A cynical odour that seemed to fill the city, that drained something good from the world.

His father nodded and said tersely, 'Good. And by the way, you've had a telephone call. From your fiancée. You may wish to call back.'

'Yes, of course. Did she say what she was calling about?'

Junius Thornton didn't answer. He stood at the door, about to vacate his own office so his son could make his phone call in privacy. But there was something odd about his expression, his posture. One part of it was that he was leaving his own office: it almost looked as though the older man was backing out, leaving the younger man in charge. But that wasn't it. He had asked *Do you understand now, Willard?* And Willard had answered *Yes, Father, then I understand*. But what was it they had been speaking about? The ultimate secret of the Firm's success? Or their shared disgust at the men who took the money the Firm so generously offered them?

Willard didn't know. He didn't have to. He turned to the phone, made his call.

120

Abe looked at Pen. He saw she was tired, grazed and foot-sore, but basically OK. He saw – he had seen with his first glance, in fact – that she held four cloth-bound ledgers flat against her stomach. The documents that McBride wanted were, for the moment at least, safe and sound.

Pen, for her part stared at Abe. He was clearly safe. Whatever kind of landing he'd had, he'd walked out of it just fine. Pen remembered the old aviator's saying, the one about a good landing being one you can walk away from. But then she looked at the plane. Its wheels had slid eight inches down into a ditch.

Eight inches. Maybe less. Maybe only six or seven. But that wasn't the point. At its deepest, the ditch went down a full sixteen inches. Any attempt to roll her forwards over the ditch would only make matters worse. If they tried to roll her back again, they risked collapsing the soft-sided trench walls and burying the wheels, their chances and themselves all in one horrible moment. And in any case, why was Pen even thinking about moving the aircraft? De Havilland built the DH-4 as a fighter-bomber. It was a big plane, heavy enough to take a cargo of bombs. She looked at the plane, perfect but immovable. Misery filled her.

'They're coming,' she said. 'They tracked me here. I'm sorry.'

Abe nodded. He didn't give her an answer directly, but his gaze travelled sideways. Pen saw a fallen palm trunk

For an instant she thought Abe must be thinking of the power of the coming storm – a storm that would soon be stripping palm trees and much else up and down the coast. Then she saw the drag marks, the sand scoured and flailed behind the trunk. She looked up, enquiringly.

Abe hesitated for a fraction of a second. He was never quite able to form a realistic picture of Pen's mechanical ignorance. At times he didn't explain things he thought were obvious, only to find that she was stumped by the problem. Other times he went the other way and decided she was so far beyond help that she needed the very simplest things explained, like how to use a screwdriver.

'I'm going to lever her up as far as I can. But first we need to get something solid under her wheels. A bridge, if you like.'

'A bridge, sure.'

Pen looked around as though hoping to find a highway bridge or a railroad bridge lying about somewhere on the camp site. Abe said nothing, just began shovelling sand and stones into the trench under the plane. Working quickly together, they filled in the ditch, so that there was solid earth coming to within an inch or so of the plane's wheels.

'OK. Now I'll get ready to lever.'

For a second or so, Pen stood uncertainly. Out to sea, the huge storm crept closer and closer. Long ragged tails of wind were already beginning to slash the palm tops, and causing white-topped waves to throw long banners of foam and spray up onto the beach. Then she collected herself. She threw her edgers in the plane, kicked off the bloody scraps of her remaining footwear and put on the flying boots Abe had brought for her. Her feet felt instantly more comfortable in the cushioned sheepskin. Meanwhile, Abe had his palm trunk in position now, threaded beneath the plane's narrow axle.

'I'll lift,' he said. 'You get the stones under her when you can. I'll lift one side first, then the other. Make sure your hands are clear when I start to lower.'

She nodded.

Abe wasn't big, but he was strong. He placed the palm trunk under the right-hand wheel and lifted. He gained only an inch or two, but it was enough. Pen thrust some stones under the lifted wheel and kicked them into place. She was just reaching for another stone, when Abe grunted and shook his head. She snatched her hand away just in time before Abe's strength gave out and he let the palm trunk and plane down with a judder. Then they repeated the same procedure with the other wheel.

They'd made two inches.

Pen wasn't sure if two inches counted as success or failure, but Abe seemed happy. He rested for a moment, then shifted his palm trunk again.

They repeated the same sequence of actions – made another inch and a half and Pen had begun to think that perhaps they'd get the old girl out of the ditch yet – when disaster struck.

Starting to lever one more time, there was a loud crack as the palm trunk broke in half just three feet from the end. Abe had only just been able to lift the plane. With three feet cut from his lever, there was no hope of lifting the plane another inch. But Abe hadn't stopped working, hadn't stopped moving. He pointed to the storm and said, 'When the storm hits, which way d'you reckon the wind'll be coming from?'

The wind was already quite strong now, still gusty but never quiet even in the lulls. But Abe's question made sense all the same. The windy outriders of a storm didn't necessarily blow in the exact same direction as the wind concealed in the bosom of the storm itself. Pen focused on the bank of thundercloud now only a stone's throw away. She concentrated on the question. She was a southern girl born and bred, a pilot too. She knew her weather. She knew storms like these.

'From there,' she said, holding out her arm.

'There exactly?'

She thought again, adjusted the angle of her arm a tiny bit, then nodded. The angle of her arm was fifteen degrees different from the angle of the airplane.

'OK. Let's get her moved.'

Then Pen saw it. And the moment she saw it, she was struck by a new wave of love so strong she could actually feel the pressure of it against her heart. Her lover wasn't just a courageous man, not just a good one, there was a flash of genius in him, a spark of something so unusual that it was a privilege to be in its presence.

'I've got you,' she said. 'Tell me what to do and I'll do it.'

'OK. I'll move her. You dig her in. Just the tail skid. Make a bowl. A flattish bowl.'

Pen nodded. Just then, in a sudden gap of wind, there was the sound of cars. The two fliers looked at each other. They said nothing because there was nothing to say. There was only one reason why anyone should want to come to Tin Can Field now, and that wasn't a reason either of them wanted to think about for long.

Abe gave a half-shrug, then went back to work, as Pen already had. She scooped out a wide flat hole in the sand. Abe used his palm trunk to lever the plane round and into the hole. The plane now had the correct attitude for take-off: facing clear into the coming wind, her body level and her wings even.

Of course, the way take-offs normally happened, this plane stood no chance at all of taking off. Her front wheels were still a few inches down into a ditch. At the rear end, Pen had dug the tail skid into a hole. A flattish hole, to be sure, but planes like a level runway, they aren't used to clambering out of foxholes.

But they had done all they could do. They finished just as the wind dropped from forty knots down to nothing. Except for the heavy smashing of the ocean, the world went suddenly silent. The sound of cars was unmistakable now. Cars arriving. Cars stopping. Car doors opening then slamming shut.

Meantime the huge curve of the thunderclouds was on top of them. Rearing ten or fifteen thousand feet in the air, the sheer immensity of the storm made them all – men, women, cars, plane – seem tiny, insignificant, as though the drama about to be played out mattered not at all.

At the top of Tin Can Field, the first men appeared. Coats and ties flapping in the wind. A couple of the goons, ridiculously, had their hats on and were moving forward, a gun in one hand, their hats jammed down over their heads with the other. Down the edge of the field, there was a glitter of black and silver in the undergrowth. Cops, Pen guessed. Determined not to let their enemy escape again, the goons had taken their time, had planned an encircling movement with the cops on the flank, the goons at the head.

Pen and Abe watched – for two seconds, no more. Then Abe nodded and climbed into the cockpit. 'Contact off! – Contact on! – Let's go!' The big propeller began to beat the air, at low throttle. Pen ran back from the propeller and jumped into the rear cockpit. Sarah Torrance's discarded shoes lay on the ground below as though the girl wearing them had simply evaporated. Behind them, the goons began running. There were little white puffs from their guns, though in the strengthening wind no sound was audible.

Out to sea, there was a band of sunshine still glittering on the water, then a huge, dense band of blackness rushing towards them. Blackness and wind. Strong wind. A wind of more than gale force.

A wind that would either save or destroy them.

121

'I'm sorry, Willard. This is the hardest thing. I hate being the one to break your heart.'

Willard still stood at his father's desk in his Washington office. Rosalind, her voice tear-stained, was trying to wind things up.

'To break my heart?' he said woodenly.

He was feeling strange. He had never been dumped, let alone dumped only weeks before a very big, very public wedding. But he didn't feel like a man with his heart broken. He didn't even feel as though Rosalind imagined his heart might be broken. It was almost as though she was hoping to script their break-up in a way she'd never quite managed to script their relationship.

'Oh, Willard, I know it must be terribly hard, but it will be for the best. You'll see in time.'

'Yes.'

She'd said that before.

He wondered at his own reactions. He loved her, didn't he? Certainly more than any of his Hollywood girls, more than any of those he'd had in France or before the war. When he thought about how glamorous Rosalind had looked by his side, about what a dazzling couple the two of them made, he felt a kind of dark fury that she should be ruining it. But love? A broken heart? He couldn't make sense of that.

'Thank you for telling me. I'm rather shocked, I guess. I think I'll get off the phone now.'

They said their goodbyes. Rosalind hung up first and the line went dead. Willard listened to the emptiness on the line, wondering if he should have protested more? He had the sudden feeling that if he'd kicked up a fuss, if he'd acted like a man whose heart *was* breaking, things might have turned out differently. Perhaps all Rosalind had needed was to be assured of the strength of her lover's feelings. The actor in Willard felt annoyed at letting a fine scene run away from him. But it wasn't too late. If that's what he wanted to do, he only had to call her right back.

He stared down at the phone. The handset stared back. To call or not to call? The part of broken-hearted lover tempted him. Willard already knew how to speak the lines that formed in his head. He put his hand to the phone and asked the operator for a long-distance line.

'Yes, what number please?' The operator's voice was high-pitched and acid, like something you could use to etch on copper.

'A New York number. Manhattan. The party's name is Hooper. Annabelle Hooper.'

122

The goons came running forwards. The cops, not wanting to miss the action, came running too. Abe saw a dozen men in the first wave, with more following after. Every man was armed and most were shooting. Most carried only hand-guns and were shooting at a range from which handguns were almost guaranteed to be ineffective. But there were a couple of men carrying rifles and still others who had the sense to run first and shoot later.

The wind increased.

It was strong enough now that the men on the ground were having difficulty running directly into its force. The two men with hats had given up the struggle and had let their hats blow off into the sky. Those who had begun the race with coats unbuttoned were having to run with a hand keeping their coats closed up. One man leaped to clear a fallen log, but misjudged how hard he needed to jump against the wind, and missed his footing as he tumbled comically in the blast.

Abe glanced around at Pen. Her eyes were in goggles now, but her mouth was visible. It wore a grin. Abe guessed he was grinning too. He had always wondered whether a plane could do what he was about to ask it to do. Well, he was about to find out. He felt very calm. The next few moments would determine whether he would find safety or find death, but the human implications of that choice had receded almost infinitely far in his mind. Even Pen, sitting in the cockpit behind him, didn't disturb his focus. He knew, of course, that she was the love of his life; that if he killed himself in the coming manoeuvre, he would kill her too. But the significance of those facts, like all other normal human concerns, had shrunk away to a tiny point the size of a pinhead.

Instead, his awareness was entirely focused on the importance of gauging the wind right, handling the plane properly. Abe sank into a state which was both hyper-conscious and entirely intuitive. While his eye and mind measured the wind, calculated forces and angles, his finger-tips simultaneously spoke to the controls, his body felt the aircraft, felt the ache in the wings, the tremble running down the tail. In this expanded state of awareness, he no longer felt like he was in control of the plane, he felt like he *was* the plane; its brain and nerves, its muscles and its will.

The wind screamed through the rigging. The cross wires that braced the wing-struts set up a howl, a hollow, whining, mournful sound that never ended. Abe had the plane's elevators fully raised, so that the force of the wind kept the plane jammed against the ground, and he could feel the wood and fabric flaps groaning under the strain.

Another second or two passed. Abe could feel the wind increase. Reading from the storm-whipped pattern of the boiling ocean ahead of him, he felt he could even see the wind.

The attackers continued forwards. There was more shooting.

Abe saw a bullet hole open in the starboard wing a few feet in front of him. It was time to go: safety or death.

He hunched over the control stick. Infinitely relaxed, but with infinite authority, he raised the stick. The aircraft responded. It began to move.

123

Mostly the way planes take off is simple. They roll along a flat piece of ground, gathering speed. When the air is moving fast enough over the wings, the plane has enough lift to take off. At this point, the pilot pulls back on the stick and lets the plane fly.

But that's the regular type of take-off. It's not one you can use if your plane has its rear end dug into a hole and its front end stuck in a sand-filled trench.

Fortunately, however, that's not the only type of take-off possible. If the wind is running hard enough, then, even if the plane is stationary, there can be enough airspeed over the wings to make a take-off possible. Not a good take-off, of course. Not a safe one. Not a controlled one. As a matter of fact, it can be the sort of take-off which sees the plane snatched into the air, only to be dashed to the ground a second later. All the same, given the circumstances, any kind of take-off would be welcome, any kind at all.

Keeping the tail held firmly down on the ground, Abe gave the engine maximum power. Angled as they were, the two pairs of wings were meeting the wind at a high angle of attack, exposing their undersurface to the buffeting force of the air.

And, in an instant, the big plane, all two tons of her, was snatched into the sky, exactly as if it had become a giant kite. There was no forward movement. There was almost no backwards or sideways movement. One second the plane was sitting on the ground, the next it was as if it had been jerked seventy feet into the air. The position, of course, was wildly unsustainable. Abe forced the nose of the aircraft down again. The wings bit into the wind at their normal angle. The big machine was no longer a giant kite; it was a plane once again.

Leaning out of the cockpit, Abe could see their recent attackers on the ground, looking up, astounded, completely beaten. A few of them had guns raised. Abe counted a few more shots, but what with the rapidly widening distance and the unpredictable ferocity of the wind, he knew they had little chance of causing damage.

But they were out of one danger and smack into another, possibly more serious, one. The storm was one of the most violent Abe had ever seen. It was possible that no pilot in history had ever flown in such weather and lived.

Still relaxed, still alert, Abe coaxed the plane into climbing. He kept her at full throttle, keeping her nose pointed into the wind, and giving her all the lift he could find.

It wasn't a predictable ascent. The wind was still gusty, and when it dropped, it dropped suddenly and hard. As soon as it dropped, the lift on the wings died away and the big plane lurched downwards. Abe did what he could to keep her steady, but it was an unnerving journey. They'd gain two hundred feet in a few seconds, then lose half of their gain in the blink of an eye. It was like being trapped in some giant elevator, with somebody else at the controls.

Abe coaxed the plane upwards. As the seconds ticked by, he fought the plane higher and higher. Two hundred feet, four hundred, six hundred, a thousand. At present, they were still on the outskirts of the storm. They hadn't yet reached the mountainous cloud wall that threatened to overwhelm them.

Abe was tempted to turn the aircraft and fly full-speed away, but he didn't dare. In those tumultuous conditions, turning the plane through one hundred and eighty degrees would expose the wings to violent and uneven forces. A couple of times, he tried nudging the plane around just a few degrees, but both times, the wings told him they couldn't stand the stress. He straightened up.

He had fifteen hundred feet beneath him now, but he needed more before attempting the manoeuvre. He wanted at least two thousand feet before risking it. He almost made it. At nineteen hundred feet, he began to relax. He adjusted position on the controls, ready to turn the aircraft, when a violent jolt of wind, the most violent yet, sprang them up three hundred feet, then threw them back almost a thousand.

Abe steadied the aircraft. There was no turning now. They were already into the grey outposts of the storm. Then, in a flash, they were inside the storm itself.

124

Henry Geddes, driving his own car, met Roeder off the train from New York. The two men knew each other, disliked each other, and used their acquaintance as an excuse to avoid courtesy.

'News?' asked Roeder.

'They didn't get her. Neither her nor the pilot nor the mechanic.'

'And the documents?'

'She has them. They're missing from the bank anyway. The only good part of it is the weather. They took off in the worst storm this year. For all we know, they've already smashed up.'

Roeder said nothing, just watched the road ahead. Geddes drove a big-engined Studebaker and he drove it fast, but somehow effetely. His hands were dressed in tan leather driving gloves and they slid around the rim of the steering wheel instead of gripping it and releasing it like a man.

Roeder half-closed his eyes. His attitude of relaxation wasn't a pose, it was for real. And why wouldn't it be? Despite the setbacks, the situation was under control. Rockwell and the Hamilton girl didn't know it, but their escape from Florida was meaningless. The stolen ledgers were already worthless, the two runaway pilots already dead.

The Firm would win, as the Firm would always win.

PART FIVE

Height and Speed

To most people, there are only two things about airplanes that scare them: height and speed. To pilots, however, there are only two things that make a plane safe enough to get into: height and speed.

Speed means air moving fast over the airplane's wings. Speed means lift. It means no risk of falling from the sky. It means the pilot has plenty to play with. It means the pilot can climb, dive, turn, manoeuvre, all without risk.

And height.

Just suppose the worst happens. Suppose the engine cuts out or a control wire snaps, the fuel pump jams. Where's the safest place to be when that happens? The answer's obvious. High up is the only safe place to be. At two, three, even five thousand feet, the world is a blanket spread out beneath the sky. The pilot can begin to glide, nose angled a little down, slowly circling as alternative landing sites offer themselves. To land safely, a biplane only needs a largish field. All a pilot needs to do is to pick a site, then wait. Why hurry? The view's great, there's no need to rush. When the field finally rises close enough to land on, the pilot simply glides in to land. Fields can be a little bumpier than a regular airfield, but who cares about bumps?

Of course, things don't always go so well.

Sod's law says that problems never happen when you're ready for them. Problems happen when you're flying low, close to the ground, when the engine's stuttering, when your airspeed's low.

Not enough speed. Not enough height. No room to manoeuvre and a loss of power. The pilot's nightmare. A recipe for death.

125

The intensity of the storm was literally stunning. Light left them. It wasn't pitch black, but the suddenness of the darkness was terrifying all the same. The ground below disappeared. The cloud was so thick that Pen couldn't see clear to the ends of the wingtips. Ahead of her, the flashing disc of the propeller was only barely visible in the tearing fog.

And the rain! The rain struck with the force of hailstones. Pen had found her flying clothes in the cockpit and struggled into them as soon as she could. But even so, her flying suit left the bottom half of her face unprotected and the exposed skin was instantly stinging and sore. Aircraft were designed for clear weather. They could take a little rain, but weren't designed to take much. Over the sound of the storm and engine combined, Pen could hear the wings sounding a new note under the driving rain.

Lightning flashed around them. Up there inside the thunderclouds, lightning wasn't as simple as a bolt or a flash. It was a change in the entire sky. One second there was blackness. The next moment Pen's entire field of view was completely filled with an awful yellowish glare that lasted an instant before vanishing again. In that chaos of sky, Pen kept her eyes fastened on the instrument panel. Like many planes of its type, the DH-4 had a dual set of controls so that it could be operated from the front or rear cockpits. The instrument panel was replicated in both cockpits. Pen read off the vital measurements.

Altitude: altering violently, but never less than two and a half thousand feet. Good.

Fuel: a three-quarters full tank. Abe must have been absolutely full before he'd left Marion. Good again.

Turn indicator and banking indicator: moving all the time, but shifting so fast and so unpredictably that they were hard to read. But as Pen kept her eye on the controls, she felt that perhaps – yes, quite likely – some kind of turn seemed indicated.

Pen swept her gaze across to the compass. When she'd learned to fly, she'd been taught to think of the compass ball itself as stationary, the needle always fixed on north. If the compass needle seemed to move, that wasn't because the needle was moving but because the plane was. Right now, the compass was seeming to swing clockwise, which meant that the plane was turning anti-clockwise. Slowly, slowly, Abe was bringing the plane around to head north-west. On that course, it would ride the curve of the storm inland – and hope at some stage to outrun the winds.

She didn't possess Abe's sense of hyper-alertness, but she too felt very calm. She was in a vastly dangerous situation, but she had long accustomed herself to the possibility of dying in a plane crash. The thought of being gunned down by one of Marion's thugs had been obnoxious beyond description. And there was Abe. She knew that perhaps no pilot in the world was better qualified to fly in these conditions than the man in the cockpit ahead of her. As the airplane surged and struggled, she felt only infinite trust, a kind of loving glow that connected her to him.

She barely glanced now at the destructive violence outside the cockpit. There was nothing to see there except swirling cloud. For all that the view out could tell her, the plane could be travelling north or south, east or west, it could be right-side up or upside down. It could be travelling dead straight for open sky, or dead straight for the ground below. In the giddy lurching of the airplane, Pen knew that she had to stop trusting the senses of her body. The human body tends to interpret any strong pull as gravitational. But there were too many other forces which confused things. Acceleration, deceleration, centripetal force all felt exactly the same as gravity. So did the shocking lifts and drops that were caused by sudden updrafts and downdrafts in the air. Any of those forces could be stronger than gravity, could simply cancel it out.

Pen ignored the blood pulsing in her head and concentrated. The altitude reading was good. Whatever other problems they had, there was plenty of empty sky beneath. Airspeed was worse. The gusting wind meant that the plane's speed was hard to control. There were moments when the wind suddenly betrayed the airplane, speed dropped away, the plane began to drop. Abe was doing a mighty job, but conditions were abominable.

Then the plane suddenly seemed to drop off a cliff. Pen experienced something like a little tremor running through the plane. The machine lost a thousand feet of altitude in a matter of seconds. Pen gulped – belched – and found herself vomiting that day's meal, seeing the solids flash over her shoulder and into the thick cloud behind. She wiped off her mouth, then her goggles. Some of the fog around had been from the spray of burned castor oil on her goggles. But there had been vomit there too, and something else, something red.

She put her hand to her head again and wiped carefully. Her hand came away with more red, little spatters of blood. And with the blood, little chips of red stone. She remembered the tremor that had hit the aircraft. Had she been struck by something? She kneaded her scalp. But her aviator's brain had already switched its attention to something else. The altitude needle was still dropping, not so fast now, but still inching down. They had less than eight hundred feet of height now. In normal cirumstances, that was plenty, but right now they were in extreme danger.

They'd just lost a thousand feet in a downdraft. If they did the same now, they'd smash into earth or ocean and be destroyed for sure.

A huge sheet of lightning filled the sky. The plane felt as though it was flying in the middle of the sheet. Lightning can't harm a plane, but the experience was eerie.

The altitude needle was still dropping. Six hundred feet. 'Abe? Abe?'

Pen yelled, knowing that Abe could never hear her. But even as she yelled, she guessed what had happened. It hadn't been her blood she'd found, but Abe's. Blood and stone that had spattered backwards from the front cockpit. Some heavy object must have been torn loose by the storm and must have struck Abe. Was he conscious or not? Dead or alive? There was no way to know, but one thing was certain, the plane was no longer under his control.

Pen swept into action. The rudder bar passed freely under her feet, but what she needed now wasn't the rudder, but the stick. The socket was right there in front of her, but the stick itself had been moved out of the way, strapped to the side of the cockpit. Pen fought the tight canvas straps. Arnie Hueffer was the world's best mechanic, but he was a man, and had a man's completely unreasonable view of how tight to make a strap. Pen fought the buckle.

The altitude was still dropping – and the compass was swinging around and around. Too fast. The lightning had probably disabled the compass. She looked at the turn and banking indicators, which seemed to indicate a tilt – not that she was sure she could trust the instruments under the current circumstances.

Pen looked up from the controls. Instinctively, she knew the problem. They were in a spin. Out of control and circling down.

Four hundred feet.

Somehow, she didn't know how, Pen freed the control stick. She jammed it in the socket. There was a bolt to thread in, a split pin to make it fast, but Pen had no time for that. Four hundred feet was an ugly enough height to attempt a spin recovery under any circumstances, but it was close to a death sentence when the control stick was out of position and the pilot was flying blind.

She reacted by instinct, by years of training.

She gave the plane a little forward stick to add airspeed, then gave the plane starboard rudder, opposite to the direction of spin. The big craft eased out of its deathly circle, but was continuing to race towards the ground. For one split second, Pen let the plane settle on its course, before pulling back on the stick. There was no view ahead. The altitude needle was so close to zero, that according to the needle she could have been driving along the highway. She pulled back harder, the big plane wrestling her for control. She could still see nothing, nothing but cloud.

And then she could.

Trees. Black topped trees, lashing furiously in the wind. Trees which would kill her if she touched them. She gave the plane full back stick, hoping and praying that it would respond.

126

Geddes had taken Roeder not to the Firm's K Street offices, but to the offices of the Inland Revenue Service. Senator Paulet had met them in the lobby, pacing up and down and smoking, flicking cigarette ash into the potted palms. Geddes had made the briefest possible introduction before the three men had walked unannounced into Jim Carpenter's fifth-floor office.

The conversation hadn't lasted long.

'We want McBride,' said Roeder. 'McBride and Bosse.'

'Mr Geddes, Senator,' said Carpenter, half-rising. 'I'm sorry, I don't –'

'McBride. Where is he?'

'Fourth floor, I'll call downstairs. Now listen, gentlemen, why not –?'

'He's not at his desk. He hasn't been in the office all day,' said Geddes. 'Nor Bosse.'

'Really? They ought to be here. I don't know where else they could be.'

'Why not?'

It was Roeder who spoke. At times like this, he had a habit of speaking very softly. So quietly, you could hardly catch his words. That meant people had to bend forwards, listen up, even quiet the sounds of their own breath if they wanted to hear him. Roeder's habit was a way of pointing up who had the power and who didn't. And Roeder did, not Carpenter.

'Sorry? What? Why not?' Carpenter licked his lips. He didn't know who Roeder was, but Senator Paulet was clearly minded to pay Roeder a lot of attention and Carpenter wasn't inclined to argue. 'I don't know why not. They ought to be here.'

'They report directly to you?'

'Yes, McBride does.'

'He's working on a major case? One that is coming close to completion?'

'Yes.'

'What case? Who is the target?'

'Hey, now. This investigation is confidential. I can't . . .'

Roeder pulled back with a flick of irritation. Paulet turned away from the window and towards Carpenter. 'You better believe you can, Carpenter. You want to hold on to your job, you better cooperate with a Senate investigation.'

'Mr Roeder, you mean? He works – you work – on behalf of the Senate?' Carpenter had turned to Roeder, but Paulet answered instead.

'I'm a Senator, aren't I? This is an investigation, isn't it?'

'Sure . . .' Carpenter's gaze wavered between the two men. There was something strange in the power structure. Paulet was the Senator, but it wasn't him calling the shots. 'Sure, OK.'

'Well?'

'The target of investigation? Right. Well, the fact is, McBride has played his cards pretty close to his chest. I've always insisted on confidentiality.'

Roeder leaned forwards. 'You don't know? You're telling me you don't know?'

'You dumb bastard, Carpenter. How's it gonna feel being fired and dumb?'

But Roeder was already heading for the door. If McBride wasn't here, they'd have to find him.

127

A cottonfield in Georgia, ploughed up and red under the aching sun.

A little way to the south and east, there's a storm coming in, but ahead of its violent battlements, there's a small plane, red and white painted, racing clear.

And it *is* clear. The storm is moving more slowly now. The plane does a hundred miles every hour, that's more than fifteen miles in ten minutes. After thirty minutes of excruciating flying, uncertain of her direction, struggling to hold height, and visibility not an inch beyond her propeller, Pen had seen a gap.

Or not a gap exactly. Not a clearing, not even a whitening in the cloud. But suddenly there had been some lessening in the darkness that surrounded her. Movement outstripping thought, she dived for the hole. The big plane had plunged through the air. For a split second she thought she had failed to escape – but then the gap appeared again: a glimpse of dirty soil far below and only a thin grey film of racing cloud in between. She plunged again for the opening and caught it.

With the storm massive over her head, she flew in the thin gap between earth and sky. But she had direction now. She could see where the landscape beyond shone gold and clear in the afternoon sun. She raced for the sunlight.

After putting enough clear distance between herself and the storm, Pen looked for a landing site and found one.

She set the plane down, jumped from her cockpit and ran to the forward one.

'Abe?' she shouted, 'Abe?'

The shape in the front of the plane stirred. Abe's face turned to hers.

There was blood sheeting the front of his goggles and more blood oozing from the flap of his flying helmet. But he was grinning. In his hand he held a red clay roof tile, broken in two. The tile must have struck him over the ear, concussed him, knocked him out.

'Abe, my love, you're OK, are you? You're fine?'

He nodded muzzily, but didn't answer her, not properly. 'Neat flying, kid.'

128

'Haggerty.'

'Ed, hi. This is my colleague, Jim Bosse. I don't think you've met.'

The three men – the two taxmen and the judge – touched hands briefly. They were in an old three-storey warehouse that fronted the Potomac. The warehouse had been built for the river trade, which had shrivelled away when the railroads arrived. The ground floor was still in use as a tobacco warehouse, and the fumes of the leaves scented the entire building. Upstairs, there was pretty much nothing at all, just bare brick walls, wooden board floors and tall iron-framed windows. It looked like a place where the after-noon sunlight came to die. But the building had power. It had space. And it had privacy.

A line of wooden tables ran under a row of unscreened bulbs. At the head of the line there was a big stack of card-board boxes. In the room, mostly seated at the tables, were half a dozen typists, four lawyers, an accountant, and Ed Styles, a judge of the District of Maryland Court.

Styles looked at the scene. His eyes had an odd way of taking hold of something then hanging on to it, no matter what. Right now, he hooked his gaze onto a secretary who was emptying and sorting one of the boxes. The secretary felt his gaze and her precise, orderly movements became flustered. McBride had known Styles since their college days together and he let the judge take his time. At last, the judge unhooked his gaze and transferred his attention to McBride and Bosse.

'What in Pete's name are you up to now?'

McBride didn't answer directly. He'd already briefed Styles somewhat over the phone.

'It's been a long haul getting here,' he said. 'And not my work mostly.'

'Tax evasion, huh?'

'We gotta stick 'em with something, Ed.'

Jim Bosse, nodding, muttered in agreement.

The judge walked over to one of the cardboard cartons and took the lid off. The carton, like all the others, was full of papers. Styles picked the first document from the box. The document was headed 'Powell Lambert Incorporated, IRS Statement March 6, 1922, Supplementary Material, Appendix IV.' The judge flipped through the document quickly. He put the document back, carelessly, not getting the edges to line up with the ones beneath. McBride, who couldn't tolerate disorder, put his hand into the box and straightened it.

Over to the side of the room, under one of the long windows, stood a little table with a Primus stove and a jug of hot coffee. Bosse poured three cups without milk. McBride meanwhile found some hoop-backed wooden chairs that looked like they belonged in a schoolroom and placed one in front of Styles. The judge took the cup and seat as though being released from a trance.

'Start me from the beginning, guys.'

'OK, it's like this,' said McBride. 'We've known for some time that we've been missing huge amounts of revenue. Vast amounts. It's taxation on criminal earnings, but the law doesn't make a distinction. Income is income. Tax is tax. And we're missing it. I'm not just talking about one-man bootlegging operations. I'm talking about substantial business organisations, large corporations in effect. We've known this for some time. Had hints from all over.'

Bosse indicated the box of documents that Styles had looked at.

'Want to know what that is? It's the federal tax returns filed by a Wall Street finance house, Powell Lambert. Now the funny thing is this. The firm seems to do well. Each year its business revenues are up. It owns some pretty nice real estate. Its payroll gets bigger each year. But it makes no profit. Hardly any. No profit it feels like it wants to pay tax on. We've audited them in the past. Hit the numbers pretty hard, but it all meshed. I had the feeling at the time we were missing something, and it turns out we were.'

'Booze.' Styles spoke the word not as a question, but as a statement of fact.

McBride nodded. 'Yes. We might never have made the connection, except for this guy, a flier, who crashes his plane in the middle of some hick town in Georgia. The locals there have got bootleggers for neighbours and aren't enjoying the experience. They ask this flier for help. He agrees. Now, how he gets where he gets is a long story. I don't think I know the half of it. But the point is, he makes the connection we've been looking for. He has a mountain of documents demonstrating that the local operation is making huge money out of bootlegging. Easily enough that they ought to be paying tax on it. Only they aren't. Of course they aren't. We asked him to go one step further and help us connect the local operation to the centre. He took a deep breath, but he went right ahead and did it. Him and some others. There was a girl as well. A flier too.'

'A girl? A pilot?'

'Yep.'

The table they were sitting at had a single drawer on McBride's side. He slid it open and pulled out four banking ledgers, bound in black cloth.

'I took delivery of these this morning. The girl managed to obtain them from a local bank. The two fliers arrived here this morning, first thing, by airplane naturally enough.'

'Bank records.'

'Right, bank records. These books show huge finance flows from Powell Lambert in New York down to Marion in Georgia. We can trace those cash flows on from there to Havana, Cuba. We have a signed, notarised deposition from the Havana buying agent affirming what those monies were used for. We have a complete picture of the Marion side of things. With these records, I think we can demonstrate that Powell Lambert is involved up to its eyeballs and beyond.'

Styles had his eyes hooked on the bank ledgers now. When he blinked, his eyelids drooped slowly and heavily like a man about to fall asleep, before rising again the same way.

'And you want what?'

'A search warrant, Ed. A handful of them, in fact. And arrest warrants. The sooner the organisation is headless, the better our chance of smashing it completely.'

'You've got a list?'

McBride tossed a couple of typed sheets across the table. The list began with Powell Lambert: its Wall Street office, its Washington office, its handful of regional offices. Every name and address spelled out in full, just the way a lawyer liked it. But then there were other names too. Edward 'Ted' Powell. Junius H. Thornton. Their addresses, town and country. And other names too. The names of the bank's senior officers. The name Willard T. Thornton, the boss's son. The name Robert Mason, with an address in Marion, Georgia. Fifteen names altogether.

'Each one of these?'

'Uh-huh.'

'That's not a handful of warrants, that's a plateful.'

'A plateful, then. And if we get these, Ed, we'll locate material which leads us to more people. And those people will lead us to others.'

'Right. Including folk that live right here in Washington.'

'Right.'

'Including some that work in a big white building on a hill.'

'Right.'

Styles whistled again. 'You've got all your evidence here?'

'Yep.'

'I'm gonna need help. I'm no accountant, Hag. It's not that I don't trust you, but we gotta do this properly. There's no point in cutting corners, then finding your guys wiggle out of a charge because we didn't do things right.'

McBride went silent and Jim Bosse continued instead. He pointed down the tables to the men in suits.

'We've laid on four accountants for you, Judge. They're all well acquainted with court procedure. We've got lawyers too, secretarial support. You need help looking things up, getting clear on points of law, we've got everything we need right here in this room.'

'It's gonna take time.'

'It can't.'

'Two weeks.'

'Two days.'

Styles shook his head. He addressed McBride directly. 'You've asked for fifteen warrants, Hag. That's fifteen cases you got to prove.'

'And I need all of them together. If we hit one address early, we'll never find nothing in the rest.'

'Why two days? What's the rush?'

'These ledgers. We'd hoped to sneak these out so no one saw. We failed. They saw.'

'Hence this place.' Styles gestured at the grimy building, the rickety tables, the bare bulbs, the Primus stove.

'Right.'

'Two days?'

'Less if we can manage it.'

Styles shook his head. 'We'd better get to work, Hag.'

129

Pen sat on a train, steaming north.

Little by little the landscape changed under her gaze. Long gone were the red fields and baked cottonfields of the south. In their place were the smokestacks and dark industrial buildings of the north-east. The deep green of pine trees began to speckle the clearer greens and browns of the deciduous forests. She was heading north, heading for the Canadian border and safety.

She travelled under her own name, Miss Penelope Hamilton. She had her passport in an inside pocket and two thousand dollars, cash. Although she had friends in Toronto, she wouldn't stay with them. She'd rent a car, move around, stay in no one place for long.

And for now, she didn't need to think about the future. She was happy to let the miles run away under the train and not think too much. Ordinarily, a train stifled her. She hated the stuffy cramp of a train compartment, compared with the speed and openness of the skies. Often enough in the past, she'd let her family or servants travel by rail with her baggage, while she'd flown on ahead by airplane.

But things were different now.

Just for a while, she'd had enough of flying. And, what's more, for the first time in her life, she was in love, and in love with a man who was as perfect for her as she was for him. He'd never stop flying, of course. She wouldn't ask him to, wouldn't want him to. But maybe the kind of flying he'd do would change. Arnie Hueffer wanted to design airplanes. Abe wanted to help, wanted to be test pilot to the planes Arnie built. There was a future there, a good one. There was no money in airplane design, of course. Not a dime. But that hardly mattered. Pen had plenty.

The train slid forwards. The north drew closer. Pen dreamed or dozed. She travelled alone because Abe wasn't with her yet. He was in Washington, lying low, with one last thing still to do.

130

'Shawcross?'

'Yeah, got him. Fishing trip. Seems for real.'

'Seems?'

'Left ten days ago. Planned from way back.'

'Says who?'

'We got to one of the maids. Boss, it ain't Shawcross.'

'OK.'

Roeder nodded. His clotted eye with its purple iris was sometimes made painful by excessive light and he had pulled down the blinds in his K Street office window so that the room was heavily shaded. Even so, he sat turned from the window, staring into the deep shadows that edged the room.

His task in Washington was simple. The two fliers had made their way through to McBride. McBride was presumably holed up somewhere right now with a stack of incriminating documents working to get the warrants that he needed to proceed further. Over in New York, Ted Powell had told his subordinates to inventory their documents, ready to destroy the most dangerous. But nobody wanted to take such a step if it could possibly be avoided. The thing was to stop McBride.

And clever though McBride might be, he had a chink in his armour. To get the warrants, he needed a judge. If Roeder could find the judge, he'd have found McBride.

Roeder went back to his list. Thompson, Roeder's chief

lieutenant, stood ankle-deep in the shadows, waiting for his boss.

'How about Styles?' asked Roeder. 'We got a fix on him yet?'

'No.'

'No?'

'We ain't got a fix on him, but he ain't at home and he ain't at work.'

'Ha! How long?'

'Thirty hours.'

'OK. Keep on looking –'

'And that ain't all.'

'Huh?'

'We just found out. They're friends. Him and McBride. They boxed together at college. They go way back.'

'Hah! It's him.'

'Yeah, boss, it's him.'

Roeder stared down at the dim carpet, red and violet, on the floor. He pushed something that didn't exist with his toe, out in front of him, as though to see it better.

'OK,' he said, 'we know what we gotta do.'

Thompson nodded and slid silently from the room. He knew all right, he knew.

131

Willard felt like the ugly sister at the dance.

Washington was filling with men from Roeder's private army. If Willard was anywhere there was something going on, he was in the way. If he was any place else, he was ignored completely. In the meantime, the Wall Street office was being turned upside down, crisis meetings were being held every day, every hour. The world, it seemed, was in turmoil and Willard had no part to play.

Except this.

He had either saved the Firm or he had ruined it.

He'd been the first one to warn against Rockwell. He'd disposed of Lundmark, scared off Hennessey, cleaned Marion, hired pilots, taken precautions. He'd brought the whole Rockwell-Hamilton-Marion business right to the forefront of the Firm's attention. That was the list of his achievements, and it was a good one, one that should earn him plenty of credit.

But there were also negatives, or one in particular. Roeder had wanted to kill Rockwell right away. Willard had refused.

Maybe that fact wouldn't be enough to damn him. Maybe the credit list would blot out that single negative. Only maybe not. Willard couldn't tell. He couldn't get his father to speak to him. He'd spoken to Powell on the phone, but only briefly and not in any way that meant anything. Was Willard still the natural inheritor of Powell Lambert?

Or would his father, ruthless as ever, choose to blame his son?

Willard didn't know. He had no way of knowing.

In his pocket, he still carried an envelope containing the liner ticket, passport and money. If Willard could have thought of a way to get them to his old commander, then he would have done. But he couldn't. He knew the whole dangerous game was in its last explosive stages, but how to get Captain Rockwell to a place of safety, he just couldn't work out.

Also one other not-so-little fact. Willard had been dumped by his fiancée. And nobody knew. Nobody was interested enough in Willard to give a damn. There was literally only one person in the world whom Willard had confided in: little Annie Hooper, all the way over in New York.

And she'd been a sweetheart. She'd cried on his behalf, with immediacy and naturalness. She'd taken his side. She'd comforted him. There was a tone in her voice which expressed astonishment that any woman in the world could be lunatic enough to ditch Willard. It wasn't a lot to boast about, maybe, but there was at least one person in the world, Annie Hooper, who still thought that Willard was really quite a guy. In time perhaps, he'd get consolations from elsewhere. Other friends. Family. Other girls. But in the meantime, it mattered. He spoke to Annie at least once a day. Usually twice or three times. They told each other things they wouldn't have said to anyone else. Each time he got off the phone to her, he found himself thinking about her a little more.

And in the meantime?

In the meantime, he was forced to hang around Washington like the ugly sister at the dance. He got drunk in his hotel room. He visited the museums. He got Gregory, the chauffeur, to take him on car rides into the country. On one occasion, they'd driven out to nowhere in particular.

Willard had produced a bottle of whiskey bought from the hotel bellboy, and the two men had got shit-faced together, Willard and his driver, master and servant. Normally, Willard had contempt for men who let themselves go to that extent.

But not now, not at the moment. Because things weren't normal. Things were anything but.

132

Judge Styles kept to his word. He'd promised McBride to be done in forty-eight hours and he would be. He'd put in the kind of hours that would have exhausted a man twenty years younger. He worked hard, slept little, worked through the evidence.

And the evidence was dynamite!

Deep in the piles of facts and numbers, tax returns and accounting estimates, there emerged the picture of a criminal organisation so huge that even Bosse and McBride were taken aback. In his heart, Styles had no doubt that there was enough evidence to justify each one of the search warrants that the two taxmen had asked for. But the law isn't about hearts and hunches. Both men knew that the warrants would be challenged in court, by expensive lawyers with ruthless clients. There were legal hoops to be jumped through and they had to be jumped right.

But Styles was a lawyer to his fingertips. He knew his procedures. He knew what would work and what wouldn't. He read the documents, made summaries, dictated his notes with patient, unrelenting, forensic brilliance.

And once, just once, he'd gone home. He'd dropped straight into bed, slept for three hours, then woken up, exhausted but refreshed. He'd showered, dressed, and driven back the way he'd come.

McBride had begged the judge not to leave. Styles had insisted. Then McBride had begged Styles at least to be careful on his return. He told the judge to assume that he was being followed. He'd insisted that Styles take Jim Bosse to look out for him. And Styles agreed.

All the time the judge had been at home, even the three hours that he'd been lying in bed asleep, Jim Bosse – the taxman with a farmboy smile – had been patrolling the dark perimeters of the judge's garden, with an ex-army revolver loosely holstered at his hip. Bosse never once closed his eyes. Though every bit as short of sleep as the rest of them, he'd stayed alert and watchful the entire time. And on the long and circuitous drive back to the warehouse, Bosse told the judge how to drive, when to accelerate hard, when to brake to a halt, when to feint left or right, when to double back on his tracks without warning. On two occasions, a car seemed to be following them for a short distance, but both times it moved away again just as Bosse had started to get uncomfortable. Aside from that, they saw nothing. It was just before dawn and not many people were around, not many cars. Bosse thought it had gone OK. He hoped.

133

A knock at the door.

It was dawn, or almost. A thin grey light tested the edges of Willard's curtains. A thin grey light tested the edges of the hangover which was kicking like the hind legs of a mule.

He sat up in bed, unsure if he'd heard what he'd heard.

Then it came again. A small knock. Timid. The second knock even quieter than the first. The suite was large and the door was in the living room, so Willard could only just hear the sound at all.

Who the hell arrived anywhere at dawn? Who the hell knocked like that?

Willard moved in bed. His hangover caught him before he'd moved far. That was the trouble with Prohibition. You could pay top dollar for your hooch, but unless you were damn sure where the booze came from, you could still find yourself drinking something only one shade different from poison. Willard groaned and rolled over. He'd ignore the knock, whoever it came from.

But the person outside must have heard him move or groan.

Willard knew that because of the silence, the silence which was suddenly charged because it was shared. He became scared. What if McBride had beaten Roeder? If he had, then the person outside could easily be a federal agent.

His head told him that federal agents didn't knock like

pussycats, probably they didn't even knock at all. But his heart wasn't always connected to his head, and right now his heart was doing one-twenty beats to the minute. What if it wasn't the cops, but one of Roeder's men with an urgent message? Or the hotel bellhop, warning him to get the hell out?

Willard rolled out of his bed, scared white and cursing himself. He found a robe, pulled it on, got the sleeves muddled, set them right, tied the cord, entered the living room and went to the door. He stood with his hand on the handle, listening to the other person just outside. He remembered once being like this with Rosalind. The time she'd been in her Temperance Army uniform and had rung the bell outside his apartment door. The memory hurt. He swung down hard on the handle, yanked open the door.

It wasn't cops. It wasn't Roeder. It wasn't the bellhop. It wasn't Rosalind.

'Gosh, Annie, gosh!'

She had her hand up ready to knock a third time. Then the door had opened so suddenly, that she almost fell into the space it left. She actually rocked forwards so that Willard had to put a hand out to steady her. *She was so small*, he thought, physically small, like a member of a species subtly but definitely different to the one Willard was a part of.

'Sorry.'

She stepped back. She had a small travelling bag at her feet, small and cheap.

'Annie . . .'

'Oh, I'm sorry, it's terribly early, isn't it? I should have waited, I know. There was some problem with the train engine on the way down. We didn't get in until very late. I didn't want to come until later, only I was on my own, I didn't know where to go . . .'

It wasn't much of an explanation, really. Why had she come at all, was the question which needed answering, not

572

why she had chosen to arrive at dawn. All the same, Willard thought of little Annie wandering the streets of Washington and he instinctively pulled her into the room.

'That's good. It's fine. Don't worry, I usually get up around now anyway,' – a lie – 'look, do sit down. No, take the chair or, no, I'm being silly, I've got a suite, we may as well go next door.'

He ushered Annie to one of the suite's large, heavily cushioned sofas. It was just about light enough to be worth opening the curtains, but he didn't want to, not yet. They sat down. Annie primly removed her little travelling cap and laid it down beside her. She smiled anxiously. He smiled back reassuringly.

'Tea? Coffee?'

'Oh, I don't . . .'

She looked around, her eyes searching for a kitchen, or at least a kettle, but not finding one. Willard guessed this was probably her first time in a hotel room, let alone a suite as grand as this one. He picked up the phone and asked for room service.

'Are you hungry?' he asked her. ' You must be famished. It's hungry work travelling, I don't know why.' He was connected to room service. 'Breakfast for two please, something hot, plenty of coffee – fruit, Annie? Do you like fruit? – Yes, and some fruit, please, whatever you've got.'

The guy on the other end of the phone knew Willard a little – or at least, he'd sold him some booze – and allowed himself to smirk.

'You got company, sir? Sure. You want anything with your breakfast? Anything to drink?'

'No, no, no. Just breakfast, right away, please.'

Willard hung up. Something in him softened at the sight of Annie. She loved him, of course. He knew that. Perhaps he'd known it for a long time, but during their phone conversations of the last few days, it had become obvious to them both, a knowledge shared though unspoken.

And it was more than love. She loved him, but she also adored him, did so knowing, as Rosalind had never known, about his weaknesses as well as his strengths. She'd known his impatience, his tantrums, his petulance, his vanity. She knew the dark secret of the people he worked for. She knew that he worked for Powell Lambert not because he was obliged to but because he chose to. And still she loved him. Still adored him.

He smiled at her with his eyes. He'd be gentle with her. Even if he slept with her, he'd be careful of her feelings afterwards.

'You haven't exactly told me why you came,' he said gently.

'You don't mind?'

'Not at all. I'm pleased.'

'I came because . . . I don't know. The office, Wall Street, it's all upside down. They've sent everyone home. Almost everyone, anyway. Before we went, we had to get all our papers together. Lots of it was taken away. I think they mean to burn it.' She looked nervous. Her hand found her hat, touching it as though to reassure herself that she could leave quickly if she needed to. 'Is it . . .? I mean, I guess it's because . . .?'

He nodded. 'Yes, Annie. They're worried about the feds. There's a possibility – a very, very small one – that the Firm could be in trouble. Ted Powell is taking every precaution necessary to make sure that doesn't happen.'

'I see.'

Annie's eyes blinked. One second they were wide and worried, but perfectly clear. The next moment, they were full of tears and crying hard, though soundlessly. Willard realised she was worried about his safety, but not only that. She was worried for herself too. He actually had to repress a smile at the thought of the feds taking an interest in little Annie Hooper. He waited until her tears were over, then passed her a handkerchief.

'Sorry. I'm being silly. I didn't know where to go. I was scared.'

'You don't need to be. But I'm pleased you came.'

Breakfast arrived. Annie was hungry, but she was more tired than hungry. She ate some fruit, started on some eggs and bacon, but didn't get far. She yawned. The yawn made the little freckles on her cheeks bunch up, then relax. Her light brown hair was very fine and had got a little rumpled on her journey. She kept smoothing it into place with her fingers. Willard got up, smiling. He kissed her full on the top of her head. Her hair felt very warm, very soft, very clean.

'You finish that later,' he said. 'Right now, I'm going to put you to bed.'

134

The tall windows were griddled by little iron panes. When the first sunshine of the day came down across the Potomac it sketched those panes one by one across the board floor, the wooden tables, the bare brick wall. Styles had a slice of bread in one hand, a cup of coffee in another. His eyes were hooded, almost closed, but his voice and mind were as clear as polished glass.

'You were retained by Robert Mason on what date?'

Abe had his back against one hoop-backed chair, his legs stretched out across two others. In that last, crazy flight from Jacksonville, he had brought nothing with him except the clothes he stood up in. So, slightly incongruously, he wore flying boots, some borrowed flannel trousers, his own white shirt, open at the neck, and his flying jacket unfastened. This was the final stage of Styles' examination of the evidence: the opportunity to interrogate the principal witness. Styles had already had Abe confirm his identity, his war record, his haul of medals, including his Congressional Medal of Honour. The facts were already well-known to Styles, but his interrogation placed the whole thing on record, transcribed verbatim by a pair of stenographers beside him.

Abe lit a cigarette as he answered Styles' question. 'I was retained on 1 August 1926.'

'And the nature of your arrangement?'

'Mason paid me four hundred dollars a week to fly goods for him, Havana to Miami, six days a week.'

'The nature of those goods?'

'Primarily alcohol, but other items too. Gold watches, jewellery, cash and securities, other high-value items.'

'To your knowledge, was the importation of those other items ever declared to the United States Customs authorities?'

'I am certain that they were not so declared.'

'And the volumes of alcohol transported by you during that period?'

Abe answered with precision.

The two men had entered a kind of intuitive double-act. Styles already knew all the answers. Abe already knew all the questions. The only purpose of the conversation was to have itself put on record, one more defence against the legal challenges that would lie on down the road. McBride was close by, his prosecutorial mind rejoicing in the accumulation of destructive evidence. Jim Bosse was over by the door on the main staircase, listening out and smoking.

Then suddenly, he stiffened.

With one elastic movement he took the cigarette from his mouth, threw it to the floor and trod it out. For one brief second, he stood at the door, his fingertips pressed against it as though they were some kind of listening device, then he stepped quickly back. He whistled twice. The hum of business in the room was instantly silenced. Everyone looked up. Unholstering his gun, Bosse moved quickly to a position sheltered by the swing of the door. He held the gun out with both hands, his knees bent and legs apart.

For a second, everything was silent.

Then everyone heard it. Steps moving rapidly up the concrete staircase. Bodies fanning out just the other side of the door. The sudden silence seemed loaded down with threat, as though a wild animal were moving outside.

The only person who moved at all was Abe.

Moving as though he were a dancer running through long-choreographed movements, he snatched up a carton of documents – Powell Lambert financial documents, which were on record in a dozen other locations – and threw the contents in a wide semicircle across the floor. McBride and the judge stared at him, uncomprehending. Still not losing a moment, Abe snatched up the little Primus stove they'd been using to brew coffee. The tank was still half-full and there was a flask of further fuel if needed. Abe took both. As he moved, he spoke to the taxman and the judge. 'Get all the papers out of the window. And meantime, get everyone back through there. Call the fire service as soon as you find a phone.'

He jabbed his hand behind him, to the wall furthest from Jim Bosse, where there was a small wooden door leading to a second staircase. There was no exit from the building that way, but there was access into the main tobacco warehouse and a ramshackle collection of offices and outbuildings. The complex was large enough and crowded enough that at least some people would be able to find hiding places from even a large team of searchers. As the two men began hurling boxes of papers out of the window, there was the sudden bellow of gunfire.

Jim Bosse, at his post by the door, had watched the handle begin to turn. As it did so, he leaped forward and pumped three bullets at chest height through the wooden door. There was nothing. No cry. No muffled groan. No sound of a body slumping to the floor. Just a tiny pause before a torrent of automatic gunfire ripped through the woodwork, almost sawing the door in half horizontally. Jim Bosse, somehow, had managed to leap back in time but there were screams from elsewhere in the room.

Following Abe's urgent signals, most of the lawyers and accountants and secretaries had begun piling out through the rear door. Abe guessed that the screams were mostly of fear, not of pain, but he didn't spare the time to look. Instead, he just ran down the line of strewn paper pouring kerosene over it. Behind him, McBride, together with couple of helpers, was beginning to hurl the other boxes of evidence out of the window. They emptied the boxes as they threw, making sure that the precious papers were scattered over as wide an area as possible. It wasn't a windy morning, but there was enough breeze to send the papers rustling and fluttering across the dirty Tarmac. The first few pages began to fall into the Potomac, where they lay, as though flattened by a smoothing iron, moving slowly downstream on the turbid current.

There was more shooting at the door.

As the first boot began to smash the collapsing door away, Bosse fired again and again. He probably scored a hit with every shot, but if so it was a brief victory. There was another smashing hail of gunfire. Bosse was physically lifted on the stream of bullets, was carried backwards, was deposited on the floor, a smashed, bloody, unrecognisable thing.

Abe put a match to his papers. Flame rippled along the paper ring. Smoke and flame filled the air. The room was now divided in two. The door and the broken shape of Jim Bosse was on one side. The rest of the room lay on the other. Box after box of papers was hurtling outside, but there wasn't much left to go. The room was mostly clear of people now. Abe wanted the judge and McBride to get the hell out. Abe began throwing chairs and tables onto the flames.

But he was out of time. Men were now pouring through the door into the room. Around half of the men carried Tommy guns. The rest all carried handguns of some description. But the wall of flame was right in their faces. Their onward surge through the door had brought them directly into the heat and smoke of the blaze. The open windows at one end and the smashed-open door at the other end of the room formed a perfect tunnel for a draught, which fanned the heat and smoke in the direction of the attackers.

More people fled through the door at the back.

But, as Abe had known, the flames would be a diversion and a delay, little more. On the far side of the blaze, a short man, with the unmistakable authority of a leader, took stock of the situation, then gestured forwards. His men collected themselves and ran forwards through the smoke. A Tommy gun jabbed into Abe's ribs and threw him against the wall. Abe looked around to check who had managed to get away. Nearly everyone was the answer. The judge had made it out. It was only Abe himself, Jim McBride and two of the accountants who hadn't got out in time. The four of them were backed up against the open windows, by the low table that held the coffee pot.

The short man's face flickered with a smile. Abe guessed that he was the chief of Powell Lambert's peculiarly nasty police. Putting two and two together from some of the financial documents they'd been studying, Abe guessed him to be the 'Vice President of Insurance', Dorcan Roeder. Roeder sent half a dozen of his men off through the back door to go and search for the escapees in the warehouse. He sent another two men downstairs to start collecting up the paper which was blowing about on the asphalt outside. Abe felt a tiny, temporary jab of triumph. Picking the paper up from outside would take a lot more than two men, but, with his force as divided as it was, Roeder couldn't yet afford to send more. The insurance man's eyes blinked at the eddying smoke. Then he put his revolver away in his pocket and approached his prisoners.

'Judge Styles?' he asked, raising his eyebrows.

Nobody spoke.

'Mr McBride?'

Abe hoped that McBride would keep his mouth shut, but the taxman was too proud.

'I'm McBride. My colleague, Jim Bosse, is lying dead over there. Judge Styles has already made his exit. These two men –' he indicated the two accountants '– have been assisting us on points of detail. They're not more than partially aware of the case against Powell Lambert. I will ask them to keep silent about all this, and I therefore request you to let them go.'

'Nice. Nice speech. But they can stay . . .' Roeder approached Abe, coming up close, just a few inches away. 'Captain Rockwell, how nice to meet you.'

Roeder didn't make it a question, or a statement, or even a greeting. It was a gloat, pure and simple, the gloat of a predator pleased with its trapped and cornered prey. The man's eyes were strange, Abe noticed. One eye was inflamed, had dark clots over a purple iris. Abe saw the way the man had difficulty looking directly into the light from the windows, and he shifted position carefully so he was framed against the wide and empty pane behind him.

Roeder looked away. The fire didn't have the rage of a paper blaze now, but the tables and chairs were still sending up a crackling heat and bursts of sparks and smoke. Abe noticed some of the timber rafters beginning to blacken with the heat. Beneath the fire too, the floorboards were beginning to be eaten away. Roeder's bad eye was giving him trouble. He rubbed it once, making it worse. The men with Tommy guns stood silently watching their boss, waiting for instructions.

Abe nudged McBride's foot with his boot. His thumb turned backwards, indicating the window. It would be a huge jump, possibly a bone-breaking one or worse, but the alternatives waiting inside the room were hardly better.

'No,' said McBride in a loud, confident voice. 'Not me, you.'

Roeder's eyes leaped to the taxman, suspicious and calculating. Part of him – the sadistic, blood-delighting part – visibly wanted to prolong his moment of triumph. The other part, the professional servant of the Firm, decided it was better to get the job done fast and smoothly. He indicated the two accountants, and spoke to a couple of his men, 'Get them down there, hands and feet tied, stand guard.'

The two men took the accountants down to a corner of the still-burning room.

Now it was just Roeder and four guards left for Abe and McBride. He was clearly planning to kill them then and there.

'May I smoke?' said Abe, gesturing at his pocket.

Roeder didn't say yes or no, but he took one pace back, expecting trickery. Four Tommy guns tightened their aim on Abe's forehead. He felt his skin freeze, knowing his face was taut and empty. Trying to act normally, he fished slowly in his pocket, making no sharp or sudden movements, and drew out cigarettes and matches. He took one out, lit it, and inhaled. Then, as he was returning the boxes of cigarettes and matches to his pocket, his hand trembled briefly and he dropped them both.

'Sorry,' he said.

He got down on his knees to pick them up. He was the only moving thing in a silent room. Down low, the air didn't have the fierce heat of the fire in it, but the air still pricked with the sharp smell of unburned soot. Abe could feel four sets of eyes and guns following his every move.

And then he did it. The magic show of his career. He reached for the packet of cigarettes. He allowed his right hand to close over them – or seemingly close over them – while in reality, a sharp flick, concealed by the sleeve of his jacket, sent them into his lap. He held his right hand out and opened it: nothing.

He hardly dared to breathe. All conjurors, even the best, like to practise their tricks before exposing them to an audience. It's no use having a general facility for sleight-of-hand, you need to know the exact weight of the item you're using for the trick. Even substituting one deck of cards for the one he'd practised with could cause Abe difficulties – and he'd never even taken his limited interest in conjuring beyond fooling around with playing cards.

All the same, he had one thing on his side. Just as

conjurors need to train to do tricks, people need to train to see through them. It's not that easy to do. People see the laws of nature being bent under their eyes. They almost can't help but watch.

Abe put out his left hand. The cigarette box was there now – but empty. It had been full just moments before. Abe dropped the box. He showed one hand, then the other: no cigarettes. He began to straighten, right up by Roeder's feet now. He shook the cigarettes invisibly from his sleeve to his right hand, which his audience still took to be empty. Still straightening, he fluttered his hand. Cigarettes seemed to fall out of thin air across the floor.

'Funny guy,' said Roeder, moving back.

'I try.'

Abe stepped back.

Misdirection: the oldest and best of the stratagems of war. Even though Roeder's eyes had been gluey with suspicion, he'd looked the wrong way. While he and everyone else had been looking at the fluttering cigarettes, Abe had used his left hand to sneak the gun from Roeder's pocket. It was in his waistband now, at the back. He backed into Haggerty McBride and felt the taxman's fingers take the gun. Abe paused for a second, to give the taxman time.

'So long, buddy,' he whispered.

Then he moved. He stepped back to the window sill. McBride's gun barked sharply once – twice – a third time – but Abe heard nothing more.

His first leap took him to the window ledge. The next leap took him well beyond.

From inside the room, it seemed as though his leap took him into the clear blue light outside and nothing else. But Abe had already checked his position. Five yards beneath him and as many as three or four yards to the side, an old rusted winch jutted out over the Tarmac. Abe jumped with all the spring his legs could provide. He sailed through the air – a moment of terrifying freedom – then, just as he thought he'd misjudged, his outstretched hands found the rasp of blunt metal. His fingers locked. The swing of his body threatened to tear him away, but he hung on until he could hook his legs over the diagonal support strut. Up above now, he heard shooting: not the snap of McBride's revolver, but the long roar of Tommy guns. McBride too was dead now: joining Brad Lundmark and Jim Bosse among the heroes who had died to help Abe.

Steady now, and feeling his fear for the first time, Abe slid down the rusty steel to the red brick wall. He was still twenty feet above ground and there was little or nothing to help him down. Hanging at full stretch, so his feet were perhaps a dozen feet above ground, he dropped. Landing like a parachute jumper – legs bent and ready to roll – he hit the ground hard but OK.

Roeder had two men down there on the waterfront in between the warehouse and the Potomac. But they were downwind, trying to catch the swirling papers as the wind lifted them. They had looked up at the noise of shooting, but hadn't noticed Abe's figure dropping in the shadows under the old winch. Down on the asphalt, there was a litter of broken glass from the windows above and a mass of documents – mostly the heavier ones, that hadn't yet been lifted by the wind.

Abe knew what he was looking for and found it quickly

One of the black-bound banking ledgers; the most recent of them; the one that hadn't yet been completely filled in There were other priceless pieces of evidence lying close a hand, but Abe couldn't afford to waste a moment.

He snatched up the ledger and began to run.

There was a shout from the windows above and bullet began to spatter the ground away and to the left of Abe The hum and zing of ricochets filled the air. But for th gunmen above, the shooting wasn't easy. The angle wa bad, worsening all the time, and perhaps McBride ha managed to do some damage before he'd died.

There was another burst of fire, closer this time, but Abe had reached an alley at the end of the warehouse. He ran into it, lungs bursting, but close to safety now. Somewhere a long way away still, he could hear fire engines clanging their bells. He guessed that someone had managed to find a phone and get help. The fire service would make life tough for the mobsters. The people now trapped in the bottom section of the warehouse would be able to get clear to safety. Maybe the fire service would collect up the fluttering documents; bundle them up and take them downtown for processing.

But those were subsidiary thoughts. Abe's priority lay elsewhere now, close by, as though destined.

135

Willard sprawled on the sofa in his bathrobe.

He had eaten his own breakfast and had begun picking at Annie's. His hangover still muttered at the edge of his brain. The curtains were still drawn, the light outside still unwelcome, the room inside still dark. Next door, Annie was asleep and would be for some time.

What to do?

Willard hadn't really slept enough, but he was too awake now to think of returning to sleep. His hangover was a nuisance, but he didn't feel ready to take the few glugs of whiskey which would drive it back into hiding. Really, he wanted to get up, do something, be useful, but both his father and Ted Powell still wanted him sidelined.

The whole Rosalind mess stirred uneasily at the back of his mind. Even now, nobody knew or cared that Rosalind had dumped her fiancé. The odd thing was how strangely unmoved Willard seemed to be. At one level, he felt a breeze of sudden freedom. He felt relieved. But at another level he felt flat dismay. He remembered some of those old, scary interviews with his father – about his bad results at Princeton, about his move into movies, about the disaster of *Heaven's Beloved*. And this time promised to be the same. Junius Thornton wouldn't say much. What he said would sting. What he didn't say would sting even more. His son had been dumped. The news would be public. There was no explanation.

Willard's solution to the problem was an old one. He didn't think about it. At some point, he'd have to, but that point wasn't yet. In the meantime, he had no idea how he had ended up with his former secretary curled up in the bedroom next door, but he liked it that she was. He looked forward to the moment when she woke up. They'd have sex together, of course, but nothing brash, nothing showy. Willard would enjoy having a different sort of relationship. Something quieter, more private, intimate.

He poked at the mess of egg on Annie's plate. The egg was cold and hard, like the light outside. He picked up a slice of bacon in his fingers and ate it. Then he threw himself back on the sofa, a cup of coffee within easy reach.

He lay like that for a minute or two, then became aware of something strange in the room. A little chill of fear swept through Willard's body. He caught his breath, then jolted himself upright.

Over in the corner of the room, between door and window, there was a man, no more than middling height, not large, very close-cropped blond hair, motionless and silent. The window was open a crack and the thin curtain moved a little in the draught. For one idiotic moment, Willard wondered whether the man had come in by the door or through the window, from the sky itself. The two men stared at each other for a quarter of a second. Willard's throat was too tight to speak. Then the newcomer moved.

'Willard, hi!'

Abe walked forwards, smiling. Long afterwards, that was how Willard would remember him: in that first moment, smiling.

'Gosh – sir! – I mean Captain.'

Willard thrust his legs to the floor, stood up, raised his hand in what started out as a military salute and ended as a strange kind of wave.

'When you dropped that note to me, the one you enclosed

with the movie poster, you said I should look you up. I hope now's OK.'

'Gee, Captain, I didn't hear you knock. How did you get in for that matter? The door was locked, wasn't it?'

Abe smiled, dangled a passkey from his hand, and dropped it into his pocket. This was the man Willard remembered: the pilot who was always in the right part of the sky at the right time; the pilot who couldn't be followed, couldn't be tracked.

'Is that coffee?' said the airman.

'Yes, you want some?'

'Please.'

'You want milk? Sugar? The pot's gotten a little cold. We took breakfast kind of early. If you want, I could call room service. They're not always too fast, but I could hurry 'em up, if you –'

'Black. It's fine. I don't mind it cold.'

Willard poured coffee from the hotel's silver coffee pot into a white porcelain coffee cup. He put the cup on its tiny saucer and passed it over to his one-time commander. While cup and saucer were in Willard's hand, they jigged a tinkling dance of nervousness. When Abe took the saucer, the cup went instantly still.

Abe smiled again.

'Nice suite.'

'Yes, it's OK, isn't it?' said Willard, before instantly regretting the word 'OK'. He knew his old commander had never been well-off before, wasn't well-off now. This suite must seem like an unthinkable luxury to him. 'I mean, it's great, really. Terrific.'

'May I?'

Abe pointed to a small wooden chair with a covered seat.

'Huh, sorry? Oh, sure.' Willard had already sat down, but now got half-up again, waved at Abe to sit, then sat again. 'Sorry.'

'I called unexpectedly.'

'No, that's fine. I wasn't doing much . . .'

Willard gulped. His brain was in turmoil.

Here was the situation. Abe Rockwell had voluntarily walked into Willard's room. Willard was bigger, stronger, younger, taller. Abe would hardly be a pushover, but if Willard really wanted to, he was pretty sure he could jump on Rockell, fight him, beat him – capture him, in fact. To put it bluntly, Powell Lambert's most dangerous enemy had placed himself in Willard's power.

But here was the strange thing: Willard had no impulse to do anything of the sort. Get up and punch Abe Rockwell in the face? It was unthinkable. He'd likelier punch his own father. Meantime, though he knew he ought to call someone, or interrogate his visitor, or do something, he did nothing at all. He just got tongue-tied, embarrassed, flustered.

'Things OK on Wall Street?'

'Sure. Yes. Fine. Busy, always busy.'

'I'm sorry I never got to see your pictures. I knew others who liked them though. You did well.'

'Thanks, yes. Some of them weren't so good, but you know one or two, they did OK. And they're only pictures, I mean. After all, what can you expect?'

'That kid you sent the movie poster to, he was thrilled.'

'Great, that's great.'

There was a pause. Abe looked down at his coffee cup, swigged it all in one go, then put the cup down.

'The booze, where did that come into things? How did you get mixed up in all that?'

Willard could hardly be surprised that the question arrived, but he was thrown by it all the same. There was no anger in Abe's voice, no accusation, not even sadness.

'The booze? Well, you know, who isn't mixed up in that? Do you know anyone who doesn't take a drink now and again? I don't.'

'I wasn't talking about taking a drink now and again.'

Willard felt a moment's anger. He felt angry at his hangover, angry at Abe's intrusion, angry at the world. And then he did something odd. He spoke the truth.

'I got into debt. I made a movie. I mean, my own movie. Produced it, directed it, everything. It wasn't too bad, only . . . well, no, I guess looking back, it was a stinker. It's harder than you'd think. Anyway, I owed money I didn't have. One thing led to another. I didn't know about Powell Lambert before I joined them.'

Abe's quiet eyes rested on the younger man for a moment or two.

'I'm sorry, Will, that sounds tough.'

'It was actually. You wouldn't even guess how tough.'

Willard looked up as though asking forgiveness. Abe nodded as though giving it.

'These things happen.'

The silence came back into the room. Willard remembered the long pauses of his old commander. To begin with, they'd worried him. He'd tried to fill the gaps with chatter. Later on, he'd come to realise he didn't need to. These silences weren't like his father's domineering silences, they were different, shared. Willard could talk if he wanted to, not if he didn't. Willard relaxed. He was about to help himself to more coffee, when the phone went, crashingly loud in the quiet room.

'Excuse me.'

He took the call. It was his father.

'Willard, my boy, are you up already?'

'Yes, Father.'

'Mixed news, mostly good. McBride is dead. So is Bosse. We haven't got the judge yet, but we know where his family lives. We don't see him causing us difficulty. There were some others who got away, but nobody of importance.'

'And the evidence, Pa? The papers?'

'We have some of it. The fire service has most of the rest. We'll ask our friends in the police to retrieve it from the fire service in due course. The police will hand it on to us.'

'Excellent. That's excellent. Did you . . .? Was there . . .? I mean, was a lot of force required?'

There was a half-second's pause, which was Junius Thornton's way to register his irritation at his son's tongue-tied tendencies.

'There was very little shooting if that was what you wanted to ask. McBride and Bosse virtually killed themselves, it seems. Our own men took some casualties. Three dead, I believe. Some others wounded.'

'I see.'

'And I wanted to thank you. You saw the danger. You alerted us. You were right.'

'Really, Father, gosh, I had no idea. I didn't know if you were sore at me. All this waiting around in Washington has been driving me crazy.'

'Has it? Why?'

'Well, you know. Nothing to do. Communications cut. That type of thing.'

'I don't understand. You were able to speak to whomever you wanted, weren't you? To come and go as you wanted?'

'Yes, only . . . it felt strange, you know, what with everything going on.'

'Powell felt you might feel close to Rockwell. If so, I can understand it. But feelings can get in the way of good commercial judgement. It seemed to make more sense to keep you away.'

'Yes, Father. I see.'

'I had intended for you to enjoy your vacation. Geddes made sure you had everything you wanted, I suppose? Car, driver, arrangements made, that kind of thing.'

'Oh yes, it wasn't that.'

'Good.'

There was a short pause. Willard felt the heat of Rockwell's gaze on the back of his neck. He felt the pressure of his father's presence looming from the telephone. He felt squeezed between the two men.

'I am sending Roeder to you now. That was the reason I phoned.'

'Roeder?'

'Rockwell is still at large. He managed to escape. Roeder thinks you may be able to assist.'

'Me?'

'Yes.'

'Roeder's coming here?'

'Yes . . . Are you drunk, Willard?'

'No, Father.'

'He'll be with you in twenty minutes. And well done. I wanted to say well done.'

'Thank you.'

The two men hung up. Willard swivelled to face Abe, who nodded an enquiry at the phone.

'Your father?'

'Yes.'

'Powell Lambert.' Abe pronounced the two words as though he'd never heard either of them before. 'You know, my colleague – my late colleague – Haggerty McBride found Mr Powell easily enough. He never found Mr Lambert.'

'That was him, my father.'

Abe smiled, as if he had found something to smile at. 'It makes sense. I couldn't see you mixed up with mobsters. I thought there was something I wasn't seeing, else I'd got you figured wrong. Well, your Mr Lambert makes sense of it. I had you right, after all.'

Willard began to say, 'We aren't mobsters. We only sell the stuff wholesale. We're not mixed up with all the rackets on the street.' But he didn't. He didn't get any further than the first two words. Because of course it was true. Roeder and Mason and all the others. They were mobsters. Just because Willard worked on Wall Street and wore a fancy suit didn't make him any less of a mobster. Instead, he said something that surprised him.

'You thought I couldn't be mixed up in it? Because of who I was?'

'I knew you weren't perfect, Will, far from it. But I couldn't see you mixed up in that. Not you.'

Willard scowled at the floor, pleased at what Abe had just said, but scowling because he was about to say something he knew he shouldn't.

'McBride and Bosse are dead – but you knew that?'

Abe nodded.

'The judge is still free, but they have his family . . .'

'I understand.'

'The other folks mostly got away, it seems. As for the evidence you folks collected. It seems like the fire service has most of it. We think . . . that is, my father thinks . . .' Willard tailed off, not wanting to tell his old commander that his final mission had comprehensively failed.

But Abe nodded. 'You'll send a few friendly cops down to the fire station to collect it up. The fire guys will hand it over, thinking they're doing the right thing. Yes, I thought that might happen. We gave it our best shot.'

There was another pause.

'They're on their way here now,' said Willard.

'Huh?'

'Roeder.'

'Oh, I'm sorry, Willard. I came by here to dig you out of trouble. I think maybe I just created some.'

'To dig *me* out of trouble?'

All through their conversation, Abe's hat had lain beside him on a little side-table. He moved the hat to reveal a black cloth-bound ledger.

'We took four ledgers from the bank. Your name didn't figure in three of them. It figured a whole lot in this one. I wanted you to have it. To destroy it, or do whatever. If we had won out down there at the warehouse, I wanted

593

you to make yourself safe. But as it is, I guess your man Roeder noticed the missing book. I reckon that's why he thinks it's worth a trip over here.'

Willard took the book uncertainly. To be found with it now would be catastrophic. God only knew what his father would think if Willard were found with gifts from the enemy. He shoved the book under the sofa, wondering if Roeder would attempt to search the place. His mouth went dry.

Abe said, 'Sorry. I was trying to do you a good turn.'

'I appreciate it.'

'Do you have any friends in the hotel?'

'Huh?'

'I don't think the couch is the best place to put that. The hotel will have an incinerator in the basement. Perhaps you know someone who could take it there.'

Willard nodded, still dry-mouthed. 'Good idea.' He went to the phone, called down to the lobby, asked for the bellhop he knew. The bellhop was there and promised to come up right away. Willard paced the room impatiently until he arrived, then gave the kid the book and a twenty-dollar note. The boy promised to have the thing destroyed immediately.

'Be sure you do,' said Abe.

'Yeah, OK mister, sure.'

The boy left. Willard watched the door close with relief. 'Gosh, I hope it's OK to trust him. Maybe I oughta go and watch. These kids, you never know –'

'He's fine. You can trust him.'

'Really? It's just that –'

'Will, you don't want to be running up from the incinerator when Roeder comes knocking.'

'Jeez, no.' Willard looked at Abe for a moment, before his belly gave a sudden lurch. 'But, *jeez*, Captain, you need to get going.'

Abe nodded.

'But I mean *now*.'

Abe nodded again. He indicated the open window. 'I can
ways step out there, if necessary. Don't worry. I won't let
em find me with you.'

Willard looked, jaw dropped, at the window. Just as he
d done when Abe arrived in the room, Willard had the
rie sense that Abe could just step in and out of the sky
will. 'The window? We're fourteen floors up here.'

'There's a ledge. It runs along to the elevator lobby. If I
ve to use it, I will. I'll be fine.'

'Gosh.'

The pause returned. Then Willard remembered some-
ing. He scrambled for his jacket and produced the enve-
pe he'd been carrying around with him. He thrust it into
be's hands.

'Look, I'd got this to give to you if we ever met up. Then
erything got so complicated, I couldn't figure out a way
find you. It's cash, a passport, and a liner ticket to Sydney,
ustralia. I figured you'd be safe there.'

Abe didn't open the envelope. He didn't even toy with
He just held Willard's gaze.

'That's big of you, Will. I hadn't expected it.'

'You need to leave. Now. Nobody knows about the boat,
swear it. You'll be safe there. I thought Australia would
it you. Plenty of sky.'

'Yes, plenty of sky.'

Willard stood up. 'So long, then.'

Abe shook his head very gently and tossed the envelope
ck to Willard.

'I can't take this, Will.'

'What? Why not? Don't worry. It wasn't much. If you
ally want, you can pay me back some time. Only you
edn't worry about it. Honestly.'

'I wasn't thinking about the money.'

'Huh?'

'I'm not leaving. I mean, I won't be in here when your

guy Roeder arrives. But I'm not leaving America. I started a job, you know.'

'You're not giving up?'

Abe shook his head.

'Christ, Captain, we've got everything. We've got McBride. We've got Bosse. Quite soon we'll have the papers and the judge as well. We've got everything. We've got half of Washington.'

Abe smiled. 'I know. That's why I can't quit. You understand.'

There was a pause. Willard looked at his watch.

'How long?' asked Abe.

'About fifteen minutes.'

'OK. I'll be gone in ten.'

Willard nodded. Abe turned away and rummaged amongst the breakfast things for more coffee and some cold toast.

'May I?' he asked.

'Of course.'

Abe munched on the toast. Willard remembered this about his old commander. In one way, Abe was naturally spartan. He had never used his rank or his fame or even his army salary to buy himself any extra comforts, not even an extra blanket for his bed or a picture to hang on his bare office walls. But in another way, Abe always managed to make himself comfortable. Here he was, with danger advancing by the minute, lolling on a chair, munching toast. Abe looked up.

'Remembering old times?'

'Yes.'

'D'you miss it? The squadron, I mean.'

'Yes. I do, I guess I do.'

'Despite everything? Despite the fear?'

'Yes.'

'D'you remember early on, those speeches of President Wilson's?'

596

'Jeez, those speeches!'

In the first months following America's entry into the war, the American airmen had been called on to drop propaganda speeches over enemy lines. The propaganda was of a strange sort. No flimsy leaflets, but instead long, wordy speeches by the then President, Woodrow Wilson. The speeches were idealistic, innocent. They exhorted the German troops to cease fighting. The speeches painted a picture of a world in harmony, working together for peace. The message was utterly well-intentioned, utterly useless.

And dangerous.

Not to the Germans below, but to the American airmen above. The speeches were big, heavy things. The aircraft dropping them were designed as pursuit planes or perhaps observation planes, but certainly not bombers. The unlucky airmen assigned to delivering the manuscripts had to fly low over enemy lines, chucking ungainly chunks of paper, handful by handful, from the cockpit. Sometimes the speeches wrapped around the airplane's tail fin and rudder, or snuck into the control wires running along the fuselage. As the airmen wrestled with their planes, the Germans below amused themselves by turning every gun upwards hoping for a lucky hit. After months of near-accident, high command was eventually persuaded to drop the venture.

'We sure took some ribbing from the Frenchies, huh?'

Willard nodded. He remembered.

'But, Will, let me ask you something. What did you think, what went through your head, when you had to drop those speeches.'

'I thought our President knew damn all about aviation.'

'Sure. What else?'

'I thought our President knew damn all about the German fighting man.'

'Sure. What else?'

'I thought . . . Shit, I was scared doing it. And what was the point anyhow?'

'Yes.'

There was a pause. Abe was driving at something, but Willard didn't know what. Abe tried again.

'You remember how some of the Frenchies were given those same speeches to drop? They didn't want to, so they just put their allocation on a truck and drove it around to our aerodrome.'

'That's right,' Willard laughed. '"*C'est votre Président.*" I could see their point of view.'

'Right. And what did you think then? When you took those speeches off the Frenchies, knowing it would be your job to drop them?'

'Heck, I thought . . . D'you know what, Captain? I felt proud, actually. I felt proud of my country and proud of my President.'

'Yes.'

'I mean, the speeches were useless. We all knew that. But they said something. They said something about America. About how it was our destiny to be different. To make peace, not war. To bring freedom. You know what? I felt honoured to drop those speeches. Dangerous or not, stupid or not, I wanted to drop them. To say to the Germans and the French and the Brits and everyone else, look at me. I'm an American and proud of it, Goddamn it.'

'Yes.' Abe's look was unusually direct, unusually intense 'Yes. So you do understand.'

'I'm sorry. Understand what?'

'Will, how come you miss being a part of the squadron? It was dangerous, frightening, relentless. But you miss it. do too. Everyone who was a part of it does. How come I'll tell you. Because you fought for something you believe in. Fought for something that was bigger than you. And what's become of that, Will?'

'I'm not getting you.'

'What's happened to our country? Freedom and democ racy, we invented them, Will, or at least we put our stam on 'em. And what's happened? What the hell have we let happen? We've let bootleggers buy the country. We've got enforcement officers who take bribes. We've got cops who are crooked. We've got entire cities owned by the mob. Even Congress isn't straight, Will, even Congress.'

Willard thought about the Powell Lambert bar, operated in the heart of the Senate. Abe was right and he didn't even know the half of it.

Just then, there was a quiet commotion at the door. Not the door to the corridor outside, but the bedroom door. Annie was there, dressed only in nightgown and bathrobe, hair messed up, sleep still in her eyes. She saw Willard, saw Abe, blinked in surprise. Abe was getting ready to go, hat in hand. He nodded to the newcomer.

'I guess you must be Rosalind. I'm Abe, an old friend of –'

Her face told him he had goofed. Annie looked at Willard for help. Willard gave it.

'Annie, actually. A friend of mine. Rosalind and I – she isn't – she didn't want –' Willard pulled himself up. Abe wasn't his father. He didn't have to be tongue-tied with Abe. 'Rosalind broke off her engagement. Annie is just a friend who dropped in unexpectedly.'

Abe smiled and nodded. 'Nice to meet you, Annie. I'm sorry but I need to get going.' He looked quickly between the two of them again, reading that even if there hadn't yet been sex, there was certainly more than friendship. He spoke again to Annie. 'He's a good man, you got there. You be sure to hold on to him.' He turned to Willard. 'So long, Will. Take care.'

'So long, Captain.'

'Captain?' It was Annie who spoke.

Willard looked at Abe, who answered her.

'Captain Rockwell, ma'am, only you might want to keep that quiet for now. Willard can tell you why later.'

'Captain Rockwell? Will's old commander?'

Abe grinned. 'Not that old.'

The sleep still caught in Annie's eyes made her face wider, softer, more innocent than usual.

'You saved his life. You kept him safe. Thank you.'

'He told you that?'

'He doesn't talk about anyone the way he talks about you.'

Abe put his hat on. He opened the door to the corridor, looked quickly out. There was no one there.

'He saved my life too, Annie. He ever tell you that?'

And then he was gone.

Through the door, down the corridor, away from the elevators, heading towards the concrete service stairs which would lead down to the hotel basement and safety. And Annie was staring at Willard, Willard at Annie.

Because, no, Willard hadn't told her that. Hadn't ever told anyone.

136

France, Somme sector, October 1918.

A dogfight. Two American planes – a Spad and a Nieuport – fighting four Germans, three Fokkers and a clumsy two-seater Albatross. Willard had been one of the American pilots. Captain Abraham Rockwell had been the other.

The dogfight proceeded with the usual terrifying swiftness. Willard couldn't remember the detail, only the broad outline. Rockwell, somehow, was pursuing the Albatross, but using his pursuit as a ruse to close on the Fokker that protected it. Willard was having a fierce encounter of his own, with neither pilot able to gain a decisive edge. But then the last German plane saw an opportunity to dive at Rockwell, who was now fighting three.

Twist as he might, Rockwell couldn't avoid placing his aircraft in danger from one gun or another. The first Fokker found his tail, began to close range. Willard, still fighting, was unable to help.

Except that he did.

On an impulse, he turned his plane. He flew towards the Fokker that endangered Rockwell, but at the same time let his own tail appear huge and steady in the sights of his own attacker. For three, four, five, ten seconds he flew, expecting the sudden flare and shock of bullets, the roar of flame, the hot red touch of death.

It never came. Nothing happened. The Fokker closing on Rockwell saw its own position worsen and pulled away.

Willard turned to face his own pursuer, whose gun, he now saw, was badly jammed. With the German gun jammed, the odds had shifted: two Americans against the three Germans and one of the Germans an unwieldy two-seater. The conflict sputtered on for a minute or two, before the two sides chose to pull away.

And that was it. Willard's one moment of perfect heroism. He had saved Rockwell's life at the risk of his own. Back at the aerodrome, Captain Rockwell had put his hand on Willard's shoulder and said, 'Thank you. That was a noble thing you did.'

And that was all. Rockwell had never spoken of it again. And in all his years of boasting, Willard had never mentioned it to a soul.

137

Annie smiled a proper hello to Willard.

What was she, a friend, a girl to have a fling with, or a life partner? He didn't know, but he did know he liked her better than any of his other girls. More than Evie Moroney. More than Rosalind. More than anyone. He walked to the windows and pulled back the curtains. Light flooded the room.

'Sorry,' said Annie, 'did I interrupt something? I didn't know you were –'

The phone went. Willard picked it up. It was the hotel reception, telling him a Mr Roeder was here to see him.

'Don't send him up. I've a guest staying. I'll be down in two minutes.'

Willard looked at Annie. He felt light-headed, but joyous. Joy poured through him, as though it were an emotion he'd never experienced before.

'How fast can you get dressed?' he asked.

'Already?' Her voice sounded upset, as though she thought he was sending her away.

He kissed her softly on the lips. 'I'm coming too.'

They went into the bedroom and began to dress quickly. Annie wanted to go into the bathroom to look after her make-up, but Willard told her not to bother.

'Annie, listen to me, I have a question to ask. I want to do something rather dangerous, but worth doing. There may be a little danger in it for you too, though I hope not. I expect I shall need to go to prison for a little while. Will you . . . will you still be there for me when I come out?'

'Oh Willard, it's the Firm, isn't it? Do you have to –?'

He shook his head. 'It is to do with the Firm, but not the way you think. Annie, are you happy selling booze? I mean, booze itself is fine, we both enjoy it. But are you happy with the way we sell it? The violence and the graft and everything?'

'No. No, I hate it.'

'Me too. It's time to stop.'

Willard knew that Washington was half rotten – but that still left one good half, even so. He remembered walking through the Senate Library. There had been some men there on the right side of the curtain, men with no drinks in their hands, men who had spoken out against corruption and had actually meant it. He'd enlist their help, senators of the United States, men as honourable as the positions they held. Willard would go to them, seek their protection, resurrect the case.

And as for the physical evidence which might even now be making its way into the Firm's hands, who needed it? Willard *was* the evidence. What he knew – names, dates, papers, files – what he knew was enough to blow Powell Lambert to kingdom come. The phone rang again.

'The gentleman you were expecting got tired of waiting, sir. He's on his way up.'

'OK. Thanks.'

Willard was calm, as calm as he'd ever been.

'Time to go.'

He steered Annie out of the room, down the corridor, away from the elevator, heading in Abe's footsteps for the concrete service stairs and safety. She clung tightly to his arm, matching two of her tripping little steps to each of his long, decisive strides.

He loved her and she loved him. And they'd marry. Some

day. Not too soon. Willard didn't know if he could avoid prison, but he wasn't worried by the thought. Annie, sweet little adoring Annie, would be there for him afterwards. And, in a funny kind of way, he'd be serving his country once again.

There were different ways to do these things, after all. Different kinds of heroes. Not everyone could be an Abe Rockwell. Most people couldn't. But Willard could hope to become the best version of himself. Better than any version his father had ever shown him. And the best version was a good one. Not just good, heroic.

By the time they walked out of the service stairs, down through the loading bay, out along the concrete yard at the back of the hotel, Willard wasn't just smiling. He was laughing, actually laughing.

EPILOGUE

✍

Willard watched Annie go.

She was dressed in a neat grey suit and a matching hat with a blue silk flower on it. She had got thinner than she'd been back in Wall Street days and she'd never had a spare ounce even then. She walked quickly, not because she was pleased to be leaving, but because she could hardly bear it. She wouldn't even turn to wave because she wouldn't want Willard to see her streaming eyes. She reached the end of the corridor and turned right. Willard fancied he could still hear her footsteps clicking down the concrete floor, but that was probably fantasy.

The big Irish guard, who had been waiting sympathetically, tapped the table.

'OK, buddy,' he said.

He meant: time to go back to your cell. Time to bite off another whole week before the next visit. Time to bite off one more week of the forty-six weeks remaining.

Because Willard had done it. He'd gone to the Senate Library of all places and found two senators whom he knew to be non-drinkers, non-hypocrites, non-corrupt. He'd made them a proposal and they'd bought it. Willard, the two senators, and eight cops hand-chosen by the senators themselves went down to the Firm's K Street offices. The office building had just one entrance. The eleven men went straight

606

up to Junius Thornton's office. Willard entered first, then the senators, then two of the cops.

The heavily-built businessman was drinking coffee as his visitors entered. He had the cup raised halfway to his lips – paused – then drank slowly before putting the cup down again.

'Willard,' he said carefully, as though it was only his son who had entered.

'I'm sorry, Father.'

'Sorry? For what are you sorry?'

Willard said nothing. Junius Thornton stared at his son with a face of thunderclouds over ocean. He too said nothing. When the cops came forward with the cuffs, he shot his wrists out wordlessly, his gaze unwavering from Willard's face.

It was a strange gaze. All the things that Willard had expected to see there – fury, contempt, fear, rage, even brutality – were completely absent. Partly it was just the old man's habit of clearing his face of visible emotion. Partly, it was Willard's age-old difficulty in making any real connection with his father. But in the weeks and months that followed, Willard had decided he'd seen something else too; something that was very far removed from brutality; something a little like respect.

But it was only a moment. The cuffs were snapped on to the big man's hands, and he was pushed away, out of the room. Willard asked the one remaining cop to leave, so that only he and the two senators were left. Wordlessly, Willard went to his father's desk and took from it the small black book with its list of names and gifts that he and almost nobody else in the world had ever seen. He gave it to the senior of the two senators.

'What you do with this is up to you, senator. I hope you use it well.'

After that, time and events had slid into confusion.

Everyone else in the building was either placed under

arrest, or herded into a single room and held under guard. Then they just waited. After an hour or so, Roeder returned back with a couple of men. They weren't expecting any trouble in their own offices, so they simply walked straight in and into the hands of the waiting cops. They too were arrested. After that, more of Roeder's men arrived and were arrested. Then some cops bringing the paper evidence retrieved from the fire service arrived. They too were asked to stay. Then somehow word got out, and a cluster of newspaper men began to form. One of the senators went out in front of the popping flashbulbs and made an oration. The radio airwaves began to fill with the story.

But Willard avoided the public clamour. He went back to the Senate, where he spent four days solid, telling everything he knew. There were at least three policemen present the entire time, plus at least two senators, sometimes more. Willard told everything without reserve. He told enough to damn his father, Ted Powell, Bob Mason, Dorcan Roeder, as many of his former colleagues as he could incriminate.

And himself. He damned himself a dozen times over. Afterwards, his lawyer told him he should have secured immunity from prosecution before saying a word. But Willard had been talking for two days solid before he even thought to get a lawyer, and by that time it was far, far too late. But he didn't mind. Genuinely not. In a strange way, as the prosecutions began to unfold in a roar of publicity, Willard began to feel himself connected to his father, for the first and perhaps last time. They had both done wrong. They would both face jail.

And, unlike his father or Ted Powell or Dorcan Roeder or any of the rest of them, Willard knew he would be treated leniently. He had sinned, of course, but he was, beyond question, the hero of the whole adventure. Neither Abe nor Pen had wanted to draw attention to their role in things. McBride and Bosse were both dead, Judge Styles was hardly a factor. So Willard was the hero. His handsome face wa once again one of the best known faces in America. More famous now than he'd ever been, no court in the land would have put him away for the maximum term. He'd been sentenced to two and a half years and was expected to serve just sixteen months. The prison was bad, but even there Willard found himself curiously respected, even popular.

And he was engaged to Annie.

When he came out of prison, they'd marry. Although his family was still very rich, none of the money would come to him now. His mother had refused to visit him in jail. Of his four sisters, only two had yet visited and even then had spent half their time recriminating. So when Willard came out, he'd be just a regular guy: famous, of course; a figure heaped around with the nation's praise; but not rich. Any money that came his way, he'd have to go and earn himself, dollar by dollar.

Sometimes, during the long and empty prison nights, Willard found himself feeling regret. But not most nights. And not by day. Most of the time, with most of himself, Willard was happy; proud and happy. He knew that Abe was proud of him too.

No matter where it may be, every airfield in the world feels the same as every other. And that's how it ought to be. Because a runway is only a jumping-off point for the sky and the sky is always the same and always different, no matter which part of the world it may cover.

The wind skittered in the dry grass, making a low moaning over the airplane's metal wings. Metal, because Abe's new plane was an all-metal monoplane. It was a high-wing, single-engine machine. It was a shape that had first been designed from Abe and Arnie's experiments with the water-chute. When the engineers had translated the plans into a life-size model, the plane had beaten all previous wind-tunnel records for an aircraft of its size.

Arnie Hueffer fussed around the airplane. A fuel tanker had accidentally splashed mud on the plane's nose cone. Tiny splashes, the sort of thing that nobody in the world would care about. Except that Arnie did. Because every splash of mud made for a tiny imperfection in the way the plane flew. And this plane was currently in New York and aimed to fly non-stop right from here to Paris, France. The journey would weigh in at over three thousand, six hundred miles and would, if successful, set a new world record.

But it was more than that.

The flight wasn't about records, it was about showing that there were no horizons in aviation. None. No barriers to what was possible. Oceans could be crossed. Continents could be joined. Trade could knit countries together. The world could be made a safer, wealthier, better place.

Pen stamped her feet in the cold.

They had got engaged, she and Abe. They hadn't wanted to make a big deal out of it. They'd made their announcement quietly, while the newspapers were full of ballyhoo about Willard Thornton and Powell Lambert. But all the same, the announcement had made a splash. How could it not have done? America's greatest war hero to marry the country's leading female flier? Then throw in the attempt to snatch the Orteig Prize and the story became an irresistible one.

So Pen stamped her feet, which weren't shod as she liked them to be, in flying boots below leather trousers. Her feet now had to look pretty and wife-like for the waiting cameras. Her comments had to be just right for the throng of waiting newspaper men.

But there was something that the newspaper guys didn't know. Something that nobody in the world knew except her and Abe. And that was this. In the weeks and months of final preparation for the flight, the risks that Abe was choosing to undertake had become progressively more obvious. There was so much that could go wrong. The plane was a flying fuel tank. What if there was a leak? A spark? What if headwinds were worse than expected? What if he lost course by a degree or two? What if he fell asleep? In the journey across the sea, the engine would fire approximately fourteen million times: fourteen million opportunities for something to go wrong. Nobody knew if the engine could do it. Nobody knew if a single man could do the job.

And that fact had begun to weigh on them both. They were engaged. They would shortly be married. The plan was to raise children, be a family. And flying the ocean was a risk that no responsible family man should ever take.

One day the whole business had come to a head. Abe had come back from the engine manufacturers, shaking his head. He'd had some story about firing ratios, carbon build-up, poor test results – Pen couldn't follow the tale.

'So what?' she'd said. 'Get it fixed.'

'Maybe it's not fixable. Not by me, anyhow.'

Pen opened her mouth to argue, then closed it. She understood her fiancé well enough by now, and she had seen straight through him. She felt very sad and very moved.

'There's nothing wrong with the engine, is there?'

Abe opened his mouth to protest, but then just shook his head. 'The tests are fine.'

'I thought so.'

'Listen, if it's not me, it'll be some other guy. Aviation doesn't need me to do it. Aviation doesn't much care who does it. I've got other things to care about now.'

'Me.'

'You, and the kids we'll have. What kind of a father would go fly the ocean? What kind of a husband?'

Pen's sadness increased, but she knew what she was about to do and knew that she would never regret doing it.

'Then I can't marry you,' she said. 'I'll not be the one

to stop you flying. And please don't argue. You will never get me to change my mind.'

Abe had argued and he never showed his love for Pen more than he did by arguing as hard as he did. But Pen never budged. And she was right. The world had plenty of husbands and plenty of fathers. It didn't hold a whole lot of men like Abe.

But the newspapers knew none of this. Wanting to avoid the furore that a break-up announcement would create, the two of them had decided to say nothing. As far as the world was concerned, Abe and Pen were still the perfect husband-and wife-to-be.

Abe was ready now. He was dressed in his flying clothes. He had a pile of sandwiches and a flask of coffee in the cockpit, along with his maps and navigation instruments. The wind was set fair. The horizon was clear. Weather reports from Newfoundland, Cork, London and Paris were all sound.

Pen didn't want him to go. Part of her, of course, wanted him to change his mind, come back to her, restart their future.

But that was only a part of her. The rest – most of her – did want him to go. Why did she love Abe, after all? She loved him because he was the sort of man who had to do these things. Who had to fly, had to travel, had to push hard against the limits of God and the sky. Pen felt proud of being the one who had found him and set him free. Proud and happy as well as also sad.

Abe hugged her. She hugged him back. They kissed. Flashbulbs popped. They offered a second kiss for the cameras, then turned away and kissed privately and longingly for themselves alone.

'Break a leg,' she whispered, using the old good-luck message from the war.

'We'll be fine.'

She nodded. 'I know you will.' She meant it.

They kissed one last time, then stepped back. Abe climbed into the cockpit. A newspaper man, a decent guy, who flew a little himself, stepped close to Pen.

'You want to know how we're gonna be covering this tomorrow?' he said. 'I'll tell you. THE GLORY BOYS FLY AGAIN. That'll be our headline. We've got that guy Thornton taking the rap for the whole Powell Lambert thing. We've got your Captain Rockwell doing this. It's kind of like the war again, ain't it? Only better. The war, really, what was that? The further it slides back into the past, the more damned I am if I can remember what it was all about anyway. But this, this stuff is real. Cleaning up America. Crossing an ocean. Now that I can understand. THE GLORY BOYS FLY AGAIN. Yep, that feels like a story all right.'

'The Glory Boys fly again.' Pen said the phrase over to herself in her head as Abe was done with his checks. The big propeller blade flashed into action. Abe looked back at the crowd, sought out Pen, raised a thumb and smiled. Had he heard the newspaper man speak? She didn't know why, but she felt he had the same phrase in his head too. Maybe he was even thinking of Will Thornton, the booze-dealer who'd come good.

The two fliers, Abe and Pen, took a long look at each other.

He saw in her the woman he loved: tall, boyish, quiet, inward, but also alive, quick to smile, young.

And she saw him: the man she loved. Middling height. Not big-built. Poised. A sense of athleticism held a long way in reserve. Eyes of astonishing blueness. His face lined but still somehow young. Or perhaps not young exactly, but alert, watchful. And smiling. That was how she held him in her heart.

Smiling.

HISTORICAL NOTE

One of the pilots to have survived the First World War told of a friend who, returning to his aerodrome one day, had emerged from a cloud upside down and heading fast towards the steeple of the local village church. Only lightning-fast reactions saved the day on that occasion. (The pilot concerned subsequently lost his life due to enemy action.) But the strange part of the tale was this. The pilot concerned reported that all the time he'd been stuck inside the cloud, he had been absolutely convinced that he was flying straight and level and true. His first reaction on finding himself zooming upside down towards a steeple wasn't fear, but amazement.

With jet planes, of course, and modern instruments, nothing like this could possibly happen now. But any reader who doubts that a sober human being could lose orientation so completely can easily try the following simple experiment. All you need to do is buy yourself an hour's instruction in a microlight aircraft and ask your instructor to head for the nearest cloud. Once you get there, take the controls yourself. (Don't worry. The plane will have dual controls and the instructor will watch you like a hawk. I'm certainly not suggesting that you go out there and kill yourself.) Then do it. Fly straight and level in zero visibility

You won't be able to. You'll think you are doing it, but then your instructor will point out that your wings are beginning to tilt, you're beginning to turn, your nose is starting to dip. At this point, you'll take your hands gratefully off the control stick, and your instructor will guide you out of the cloud. (Even top-notch pilots don't like to hang around in nil visibility.) But there it is. Your lesson. Of course, all that happened is that you *started* to tilt, you *started* to nose downwards. But that's how it always starts: gradually. Bit by bit, the plane's flight will diverge wildly from normal. And all the time, your sense of your aircraft's attitude will get further and further away from reality.

Writing novels can be rather similar. It's a journey that can start out confidently, then lose visibility, diverge hopelessly from reality, and end in a catastrophic smash. If *Glory Boys* has managed to avoid this outcome – and a good landing is any one that the pilot, or writer, can walk away from – then I owe a lot to my in-flight instruments. Most important among these are the friends and colleagues who support my writing in a thousand and one essential ways – and most important of all is my wife, Nuala, who is compass and turn indicator *par excellence*. It if weren't for her unerring eye for false positioning, this entire business of writing novels would have crashed and burned a long time back. I also owe a major debt of gratitude to Mark Buckland, who was extraordinarily generous with his help on the technical flying aspects of the manuscript.

But I've also been helped by one other thing: namely, keeping a close eye on historical truth. As far as possible, *Glory Boys* is faithful to the aviation achievements of the day, and to what is and isn't possible in the air. Of all the reference books which have helped me construct this narrative, the one that has most often been close to me is the *Aircraft Handbook* by Colvin and Colvin, the 1921 edition. The book instructs the reader in everything from how to assemble a plane (yes, really) to the ins and outs of aerial navigation. Inscribed inside the front cover, in March 1924, by a lieutenant belonging to the First Observation Squadron of the US Air Service, Mitchell Field, New York, the book has a period flavour like nothing else.

As for the stunts, I've sought to make these extreme, but possible. Movie pilots certainly did drop off towers, much as Willard did for *Heaven's Beloved*. Willard's bob and dive over the pine trees in Ruxion was adapted from a true life account of a similar incident, where the obstacle was, amazingly enough, the Taj Mahal in India. As for Abe's vertical take-off in the final storm, most real pilots are bound to dislike the idea of anything so horribly contrary to the way planes are meant to fly. All the same this kind of thing really can happen. If anyone doubts me, then I encourage them to read *Propellerhead*, by Antony Woodward, in which a vertical take-off of exactly this sort is described with extraordinary humour and accuracy. (As a matter of fact, I encourage you to read *Propellerhead* in any event. It's a terrific book, with a splendid flavour of the air. It might even get you down to your local airfield for an hour or two's flying. What did you do last weekend which was more interesting than that?)

The other theme in the book is booze and, once again I've tried to be as accurate as I can. Most people think that Al Capone was the biggest distributor of booze in the Prohibition era. He wasn't. That accolade goes to a man named George Remus, the possible model for Gatsby in Fitzgerald's famous novel. Remus was a larger than life character. He sold more booze than anyone else. His parties were bigger than anyone else's. When he was finally jailed for his boot-legging he arrived at the jail in spats, a pearl grey suit and a diamond tie-pin, promising journalists that he planned to lose a little weight while inside.

But the showbiz stuff isn't what mattered about Remus or about Prohibition. What mattered then – and matters now – is the effect that one bad law had on the entire nation.

his swaggering prime, Remus had been absolutely confident that he could never be imprisoned. Why? Simply because he had bribed everyone who mattered, right up to the level of the Attorney General himself. Just like my fictional Junius Thornton, George Remus handed out bribes on a colossal scale, including the Prohibition Directors of virtually every state in which he operated. He once stated that in his entire career he only ever found two people who wouldn't take his bribes: Burt Morgan, the Prohibition Director of Indiana, and Sam Collins, who held the same post in Kentucky. Given the amount of money on offer – quarter of a million dollars in the first case, a hundred thousand bucks in the second – the honesty of this pair does them remarkable credit.

Another common misconception about Al Capone is that his eventual conviction for tax evasion was somehow a ridiculous fluke, one of history's little absurdities. It was no such thing. The problem, quite simply, was that the Chicago police force had become so grossly corrupt that no regular type of investigation was going to trap the chief gangsters. While the city had seen well over five hundred gangland homicides by 1930, almost none of them had been successfully prosecuted. Something special was needed, and that special something was the Supreme Court ruling in the Sullivan trial. Following their verdict, criminals were obliged to report and to pay tax on their *illegal* earnings. Though the Chicago 'untouchables' were best known for smashing breweries and breaking kegs of whiskey, their most important work was in gathering the evidence that would end up convicting Capone for tax dodging.

And the corruption went all the way. My account of the bar in the Senate isn't fiction: there really was one, well-stocked and well-attended. There was an office set aside in the basement for the people who handled the alcohol. And bear in mind, this came at a time when the sale of alcohol wasn't just against the law, it was against the country's Constitution. Meantime, if the lawmakers were bad, the executive arm didn't have a lot to boast about. Warren Harding became President in 1920, symbolising the American desire for 'normalcy' after the years of war. But if this was normalcy, then it was the normalcy of the wild west. Here is Alice Roosevelt Longworth, the daughter of a former President, writing about her first trip upstairs to President Harding's study.

> No rumor could have exceeded the reality: the study was filled with cronies . . . the air heavy with tobacco smoke, trays with bottles containing every conceivable brand of whisky stood about, cards and poker chips ready at hand, an atmosphere of waistcoat unbuttoned, feet on desk, and spittoon alongside . . . [President Harding] was not a bad man. He was just a slob.

To get an accurate picture of how low Prohibition brought the moral authority of America's governing institutions, you would need to imagine today's President shooting up in the Oval Office. You'd need to imagine a smack house somehow incorporated into the fabric of the Senate itself. You'd need to imagine that all this was half-known, half-denied by the public at large. When Prohibition finally collapsed it took years to squeeze out the crime which one bad law had fostered.

Glory Boys is the soubriquet I've given to a fictional bunch of American fliers. But there are glory boys aplenty in the territory covered by the novel. Sir George Cayley, who worked out how humans were going to conquer flight; the Wright brothers, who went ahead and did it; the fliers and engineers who took things forward; the countless pilots of both sides who died to so little effect in the First World War; and the good guys of Prohibition – the Burt Morgans and the Sam Collinses – who stayed straight no matter how bent the world around them had become: this story is their story. I hope it honours them.